KU-719-154

A FAMILY CHRISTMAS

It was a time for dreams to come true…

Lucy Gabbitas is excited about joining her sisters at the local umbrella factory, but then her beloved father dies, leaving Lucy and her siblings heartbroken. The family receive no sympathy from their tyrannical mother, Annie, and their first Christmas without him holds little comfort and joy. Lucy meets John Grey and falls in love, and things seem brighter until Annie falls ill and dies and Lucy is forced to put her family first. She resolves to turn their home into a happy one for her brothers and sisters, and is determined to make Christmas a joyous occasion once more…

For my husband and family,
with love, as always.

A FAMILY CHRISTMAS

by

Glenice Crossland

Magna Large Print Books
Long Preston, North Yorkshire,
BD23 4ND, England.

British Library Cataloguing in Publication Data.

Crossland, Glenice
A family christmas.

A catalogue record of this book is
available from the British Library

ISBN 978-0-7505-3257-0

First published in Great Britain in 2009 by Arrow Books

Published in Large Print 2010 by arrangement with
Arrow, one of the publishers in the Random House Group Limited

Magna Large Print is an imprint of Library Magna Books Ltd.

Printed and bound in Great Britain by
T.J. (International) Ltd., Cornwall, PL28 8RW

Acknowledgements

With thanks once again to Georgina Hawtrey-Woore and everyone at Arrow for all their hard work on my behalf. Also to Magna Books. Thanks also to the creators of the beautiful book cover designs which I am sure go a long way towards selling my books. Also to my late mother and her sister for sharing with me their memories of the days they worked as umbrella girls. Thanks to my husband and family for their encouragement and to the staff of Stocksbridge Library for their support. Most of all, thanks to all the readers who continue to buy my books. Your enjoyment is my pleasure.

Prologue

Lucy opened her eyes and peered into the darkness. She could just make out the stockings hanging over the brass knobs on the iron bed. She slid out onto the cold lino and ran to open the curtains. Jack Frost had been in the night and left pretty patterns on the window pane but she hadn't time to stay and admire them this morning. 'Wake up, Jane. Father Christmas has been.' Lucy lifted down the bulky stocking and hurried on bare feet across the landing to her parents' room. She climbed up onto the bed and scrambled over her dad until she could snuggle down between them.

'He's been.'

'Well I never. I wonder what he's brought.' Annie helped the five-year-old to empty her stocking. She loved the excitement of Christmas almost as much as her children.

'Just a minute, little lass. Let's have some light.' Bill Gabbitas reached for the matches and lit a bedside candle, sending shadows dancing on the wall, and setting himself off in a fit of coughing. Jane was the next to crawl up the bed. Annie pulled her down between the blankets and warmed her cold feet between her hands.

The toys didn't amount to much: a couple of skipping ropes and yoyos, knitted teddy bears which Annie had stuffed with bits cut from an old vest. Annie noticed that one ear had been stuffed more than the others but neither Lucy nor Jane seemed to notice. There were brightly coloured scarves and caps, too. Both little girls decided to wear them. In the toes of the stockings were shiny new pennies and a sugar mouse.

'Can we come in, Mam?' Nine-year-old Nellie and Mary, the eldest, perched on the bottom of the bed and opened their stockings, keeping up the pretence of Santa Claus for the benefit of their little sisters.

Ben came clattering down the attic stairs. 'Thanks, Mam. Thanks, Dad.' He shoved in between his sisters until he was up on the bed. Ben had a cricket bat – lovingly made by Bill – in his hand and Annie protected her heavily pregnant belly from her boisterous son. Laughing, she reached over and took hold of her husband's hand.

'Looks like we shall need a bigger bed next year, Bill love.'

'Aye lass. It'll be grand with a new bairn in the house, and perhaps it'll be a little lad.'

Chapter One

Mrs Rawlings told the two girls to sit at the table and she cut two wedges of chocolate sponge. Then she poured two glasses of lemonade. Whilst they were partaking of the refreshment she counted out the money for the bread and popped it in the basket.

'Our William'll be coming after today,' Lucy

said. 'I'm starting work on Monday.'

'Never. Don't tell me you're thirteen already.'

'I am, on April the nineteenth my birthday was.'

'Well! Why ever didn't yer mention it? Here, let me find you a few coppers then.' The woman searched in a huge leather purse and gave Lucy a sixpence.

'It's all right,' Lucy blushed, 'I didn't tell you so you'd give me something.'

'Course yer didn't, love, but yer a good lass, so take it. And I hope yer enjoy yer work. If your William's as reliable as you he'll do me fine.'

'Oh he is, Mrs Rawlings, you can depend on that.' Bill Gabbitas had brought all his six children up to be reliable and dependable.

On Monday morning Jane and Lucy set off to work with Kitty nervously following in their wake. Mary had been gone a good half hour ago. Mary was saving up for her wedding and working all the hours she was offered. The girls hurried up three flights of steps and then Lucy began to panic when Jane instructed them to wait here for Mr Blackmore to set them on, before hurrying away and leaving them there. What if she and Kitty were separated too and she didn't know anybody?

Kitty's face was as white as the cloth in which her bread and cheese were wrapped. 'Look at all them machines,' she whispered. 'I'll never know what to do wi' 'em.'

'I expect they'll show us what to do,' Lucy murmured.

'So there you are.' Mr Blackmore looked at

Kitty. 'By gum, you're a little 'un, aren't yer? We'll 'ave to find a box or summat for yer to stand on. Come on then, let's get on.' Twenty pairs of eyes followed the girls along the shop floor. Lucy recognised one or two of them from their school days and began to feel a bit better. Mr Blackmore called to one of them and told her to fix the two girls up with aprons, then Kitty was taken further along the bench and Lucy was shown what to do.

'Put on the apron and then this pad on top,' the girl told Lucy. 'Your job is to straighten these ribs by knocking 'em on this pad, like this. Sometimes if the metal's too soft they bend and you 'ave to straighten 'em with yer hands, so you 'ave to wear these little leather caps to protect yer finger and thumb.' The girl showed Lucy how to do it. 'When we finish at end of shift yer've got to sort 'em out into two bundles, twenty-one-inch and twenty-four. Yer'll 'ave to do it yerself now or I shan't earn any bonus.' The girl left Lucy to get on with it and then came back. 'Oh I forgot, because yer a new lass yer've got to keep that bucket filled so we can wash our 'ands.'

'Where's the tap?'

'In't hardening shop.'

'Where's that?'

'On't next floor, and don't slop it all over't floor when yer fetch it, else somebody might slip and break their neck.'

Lucy started on the umbrella ribs, thinking she would never remember everything she had been told and wondering what Kitty was doing. The girl next to her was working so fast Lucy could hardly see her hands moving. She would never be able to do that. Perhaps Mr Blackmore wouldn't keep them on if they couldn't keep up with the others. Then what would happen? She'd be in for a beating from her mam, that's what.

'How's it going, Lucy?'

Lewis Marshall came up to her carrying a huge bundle of ribs. She was relieved to hear a friendly voice but she hoped he wouldn't become too friendly and want to kiss her like he usually did. She daren't take her eyes off what she was doing. 'I'll never keep up with the others,' Lucy told him.

Lewis laughed. 'Of course yer will. Everybody's slow on't first day. I'll tell yer what, I'll keep bucket full, just for today and then you can concentrate on yer job.'

'Oh lor, I'd forgotten all about water,' Lucy moaned.

'I know, I've done it for yer, don't let on to old Blackmore, though,' Lewis laughed. 'I'll expect a kiss in return.'

Lucy blushed, hoping nobody had heard him, but the girl next to her was giggling. Lucy was relieved when the buzzer went, signalling dinner time. At least half a shift was over and it hadn't been too bad, even if Lewis Marshall did come pestering whilst she was eating her bread and cheese. 'I'll tell our Ben if yer don't go away,' she told him when yet again he leaned over trying to kiss her. He had fancied her for months.

'I'm not scared of 'im,' Lewis said, but she noticed he moved away. Everyone was in awe of nineteen-year-old Ben Gabbitas. At six foot two Ben only had to scowl at someone for them to make themselves scarce. If they had known Ben as well as Lucy did they'd have known he was one of the gentlest people in Millington and no troublemaker.

When Lewis had left, Kitty moved over to where Lucy was finishing her lunch. 'Don't take any notice of 'im,' Kitty said. 'He's a pest.'

'Well I wish he'd behave 'imself, embarrassing me like that.'

'Nobody would think owt; everybody knows what ee's like, they're all used to 'im.'

Even so, word had reached the ears of Jane Gabbitas by the end of the working day.

'What was Lewis Marshall saying to you at dinner time?' Jane enquired when they set off up the hill.

'Nothing.'

'Don't let him touch you, or you might have a baby.' Jane was fourteen and knew lots of things that Lucy didn't.

'He did touch me, on my arm,' Lucy panicked.

'Well, that doesn't count, but don't let him touch you anywhere else.' Jane decided to ask their Mary to have a talk with Lucy and explain to her about boys and babies and things. Jane had learned everything she knew from chats in the playground with her friends but Lucy seemed rather ignorant about such matters. However, she was far too embarrassed to talk to her sister herself. Besides, she wasn't sure if some of the things she'd heard were true or not.

Lucy was wondering why their Mary didn't have a baby; Jacob touched her on her knee when they were sitting together in the front room on

Sunday afternoons. She and Kitty had seen him once when they had peeped through the window to see what they were up to. And Jacob always put his arm round her waist when they walked home from church. If their mam saw him their Mary wouldn't half cop it. Annie Gabbitas would think nothing of lashing out with the carpet beater, even if her young man was there. Lucy had had a walloping only yesterday for leaving the kitchen door open when the bread dough was rising on the hearth. Thinking of bread, she wondered what was for tea; the bread and cheese hadn't been enough to feed a bird. 'I'm hungry,' she told Jane.

'I am too. I could eat the coalman's horse. I expect it'll be stew again.' Stew was the usual meal in the Gabbitas household. Mr Brown the greengrocer always made Top Row the last call and dropped off any greens that were turning yellow, half-rotten root vegetables and bruised fruit at their house. Annie repaid the man by sending young William to run errands for Mrs Brown on Saturday mornings. The old vegetables made a decent stew when simmered with a few neck of mutton bones. An oxtail would be added after a few days, providing dinners for at least a week.

'I'm fed up of stew,' Lucy moaned.

'Aren't we all?' Jane rolled her eyes, then she blushed as she noticed one of the lads from Next Row walking towards them. Jane thought he was one of the most handsome lads in Millington, but he was sixteen and didn't even glance at her. If any of the Gabbitas girls had attracted the attention of Josh Smith it was Nellie. At sixteen, Nellie's curves showed through her frock – which she had long since outgrown. Nellie, like her sisters, would have to wait until Whitsuntide, when Mary, being the eldest, would have a new dress made by Annie, so that her old one could be handed down.

Poor Lucy, being the youngest, always had to make do with a faded fourth-hand dress. Not that she dared complain. So Lucy Gabbitas fixed a smile on her pretty, animated face and said her prayers every night that one day something nice would happen. Up to now nothing had, but Annie's family had long since learned that if nothing good was expected, then nobody would ever be disappointed.

Bill Gabbitas was home when his two daughters arrived from work. Lucy's heart seemed to miss a beat as she realised her father must be ill again to be home at this time. She ran to where he was lying on the old horsehair sofa. Lucy idolised her dad; he was a loving and generous man. Everyone loved Bill Gabbitas. It was only her mam who had changed and become miserable.

'Hello, little lass.' Bill held out his arms as Lucy fell into them. 'How did yer day go?' His daughter planted a kiss on her dad's cheek, setting him off coughing. Lucy fetched a clean piece of linen from the cupboard by the fire and handed it to Bill. Her face turned pale as she saw the bright red streak of blood he coughed up onto the white rag.

'Now look what you've done,' Annie chastised Lucy. 'Throwing yerself about. Get out to play.'

'Leave her alone,' Bill managed between the coughing. Just then Ben Gabbitas walked in and went towards his father. 'Are yer bad again,

Dad?' He placed a cushion behind Bill's head. 'It's time yer gave up that job. It'll be the death of yer, if yer keep on much longer.' Bill was a ripper in Millington Colliery, the same pit where Ben was employed.

'He can't. What are we to live on?' Annie snapped.

'We'll manage; we're all working now, except our Will. Isn't me dad more important than money?'

'The rent'll 'ave to be paid if yer dad leaves work – have yer thought about that?' The rent was deducted from Bill's wages every week by the owners of the pit.

'It'll 'ave to be paid if owt happens to me dad anyway. Unless we get the house transferred into my name. We can do that.'

'I don't want owt to happen to me dad.' Lucy began to cry.

'What did I tell yer? Get outside and play.' Annie grabbed the carpet beater and whacked Lucy hard.

Ben grabbed the beater out of his mother's hand. 'Leave her alone. The child's done a day's work. She wants some food inside her. Not that we get much to say we're all tipping up our wages; I'd like to know what yer do with it all.' Ben snapped the handle of the beater in two and threw it out of the door. Lucy couldn't help admiring him for standing up to her mother.

'What did yer do that for? Yer like a mad man.'

'Aye well, it's time somebody opened their mouth around here. Our Lucy's a good lass; yer always on at her. Besides, what do yer want with a carpet beater when we've no bloody carpets?'

Bill began coughing again, the rag turning scarlet when he couldn't stop.

'Fetch the doctor, Jane,' Ben ordered.

'We can't afford no doctor,' Annie snapped.

'Fetch him, go on.' Ben ignored his mother. He had had enough of her penny-pinching ways. Jane ran all the way down past the three other rows of houses, all identical to Top Row, and up the hill by the clock till she reached the doctor's house. She might as well have saved herself the trouble. By the time Jane returned with the doctor, Bill Gabbitas had breathed his last breath.

All Top Row was in mourning. Neighbours came from every house offering help, a loaf of bread – though God knows they had hardly enough to feed their families – and most importantly they offered a shoulder to cry on. Annie did her fair share of weeping, never considering the sadness her children were experiencing, and regardless of the fact that she had given little thought to the suffering of her husband over the last few years. In fact Annie seemed incapable of caring for anyone.

Ben comforted William and Lucy as best he could, knowing they were the two closest to their father. Mary sent Nellie and Jane off to work, knowing not only that it would be good for them but that her mother would expect a full wage packet from them at the end of the week. She kept Lucy at home. The lass couldn't be expected to master a new job in the state she was in.

Arrangements were made for the funeral at Cragstone Parish Church, even though Annie grumbled that the carting of the coffin all the way to Cragstone would cost more. Ben put his foot down and insisted that as his father's birthplace had been Cragstone and as he had been baptised there, he would be buried and laid to rest close to his parents and grandparents. Ben considered his father would be at peace away from his nagging misery of a wife. Annie complained, but Ben told her she could argue till kingdom come; if he was arranging the funeral that was where his father would be interred. He sent William to the insurance agent's house with a message and was relieved when the man came with the news that the premium was up to date and money for the funeral would be forthcoming.

Annie set Lucy to work cleaning the front room so that Bill would look nice laid out in his coffin. After that Lucy baked a batch of loaves. She thought she'd be better off at work, but didn't dare say so, even though the broken carpet beater had been dumped in the midden behind the lavatories. The heartbroken girl sobbed all the time she was kneading the dough, grief-stricken that her kind, loving dad had gone for ever. Lucy hated her mother on that day, remembering how she had tried to prevent their Jane from fetching the doctor. She hoped her mother would cough herself to death, just like her father had from the consumption. It would serve her right if she did. Then she wondered who would look after them if their mother died as well. Perhaps Lucy shouldn't wish her dead after all; she didn't love her, though. Her mother had been mean to her father and Lucy would never forgive her for that.

She wondered if the others were remembering

all the times their dad had been too ill to go to work but had gone anyway, knowing his life wouldn't have been worth living if he hadn't made the effort. Lucy could remember when her mam had been different, affectionate and smiling a lot. She didn't know why she had changed, but she vowed that if she ever had a husband and family she would never treat them the way her mother had treated her dad and her brothers and sisters.

It was the first Christmas without Bill Gabbitas and even the younger ones would be glad when it was over. The older ones could remember a time when the house had been a wonderland of holly, ivy and even a mistletoe bough. Even in the latter years when their mother had moaned about the extra work Christmas caused – not that she had made much of an effort – there had been the excitement of Christmas morning. A sugar mouse, a penknife, a picture book or a pretty lace hankie, all supplied by their father. Even Annie complaining about the wasting of money hadn't spoiled the fact that their father had given each of them something personal, and given it to them with love. There had been the carol singing, accompanied by Bill on the old melodeon brought down from the attic, with neighbours calling in to join in the jollity. Now it was just like any other day, except that the fact that it was Christmas meant that their hearts were heavier and the memories more poignant without the presence of their beloved father.

When Ben tried to add a little cheer to the special day by handing each of them a few shiny new pennies and a small bag of sweets, his mother accused him of being uncaring, with his father not yet cold in his grave. Ben knew he would only cause a scene if he spoke his mind and, not wishing to make the day even more miserable for his sisters and brother, walked out of the house and along the row. He would go for a walk in the peace and quiet of the Donkey Wood until he had calmed down. He brushed the tears from his cheeks as memories of his dad invaded his thoughts.

'A bloody right family Christmas this has turned out to be,' he muttered. As he turned down Side Row Ben wondered if he would ever know a merry one again. Not in his mother's house, that was for sure.

Chapter Two

It was a lovely April day and Lucy's sixteenth birthday, though no one except Kitty Marshall had remembered. Kitty now worked next to Lucy on the same bench and had grown tall enough to dispense with the box she used to stand on.

'It's your birthday, Lucy,' she said as they walked to work.

'How do you know?' Lucy asked, surprised.

'Me mam said. She said your birthday's on Primrose Day, that's how she remembers.'

'Is it Primrose Day today then?' Lucy wondered why Kitty's mam had remembered and her own mam hadn't.

'Well me mam says it is.' The girls hurried as the buzzer sounded. Their Jane would be late again; she was staying out too late talking to the lads on Next Row. Her mam'd go mad if she got the sack and she wouldn't be given a second warning. Lucy had almost dragged her out of bed but she was still nowhere in sight. Mr Blackmore was standing in his usual place by the door, glancing at his watch as each employee entered the building.

'Good morning, Mr Blackmore. It's a lovely day.' Lucy tried to engage the boss in conversation in order to distract his attention from the fact that her sister wasn't with her.

'And it's Lucy's birthday today, Mr Blackmore,' Kitty added.

'Is that so? How old are yer today then?'

'Sixteen, sir.' Lucy really missed her dad on special days like birthdays and Christmas. It never felt the same without her warm and loving dad.

'And never been kissed, eh?' The man chuckled at his own humour.

'She'll not tell you even if she has,' Kitty laughed. Lucy sighed with relief as Jane came rushing up the steps.

'Oh well, many more happy ones to follow, Lucy.'

'Thank you, sir.' The girls hurried to their bench and began work.

Lucy sang as she worked. She would be getting a rise in wages now she was sixteen. She wasn't sure how much, but it would be better than the nine shillings she was taking home now. Not that she would see any of it. Her mother was waiting at the door every Friday for the wage packets to be handed over. She would give them back a measly one and sixpence for spending money. Kitty's mam gave her half a crown, but then Kitty had a dad, and her mam wasn't a tyrant like Annie.

When they got home that night Ben gave Lucy two shillings as a birthday treat. He gave it to her on the quiet, telling her not to let her mother know or she wouldn't rest until she got her hands on it. Lucy hid it in the brass knob on the black iron bed she shared with Jane. Unlike Ben, who still lived at home, Mary had left home now and married Jacob, who had been her young man since school days. Of course she had been forced to leave work on her wedding day, but Mr Blackmore would often send for her back if they had a rush order, then Mary would be given the sack again when the work was done. Mary didn't mind; she loved Jacob and was quite content cleaning for one or two Millington ladies such as Mrs Rawlings and Mrs James, the wife of the schoolmaster. Jacob had found them a little house on the opposite hillside. Like Mary told her sisters, the further away from her mother, the happier she would be.

Annie Gabbitas's temper was worse than ever, not helped by the pain in her leg, which sometimes became so swollen it felt near to bursting. Lucy was the only one who seemed to feel any sympathy for the woman, despite her mother's foul moods. Ben scowled as the dinner was served out. 'I thought we might have had summat a bit different than stew seeing as it's our Lucy's birthday,' he said.

Annie sniffed. 'What's so special about birthdays? All they do is make you a year older. Though now she's sixteen I'll look forward to a rise in her board.'

'Oh aye, I didn't think yer'd forget that.' Ben took a mouthful of bread dipped in stew, swallowed it and then said, 'Anyway, I've decided our Lucy's to have a new frock. You can wait an extra week for the rise. Next week you can go to Sheffield, Lucy. I'll take yer. You can buy some material and if me mother won't make it up for yer we'll ask our Mary.'

Annie Gabbitas had a look on her face enough to turn the milk sour. 'So you're the boss in this house now are yer?'

'No, but our Lucy's sixteen and never once in all those years has she had owt new to call her own and it's about time she had.'

Lucy's eyes were lit up like stars, but she was frightened by the look on her mother's face. Annie was liable to throw something if she was that way out.

'I'll say when she can 'ave a new frock, nobody else. She'll bring her wage packet to me next week the way she always does, and that's the end of it.'

Lucy felt her lip tremble. She mustn't cry. She should never have listened to their Ben.

'Right then, you do that, Lucy; you give her yer wage packet and I'll buy the material for a dress out of my wages.' Ben stood up and carried his empty plate to the sink in the corner. 'And from now on she'll get two thirds of me wages and I'll 'ave the rest to do what I like with, like other men my age.'

'Yer can't do that. You'll bring home yer wages to me, just like you've always done.'

'But that's where you're wrong, Mother. I should 'ave put me foot down years ago but I wanted to be a dutiful son. But do you appreciate anything anyone does for you? Do you hell as like. Well, perhaps you'll realise what you're missing when you aren't getting it any more. Though I doubt it, because all you think about is yerself.' He grabbed his jacket from the hook behind the door and stormed out, slamming the door behind him. Just then young William came in carrying a bundle of firewood. He looked round at the pale faces. 'What's up? It looks like a funeral in 'ere.'

'Get yer coat off and I'll put yer dinner out,' Lucy told her brother. Her mother had sat herself down in the rocking chair, her face like a thunder cloud; she didn't say a word, knowing she had gone too far this time.

Always one to keep his word, Ben came home from work on Saturday at dinner time, got washed and changed out of his pit clothes, polished his best boots with spit and flattened his hair down with water. 'Well, Lucy, are yer ready?'

Lucy had been ready all morning, hopping from one foot to the other until Kitty had told her to concentrate on her work or Mr Blackmore would notice. Even though Lucy no longer helped her, Annie had craftily told Mrs Rawlings that Lucy would go round and see her after dinner, but Lucy had arranged for Will to go in her place. William didn't mind; he enjoyed helping her and Mrs Rawlings always gave him a slice of bread and jam. Mrs Rawlings's jam was delicious, even though he had once worried for weeks after swallowing a plum stone, when Albert Marshall had told him it might sprout inside him and grow into a tree.

Lucy had only ever been to Sheffield once, when her dad had taken them all to the station to wave his sister Kate off on the first stage of her journey to America. It had been a lovely outing, even though her dad had had tears in his eyes at the thought of never seeing his sister again. Then her mam had gone and spoiled it all by saying Aunt Kate was no better than she should be – whatever that might mean – because she had the courage to go off and try to make something of herself. Lucy wished she could go off to America instead of living with her miserable mother.

Lucy shook herself from her reverie. She had changed her mind half a dozen times at least about what colour her dress would be. First she thought she would like a brown dress which would be serviceable, then she thought if it was to be the only dress she would have in the next few years she would like a pretty one in pink or cream.

As it turned out her mind was made up for her as they approached the market stall. The first roll of material she saw was blue muslin, sprigged with tiny white flowers. None of the others could make her change her mind, especially when Ben told her it was the exact colour of her eyes. The man told her how many yards she would need and Ben said, 'Right, we'll take it.' Then he said, 'Now, help me choose some for our Jane.'

Lucy danced with excitement; she had worried about what Jane would think about her new dress. She chose a pale-green crepe de chine. 'That'll suit our Jane's hair,' Lucy said. Jane was as dark as Lucy was fair. Ben agreed the material was lovely. After he had paid the man he told Lucy he was going to splash out on dinner in a small restaurant in High Street. Apparently he had been there before with one of his many girlfriends. All the girls were after Ben Gabbitas but up to now he had not yet settled for one. Lucy hardly dared speak as they climbed the stairs to the cafe; she had never eaten out before. She sat primly on the edge of her chair until Ben told her to relax and enjoy herself. Lucy read the menu and chose fish-cakes and fried potatoes with peas. The meal was the most delicious Lucy had ever eaten. Ben told her to pour the tea and her hand shook as she lifted the silver teapot. She thought she would die if she spilt it on the white damask cover. 'Oh Ben, are yer sure you can afford this and the material as well?'

Ben laughed. 'Oh aye, me mother did me a favour when she refused to buy you a dress. Now I'm keeping a third of me wages I'll be much better off and besides that, anything I make on piecework I'm going to keep from now on.'

'And knowing how hard you work you'll make quite a bit.'

'Aye, and do yer know, Lucy? I don't feel guilty at all. Me mother's a greedy old bitch; she's all take. Yer shouldn't feel sorry for her. She's doing well out of us all and on top of all we tip up she's a pension of fifteen shillings for her and our Will. She should be rolling in it and could keep a good table, but all she does is stash it away. God knows what for.'

'I expect it makes her feel secure.' Lucy always tried to see the good in anyone, even her miserable mother. 'Besides, she works hard and keeps the house clean.'

'Oh aye, with the help of you lasses. And you're like a little mother to our Will. Don't think I 'aven't noticed how she has you all running around after her. Have yer finished? If you have we'll have a walk on the Moor and a look in Cole Brothers.'

Lucy could have sauntered all day looking in the shop windows and planning what she would buy if she had the money. They walked back through the gardens and took a short cut down Chapel Walk towards Haymarket. She decided to go to Woolworths and spend the two shillings Ben had given her. She bought pearl buttons, a paper pattern and enough lace to trim the two dresses, then she remembered she would need sewing thread. Everything cost sixpence so her precious two shillings were gone, but it would be worth it when she and Jane walked out on Sunday evenings in their new dresses.

The house where Lucy lived was identical to all the others in the four rows known to everyone in Millington as Top Row, Next Row, Second Row and Bottom Row. Although they had proper names like Saunders Street, no one ever used them except on correspondence delivered by the Royal Mail. Each house had two downstairs rooms, two bedrooms, an attic and a cellar where the coal was kept. The top of the cellar was fitted with shelves where the food was stored, not that there was ever much on the shelves of the Gabbitas residence. Outside the houses on Top Row was a large yard overlooked by a pretty flower-strewn bank leading to the allotments. In the yard were two blocks of water closets, one to every two houses. The attic served as a bedroom for Ben and Will, with Nellie, Jane and Lucy in one room and Annie in the other. Mary's marriage had given the girls a little more space.

All the families were friendly and always ready to lend a hand or a bite to eat in times of need. Even Annie could not be faulted by the neighbours. They saw her as a good mother, spotlessly clean and a woman who had carried on regardless after the loss of her husband. No one outside the family would have believed how cold and unfeeling she could be.

The only one who had ever got herself talked about on Top Row was Evelyn Smithson. Evelyn was rumoured to entertain men in the afternoons when the curtains were drawn; Lewis Marshall often commented that Evelyn was dropping her bloomers again. Mrs Slater said none of it was true and the only reason the curtains were ever drawn in the daytime was when Evelyn's baby boy was napping on the couch and the sun was in his eyes. Mrs Slater said the only man ever to have visited the house had been little Bernard's father, and she should know, living next door. Still the rumours persisted and the Gabbitas girls considered this unfair as they thought Evelyn was lovely, always good for a laugh and a cup of tea. Besides, she was a wonderful mother to her little boy, despite finding it hard to make ends meet.

Another character on Top Row was Mrs Murphy, who seemed to have a new baby every year. Because Mrs Murphy was so fat nobody ever knew she was carrying until she actually gave birth. She would simply go to bed, bear the child and get up again, resuming her place in the chair in front of the fire where she would sit, day in and day out, leaving the kids to get on with life. Amazingly, they all seemed to thrive amongst the clutter and grime, unlike the babies Mrs Cadman had borne. Although Mrs Cadman's house was well furnished and clean and although she attended the clinic regularly, two of her babies had died, one poor little mite at birth and another of a fever. Now her third child had been taken to a hospital on the other side of Sheffield suffering from typhoid. The little boy had been seriously ill on admittance but was said to be recovering slowly. Lucy hoped the baby would pull through as Mrs Cadman would make a perfect mother. Lucy tried to compare her to her own, though it was difficult to imagine Annie travelling miles every day if any of them were ever ill and taken to hospital.

All in all Top Row was a decent place in which to live, just a short walk from the main road where all the shops and the town hall were situated, then there was the market on Fridays, the church school at the bottom of the hill opposite the parish church and the Miners' Club. Lower down were the steel-works, trailing the length of the valley with the river Don flowing alongside them. The opposite hill was sparsely populated and usually blanketed by smoke from the works and coke ovens. On the far side of the hill was the colliery where most families on Top Row had at least one member of the family working. The pit was hidden from view in the midst of Sheepdip Wood, a popular walk on Sundays for the people of Millington, especially courting couples. Lucy was glad they lived on this side of the valley, which was much more populated but greener and seemed untouched by the smoke or grime. Close to the rows were the Memorial Gardens and the clock tower.

Then there was the Donkey Wood leading to the football field and the new council school. Council houses were already springing up in one area and Lucy was sad that the strawberry fields would be lost for ever to make way for the new developments. At least the Donkey Wood would remain intact; Mr Blackmore said it had been bequeathed by the owners of the works to the good people of Millington to be used for their enjoyment and pleasure in years to come. The Donkey Wood was used for walks, blackberrying and for picnics. It was a good place to play, with a stream to paddle in and trees to climb. Of course Lucy had been too old for playing for a few years now, but it would be good to walk in the Donkey Wood in her new dress. She wondered if their Nellie would lend her her new button-up boots just for once, so she could show off and look beautiful for a change.

Nellie Gabbitas had more on her mind than button-up boots. She wondered how to tell her mother the news without her starting to rant and rave. She would wait until their Ben and Lucy came back from Sheffield; Ben would be on her side and would protect her. How awful to need protecting from the lashing tongue of one's own mother. Nellie worked at a large, rambling old house known as Cragstone Manor, situated on the edge of Cragstone. The manor had recently been renovated and opened to accommodate paying guests, mostly gentlemen visiting the steelworks or colliery for conferences or merely an excuse to party and get drunk. Nellie had worked in service from leaving school, starting as chamber maid and progressing to assistant cook. Now the cook was retiring and Nellie had been offered the post with an increase in wages. The position was a living-in one and Nellie had not had to think twice before accepting. The trek to Cragstone – a distance of several miles – was arduous on dark mornings and nights, particularly in winter on the country lanes. Besides, she would have her own room and as much food as she could eat. The only thing worrying her was her mother's reaction. Of course she would miss her sisters and brothers, but it would be a relief to get away from her mother. In fact, she couldn't wait to get away and begin her new job the day after tomorrow. Oh, she wished their Ben would come home; she thought they would have been back by now.

'What's up with yer? You're like somebody with St Vitus' dance,' Annie admonished her daughter.

'Nothing, nothing's wrong with me. I just thought they'd have been back by now. I hope nothing's happened to them.'

Annie grimaced. 'What can possibly have happened to them?'

Nellie didn't need to answer as the door opened and in skipped Lucy, who couldn't wait to show off the new material. 'Oh Nellie, you'll never believe how beautiful it is. Where's our Jane?' Lucy thought she ought to show Jane first, seeing as it was a surprise for her.

'Upstairs, changing pillow cases ready for washing on Monday,' Annie said, 'unlike some who's time to go gallivanting.'

Lucy went clattering up the stairs, bearing the parcels of cloth. Jane was in Annie's room, mending a hole in the striped pillow to stop the flocks falling out. 'Look at this, Jane.' Lucy opened the parcel, exposing the beautiful lime-green material.

'Oh, Lucy, it's gorgeous.' Jane tried to hide the envy she couldn't help feeling. 'You'll look lovely in that.'

'No, you will. It's yours.'

'Mine?'

'Yes, yours. This is mine.' She showed Jane the blue.

'Mine! I can't believe it.'

'And I bought a pattern and some lace and buttons.'

'Oh, Lucy. I love the material; I'm not sure about the style, but it'll look lovely on you.' The picture on the pattern showed a tight-fitting bodice and a full skirt. 'I'd prefer a shorter, sexier style. After all I'm older than you.' Lucy felt a little bit disappointed that Jane didn't like the style she had chosen, but she didn't let her sister know. 'I'm sure our mam'll be able to make one to suit you,' she said. 'Or shall we ask our Mary?'

Jane frowned. 'Oh I don't think we should let our mam make 'em. She'll only spoil the material by changing the styles to suit her. She won't be satisfied unless they're old-fashioned as Methuselah. You know what she's like.'

'Yes, you're right. I'm sure our Mary'll make them up for us.' The two girls wrapped the material up carefully and went downstairs, pausing to listen as their mother's voice rose. 'Yer can't leave home. It's indecent living there with all those men.'

'Don't be ridiculous, I shan't be living with them. I shall have my own room, next to Mrs Cooper, the housekeeper.'

'No! I won't allow it.'

Nellie began to laugh. 'I'm afraid I'm not going to let you stop me. You've ruled my life long enough. Besides, it isn't my reputation you're concerned about, it's the money you'll be losing, isn't it?'

'It's nowt to do with the money,' Annie snapped. 'Though a proper daughter would be considering that, with a widowed mother.'

'I shan't abandon you. I'll still be coming home and paying a bit towards our William's keep.'

Ben decided to put a spoke in. 'No Nellie, yer don't need to do that. It's time you were putting a bit away for when yer decide to wed.'

'It's nowt to do with you.' Annie glared at her son.

'Well, I'm taking the job whether you like it or not. I've been working hard for it and I'm lucky to be offered a job like that. I shall never be offered a chance like this again.'

'I'm not against the job; it's the living in I object to.'

'But that's one of the conditions of the job. I need to be there early in the morning to see to the breakfasts. Besides, it's a long way in winter when it's dark and the weather's bad. I should have thought you'd be pleased that I shan't be walking all that way on my own.'

'If yer go yer needn't come back.'

'What?' Nellie couldn't believe she wouldn't be welcome in the family home.

'You 'eard.' Annie's face was as hard as granite as she turned her head away from her daughter.

'Right, if that's what you want.'

'No.' Jane ran and threw her arms round her sister. 'You can't turn our Nellie out.'

'I'm not turning her out. She's decided she wants to go, not me.'

'But you've got to let her come home to see us.'

'Don't tell me what I've got to do. This is my house.'

'Is it now?' Ben went to the cupboard and brought out a folded sheet of paper. 'What's this then? The house is in my name now. Go on, read it, woman; the contract says that only employees of the colliery are allowed these houses. Well, I say our Nellie can come home whenever she likes.'

Nellie's face was as white as the sheet of paper.

'No, Ben, I won't be coming home again. I know where I'm not welcome. I'll go get my things.'

Lucy began to cry. 'Don't go, Nellie.'

'I have to, Lucy. I'm sorry.' Nellie went upstairs and found her few items of clothing, wrapping them all in her winter coat, then she unwrapped the new material Lucy had bought and used the brown paper to wrap her boots in. Then she went sadly downstairs to where her sisters were consoling each other.

'Come and see me sometimes on a Sunday. I'm sure Mrs Cooper won't mind,' Jane nodded her head. The two girls were too upset to respond.

'I'll carry those.' Ben took the bundle from Nellie as she prepared to leave. He turned to his mother. 'It won't end here. Our Jane'll be next, then our Lucy, and I'll tell yer this, I'll not stand for yer vindictiveness for much longer and what will yer do if I leave? Eh? You silly, stupid woman, 'ave yer thought about that?'

Nellie couldn't stop the tears as she made her way back to the manor. She loved her brothers and sisters and not being able to see them didn't bear thinking about. But she also loved her job. She would find a way to see her family somehow. Her feet were hurting as she climbed the last mile and her arms were aching with the weight of her belongings, She began to feel better as she breathed in the air from the moors and caught sight of the cherry trees, which were heavy with blossom. Besides, Mrs Cooper would make her feel better. The housekeeper was like a mother to Nellie. Like the mother Nellie could remember from when she was a little girl. But that was a long time ago, and things had changed.

Chapter Three

'Are we nearly there?' Young Robert Grey stopped and leaned on the dry stone wall. 'Is that it?'

John looked towards the circle of smoke in the distance. 'It could well be. What do you think, James?'

'We can't be far away. We'll see more when we reach the top of the hill.'

'I don't know if I can.' Fifteen-year-old Robert sat down on the grassy bank and examined his feet. His boot soles had worn through and his feet were thick with blood and dirt from the road. James took off the muffler from round his neck and tied it round his brother's foot. 'Give us yer scarf, John.' John took off the length of dirty material and bound up his brother's other foot. 'We won't be long now, then we'll get yer feet seen to.'

The journey from Lincoln to the West Riding of Yorkshire had been long and torturous, but the promise of a home and job had kept the brothers going. They had taken shelter in a barn at West Markham but had been fired at by a farmer in the early morning. Another night they had asked permission to take shelter in an outbuilding somewhere near Worksop, but the man had tricked Robert into going to the house for drinking water only to try luring him into his bed. Twice they had taken a wrong turning and gone miles in the wrong direction. Now they were nearing the end of their journey a feeling of dread was replacing the exhaustion, a fear that the promised home would not materialise.

John took out the hard bread and stale cheese. 'Well,' he said, trying to keep up their spirits. 'This is it. Once this has been eaten we should be there. That's if we calculated properly.' He hoped to God they would be; the money they had allocated for food on the journey had gone and he didn't want to dip into the rest of it. 'So come on, let's eat and be merry. Then it's off we go to Millington.'

'There's a hell of a lot of hills round 'ere.' Robert moaned.

'The Pennine hills,' James said. 'It's supposed to be a beautiful part of the country.'

'They're more like mountains. Give me Lincolnshire any day. I don't know why we had to leave,' Robert grumbled for the umpteenth time.

'Because we'd nowhere to live – you know that.' The Greys had lived in a small, rundown cottage on a large private estate. Jonas Grey, their father, had been in the owner's employ as a gamekeeper. The two elder brothers had both found work in a corn mill, not very highly paid, but constant. Then tragedy had struck the family in the form of a particularly virulent type of influenza. Young Robert had recovered, but Jonas and his dear wife Maria had both died. Of course they had been evicted from the cottage despite pleas from the minister of the church to the affluent but miserly owner. The brothers had been given temporary shelter by the minister, who had passed word amongst his friends and acquaintances about the boys' plight. Amazingly, the vicar of Millington had heard the story and he and his wife had offered a home to the desperate brothers. The vicar, also chaplain of the steelworks in the town, had sought employment there for James, wheedled a job in the mine for John, and been given a chance for young Robert to further his education as apprentice to a local joiner.

'Well, the sooner we get going the sooner we arrive.' James rose wearily to his feet. At twenty James felt responsible for his youngest brother Robert and John, the middle one.

'I don't think I can walk with these on me feet.' Robert hobbled as best he could. He could feel the scarves already unwinding and his feet hurt more than ever.

'Try and put up with it. We won't be long before we're there.' Neither of the elder brothers mentioned the festering blisters on their own heels. The smoke was nearer now as they entered the field that led over the brow of the hill.

'Would yer just look at that?' John was the first to see the view. 'You can see for miles.'

The distant hill spread in both directions for as far as the eye could see. A reservoir shimmered in the evening glow, reflecting the trees of Sheepdip Wood and beyond that the stark, beautiful Pennine moors stretched upwards to meet the sky. Beneath them the steelworks sprawled alongside the river and what looked like the main street.

'That must be the church we're heading for,' John decided, 'so it looks like downhill all the way from here.'

'Well I'm glad about that.' Robert brightened up a bit. 'It looks like a big place.' He began to feel excited.

'Well compared to our village it definitely is.'

'Will that be the vicarage where we're going to live? Next to the church.'

'I don't know, but we shall soon see.'

'I don't like all these hills though,' Robert moaned.

'I do. It's far more interesting than flat country.'

James agreed. 'Aye and look how far we can see; it's beautiful.'

They were going at a faster pace now – in fact the hill was so steep it was hard to hold back. A herd of cattle came to meet them, mooing a welcome so loud a farmer's wife came to see what all the fuss was about.

'Good evening, is that Millington down there?' James enquired.

'It is that, and the place in the distance beyond the dam is Cragstone, though yer can only see't smoke from chimneys, it being several miles away.'

'Eight.' A girl about Robert's age corrected the woman, who glared at the girl. 'Aye well, we won't split hairs,' the woman said, and turning her attention back to James she pointed in the opposite direction. 'And if yer followed the main road in that direction you'd come to Sheffield after ten miles.'

'Eleven.'

The woman gave the girl a clout round the head with a cloth she was carrying. ''Ave yer come far?' she enquired. 'Yer look fair done in to me.'

'About forty miles to my way of reckoning.'

John glanced at the girl, half expecting her to add a few miles to his estimate.

'Forty miles? All on foot? Why, no wonder you look jiggered. Dot, go put kettle on and mek 'em some tea.' The girl hurried indoors and the woman offered her hand to James. 'Boadacea Greenwood and her theer's me daughter Dot.'

'Boadacea? That's a right grand name.'

'It's a bloody daft name if you ask me. That's why I gave her a little name and yer can't get much smaller than Dot, can yer now? I wasn't 'aving her laughed at every time the school register was called, no, I told my little Arthur we'd call her summat sensible, and she's not a bad lass really, even though she's a cheeky young whipper-snapper sometimes. Anyway, bring yerselves in. Chuck yer bundles down theer, nobody'll touch 'em. Dot. Is that tea mashed yet?'

'Yes, Mam.'

'Well, cut three doorsteps while we're waiting for it to brew and smother 'em with pork dripping.'

Robert felt his mouth watering at the thought of bread and dripping. Oh but they didn't half speak funny, the people of Millington. Boadacea led them into a farm kitchen with a flagged floor and a huge square table in the centre with a bench at each side of it. A huge black fireplace took up one wall and on another was a low stone sink, which reminded Robert of a horse trough, with a pump at one end of it for the water.

'Sit yerselves down,' Boadacea ordered them. 'We might not be posh but everybody's welcome.'

'I can see that,' James said, 'And we really

appreciate your hospitality.'

'Oh it's nowt, just a pot of tea and a bite. I'm sorry my little Arthur isn't 'ere to meet yer. Ee's gone to fetch bull to put to't cows.'

'So, is he a little man, your husband?' John asked.

Boadacea let out a laugh that set the old sheepdog howling as if in pain. 'Aye, no more than five feet tall, but that don't matter, theer's many a good thing wrapped in a small parcel.' She laughed again as her guests gobbled the bread and dripping, which tasted better than any feast to the young men. When they had finished John rose from the table. 'Well, lads, we mustn't keep Mrs Greentree any longer.'

'Greenwood,' Dot corrected, then she turned to Robert. 'Do yer want to stay till me dad comes back and watch bull with cows? Yer can come up to my room; it's a good view from up there.'

'What?' Boadacea puffed. 'Why you cheeky young rascal, you'll do no such thing.' She turned to John. 'She doesn't mean any harm but I can remember how exciting it can seem at her age, watching't bull on't job and we don't want to go putting ideas into their heads now, do we?'

By now the elder brothers could hardly keep their faces straight and young Robert's face had turned the same colour as young Dot's cheeks.

'It's all right, Mrs Greenwood; we were brought up in a village and we're quite used to farming ways.'

'Oh well, that's all right then. I say do yer want a few hours' work? We could always do with an extra hand.'

'Well, we hope there are jobs waiting for us, but we'll certainly keep your offer in mind. Now we really must be off. Reverend Goodman will be expecting us.'

'Oh if you're visiting 'im, he won't mind if yer late. Yer'll be as welcome there as you are 'ere.'

Dot had sidled up to Robert. 'I'll see yer at church then on Sunday.'

Robert nodded as he moved to the door, 'I expect so,' he answered grudgingly. He hoped she wasn't going to be pestering him all the time. Then he admitted to himself that she wasn't bad-looking – not bad-looking at all. It would have been all right staying to watch the bull with her.

'If yer come back tomorrer I'll make yer feet better with spirits and some candle wax,' Dot's voice rang out as they closed the gate.

'Looks like yer've got yourself an admirer, Robert.'

Robert blushed even redder as they descended the hill into Millington.

'Will you stop fussing? You're like a moth round a candle flame.' Reverend Goodman admonished his wife good-naturedly as she moved the cruet yet again and shifted the sugar basin a little to the left. 'They won't be bothered about the state of the table; it'll be what you serve that counts. Besides, they might not arrive until tomorrow.'

'Oh Herbert, they must come today. They'll surely not survive another night in the open. We really should have sent them money for the train.'

'I know that and I certainly would have if I'd known Mark was sending them off on foot. What in God's name was he thinking of?' He cringed at his blaspheming, and him a man of the cloth, but he was so shocked that his friend hadn't been charitable enough to buy train tickets for the homeless boys.

'Anything could have happened to them. Still, I always did think he had a mean streak about him,' Louisa admitted.

'Well, he never used to be mean. Perhaps it's that wife of his.'

'I wish they weren't coming at all.' At fourteen years of age, daughter Prudence was dreading the presence of three young men in the house.

'We must show a little kindness to those worse off than ourselves, Prudence, so please try and make them welcome.' Louisa wondered from where their daughter had inherited her miserable disposition. She hoped she wasn't going to sulk in their presence, or worse still suffer one of her tantrums.

'They could have changed their minds and decided not to come.' Prudence sounded hopeful, but then the door knocker made them all start and her father hurried to let in the weary travellers.

Chapter Four

Nellie Gabbitas sighed with satisfaction as the empty plates and tureens were brought back to the kitchen.

'We shan't be getting any leftovers tonight

Nellie; they've only gone and eaten the lot.' Lily the kitchen maid dropped the crockery in the scalding water.

'Don't worry, I've kept plenty back for us.' Nellie smiled to herself. One of the conditions she had insisted on when she accepted the job had been that she and the rest of the staff be allowed three good meals a day. 'After all,' she had pointed out, 'I need my helpers to be healthy in order to put in a decent day's work.'

'Of course you must do as you think fit,' Nellie had been told. The only condition in return being that no food must be taken off the premises. So that had put paid to sneaking out a ham shank for their Mary or a fruit cake for her brothers and sisters. Nellie would keep her side of the bargain; she would never do anything to risk losing her job. Cooking was much more satisfying than making beds and emptying chamber pots. Besides she was safe in the kitchen; in the bedrooms she had often had to escape the advances of randy young men and dirty old ones. Now she was safe during the day and had her own key to her room, just like the housekeeper.

'Right then, Lily, if you've finished those dishes we'll mucky some more.' Nellie opened the door of the great oven and took out a dish of steak and kidney sizzling away in thick brown onion gravy. The aroma of roast potatoes and vegetables filled the room.

'Run and fetch young Larry.' Larry was the odd-job boy, who amongst other things looked after the stables and the occasional motor car. Lily didn't have far to look for the lad. Since

Nellie Gabbitas had taken over the cooking he was always hanging around at this time, knowing she would be feeding them a meal fit for a king. Larry wished he was older. He would have asked Nellie to marry him – she was a right good-looking lass and nobody could cook like her.

'Right then.' Mrs Cooper came and sat at the head of the kitchen table. 'That's me done for the day, so come on, let's eat.' The four of them served themselves, Nellie making up for the measly meals her mother had served. She fought back tears as she thought about her sisters and brothers. She missed them so much and the daft thing was, she actually missed her cantankerous old mother too.

'Oh, Jane. You'll have all the lads in Millington after you.'

'I don't think so – it'll be you they're after. You look beautiful, Lucy. Not that there's many lads in Millington worth having,' Jane giggled, 'unless you've suddenly taken a shine on Lew Marshall.'

'Oh! For heaven's sake. He drives me mad, hanging round me all the time.'

'There's nothing wrong with him; the poor lad's mad about you.'

Lucy wrinkled her nose. 'I know, I suppose I do care about him in a way, I just don't fancy him.'

'Then for goodness sake tell the poor soul so that he knows to find himself another girl.'

Lucy blushed. 'It's not my fault. I've never encouraged him. He just won't take a hint. Will you tell him, Jane? Let him down gently I mean.'

'Oh yes, and then he'll hate me for the rest of

his life. I don't think so.'

'Oh go on, please.'

'No, I can't.'

'Well then, he'll just have to wait until I find someone else, then he'll have no option but to make himself scarce.'

'Come on, or we'll be late.'

Annie was waiting, as usual wearing her grey coat and best Sunday hat. She stared as her daughters came into the kitchen. Even her hard heart softened at the sight of them. She couldn't hide the pride from her voice – even though she was always stressing the evils of pride and vanity. 'Well, I must say our Mary's made a good job of them frocks.'

She bent to examine the stitching on the hem of Lucy's new dress. 'Aye, it suits you, lass; you chose the colour well, and our Jane's.'

Lucy couldn't believe her ears and Jane's eyes widened; it was the nearest thing to a compliment Annie had paid either of them, or their Mary, for many years.

'Come on then – the bell's been ringing this last ten minutes.'

The church bells could be heard all over Millington. The congregation liked to hear them, except at eight o'clock on a Sunday morning. Most people tended to attend the evening service, so the church was usually packed. Annie preferred to sit near the back where she could see what the other worshippers were wearing. The conversation on the way home would usually consist of who had a new hat, or who was courting who. The same conversation would be repeated the next morning for the benefit of any neighbours who hadn't attended the service. Reverend Goodman always gave an interesting sermon; he preferred to emphasise the qualities of goodness and kindness rather than the evils of sin. Tonight he began by welcoming three newcomers into his fold.

'I hope you will all make them feel wanted and welcome in our church and community,' he said, causing every eye in the place to turn in the direction of the Grey brothers, much to their embarrassment. Jane nudged her sister. 'I bags the one nearest the aisle.' She winced as her mother dug her in the ribs with a bony elbow.

'They're all lovely.' Lucy's eyes shone. Even the young one had the makings of a handsome man in a few years' time. Neither girl heard much of the service, concentrating all their attention on the newcomers. Both were glad to be wearing their new dresses, the first new one either girl had ever owned. Annie wasn't sure about Jane's – it looked a bit short and flirty to her – but she let it pass, knowing it would annoy their Ben if she showed any criticism. Annie frowned as the pain in her leg intensified. Neither the Germolene, salt baths or Borax had made any impression on the sore. She decided she would see a doctor next week if there was no improvement.

When the service ended the two girls waited until Annie and William had gone home with neighbours, then they set off in the direction of the Memorial Gardens, where the young folk congregated every Sunday. For most of them it was the highlight of the week. Apart from the occasional dances at the Victoria Hall – which most of them couldn't afford – and the cinema which opened a few nights a week there was little in the way of entertainment for the youth of Millington.

Dances at Cragstone or Longfield meant a walk of several miles and most parents objected to their children being subjected to the temptations they were sure were waiting in such places. So every Sunday the girls would saunter up the path by the clock, where there were seats hidden amongst the laurels and rhododendrons. There they would watch the young men walk along the bottom path, up the forty steps and down to where the girls were giggling and flaunting their Sunday dresses. The evergreens provided a hidey hole away from the eyes of any parents who would think it unseemly for their daughters to be in the company of young men when darkness was falling. The only one who was there with the consent of her parents was Dot Greenwood. It was a lonely life up at the farm and because Dot worked hard all week Boadacea thought her daughter deserved the company of people her own age. Dot was also considered trustworthy enough to protect herself, having being brought up on the farm and being familiar with the ways of procreation. 'Just remember,' Boadacea had reminded her daughter for the umpteenth time, 'never give the lads an inch or they'll expect a yard and always keep their hands, not to mention their you-know-whats well away from yer tuppence, and you'll come to no harm.' So when Dot had caught sight of young Robert in church she had waited in the lych gate and offered to show him and his brothers the meeting place of all the young people.

'If yer want to come with me I'll show yer where all our friends hang out. Come on, we usually have a bit of a laugh and I'll introduce yer to 'em all.'

So, accompanied by Dot, who looked a picture in her Sunday hat and her best skirt and blouse, the three incomers set off to meet the youth of Millington. 'We don't allow any hanky-panky so just you lot behave yerselves,' she warned them. 'We're all respectable round 'ere.' Robert felt his face redden at the thought of any hanky-panky at all.

'We'll go this way tonight, but the lads usually go that way.'

'Why?' James was curious.

Dot considered a bit. 'I don't know, they just do. Tradition, I suppose.' The crowd of girls could be heard from amongst the greenery surrounding the clock.

'Hiya,' Dot called. 'I've brought some friends to meet yet. This one is Robert but we'll call him Robbie. This one 'ere is John and he's James. They've come forty miles to live 'ere. Now this is Kitty, then there's Jane and Lucy Gabbitas. This is Mable. So now we all know one another that's all right. The lads'll be here in a minute. They like us to think they've come up 'ere for a breath of fresh air, but we know different; they've come to see us, that's because we're all so beautiful, yer see.' Dot laughed at her own joke and the others giggled. They all liked Dot Greenwood and were always made welcome at the farm by Boadacea.

'How're yer feet?' Dot asked Robbie, as he was to be known from now on.

'Not so bad.' He felt embarrassed to be singled out for attention.

'Aye well, if they don't get better, me mam'll soon make 'em right.'

'Yes she will,' Kitty Marshall agreed. 'She can cure owt can Mrs Greenwood. Better than any doctor.'

'The liniment she gave me dad cured his bad back in no time,' Mable said.

'We'll remember that,' John answered Mable, but his attention was on Lucy. He thought she was the most beautiful girl he had ever set eyes on. He blessed young Dot for bringing them up here. 'So where do you all work?' he enquired, glancing round at them all, but it was really only Lucy Gabbitas he was interested in.

'The umbrellas,' Lucy said. 'All us girls except Dot. She's lucky she can stay at home all day.'

'Oh I don't know about being lucky; I don't have half as much fun as you lot and it's not the best of jobs tramping about amongst the pig muck.' Dot loved her work on the farm really and wouldn't have swapped her life with any of them.

'That's where we work.' Jane pointed to the building down in the works, surrounded by tall black chimneys and other buildings Jane went on to describe. 'That one there is the rail mill and behind it the spring mill. This one in the bottom is where they roll the steel and cut it into strips to make our umbrella frames and all sorts of things. In the distance you can see the wire mill and the coke ovens and further still, though you can't see it from here, is the coal mine; it's hidden away in Sheepdip Wood.'

'So that's where I'm going to be working, starting tomorrow morning,' John said.

'Really? So you'll be on the same shift as our brother, Ben.' Lucy smiled. 'I'll tell him to look out for you.'

'Thanks,' John laughed nervously. 'I've never done anything remotely like coal mining.'

'You'll be all right. It's hard but they're a good crowd to work with, give you their last penny the miners would.' Lucy's face clouded as she remembered the money the colliers had collected for them when their dad died. She wondered what had become of it. Certainly none of them except her mother had seen a penny of it.

'Well, like it or not, that's what I'm going to be doing.'

'What about you?' Jane turned towards James, the one who had caught her eye in church. He looked even handsomer close at hand. James looked into Jane's warm brown eyes and knew he was going to enjoy living in Millington. 'What?' He tried to recall what she had said. 'Oh! I'm to start in the wire mill, or so Herbert told me. Sorry, Reverend Goodman. That's where we're staying at present and although it seems strange calling him Herbert, that's what he's told us to do.'

'He would, he's lovely. So is his wife. Nothing's too much trouble for either of them,' Kitty said.

'Not like that miserable lass of theirs. If she ever smiles her face'll split in two,' Dot said to the amusement of Robbie. He certainly liked Dot Greenwood. So long as she didn't think she was his girl or owt like that they would get on fine. There was a hoot of laughter as the bunch of lads approached them.

'Hiya.' Dot took charge again. 'Before you all start acting the fool may I present the vicar's guests: John, James and Robbie Grey. John'll be starting in't pit tomorrow and James in't wire.' She suddenly realised she hadn't enquired what Robbie would be doing. 'What about you?'

'I'm to be a joiner apparently, though I don't know where. Herbert is to take me tomorrow.'

'That'll be with old Smiler,' one of the young men laughed.

'Smiler? Is that his real name?'

'Oh aye.' The lad winked at the others.

'No it isn't,' Dot said, 'Don't take any notice; they're playing tricks on yer so that you'll call 'im Smiler when he's never smiled in 'is life. Him and that Prudence Goodman'd make a right pair. No, his name's Mr Grundy. Ee's a bit miserable but he's all right, he's a good joiner and ee'll treat you fair. He made us two new hen houses and right strong they are.'

'Spoil sport,' Lewis Marshall laughed. 'I'd just like to have known what his reaction was if Robbie had addressed 'im as Smiler.' Lewis didn't like the way Lucy was looking at one of the brothers. He'd give anything for her to look at him like that, but he was beginning to realise it would probably never happen. Even so he would still look out for her, no matter what. All he wanted was Lucy's happiness. And he had better start looking for another lass, too. He'd go to Cragstone to the dance on Saturday, get some of the lads to go with him. Perhaps the newcomers would like to go. If the dark one went he might meet a new lass too, leaving Lucy free for him. No, he'd waited long enough for her. Besides, the way she was gazing all cow-eyed, she looked like she was already smitten with John Grey.

'Would yer like to go to the dance next Saturday? It's a fair walk but it's all right once we get there.' Lewis looked from one brother to the other. John considered himself fortunate to be included in the gang and though he wasn't too bothered about dancing he decided he wouldn't throw kindness in his new friend's face. 'Well yes, though I'm not much of a dancer.'

James was trying to work out how much money they had left from the sale of the contents of the cottage. Some of the things had been given away to neighbours but a few heirlooms had fetched quite a bit in a shop in Lincoln. They had decided to walk to Millington in order to save on travelling expenses, enabling them to give something to the vicar for their keep until they earned their first wages. Herbert had given them most of it back, saying they must keep it until they were settled in their new neighbourhood. He had also advised them to replace their worn-out boots before starting work. He had taken them to Whitaker's shoe shop and wangled a discount for the lads on three pairs of shoes, two pairs of working boots and a pair of clogs for John. James estimated that there was still ample to last them until payday. So he would take Herbert's advice and accept Lewis's friendship. 'Yes, we'd like to come.' He glanced at Jane. 'Will you and your sister be going too?'

Jane blushed. 'Oh I don't think so.' She could imagine her mother's reaction to them suggesting going dancing.

'We could, Jane, if we asked our Ben to have a word with me mam,' Lucy said.

'No, it wouldn't work.'

'Oh come on, Jane, let's all go,' Kitty pleaded.

Kitty and her brother were very close and Kitty knew how much of an effort Lewis was making to welcome the newcomers, despite his feelings for Lucy. Still, that was the type of boy her brother was.

'Yes, let's all go,' Lewis added.

'Not me.' Robbie shook his head. 'I can't dance.'

'Nor me,' Dot agreed. 'I've got two left feet. Tell you what though, you and me could go to't pictures.'

'Oh yes, I'd like that.' A visit to the cinema had been a rare treat indeed for the village children.

'So if we can, we'll go dancing with you.' Lucy really wanted to go, and was prepared even to do battle with her mother if necessary.

'All right, but don't be surprised if Mam gets in a rage about it.' Jane knew what her mother's reaction would be.

'Our Ben'll sort her out. Now we'd better be going; it's getting late.'

'Aye, and it's getting dark. Me mam likes me in before dark.' Dot had achieved her aim, getting to know Robbie Grey.

Poor Robbie had fallen for it and got himself involved in a date with Dot Greenwood and somehow he didn't care, even if she considered herself his girl.

The walk to church and back had intensified the pain in Annie's ankle. On their return the girls were shocked at the agonised look on their mother's face. 'Mam, you look awful. What's the matter?' Jane asked.

'Nowt. I shall be right as rain when I've rested me leg.'

'You said it was getting better. Let's have a look.'

'No, I've told yer all it needs is a rest. In fact I'll be going to me bed if yer don't mind.' Annie had never been known to retire for the night until everybody was in and the house locked up.

Jane and Lucy exchanged glances. 'Let me have a look at your ankle, Mam.'

Annie ignored her daughter and set off towards the stairs but Jane blocked her way. 'Come on, Mam. Let me look at your ankle.'

Annie sighed and hobbled back to her chair. 'It's just a bit inflamed.'

She lifted her skirt and pulled down her stocking, then she began to unwind the bandage, releasing a stench more vile than anything the girls had ever experienced.

'Oh my God.' Jane couldn't believe the sight of her mother's ankle. It was double its normal size, an open sore was festering, and surrounding it the ankle had already turned purple as if it was already dead. 'I'm going for the doctor.' Jane had already reached for her coat.

'No, not tonight. I'll go see 'im tomorrow.'

'But he'll give you something for the pain.'

'Doctors! What do they know?'

'I'll go and ask Mrs Greenwood; she'll know what to do,' Lucy said.

'Aye, that might be best,' Annie agreed. 'Boady'll give me summat to take the pain away.'

'But it's all septic, Mam. Why didn't you do something sooner?' Jane spooned tea into the teapot and placed the kettle over the fire. 'I'll make some tea and then when our Lucy comes back we'll get you to bed.'

'Nay, I'll wait till everybody's in. I were only going out of't way so yer wouldn't see 'ow bad me leg were.'

'Well, now we've seen it and we're going to get it better.'

Mrs Greenwood was just on her way to bed. She was wearing a white winceyette nightgown which resembled a tent. They were an early-to-bed, early-to-rise family. She couldn't imagine who would be knocking at this time of night. 'Who the hangment can that be?' she asked Little Arthur, as if he was a mindreader.

Lucy was nearly knocked down by Bob the dog, who slobbered all over her face the moment the door opened. 'Hello, Mrs Greenwood. I'm sorry to come at this time of night but it's me mam; she's in agony with a bad ankle.'

'Well, I'd better come then.' Boadacea set off to get dressed.

'Oh no, I don't want you trailing out at this time of night. We just thought you'd give her something to take the pain away. She'll have to see a doctor tomorrow, it's really bad.'

'What's it look like?'

'Well, her ankle and foot are both swollen and purple and the sore's all running with pus and it smells horrible.'

'Oh I don't like the sound of that at all. She will have to see a doctor. I can make 'er a poultice of slippery elm powder. It might 'elp for tonight but yer must get 'er to a doctor tomorrer.'

'What do you think it is, Mrs Greenwood?'

'Well, it's hard to say without seeing it. Might be an ulcer but I don't like the sound of the purple foot, or the stink. 'Ang on love, I won't be long.'

Lucy was scared. Mrs Greenwood didn't usually recommend doctors.

''Ere you are me love. Warm the poultice and apply the slippery elm powder on the poultice. This 'ere is some camomile. Make yer mam some good strong camomile tea; it'll ease the pain and calm 'er down a bit. Help 'er to sleep.'

'Thanks, Mrs Greenwood. How much is it?'

'Don't be daft, you're our Dot's friend. Besides, I've known yer mam for as long as I can remember.'

'I'd rather pay.'

'And I'd rather yer didn't. Now get on yer way. The sooner yer get 'ome the sooner yer mam'll get a bit of relief, but think on, yer must get a doctor, I mean it.'

'I will.' Lucy ran all the way down the hill. It was a bit scary up here with no houses or anything and the sound of clanging metal from the works echoing along the valley. She was relieved when she reached the main road.

Annie didn't need much persuasion to go off to

her bed and when she was made comfortable the two sisters sat down to wait for Ben to come home and discuss Annie's condition.

'I think our Ben must be courting,' Jane said. 'He's been staying out much later than usual this last few weeks.'

'Yes, I've noticed. He must be wanting to settle down at his age.'

'I hope he finds someone as nice as himself.'

'Yes, so do I. Oh Jane, I do like John Grey, but I don't suppose we shall be free to go to the dance if me mam's no better.'

'It looks awful, her leg I mean.'

'I know. Mrs Greenwood insists we get her to the doctor, tomorrow, she said. She thinks it might be infected.'

'Yes, we'll tell our Ben to make sure she goes. Thank goodness he's on mornings and he'll be home by two. There's a surgery in the afternoon.'

'I do wish we could go to the dance though,' Lucy frowned.

'Yes, so do I, I really like James Grey.' Jane hadn't really expected to go. Nothing nice ever happened in the Gabbitas household. Her mother was right: if you didn't expect anything, you would never be disappointed. But on this occasion she was, very disappointed, so disappointed she felt like crying.

Chapter Five

Lucy found it difficult to concentrate on her work the next day. It had been gone midnight when she had finally finished talking to Ben. Her wage had risen to fourteen shillings on her birthday and she could usually add to that being on piecework, but she wouldn't have made much today. She couldn't get the sight of her mother's leg out of her mind and couldn't wait to find out what the doctor had to say. Lewis Marshall was in an aggravating mood – coming up behind her he blew up a paper bag and burst it, causing everyone to laugh as it startled her. Usually she would have joined in the merriment but on this occasion she snapped, 'Oh why don't you grow up?'

'Sorry, I was only trying to cheer you up a bit. Yer've been a bit of a misery all day, Lucy.' Lewis looked crestfallen.

Lucy felt a bit sorry for Lewis. 'Aye well, I've things on my mind.'

'What things? Yer know you can always talk to me about yer worries.'

'Yes, I know that. Thanks, Lewis.' Just then Mr Blackmore came striding down the shop. 'What's going on up 'ere then? What was that noise all about?'

'Noise? What noise? I didn't 'ear a noise Mr Blackmore.' Lucy looked the picture of innocence.

'Was it thee? Lew Marshall, tha'll be getting

sack one o' these days if tha not careful.'

'Not me, Mr Blackmore, I didn't 'ear any noise either.' Lewis looked at his sister on the next bench. 'Did you 'ear a noise, Kitty?'

'What sort of a noise did it sound like?'

'I don't know, I didn't 'ear owt.' Lewis looked questioningly at his boss. 'What sort of noise was it? Mr Blackmore?'

'Oh, get on with thi work.' Exasperated, Mr Blackmore walked away. 'Get on with thi work, I said. NOW.'

Lewis hurried away in the direction of the gitting shop, carrying a bundle of ribs and stretchers he had already inspected, wondering as he went what it was Lucy was worrying about. No doubt he would hear about it sooner or later. There weren't many secrets to be kept amongst the families on Top Row.

'Your mother will have to go to hospital; I'm afraid there isn't anything I can do for her, Mr Gabbitas. You should have called me sooner.' The doctor turned to Annie. 'How long has it been like this?'

'A few years, but not as bad as this.' Annie frowned. 'Can't yer give me owt without me leaving me kids?'

'No! I only wish I could. I believe you might need surgery.'

'What do yer think it is then?' Ben asked, becoming alarmed at the mention of an operation.

The doctor stood up and walked round the room. 'I'll be honest with you, Mr Gabbitas. I think your mother is suffering from Necrosis, commonly known as fever sore. If this is the case it must be dealt with urgently. In your mother's case it has been neglected for far too long. She needs to see a specialist and I shall arrange this immediately. You must take a letter to the Royal Hospital. Your mother will be seen today.' He sat at his desk and began to write. 'If you will wait in the waiting room I shall be with you directly.'

'How much will it cost?' Annie worried.

'Oh Mother, what does it matter? Come on, let the doctor get on with his letter or we'll never get anywhere, let alone Sheffield.'

Annie sighed. 'Aye, I guess I shall 'ave to go whether I like it or not.'

The Royal was a spooky place. A nurse led them into a room and ordered Annie to take off her stocking and lie on the bed. Then the nurse undid the bandage and took off the matter-encrusted lint, releasing the stench of rotting meat which seemed to be growing stronger by the minute.

'Bloody 'ell.' Ben felt sick. 'Sorry, nurse.'

The young nurse gulped. 'It's all right. I agree it is a terrible smell.' She left the room and when she returned she was accompanied by an elderly white-haired man who took one look at Annie's leg and left the room. He obviously needed a second opinion. The second man, this time in a white coat, put on a pair of surgical gloves and examined Annie more closely. 'Mortification, sir.'

'Yes, good man. What are we to do about it?'

'Remove the dead bone, sir.' The elder man nodded.

'We shall operate first thing in the morning as a

matter of extreme urgency,' the specialist told Annie. 'The nurse will attend to you now.'

'Come with me, Mrs Gabbitas. We'll find you a bed and make you comfortable.' Annie followed her out of the room, speechless with shock.

'Mr Gabbitas.' The elderly man, immaculate in a black suit, white shirt and black tie, addressed Ben. 'Your mother's condition is extremely serious. If we are fortunate we shall be able to remove all the infected bone. If, as I suspect, it has been neglected too long and the necrosis has spread too far, we shall have no alternative but to amputate the affected limb. Even then it could prove fatal to your mother. Be of good hope; we shall do our best. And now I must proceed with my work. Good day to you, Mr Gabbitas.'

'And to you. Thank you for treating my mother so promptly.'

Nodding, the man left the room with the specialist. Ben wondered what to do now and waited until the nurse came back.

'I should go home now if I were you. Your mother'll be kept comfortable until her operation. You can come at visiting time tomorrow, but I should wait until the day after – she'll be all day coming round after surgery. Visiting is seven till eight and two till three at weekends.'

Ben felt dazed. What the hell had his mother been playing at, letting her leg get into that state? What if it needed to be amputated? How would they manage? What if it proved fatal? What about young William? Oh God, just when he was on the verge of asking Emma to marry him. Well, that would have to be postponed. He only just caught the bus to Millington; the lasses would be waiting for news and he dreaded having to give it to them.

It had been a strange day for the Grey brothers too. John had found the pit terrifying at first. After the corn mill it was not only hard work – which he didn't mind – it was also claustrophobic, which he did. Working in a space too low to be able to stand upright meant an aching back after just a couple of hours and kneeling in a foot of water didn't go down too well either. What he did like about the new job was the camaraderie amongst the men. The way they shared their drinking water and advised him on which sandwich fillings would have turned stale by snap time. The most embarrassing and sickening thing about the pit was the lack of facilities for use as a toilet. The men had no alternative but to relieve themselves by squatting down in the presence of work mates. At the end of the shift his muscles felt as though he had been in a fight with Little Arthur's bull. However, he accepted Ben Gabbitas's invitation to join him for a pint at the Rising Sun and felt better after the liquid refreshment and a dip in the slipper bath at the Miners' Club.

'Don't worry,' Ben told him, 'the first day is always the worst. Now if yer don't mind I've got to go take me mother to see the doctor. See yer tomorrer.'

'Thanks, Ben. It would have been a lot worse without somebody to talk to.'

'Oh, somebody'd 'ave looked out for yer; they're not a bad bunch of mates.'

'No, I've realised that.' Ben Gabbitas had

already gone, intent upon persuading his mother to get her leg seen to.

James Grey had felt just as strange in the wire mill, even if not quite as overworked. In fact he was embarrassed during the first couple of hours to be given a brush and ordered to sweep up. However he set to willingly and was then given what he considered real work: die polishing. The dies consisted of a series of steel cone-shaped devices through which metal rods were drawn until they reduced to the size of wire required. The work wasn't as heavy as James had expected, the most important task being the setting up of the machine and making sure it was kept maintained. When the two brothers compared jobs later James realised how fortunate he was to have landed himself in the wire mill rather than the mine.

Young Robbie thought he was the luckiest lad in Millington. Like James he had begun by sweeping the floor. A whole sack of shavings had been gathered up as Robbie made sure he swept in all the corners and beneath the work bench. Mr Grundy didn't say much but he didn't complain either, so Robbie thought he must be satisfied. After that Robbie had been told all about the various kinds of wood and what each could be used for. Then he had been set to work smoothing down and polishing a coffin lid. He loved the smell of the timber and the beeswax – in fact he loved everything about the workshop. He also liked the way Mr Grundy nodded approvingly when he came to inspect his work. It was true the man didn't smile much, but Robbie could understand why; the joiner was so engrossed in his work that nothing else seemed to matter to him. Mr Grundy was happy without having to be smiling all the time and Robbie knew that one day he would enjoy the woodworking just as much as his boss did. At home time Mr Grundy said to Robbie, 'Aye well, lad, it's time tha weren't 'ere. Aren't tha bothered about goin 'ome?'

Robbie reluctantly put down the polishing rag he was using, looked at his boss and said, 'No, Mr Grundy, I'm quite happy here.'

Then the man did smile. 'Tha'll do all right Robbie Grey, tha'r a good lad. Get off for thi tea and I'll see thi in the morning.'

'Our Mary and Nellie'll have to be told,' Ben said when he had explained about his mother's forthcoming operation. He hadn't told them how serious her condition could prove to be. There would be time enough for that after tomorrow.

'Shall I go and tell them?' Lucy asked.

'I'll go if I can borrow yer bike.' William would go anywhere as an excuse to borrow his brother's bicycle.

'Aye, that might be best. Do yer know where the place is?' Ben was referring to the manor at Cragstone.

'Yes, we went one day to look where our Nellie works; it isn't 'alf posh.'

'All the way to Cragstone. Who did you go with?'

'Albert Marshall and Ernie Slater.'

'You mustn't go in the grounds; it's private property,' Lucy warned.

'Nobody saw us.'

'Well if yer know where it is yer can take a note for our Nellie.'

'And don't go to the front door, go round the back.' Lucy always worried about doing the right thing. It got on young Will's nerves sometimes.

'I know that, I'm not daft.'

Ben gave him the note. 'Right, off yer go, straight there and back don't forget.'

'I can't do that; there're some corners to go round,' Will grinned.

'Go on, and be careful down the hill,' Lucy warned. 'Are you sure the brakes are working?'

'Positive! Will one of you go and tell our Mary?'

Ben looked from Lucy to Jane.

'Well I was just going out.' Jane couldn't meet her brother's eye.

'Oh I'll go,' Lucy snapped. 'Though how you can go out when me mam's so poorly I don't know.'

'Well it won't make any difference if I stay in, will it?'

'No, Lucy. Our Jane's right. There's no reason to sit here moping. You take the note to our Mary's and then you can go out as well, if yer like.'

'No, I'll come back and wait for our Will. You go out, Ben. You've done your share today by taking my mam to hospital.'

'Well I don't know, I reckon I ought to be here for yer all.'

'Go on, there's nothing going to happen tonight. Go on.'

Ben really wanted to see Emma and explain what was happening. He didn't doubt she would support him in any way she could; she was an understanding lass, was Emma Scott. All the same he knew she was expecting him to pop the question and he felt bad about putting it off. 'Well, I will go out for an hour, if yer sure.'

'Course I'm sure.' Lucy sat in her mother's rocking chair and picked up Annie's copy of *My Magazine* but she couldn't concentrate. She was always grumbling about her mother, but the house wasn't the same without her. She stood up and decided to give the kitchen a good bottoming, make it nice for when her mam came home. She took up the pegged rug Annie had made and took it outside to shake, then she washed the floor before replacing it. By the time Will came back the furniture was polished and the pot ornaments on the dresser and mantelpiece all washed and sparkling.

'Our Nellie's coming over tomorrow after she's finished cooking dinner. Why do they 'ave their dinner at night, Lucy, just when everybody else are 'aving their teas?'

'Because the people at the manor are all posh. Besides they are all businessmen and are at work all day.'

'I wish we 'ad a kitchen like that.'

'Did you go in?' Lucy was curious what it was like.

'Aye and she gave me some chocolate pudding with custard on. I didn't believe our Nellie had made it, but Mrs Cooper said she had. She isn't 'alf a good cook, our Nellie.'

'Right then, do you want to come with me to our Mary's?'

'I'll go meself if I can take our Ben's bike.' Will knew it was getting late and it would mean staying up longer.

'Go on then. Just tell her to pop over tomorrow after tea. Tell her our Nellie'll be here.' There was no point in worrying her until after the operation and they knew what was going to happen. Will didn't need telling twice.

This time Lucy relaxed in the chair and closed her eyes, wondering what tomorrow would bring. She knew operations were sometimes dangerous, but surely nothing could happen to Annie Gabbitas. She had always been there for them and even if she had shouted and sometimes clouted them the house wouldn't be the same without her presence. Lucy could remember a time when her mother hadn't been miserable; she could even remember her mam and dad dancing round the table and kissing each other. In fact Annie always used to kiss her dad when he left for the pit and again when he came home. Lucy tried to think when it was that things had changed. It must have been after their Will was born. That was when her dad had become ill, yes, that was it, when her dad had began having time off work because of his cough. That was when Annie had changed. Before that she had made little treats for them, like apple dumplings and ginger parkin. Even though they had never had new clothes Annie used to buy them pretty ribbons for their hair and gather wild flowers from up the banking and arrange them in a pot on the dresser.

Lucy wiped her eyes on her pinafore and told herself not to be daft: crying wouldn't help. She vowed to look after her mam for as long as she needed her. She also promised herself that when she married and had children of her own, she would always try and be of good spirits and even if her husband became ill she would make sure it was a happy home.

She suddenly saw a picture forming in her mind, a picture of John Grey, but she dismissed it before the tears started again. She wouldn't be going to the dance on Saturday – probably not for weeks if she was looking after her mam. By then John Grey would have found himself another girl; he was far too handsome to bother waiting for the likes of her.

The Grey brothers had settled in well at the vicarage. It was an old stone house next to the church – quite spooky – with three large square bedrooms and one smaller one. Louisa Goodman had arranged the smaller one for Robbie and placed two single beds in another for John and James. The food was plain but wholesome and the brothers endeavoured to repay their hosts by lending a hand with any tasks that needed attending to. The Sunday after their arrival a starling had flown down the chimney and flapped blindly around the kitchen. John had caught the poor thing, cleaned it up and released it into the garden. Then he had cleaned up the soot fall and given the walls a fresh coat of lime wash. It had all been done while the Sunday service was taking place. Louisa said Herbert always kept the commandments and on the Sabbath would never have agreed to the work being done. She did concede however that it had been a sort of emergency and since Herbert had been unaware of what had happened he couldn't really complain. Another night James had volunteered to cut the grass in the graveyard, glad of the fresh air after the confines of the wire mill.

Young Robbie was spending more and more time in the joiner's shop. Mr Grundy had suggested the boy should keep to the hours originally agreed, but when Robbie told him he enjoyed staying over and wanted to learn as much as he could, Mrs Grundy had suggested the boy join them for their main meal and then return to work under the guidance of her husband. So now Robbie could look forward to a little extra in his pay packet every Friday. He had been taught how to mix glue and how to stain wood and he also knew what all the different tools were for and how to care for them. Evenings at the vicarage were usually spent with a book from Herbert's small but well-stocked library. Sometimes they would partake of a game of dominoes and the elder brothers had been taught to play bridge.

John had been devastated when Lucy Gabbitas hadn't turned up with her sister on the night of the dance. Kitty explained about Mrs Gabbitas being in hospital and John wondered why Jane had decided to come along, leaving her younger sister with the responsibility of taking care of her brother. It made John admire Lucy more than ever and though he danced most of the dances with Kitty Marshall he never stopped thinking about Lucy. Actually John was relieved when the evening came to an end. He had been left with the impression that Jane was of a rather shallow nature, but as James seemed to be besotted with her he thought he was maybe being a little hard on the girl. John was cheered slightly with Kitty's parting words: 'I'll tell Lucy you were concerned about her mother.'

'Oh, aye, you do that. Oh and Kitty! Will you tell her I'll be waiting when her mother's better?'

Kitty grinned. 'Aye, it'll make her day if I tell her that. She really likes you.'

'Really?' John grinned.

'Aye, really.'

Kitty liked John too. If Lucy hadn't been her best friend she might have tried to entice John Grey away from her, but like Lucy, Kitty Marshall was loyal to her friends and family.

Chapter Six

On Wednesday night the whole Gabbitas family went to visit Annie, with the exception of William who, at eleven, was considered to be too young, and Jane, who made the excuse that she would stay and see to her brother, even though they all knew the real reason was that she was squeamish about hospitals. They were met by the matron, who invited Ben into her office and explained that it had been necessary to amputate his mother's leg below the knee. It was hoped that all the necrosis had been eliminated and Annie was as comfortable as could be expected. Ben and Mary were the first to be allowed into the ward. Annie looked so small and ill amongst the pillows that Mary promptly burst into tears. Now instead of fearing her mother, Mary just pitied her.

'Nay, lass, crying'll alter nowt,' Annie told Mary. 'Me leg's gone now and glad I am to be rid of it.'

'Oh, Mam, why didn't you see the doctor sooner?'

'I don't know, lass. I just kept putting it off. I expected the Borax to heal it up and get it better. Anyway, it's gone now.' A tear slid down her pale cheek and Mary leaned over and placed her arms round Annie's shoulders. 'Anyway, I shall manage once I get used to a pair o' crutches. How're me bairns?'

'Our Lucy and Nellie're here. Our William isn't allowed in.'

'And our Jane'll be too busy I expect.'

'She's keeping an eye on William.'

'She didn't need to. Mrs Slater'd 'ave seen to 'im.' Mr and Mrs Slater had always been there through any crisis affecting the Gabbitas family; in return Annie and Bill had given any assistance required by their neighbours. Unlike others on Top Row they had never fallen out over any of their children's quarrels and simply ordered them to go out and play nicely. The women had attended each other's confinements and acted as godparents to each other's children. Indeed William and young Ernest Slater had been baptised on the same day.

'I think we'd better go and let our Nellie and Lucy come in.' Ben wasn't in the mood to begin making excuses for their Jane.

'Aye, I want to talk to our Lucy.'

The two sisters were so intent on cheering up their mother that Annie never got round to saying whatever she intended saying to her youngest daughter, before the bell sounded indicating the end of visiting. For the first time in years the girls received a kiss from their mother, which might have caused the tears to start, had they not hurried out to join the others. 'What are we going to do about caring for her?' Lucy worried. 'Will I have to leave work?'

'No!' Ben was emphatic. 'We'll sort something out.'

'Aye, but what?' Nellie knew her mother would need full-time care.

'We'll get a bed downstairs for a start.' Ben hadn't thought beyond that. 'It wouldn't be fair to expect one of us to carry all the burden.'

It was a dispirited and silent foursome who boarded the bus back to Millington, each of them dreading what the future was to bring.

Whatever they had been dreading couldn't possibly have been as bad as the reality. Annie had been in good spirits and recovering well until five days after the operation. She had told Ben to bring Lucy the next day and because Ben had never missed a visit Lucy told him to have a night off and she would visit her mother on her own. Annie was sweating and her face was flushed. She didn't look as well as when Lucy had last seen her: 'Are you all right, Mam?' She held her hand on Annie's forehead. 'You're ever so hot.'

'I'm right enough. A bit of a headache, that's all. Come and sit on the bed; I want to tell yer summat.' Lucy checked to see if the stony-faced matron was anywhere in sight before perching on the bed and taking hold of her mother's hand.

'I'm sorry, Lucy.'

'What for?'

'Oh don't pretend, lass, we both know I 'aven't treated you right. I'm not making excuses, but I thought I was doing the right thing, saving every penny I got instead of spending it on summat nice for you all. Well, I still think I did the right thing, especially now. It'll come in when I've gone.'

'Mam!'

'No, let me finish. When yer father died I was frightened – in fact before he died. I knew he hadn't got long to live; I'd been told by the doctor. I began to wonder what'd become of yer all when we'd both gone. What with the worry and the pain in me leg, I turned into a wicked old woman instead of a caring mother.'

'You were never wicked and you're not that old either.'

'Any road up, I decided that if owt 'appened to me I'd leave you all right, financially I mean.' Annie wiped the sweat from her upper lip. She felt bad.

'I'm going to call the nurse. You're not well.'

'No, let me finish. I want you to go to the top drawer in me tallboy. You'll find one of yer dad's socks. Inside it you'll find me savings, and there's the money yer Aunt Kate gave me when she went away; she said it was for any emergencies.'

'But we had an emergency, Mam, when the

miners were out on strike.' Lucy cringed as she remembered having nothing in the house to spread on the bread. They had had the option of either a sprinkling of salt or a sprinkling of sugar. 'Why didn't you use the money to feed us?'

'I objected to where it came from. The man she was keeping house for left it to Kate in his will. She was keeping 'im warm in his bed more like. But I was wrong, Lucy. Kate meant well when she gave it to us. Anyway it's there for you all now.' Annie could hardly get the words out. 'It'll tide you over until our William's old enough to start work. Promise me you'll look after him, love. I know you're the youngest but I can trust you more than our Jane. She's not a bad lass, just a bit flighty, that's all. Promise me, Lucy.'

'Of course I'll look after him. What do you take me for?'

'A good lass, that's what I take yer for.'

'I don't know why you're saying all this; you'll be home next week.'

'No, Lucy. Summat's gone wrong, I know it 'as. Listen, don't give up yer job; you're too young to be stuck at 'ome all day, and don't let our Jane spend the money on daft things. It's for the three of yer. The others are old enough to be independent. Our William's well able to get 'imself off to school in a morning and Enid Slater'll keep an eye on 'im until yer come 'ome at night. There's a letter in the drawer I wrote to Enid in case owt like this 'appened to me. You can depend on Mrs Slater, remember that.'

'Nothing's going to happen. Mam.'

'Ee'll 'ave to go in't pit, our William. I were

'oping for summat better for me youngest but he'll need his name on the rent book when our Ben marries, and I expect he will soon.'

'Oh Mam, let me fetch a nurse.'

'Aye, yer can fetch 'er before yer go.' The bell interrupted Annie and she clung tighter to Lucy's hand. 'Keep the money safe, Lucy, and keep a good table. God knows I never did. Tell all me bairns I love 'em.'

'Mam, stop talking like this. You can tell them yourself when you see them.' By now Lucy was trying to control the tears.

'I love 'em all, Lucy, but you're the most like yer dad so I've a special love for you. I didn't want 'em to know that so I treated you more harshly to cover up. God bless, love.'

Lucy escaped before her mother saw the tears. She went to the table in the centre of the ward where a nurse kept a constant watch over her patients. 'Nurse, my mother isn't right; she's sweating and flushed but her hands are like ice.'

'I'll see to her.' The nurse went towards Annie Gabbitas's bed. She knew without a doctor's examination that Annie had a fever. She also realised the patient was probably suffering from septicaemia. Poisoning of the blood was all too common in amputees, and unfortunately there was little to be done except pray. She applied a cold cloth to Annie's forehead in an attempt to bring down her temperature. Annie was shivering and rapidly becoming delirious, but at least she had made her peace with her daughter. The nurse went off to find the doctor. She didn't bother hurrying. There was little anyone could do for Annie Gabbitas; septicaemia was a killer and the nurse was experienced enough to know that.

As soon as Lucy arrived home she went upstairs to her mother's room. She hadn't been in here since the day she had bought the material for the new dresses. It seemed months away and Lucy couldn't believe what a happy day that had been; even their Nellie leaving home hadn't quite spoiled the excitement. Now it was as though the family would never be happy again. How could they be with a mam with only one leg? She wished Annie hadn't told her about the money. It was as though she thought she was going to die. She opened the top drawer and shifted her mother's few possessions; a bible handed down from Bill Gabbitas's family; Annie's hymn and prayer book; her Sunday gloves, soft kid with a tiny button at the wrist and a fur cuff; a flower, pressed in tissue paper, given to her by Bill on her coming of age. She found the sock, heavy with coins and even some notes, obviously accumulated over a number of years. She found a letter addressed to My Good and Loyal Friend, Enid Slater. Another envelope, To Annie and Bill from Kate. She didn't count the money, but put it back where she had found it. It would be there when her mam came home. Lucy felt a chill run down her spine – if her mam came home.

When Annie Gabbitas did come home it was to be prepared for her funeral. Once again the family was grateful that the insurance had been kept up to date, especially as there was an added cost of fifteen shillings this time for the conveying of the body home from Sheffield. The full cost of twenty pounds and five shillings could have been reduced by ten shillings if Ben had not insisted on a wreath. 'It'll be in memory of me father as well as me mother,' he explained to the family. 'And we'll be 'aving tea for the mourners this time at the Co-op.' Lucy wondered if this was the time to tell the family about the money in the drawer, but decided to wait until her mam was buried and resting in peace.

Almost everyone on Top Row turned out to attend the funeral. Ben arranged for a carriage and two cars to follow the hearse. The Slaters, the Marshalls and Mr Brown joined the family mourners on the journey to Cragstone Church, where Reverend Goodman was to conduct the ceremony. Ben, who had kept his emotions under control as an example to the younger ones, finally gave in to his feelings at the sight of the packed church. The thought of all these friends, neighbours and relatives making a journey of several miles and probably losing a few hours' work in order to do so brought a lump to his throat and tears to his eyes. Even people Ben hadn't seen since his father died had turned up like a flurry of rooks in their black coats and hats.

After the last of the mourners had left for home Lucy asked Mary and Jacob to stay. 'You too, Nellie. I've got something to tell you.' She mashed a pot of tea and asked them all to sit down.

'You all know I was the last one to see me mam whilst she was still rational.' Lucy couldn't help showing off a bit with the new word she'd learned from the hospital doctor.

She poured the tea and sat down at the table. 'Well, she asked me to tell you how much she loved you all and apologised for being mean with the money and explained that she'd done it for a reason.' Lucy paused to take a breath, then continued. 'The reason being that she was worried about what would become of us after she'd gone. She said her leg had been worrying her even before me dad died.'

'Why didn't she tell us?' Jane was in tears. 'If I'd known how bad it was I'd 'ave gone to visit her.'

'None of us knew, Jane and anyway, me mam understood why you didn't go. She loved you, she told me she did, and she proved it by saving all the money she could have spent on herself. Every penny, so that we should have security when she had gone. She did it for our William and you and me.' Lucy stood up and ran upstairs. When she returned she emptied the sock on the table. 'She said it was for us three, but I don't think that's fair. You've all gone short, especially our Ben who's tipped up the most. I shall put my share back for when our Will needs new clothes, which he will because he's growing so fast. But you must share the rest. Me mam said I had to stop you spending your share on daft things.' Lucy smiled at Jane. 'She said you were a good lass but a bit flighty.'

Jane blushed but the tears had ceased by now and she was grateful for the chance to make amends for her neglect of her mother. 'You must have my share for our Will, and we'll come to some agreement about how much we shall be able to manage on for running the house.'

'No, Jane. If me mother said it was for you three then we must respect her wishes.' Ben looked questioningly at Mary and Nellie.

'Of course they must have it. I wouldn't dream of taking any of it. I don't need it,' Nellie said. 'In fact I can contribute a bit each week if necessary.'

'It won't be necessary whilst I live here, though if I leave I don't know what will happen. It looks like I'm stuck 'ere until you start at pit, Will.'

'I don't want to go to't pit; I'd be scared shut in all't time in the dark.' William had turned pale.

'Me mam didn't want you to go, but I can't see any alternative,' Lucy said, 'not if our Ben wants a home of his own.'

'We'll cross that bridge when we come to it,' Ben said. 'In the meantime I think this little lot should go in the bank for safety.'

'In our Will's name,' Jane stressed. 'How much is there?'

'I don't know. I haven't counted it.'

'Then we'd better do it now, and the first chance we get we'll take it to the Yorkshire Bank.

'Come on, Jacob, you work with money. Would you like to count it for us?' Jacob nodded. As an accountant he was pleased to be of assistance to his wife's family and even more pleased to be included in their affairs. Being an only child he considered this family – who admittedly had just lost their mother but had a close relationship with their brothers and sisters – to be so much more fortunate than him. He counted the money and delved into his pocket, bringing out a florin, which he added to the rest of the money. 'Exactly two hundred and forty pounds.'

'What? Bloody 'ell.' Ben usually reserved any bad language for the pit, but he was too shocked to notice. 'How did she manage that?'

'Well, I reckon she must have saved all of her pension since your father died. There's also a hundred pounds from Aunt Kate and a donation from the colliers at the time of your father's death.'

'She'd been scrimping before me dad died, she told me.' Lucy was proud that her mother had chosen her to confide in.

'Ah yes, but there would have been a time of hardship during the strike, with bills to be paid,' Jacob reasoned. Nobody informed him about how mean Annie had been. In fact they would all have been willing to exist on stew for the rest of their lives just to have their mother back. Only in one piece though – none of them would have wished her back to suffer. And each and every one of them was relieved not to have the worry of caring for an invalid, though none of them would ever have admitted it.

Chapter Seven

It was two o'clock in the morning when Lucy woke. Her pillow was wet with tears and the realisation that she would never see her mother again dawned on her for the first time. She looked to the bottom of the bed and wasn't at all surprised to see her mother standing there. She was wearing the new flannel nighty with the embroidered Peter Pan collar, which had been folded neatly in her mother's drawer ready for her laying out. Mrs Slater had done her the honour of making her look nice; she had laid her on the best cotton sheets with the lace edging ready for visitors to call and pay their last respects. 'Mam, you've let your hair down; you look lovely,' Lucy said. Annie merely smiled and floated away through the wall into the next room. Lucy sighed, snuggled down into the lumpy flock pillow and drifted off to sleep.

Jane was packing Nestlé Milk sandwiches the next morning, for the two of them to take to work and for Will to take for his school lunch. Ben would already have been slaving for a couple of hours. Lucy poured the tea. 'Me mam came last night,' she said.

'It'll be all the upset that made you dream.'

'No, it wasn't a dream. She came and stood at the foot of the bed to comfort me because I was upset. I was really sad and worried, Jane, then she came and smiled at me. She looked all young and pretty and her hair was thick and long, just like it was when we were little.'

'You're being silly, Lucy and creepy.'

'No it wasn't creepy, it was lovely. She came to watch over us and now I don't feel lost anymore.'

William came clattering downstairs. 'What are you doing up at this time?' Jane asked. 'We were going to give you a shout when we went to work.'

'I've got to go. I've got a job.'

'A job? You can't. You've to go to school.'

'Before school, I've to load up the cart for Mr Brown every morning. I shall be paid on Friday. It won't be much but it'll pay for some food I expect.'

'Well, that's wonderful,' Lucy said. 'I'm really proud of you, Will.' William blushed but he was pleased.

'As long as it doesn't make you late for school,' Jane warned.

'Oh it won't. Mr Brown needs to be off on his rounds by half past eight.' He reached for his cap. 'I'm off.'

'Here, don't go without yer sandwiches. You're to go and eat them at Mrs Slater's at dinner time.'

'Sandwiches? That's not much of a dinner.'

'No, you'll be having your dinner with us at tea time as of now.'

'Wow, does that mean we're turning all posh like our Nellie?'

'No, just that our mam's not here to cook for you at midday. We just need to get organised, then we shall be all right.'

'Well, I'm off.' Will hurried out without a backward glance.

'He seems to have recovered from our ordeal without much trouble.'

'Hmm, I expect our mam's looking after him too.'

'How did the funeral go?' John Grey enquired as Ben joined him at the pit head.

'Better than I expected. I never thought so many people would turn out to pay their respects.'

‘Aye, some people seem to enjoy funerals.’

Ben thought how horrendous it must have been for the Grey brothers to lose their parents and their home all in one go.

‘I’m just relieved that it’s over and me mother’s out of her suffering.’

‘How are the others?’

‘Not too bad. I think they’re all as relieved as I am. I can’t imagine how she’d ’ave coped with not being able to get about.’

‘How’s Lucy?’

‘Oh, our Lucy’ll cope. I shall just ’ave to make sure she doesn’t turn into a slave for us all.’

‘Aye, she needs to get out.’

‘You’re right and I’ll make sure she does.’ The conversation came to an end as the men began work. John felt happier than he had for weeks. He hoped Ben Gabbitas would keep his word and encourage Lucy to go out, then John might have a chance of seeing her, because he couldn’t get the girl out of his mind. She was there, day and night, her blue eyes gazing hauntingly into his. John Grey, for the first time in his life, was in love.

Chapter Eight

It was over a year now since Annie Gabbitas had been laid to rest. The household had soon become organised and a day-to-day routine established. At first the girls had taken turns to cook the evening dinner and clean the house, but as Lucy turned out to be the better cook it had been decided that she would prepare the meals and Jane would tidy the kitchen. On Saturday afternoons they would join forces and give the whole house a thorough bottoming. As Ben was paying the rent and making other financial contributions it was decided he would be let off any household duties. Young Will had made himself responsible for chopping sticks and bringing up the coal. He was also allowed by Mr Brown to bring home any fruit and vegetables he considered unfit for sale. The family were eating better than ever before with a real Sunday dinner of beef and Yorkshire pudding. And soon after Annie's death Evelyn Smithson had offered to do the weekly washing; it had not only been a godsend to the family but to Evelyn too. With a son to support and no husband Evelyn struggled to manage and even people who had ostracised Evelyn for being an unmarried mother had come to respect her for the hard worker she had proved to be.

A few weeks after Annie's funeral John Grey had asked Lucy to accompany him to a dance at Longfield. She had felt her pulse quicken with excitement but had told him he had better ask their Ben if he approved. Ben, who had taken young John under his wing and knew him to be hard-working and honest wasn't surprised that he had taken a fancy to his sister.

'I'd like to ask your Lucy to the dance on Saturday. Would that be all right?' John had asked as they made their way through the piles of pit props and wheel sets.

'Aye, so long as yer promise to look after 'er

and see she gets 'ome safe. Oh, and remember, she's a good lass, our Lucy. I expect her to stay that way.'

'She will, I promise.' John had set to work with a grin on his face and it was soon to become common knowledge that Lucy Gabbitas and John Grey were courting.

Although John came to Sheepdip Wood every working day he had never taken this path before, only being familiar with the ash track leading to the pit. On this Sunday evening he and Lucy were taking the path alongside the ochre stream. The air was heady with the scent of bluebells after a shower; the beeches were washed clean and seemed a brighter green than usual. They paused to listen to the tapping of a woodpecker and watched a red squirrel scurry up the trunk of an oak tree.

'I've never been to this part of the wood before.' John pulled Lucy down onto a fallen branch. 'Look at the view from up here.'

'My dad used to bring us up here when we were little. We used to walk all the way round the dam. My grandad helped to build that dam,' she informed him proudly.

'There's not many folk who'll leave a memorial like that behind them.'

'No. He died young though. The hard graft, I expect.' Lucy's face clouded. 'John!'

'Yes?'

'I wish you'd leave the pit and find another job.'

John laughed. 'Easier said than done, Lucy. There aren't many jobs to be had. Besides, it's not so bad.'

'It killed my dad.'

'Really, did the doctor say so?'

'Oh no, they said it was consumption, but it wasn't. If you'd seen the coal dust he coughed up. Every morning he'd cough for half an hour, and the rags were full of black phlegm. I don't know how he managed to work some days.'

John thought about what she'd said. On the morning shift it was normal for the coughing of the men to echo along the pit shaft. Sometimes it sounded like the barking of a pack of dogs. 'I guess all jobs have their drawbacks,' he said, trying to make light of things. 'Anyway, what else could I do?'

'Go in the works. I'm sure there must be something you can do.'

John drew Lucy towards him. 'Let's change the subject,' he said. 'I shall be back at work soon enough.' He kissed Lucy, a long, warm kiss. He felt the familiar throb in his loins and the erection he could never control once Lucy was in his arms. He moved her hand so that she was holding him. 'See what you do to me,' he said. 'You're a witch, do you know that?'

Lucy giggled. 'Sorry,' she said, but she wasn't sorry at all and began to unbutton his trousers. She still felt shy when she did this but it didn't feel wrong, not when she loved John so much. She felt the smooth, warm hardness in her hand. He had shown her how to touch him slowly, caressingly to prolong their pleasure. Lucy wished he would do the same to her but he flatly refused, telling her it would lead to other things and he'd promised her brother he'd keep her safe. She could have told him about the feelings she had when she thought about him in the privacy of her bed, but she was too embarrassed.

'We should get married, Lucy. That way we could both be satisfied,' John said when it was over.

'We will, one day. When our Will's a bit older.' She always gave him the same answer. 'Besides, we're too young; I'm enjoying my life.' At seventeen Lucy was quite content. She was just adjusting John's clothing when they heard a sound behind them. John jumped to his feet. 'Why, it's a bloody Peeping Tom.' He was about to go for the figure half-hidden in the bushes but Lucy held him back.

'No! It's only Daniel; he doesn't know right from wrong. He doesn't mean any harm.' Lucy beckoned to the lad who was known throughout Millington as Dopey Dan. 'Come on out, Daniel.' Daniel emerged from the greenery, his hair littered with twigs and sporting a wide grin. 'And what have you been doing today?' she enquired kindly.

'Birds.' Daniel pointed up at the tree under which they were standing.

'Watching the birds? What kind have you seen today?'

'Birds, thrush. Blackbirds, lots. Frogs.' He came and took hold of Lucy's hand in the hope of leading her to the pond higher up in the wood.

'Another day, I'll go and see the frogs another day. I'm going home now.'

Daniel looked disappointed as they set off

along the path in the direction of Millington. He rushed up in front of them and a wide grin spread across his face as he made a lewd gesture with his hand. Then he pointed at Lucy and then at an embarrassed John.

Further down the path Lucy began to giggle and John turned to her and said, 'I thought you implied he was a bit slow. Well he's not so daft that he didn't take in what we were doing. What if he tells someone? What was he doing up here anyway?'

'Like he said, watching the birds. He's known as Dopey Dan the bird man. He talks to them and some believe the birds talk to him too. Once when our dad brought us here looking for holly we came across Daniel feeding a robin. It was perched on the back of his hand and he was whispering some very strange sounds.'

'Where does he live?'

'Over there in the farm on the far bank of the dam. Mrs Cadman always fetches him to clip the claws on her canary. Daniel whispers to the bird and it hops out of the cage and onto his hand where it sits perfectly still until he's finished. Mrs Cadman says it won't do that for anybody else.'

'Well, I just hope he forgets what we were doing.'

Lucy giggled. 'I won't forget.'

John slapped her playfully on her firm, rounded backside. 'I bet you won't. Like I said, you're a witch, Lucy Gabbitas.'

'Aye, and if you aren't careful I shall cast a spell on you and make you invisible so you can sneak into my bed.'

'Oh aye, that'd be interesting, snuggling up between you and your Jane.' The couple laughed and joked all the way home. It was only when they reached Top Row that they became serious. It was becoming increasingly difficult to leave each other. They might be enjoying life, but it would be far more enjoyable if they didn't have to part.

Prudence Goodman watched Robbie Grey join the gang of young men and go in the direction of the Memorial Gardens. She watched a similar gang of girls wander off in the opposite direction. No doubt they would be meeting up later. 'Why don't you go with them?' Louisa asked her daughter. 'You've been invited to join them often enough.'

'Do you really think I would lower myself by wandering about making a spectacle of myself?'

'They aren't doing any harm. It would be good for you to mix more with people your own age.'

'Oh yes, some people, but not common ones like those.'

'They aren't common, they're hard-working, pleasant young people.'

Louisa wondered yet again how she and Herbert had managed to produce a daughter who could be such a snob. She even looked down on the girls who had been in the same class at school, the girls who had made their Brownie and Guide promises on the same day as Prudence.

Even on her first day at school she had found a place to sit away from the other children. Sometimes Louisa felt like suggesting her daughter be found a job of some description, but knew

Herbert wouldn't hear of it. Besides, who would employ a girl whose mood could change so rapidly? So Prudence's days were spent sewing, reading and visiting one or two old ladies in the afternoons. On Sundays she taught at Sunday school and on Monday evenings she was Brown Owl in charge of the Brownies. And that was another thing; it had been brought to Louisa's attention that one or two Brownies had left the troop because Brown Owl was too bossy. Indeed some of the younger ones were said to be afraid of her. 'Robert mixes with the group. Would you class him as common?'

'Of course, he's just our lodger, isn't he?' Prudence didn't really think Robbie was common – she thought he was handsome and mysterious because he never discussed anything with the family. If he asked her to walk out with him she wouldn't hesitate to do so, but he never even glanced her way. At meal times he usually sat at the opposite end of the table where she couldn't look at him and she daren't change places for fear of drawing attention to herself.

Prudence Grey wasn't a very nice person and though Robbie was grateful to the Goodmans for opening their home to them he couldn't stand their daughter, and not many other people could either.

Robbie wandered with the lads along the path by the flower beds, up the steps towards the clock and down the path to where the girls were chatting and laughing. New ones had joined the gang and old ones moved on, either to the pub for a crafty pint or because they were going steady with someone.

Young Will Gabbitas and Ernie Slater had taken the place of Robbie's brothers, who were thick as thieves with the Gabbitas girls. Mable, Kitty and Lewis were still hanging around and of course Dot. Robbie had gone to the pictures once or twice with Dot Greenwood, and because of that the others had begun to think of them as a couple. Actually Robbie didn't mind; Dot was fun. Besides, she hadn't objected when he kissed her in the darkness, whilst Charlie Chaplin tottered about in *City Lights* and a little woman pounded away on the piano below the screen.

'Did yer see Prudence Goodman staring at you?' Dot questioned Robbie.

'When?'

'Just now in church. I think she fancies yer.'

'Well I don't fancy her. I can't stand the sight of her.'

'You'd better watch out then; it could be awkward living in the same house as someone who has a crush on you.'

'I'm not in very much. I work over most nights. It's Sundays that are awkward. If it's raining I'm expected to play daft games like Beetle or Ludo.'

'You can always come up to our house; yer can do what yer like up there. Me dad'd be glad of a bit of help in the fields and all. You could stay for tea and go to church from there.'

'Right, I will. What time?'

'Any time yer like.' Dot grinned and the gang began to jeer. 'Oh aye, getting yer feet under the table are yer Robbie?' Will grinned.

'Here comes the bride,' Kitty sang, feeling rather jealous of the younger girl.

Robbie blushed but laughed with them. 'Yer only jealous.' He couldn't wait to go back to the farm. He had taken an instant liking to Mrs Greenwood and he would like to meet Little Arthur, but most of all be would get to spend more time with Dot.

'I've to go away for a few days,' Ben said as they were sitting down to their evening meal.

'Where to?' Young William might have put on a brave face after losing his mother but he was far more insecure than anyone would guess. It gave him confidence just knowing his brother was there.

'To a colliery in Derbyshire. I'm going to learn about a piece of machinery. They might be installing one here in the future.'

'Why is it you who has to go?'

'I 'aven't got to go; I volunteered.'

'Why?'

'Because it shows a bit of initiative, and if they know I'm willing I might be in line for promotion. I hope you'll be interested in bettering yerself when you start work.'

'Not if I 'ave to go in't pit. I shall 'ate it, I know I will.'

'Well I can't stay 'ere in this 'ouse for ever.' Ben thought this might be a good time to mention Emma. 'Oh and that's another thing. I think it's time I brought me girlfriend to meet you all. Her name's Emma. I think you'll like her.'

'I bet that's why you're going away. I bet it's an excuse to go stay with her.' Will was upset to think Ben might be considering going for good.

He was still hoping he could escape a future in the mine.

'Will!' Jane warned. 'If our Ben wants to go stay with a girlfriend he doesn't need to make excuses; he's every right to go where he likes. Besides, when has our Ben ever lied to us?'

Will suddenly felt ashamed of himself. Their Jane was right and besides, most men of Ben's age would have left home long before now. The trouble was it made him feel scared knowing he would be held responsible for keeping the house on when Ben decided to leave.

'So when are you bringing Emma home to meet us then?' Lucy asked.

'On Sunday, if that's convenient.'

'Course it is. Shall I ask our Nellie and Mary to come to tea?'

'Aye, that might be best.'

'Only I'm not sure I could cook dinner for all that lot.'

'No. Tea'll be fine. So that's settled then. And I shall be off to Derbyshire first thing on Monday.' Ben looked pointedly at Will. 'I shall be back. I promise.'

'Aye, but 'ow long for'?'

'For as long as I'm needed, all right?'

William nodded, but he didn't feel any better. It wasn't that he was scared of hard work; it was being closed in that he couldn't cope with. He had been all right until his dad died. It had been the sight of his dad's coffin being covered with earth that had done it, and it had become worse still since his mam was buried. Now it was as though he couldn't breathe, his heart would begin to pound and he had to fight for air. That was why he had refused to move with their Ben from the attic to his mam's bedroom.

The others thought he was daft, but in the attic he didn't need curtains at the rooftop window. He could lie in bed and see the sky. The moon and stars and the rolling clouds were all visible and in the mornings he could wake to the sunshine and the blue skies. Even grey skies were better than a curtained window. If he couldn't cope with a dark room how would he cope with the pit? William could see no way out, not if they were to be allowed to keep the house. Without a name on the rent book they would be out on the street, just like the Greys had been.

Lucy bought a ham shank and boiled it slowly over the fire. She persuaded Will to try and bruise a few tomatoes and any other salad stuff he could manage. On Saturday afternoon she made an apple pie, adding a bit of cinnamon for flavour. Lucy remembered the delicacies her mother had once served them before she had changed. Lucy was thankful now that Annie had taught all four girls to cook, not that Jane had been an eager pupil, but even she would get by if necessary. Both Nellie and Lucy had Annie's light hand when it came to pastry-making and the pie turned out to be perfect. She sent Will up to Barker's farm with a jug for a pint of cream. They would probably have to economise on something else before pay day came round again but she intended putting on as good a spread as possible for Ben's future wife. She frowned as she thought of young William being forced into a job he didn't want, but he wouldn't be the only one. The eldest Murphy boy was already making his way to Sheepdip pit every day and he was only a few months older than Will. She couldn't forget her mother's words though, that she would have liked something better for her youngest. Lucy added a drop more water to the ham shank; it didn't half smell good. If there was any left after Sunday tea she would slice a bit off for Evelyn Smithson. The girl was a godsend, despite her reputation. In fact if their Ben's Emma was half as nice as Evelyn their Ben would do all right.

Prudence watched Robbie combing his hair. He had already changed into a clean shirt. 'Where are you going?' she enquired as she threaded a needle with green silk thread.

'Out to tea.'

'Oh! And who do you know who would invite you out to tea?'

'A friend. Actually I'm going to do some work first.'

'What, dressed in Sunday best?' To be honest he didn't look much more dressed up than he did when he went to the joiner's shop but she noticed he had taken more care when polishing his shoes.

'You might not have noticed but it's the only suit I've got.'

'Oh yes, I've noticed.'

'Right, if you'll excuse me I'll be on my way.'

Prudence went to the window and watched him go out of the gate and turn off to go up the hill. There was only one place he could be going in that direction. She went to the mirror in the hall and studied her face closely. She wouldn't be bad-looking if she did something different with her hair. She might start wearing it loose. She ran her hands over her breasts. She liked the feeling it gave her when she did that. She felt her nipples harden beneath her dress and wondered if Robbie did that to Dot Greenwood. She felt an ache somewhere deep within her, also a feeling of intense jealousy. She wanted him to touch her, to stroke his rough workman's hands over her body. Prudence Grey was used to getting anything she desired. She vowed she would have Robert Grey. By fair means or foul, she would have him.

Robert was greeted at the farm by a gaggle of geese, well, two geese to be precise, but it felt like two dozen. One tugged at a trouser leg and the other pecked at his other leg until he cried out with the pain. He would probably be black and blue by the time they had finished.

'Come away, Gertie, yer gormless goose.' Dot drove them away, almost doubled up with laughter. 'They're worth their weight in diamonds, better than any guard dog.'

'Aye, I've noticed.'

'They didn't peck yer, did they?' Boadacea came scurrying over and proceeded to hitch up Robbie's trouser leg to survey the damage. 'Eeh, she's a proper bugger is that Gertie.'

Robbie would have liked to point out that they were both as bad, but didn't. 'What's the name of the other one?' he asked to be polite.

'Gussie. We call 'em Gormless Gertie and Fussy Gussie.'

'Nice names.'

'Come wi' me, I'll pop a bit of ointment on that broken skin just to be on the safe side.'

'I'll do that, Mam.'

'You'll do no such thing.' Boadacea sounded shocked. 'A young lass like you feeling up a lad's trousers? It's not decent.'

'Only at his leg. Yer do make a fuss sometimes, Mam.'

'Aye, well, yer only a young lass and I remember 'ow my little Arthur'd 'ave reacted to a pretty young lass massaging 'is legs. And she is a pretty lass, isn't she?'

Robbie blushed. 'Yes she is, Mrs Greenwood, very pretty.'

Boadacea sighed contentedly. Although she constantly berated her daughter over one thing or another she was intensely proud of her only child, and with good reason. Dot's dark glossy hair, her clear, healthy complexion and slim, lithe figure would have made any parent proud.

She looked Robbie Grey up and down. Eeh, they'd make a lovely couple, and not only in looks. Young Robbie was a well-mannered, presentable young man, and a hard-working one according to Dot. She'd make him welcome and see if owt developed. 'Come on, let's get some cream on that there leg.'

'No, it's all right, Mrs Greenwood, honestly.'

'Well, if yer sure. No, I've decided I'm going to see to it and be on the safe side. Come on.'

Robbie had no alternative but to go inside with the woman, who opened a cupboard containing hundreds of packets, bottles and pots. 'Me herb cupboard,' she explained. 'Passed down her knowledge to me, me mother did, been passed down through four generations at least. Cures for nearly everything in this cupboard.' She brought out a tiny pot and unscrewed the lid.

'What's in it?' Robbie was curious.

'Bergamot, eucalyptus and lavender. I grow that meself. Our Dot can show yer me garden after tea.' She rolled his trouser leg back down. 'There, does that feel better?'

'Aye, it does.' Robbie was surprised how soothing the cream was.

'Good.' Then she called, so loudly that he felt she might burst his eardrum, 'DOT! Come and take Robbie down to't four-acre field for yer dad to look at 'im.'

Dot came with the old dog fussing round her heels. 'Come on then.'

Robbie felt a bit like an exhibit at a show, the way he was going to be looked at, but he needn't have worried. Little Arthur was too enthralled in his task of repairing the five-barred gate. He looked to be all fingers and thumbs and swore as he hit his thumb with the hammer.

'Come 'ere, I can do that for yer.' Robbie picked up a two-inch nail and took the hammer from Arthur. Within seconds he had the gate secure.

'Eeh by gum, tha knows thi way round a piece o' wood, lad and no mistake.'

Robbie grinned. 'I hope so. I'm going to be a joiner one day.'

'I think tha one already by the looks o' that.' Arthur watched Robbie finish the job. 'Now then, let's go and 'ave some liquid refreshment, what does tha like?'

'A cup of tea'd be nice.'

Arthur nodded approvingly.

'And after we've had a drink I'll give yer a hand with anything else that needs doing,' Robbie offered.

'Nay, lad, I've done for today, apart from cows to bring in and milk. But when tha comes again I wouldn't mind a hand wi' mending me owd shed.' He closed the repaired gate behind them and Robbie noticed his upper arms. Arthur might be a little man but Robbie would have given anything to possess muscles like Little Arthur.

The tea table looked as though it was set for a party. Robbie had only once seen a spread like it and that had been at a party at the hall where Robbie's father had worked in Lincolnshire. The housekeeper had been ordered to arrange a celebration tea for the children of the village; it had been one Christmas and he would never forget the sight of the furnished table. Boadacea's table might not be quite so elaborate but the pork pie, boiled ham and roast chicken would have compared favourably with the food at the hall. He wondered if there were any other expected guests but there were just the four of them when they sat down at the table.

''Elp yerself. It's all our own produce. Even't pickled onions are 'ome grown.'

'It all looks wonderful,' Robbie commented as he helped himself to a slice of juicy, tender ham.

'It might look grand, lad,' Little Arthur laughed, 'but it'll taste bloody better, so let's all send in.' And Robbie didn't need telling twice.

Chapter Nine

Lucy and Jane surveyed the tea table critically. 'Perhaps we should put the meat on the individual plates before we start,' Jane wondered.

'No, we should let them help themselves. Oh I wish our Nellie would hurry up and come; she'll know what to do.'

'For goodness sake, anybody'd think the queen was coming.' Will was fed up already, what with having to suffer a haircut and cut his fingernails, even though he'd done them only last week.

'Our Will's right. Emma must take us as she finds us, and if she won't, then she's not the right girl for our Ben,' Lucy said. 'Go and borrow two chairs off Mrs Slater, Will.'

Will went off willingly, glad to escape and hoping Ernest would be at home. Ernest was nowhere to be seen but his sister Joyce and a friend were outside playing skipping with a crowd of others from Second Row.

'I'll turn for yer.' Will took hold of one end of the rope and chanted with the rest, 'Salt, mustard, vinegar, pepper,' whilst the skippers jumped the rope and tried to avoid tripping over as the rope accelerated at the call of 'pepper'.

'Will!' Jane called. 'Don't you dare to get dirty, and where are those chairs?' Will handed over the rope and grudgingly fetched two kitchen chairs from the Slaters' house. By now Mary and Jacob had arrived and Nellie was walking on the row. Lewis Marshall whistled and Nellie laughed and exaggerated the swinging of her hips. 'Have you nothing better to do, Lew Marshall, than sit on yer mother's doorstep ogling older women?'

'What could be better than watching you, Nellie?'

Nellie disappeared laughing into the house. It was good to be back on Top Row. It had upset her to be banned from the house in which she had been born. She vowed to put that awful day behind her and enjoy her visit, and anyway she and her mother had made up before she died; that was all that mattered.

'Oh Nellie, thank goodness you're here,' Lucy laughed. 'Our Jane's nattering about the table looking right.'

Nellie surveyed the table. 'Well it looks all right to me. How are you all?' According to the replies everyone was fine. 'Right then,' Nellie said, 'so we'll all enjoy our teas. What time is our visitor expected?'

'Our Ben's gone to meet her off the bus. They should be here any minute now.'

And they were. Ben came in rubbing his hands. 'Right then, Emma, let me introduce you to the family: Mary, the eldest and her husband, Jacob. This is Nellie, Jane, Lucy and... Where's our William?'

Lucy went towards the door. 'He's sneaked out again. I'll go find him.'

'No, please leave him,' Emma said. 'I'll see him later. It's so nice to meet you all at last.' Emma thought there were quite enough people staring at her for the time being without William.

'Nice to meet you too.' Mary shook hands with the pleasant, gorgeous-looking girl. 'I'll mash the tea then, shall I, Jane?'

'Yes please, and I'll go fetch our Will, if I can find him.' They managed to squeeze themselves round the large kitchen table and Mary poured the tea.

'Is it a party then?' William asked as he helped himself to salad from the cut-glass bowl that had once belonged to Grandma Gabbitas.

'Aye it is,' Ben told him. 'It's some time since a party was held in this house, so we'll have one today, to celebrate Emma's first visit to our house.'

'Welcome to our home, Emma,' Lucy said. She liked the look of Ben's girlfriend and hoped she would make her brother happy.

When the tea plates were cleared away and the tea cups replenished Lucy served the pie. 'Mmm.' Nellie rolled her eyes. 'Who's made this?'

'Our Lucy,' Jane answered.

'Hmm, you can come and bake for me at the manor.'

Lucy blushed.

'Nellie's right, it's delicious,' Emma added. 'I'm afraid I've yet to learn how to cook.'

'I'll teach you. That's if you want to come again of course.'

'Oh yes, I'd love to come again. That's if Ben invites me, I mean.'

'*I'm* inviting you,' Lucy smiled.

Ben grinned at his sister, relieved that Emma had received such a warm welcome. 'Right then, shall we adjourn to the parlour?' Ben put on a posh voice, to everyone's amusement. Young Will had lit a fire in the front room and they had placed a vase of flowers on the polished round table.

'I'll help to wash up first,' Emma volunteered.

'No, we'll see to that later.'

'Can I go back out now?' Will was itching to be outside with the other kids.

'Oh, go on then.' Jane was relieved in a way – the front room would be crowded enough without their William.

'Right, then, who's for a sing song?' Ben went up to the attic and came down with his father's melodion. Lucy's face paled. It was the first time she had seen the instrument since her dad had played it in the happy time before his illness. She suppressed the feeling of sadness and vowed to put the past behind her.

'Right, what shall we sing?' Ben blew the dust off, revealing the bright colours of the melodion.

'Let Emma decide; she's our guest,' Mary said.

'Well! seeing as it's Sunday, how about a hymn?'

'Aye, that's a good idea.' Jacob had a lovely voice and enjoyed belting out a few hymns now and again. 'What about "Onward Christian Soldiers"?'

Ben had a practice and found the key, and before long the hymn could be heard all along the row. After a few minutes half a dozen ragged-looking children wandered in to see what was happening, then Enid Slater arrived, partly because she could never resist a good sing song and partly to sneak a look at Ben's girl. She had promised to look out for Annie's family and didn't consider Ben too old to need a bit of looking out for.

'Come in, Mrs Slater,' Ben invited. 'Come and

meet Emma, the girl I'm going to marry.' Emma blushed as she shook the hand offered her.

'You'll be getting yerself a good lad. There's none better as I know of.'

'I'm sure you're right, Mrs Slater.' Emma remained standing and gave the lady her place on the sofa. After another couple of hymns Ben changed the tempo and struck up with 'I've Got Sixpence'. Then he did a medley of popular songs.

Before they had finished Mr Slater had wandered in and joined in the revelry. 'Eeh, lad, it's like old times; it's some time since there was music like this on the row. What's it all about?'

'It's to welcome my fiancée, Mr Slater.'

'Is it now? Well then, let's 'ave a look at you, lass.'

'Stop embarrassing the girl,' his wife admonished. 'If Ben's chosen her it doesn't matter what anybody else thinks.'

'Course it does, ee's as good as a son to me and I can see that this young lass'll be a wife to be proud of. I'm not a bad judge of character and I can see that Bill would 'ave been proud to have her in the family, so can we 'ave a bit more music?'

'One more, then we shall 'ave to go.' Ben had suddenly realised what time it was. 'Hey, shouldn't you lot be at church by now?'

'We're not going,' Will informed his brother. 'Our Jane says we needn't as it's a special occasion.'

'Right, well just this once then.' Ben began to play again, the hymn that had been his father's favourite. 'This one's for me mam and dad, even though they aren't here to hear it.'

'Oh but they are,' Lucy said. 'I mean, I'm sure they're here in spirit.'

'He Who Would Valiant Be' rang out across the row and the Gabbitas family were uplifted and finally felt they could look forward to the future and better times. All except William, who could foresee a wedding day drawing rapidly nearer and an escape from the mine becoming ever more remote.

On the following day, tea at the vicarage consisted of salad and roast chicken. The poultry had been sent with the compliments of Boadacea Greenwood – in appreciation of the vicar's help given to all the people of the parish, she said. Because it was Mr Grundy's Oddfellows Benevolent Society meeting Robbie was for once home to join them. James and John, both being on afternoon shift, were absent.

'Well, this is nice,' Louisa commented as she poured the tea. 'We don't often have Robbie's company at the evening meal.'

The chicken was delicious but Prudence helped herself to nothing more then a lettuce leaf and a warm boiled beetroot. 'Aren't you feeling well?' Louisa enquired of her daughter.

'I'm fine, why?'

'Well, why aren't you eating?'

'I am.'

'Have some chicken then.'

'Oh I couldn't possibly eat that, knowing where it's come from.'

'What do you mean?' Herbert put down his fork.

'From the Greenwoods. I'm sure the farm

kitchen is far from hygienic.'

'It's as clean as anyone else's,' Robbie said, not counting the flea-ridden old dog, but he didn't think he'd better mention that.

'I'm sure it is,' Louisa acknowledged. 'Anything Mrs Greenwood sends us is always delicious and very much appreciated.'

'And that's another thing: do we have to accept charity from those people?'

'It's not charity. She sent it for the vicar for all the good work he does. Goodman by name, good man by nature, that's how she described your father. Besides, what do you mean by "THOSE PEOPLE"?' Robbie could feel his temper rising.

'Well, they're so vulgar. Take the girl, Dot, so loud-voiced and common.'

'No she isn't. She might laugh loudly, but that's better than never laughing at all and having a long, miserable face like yours.'

Prudence felt the colour rising to her face. 'I won't sit here and let him speak to me like that,' she told her parents.

'That's all right. Go to your room then,' Louisa said.

'No it's all right. I'll go to mine; you can stay here. I apologise for my outburst, sir, but I don't regret the things I said. The Greenwoods are my friends. Good hard-working people who have made me welcome in their home just as you have. I'm very grateful to you for that and sorry if I've upset you.' Robbie stood up and made for the door.

'Robert, come back here and finish your meal. Prudence, I believe you were going to your room.

What are you waiting for?'

The girl stood up so abruptly she knocked over her chair and leaving it where it had fallen she flounced out of the room. Robert picked it up and placed it at the table. 'I'm sorry, I can't eat any more,' he said.

'And no wonder. What's wrong with the girl?'

Louisa sighed. 'I don't know,' she said. 'She's turning into a spoiled, pampered snob. She needs something useful to do with her life. All she does is waste her days doing useless pieces of embroidery and reading, and it's not as if she reads anything intelligent; she's taken to buying those awful love magazines. Nothing but a waste of money, money she doesn't see the value of because she doesn't have to lift a finger and earn it. She needs a job.'

'A job? Doing what?' Herbert would never agree to his daughter working.

'I don't know. I only know that she'll end up an embittered old spinster if she doesn't get out amongst people her own age.'

Robbie was embarrassed at being a party to the conversation. 'If you'll excuse me, I need to get ready. I'm going to play billiards at the Miners' Club. Thank you for a lovely meal, Louisa.'

'Thanks to Mrs Greenwood. Please give her our thanks when you see her, and for the eggs from the week before. We're most grateful.'

'I will.' Robbie escaped from what had been the most embarrassing meal of his life. Thank God his brothers hadn't been here to witness his outburst or he'd have been for it. He didn't go upstairs, unwilling to encounter Prudence Goodman. He checked to see that he had two pence in his pocket, which would pay for half an hour's billiards, and went out into the fresh Millington air. He had grown to love this town and the people in it. He felt a deep affection for the Goodmans and the Grundys and considered himself an extremely fortunate young man. Only one person was spoiling his life, but it was Prudence Goodman's home and he was just a lodger, so he had better learn to control his tongue. Otherwise he and his brothers could find themselves homeless again. Even seeing Prudence Goodman's spiteful face every day was preferable to that.

Nellie Gabbitas was more excited than she had ever been in her life. She had been asked to arrange a dinner party for twenty-four very important gentlemen who were doing business in Cragstone. Not normal everyday catering, she had been told, but something very special. If she wasn't capable – the housekeeper had told her – outside help could be arranged. Nellie had been adamant that with Lily's help and maybe a girl to help wait at the table she could definitely cope. Lily said her sister would be delighted to assist her and now the day had arrived.

'You can pluck those pheasants now, Lily. And don't forget to remove the charcoal pieces.'

'What's it for, the charcoal?'

'Keeps it fresh whilst it's hanging. Before you do that, bank up the oven and pull out the damper, I need to get these pies in soon. We could do with two ovens today.' The pies had been made with four hares and a pound of bacon. Four onions, the livers and four glasses of wine had been mixed with breadcrumbs and seasoned with nutmeg and parsley to make a forcemeat. Nellie had lined the pie dishes with the forcemeat and placed the cooked chopped hares in the dishes. For the topping she had made four pounds of rough puff pastry and placed it over the pies. These would be cooked now whilst the oven wasn't too hot; when they came out the cranberry tarts would be ready to go in. She would serve these with egg custard. She would also be serving ginger puffs with wine sauce and rice meringue decorated with cherries and angelica. Lily's sister could do the decorating.

'Are those pheasants plucked yet, Lily?'

'Nearly.'

'When they are you can get down the iron cauldron and put the ham, asparagus tops and the lettuces in; it'll need five pints of liquid in and it can go on the hook over the fire. You can use that stock we saved from yesterday and don't overdo the salt; that ham's a bit on the salty side. I ought to have soaked it overnight but it'll be all right.' Before the asparagus soup Nellie would be starting with prawns, twelve for each person, cooked but not shelled. She would stand them round half a lemon decorated with parsley. After that they would be served whitebait with thin brown bread and butter. Then would come the hashed pheasant and then the hare pie followed by the sweets. Nellie had been more worried about serving the wrong wines than not coping with the menu, but Mrs Cooper was an authority on that, her being a secret tippler.

'Sherry wi' soup. Hock wi' fish. Champagne wi'

owt. Port wi' the dessert and a nice liqueur with the coffee. You can do them; leave the lasses to serve the food and you serve the drinks. Oh and have some barley water for the teetotals, though I doubt there'll be any amongst that lot. I'll get out the decanters for young Molly to wash later.'

'I don't know how they'll get any drink down them if they eat this lot.' Lily brought out the pies, her face scarlet with the heat from the oven.

'And summat else to remember,' Mrs Cooper told Lily, 'go and ave an all-over wash before yer put that clean uniform on. We don't want 'em complaining about the smell of sweat.'

'I won't smell. I'll put some of that Lily-of-the-valley on that you bought me for Christmas.'

'Aye, well I don't mind yer smelling nice, but get rid of that sweat first. I don't want yer thinking yer can cover it up wi' scent because it won't work.'

'I might not 'ave time.'

'You will.' Nellie looked at the clock on the wall. 'We've got everything in hand.'

'I hope our Molly don't faint, she's ever so shy.'

'Faint?' Mrs Cooper shrieked. 'Why, is she prone to fainting?'

'No, not as I know of.'

'Well then, stop trying to give us a heart attack, yer daft haporth.'

'I hope there's someone tall, dark and handsome and rich who takes a fancy to me,' Nellie said.

'They'll be too busy gobbling to notice owt else.'

'Aye, I expect they will,' Nellie agreed, 'but I

can always dream and hope.'

'Aye, I suppose you're right. As my owd mother always used to say, "Where there's life there's hope".' Mrs Cooper flopped down in her own special chair. 'Though I've given up hope of a man of any sort, years ago.'

Young Lily began to giggle and whether it was due to the thought of Mrs Cooper finding a man, or because they were all wound up like clock springs at the thought of the meal to be served, all three of them were soon bordering on hysterics. When Lily's sister opened the kitchen door she called 'Is summat burning in 'ere?'

'Oh, my gawd, the tarts.' Nellie ran to open the oven door. The tarts were done to a turn. 'Oh, it's a good job you came when you did or they'd have been ruined.'

'And then where would we all have been?' Lily asked.

'Where indeed?' Mrs Cooper took off her shoes to rest her feet and wondered where she would be in a couple of years and what would become of her in her old age. She wouldn't be laughing then, would she?

The last of the dirty dishes had been removed and the men had withdrawn to the drawing room to enjoy a cigar with their coffee. Nellie kicked off her shoes and rubbed her feet. 'I feel as if I've walked a hundred miles and back again.'

'And no wonder. All I've done is supervise and I'm fair jiggered. 'Ere you two, leave them mucky pots and come and 'ave a sit down for ten minutes. There's all this 'ere stuff to eat. Lily, go and fetch that lad in and let's send in.'

'He might 'ave gone to bed, Mrs Cooper. It's past eleven.'

'What? It never is! Why, the greedy gluttons must 'ave been eating for three solid hours.'

Larry should have gone home hours ago but chose to hang about the yard and had decided to sleep in the stables. It had been so exciting with motors drawing into the grounds and one or two arriving on horseback. He knew if they were all looked after he could expect a few tips before they left. He had spent the evening grooming the horses and polishing the saddles. Anyway, it was cosy here in the lamp light and more peaceful than at home, where his dad usually came home the worse for drink and started an argument. He was keeping a lookout for Lily, hoping she would come looking for him. He had almost given up hope when the door opened. She didn't need to call his name before he was there beside her.

'Come on, we're going to 'ave us supper.' Lily was whispering in case there was anybody about; she didn't want to get Larry in trouble.

What a supper it was! Some of the tureens had hardly been touched and there was one whole hare pie left.

'We'll keep that for tomorrow's dinner and have a fuddle,' Mrs Cooper said. 'We shan't sleep by the time we've done with this lot. Now then, who's for soup?'

It was almost midnight before they had finished eating and one o'clock before they had cleared away.

'You'd better stop 'ere tonight; you can sleep

with your Lily,' the housekeeper told Molly. 'It's too late for yer to go 'ome now. Besides, there'll be all those breakfasts to cook and serve. Yer can give us a hand wi' them if yer like.'

Molly nodded. It would mean a bit more money and there was no school tomorrow to worry about.

Young Larry had taken a fancy to Lily's sister. 'I could walk 'er 'ome Mrs Cooper, if she likes.'

'Well, I don't know. What do yer think, lass?'

Molly was torn between staying and having a good breakfast or being escorted home by Larry. He had been smiling at her ever since she arrived and she quite liked him; it would be exciting being out in the dark with a boy. On the other hand, if she stayed she would be able to see him in the morning, so she chose a warm bed and a good breakfast.

'Go on then, get to yer bed you two. We shall no sooner 'ave got our heads on the pillow than we 'ave to get up again. Go on, Larry, be in 'ere at six if yer want some breakfast. We shall be too busy after that.'

'Thanks, Mrs Cooper. Thanks, Nellie. I don't think I shall be able to eat owt else for a week, never mind breakfast.'

When he'd gone Nellie raked down the ashes and banked up the fire. Mrs Cooper undid the bun in her hair and let it loose. 'You did well today, Nellie. The meal was fit for the king and no doubt about it.'

'I couldn't have done it without your guidance.'

'Rubbish. I'm getting past all the rushing around at do's like this. Me old legs are me downfall.'

'You're not that old, Mrs Cooper.'

'No? Ow old would yer say I was then?'

Nellie wished the woman hadn't asked a question like that. 'Fifty-three or -four.'

'I'm sixty-five.'

'Never.' Nellie couldn't believe a woman of that age could be as energetic as Mrs Cooper.

'Aye, I don't know what'll become of me when they kick me out.'

'Oh, they won't do that.'

'Yes they will, Nellie. Don't make the same mistake I did. Find yerself a good man and 'ave some children.' The woman sighed. 'Oh they call me Mrs Cooper, always did with me being housekeeper, like, but I was never married. Loved a man once, would 'ave given me life for 'im but it wasn't meant to be.' Nellie saw the tears brimming for a few moments, but then Mrs Cooper cheered up again. 'Then there was another one who proposed to me, but 'ee upped and married somebody else, somebody with plenty of money, a bit of a horsey-looking woman, but she had money. Thought he could 'ave the penny and the bun; married her and then came back to me 'oping I would be his bit on the side.'

'Never! You didn't fall for that, did you?'

'Did I heck – hit him over the head with a copper posher, knocked 'im out, I did. Right on this 'ere doorstep, cut his head open. The master who was 'ere at the time dumped 'im in the carriage and took 'im into Millington to the doctors. Told 'im if he caught 'im round 'ere again ee would fetch constable. Lovely the master was at that time, came back and told me to find someone worthy of me in future. But it wasn't to be.' Mrs Cooper began to laugh. 'I often wonder what ee told that wife of 'is had happened to 'is 'ead.' She went towards the door. 'You're missing yer way 'ere, Nellie. You could be cooking in your own establishment instead of being stuck in this kitchen cooking for somebody else.'

It was usual on Saturdays for Mrs Cooper to collect the wages for her staff and discuss anything of importance with Mr Smith, the manager. The day after the dinner party being Saturday, the housekeeper knocked on the office door as usual at eleven o'clock. 'Come.' As usual Mr Smith was busy at his desk, but this morning another gentleman was seated in the chair by the window. Both men stood as Mrs Cooper entered the room.

'Good morning.' Mr Smith indicated for her to be seated.

'Good morning, sir. I didn't know you were occupied. Shall I come back later?'

'No, no. Mr Johnson was one of our guests last night; he is waiting to pay his respects to you and your staff.'

Mr Johnson held out his hand to Mrs Cooper. 'Yes indeed. It was the most excellent meal I have enjoyed for some time.'

'All due to Miss Gabbitas; she's an excellent cook.'

'Under your expert guidance, though.'

'Thank you. Miss Gabbitas worked extremely hard and was ably assisted by my other staff.'

'Yes, if you tell me how many hours they worked above the norm, I'll see they are paid accordingly.' He picked up one of the pay packets. 'How about Miss Gabbitas?'

'Well, she was at it from half past five in the morning right through till gone one this morning.' Mrs Cooper added a few hours on. 'Then there was Lily, who worked the same hours, and her sister Molly, who never stopped all day and stayed over to help with the breakfasts. And young Larry gave up his night off to see to the horses and keep his eye on the motors. Polished 'em up this morning as soon as the cock crowed. Ee's a right good lad, young Larry is.' She watched him open the black metal cash box and add a bit extra into each packet.

'Anyone else?' Mr Smith enquired.

'No sir, that's all.'

'Do you mean to tell me that the only outside help you had was Lily's sister?'

'Oh aye, sir. They're all quite capable.'

'Under your supervision, of course.'

Mrs Cooper kept quiet and was satisfied knowing they were all receiving overtime for their efforts. Mr Smith closed and locked the money box and handed the envelopes to the housekeeper.

'Will that be all, sir?'

'Unless you've any other matters to discuss, I think so.'

'No, sir.'

'Right then, if you'll send Nellie up I shall thank her personally. And please give the young ones my compliments on a job well done.'

'I will, sir.' Mrs Cooper sighed with relief. Even after all the years she had worked here, she still dreaded these weekly meetings.

When Mrs Cooper came back to the kitchen she said to Nellie, 'You're to go to Mr Smith's office.'

'Oh crikey, what 'ave I done?' Nellie was very rarely called in to see the manager.

'Don't worry, there's nowt wrong. Ee just wants to thank you for last night.'

'Oh, do I have to?'

'Of course yer do.' Mrs Cooper didn't tell Nellie about Mr Johnson; it was enough of an ordeal being received by one man, let alone two.

'Come.' Nellie opened the door and the two men rose to greet her.

'This is one of our guests, Nellie: Mr Johnson.' Nellie was mesmerised by the bluest eyes she had ever seen. Mr Johnson held her hand and her gaze for far longer than necessary and Nellie felt herself blushing. 'Pleased to meet you, sir,' she said.

'And you, Nellie. I would like to compliment you on a most excellent meal. Where did you learn to cook?'

Nellie smiled. 'In my mother's kitchen; that was the plain cooking. The fancy dishes I taught myself, with a bit of guidance from the cook who was here before and a lot of help from my mother's *Best Way* cookery book.'

'Really? I would have guessed that you had had a more formal training.'

'No, sir.' Nellie was embarrassed. 'Will that be all, sir?' She turned reluctantly to Mr Smith.

The manager smiled. 'Well, I would like to add my thanks to those of Mr Johnson. I'm sure the meal last night will be discussed for weeks to come and as there were some very influential people amongst the party I'm convinced that when the word is spread our business will benefit greatly, all due to you.'

'And the waitresses, sir.'

'Of course. I have shown my appreciation to you all with a small bonus. That will be all, Nellie.'

'Thank you, sir.' She nodded at Mr Johnson, who nodded and smiled. Once again she found it difficult to tear her eyes away from his. Flustered, she made for the door.

'Come on, lass. Let's 'ave a cup of tea and celebrate our windfall.' Mrs Cooper had cut them all a wedge of the leftover cranberry tart, which she topped with a dollop of cream. 'Well! what did ee say?'

'Well, he wants to thank you all for your hard work, and he wanted to know who taught me to cook; he seemed to think I'd been to cookery school or something.'

'And no wonder. In all the years I've worked 'ere I've never seen a spread like that was last night. Here lass, 'ere's yer wage packet.'

'We've got some extra.' Lily took the packet from her apron pocket and checked the money excitedly.

'Yer'll wear that money away before yer've done,' Mrs Cooper told Lily. 'Anybody'd think you'd never 'ad a wage packet before.'

'Well I 'aven't, not with so much in it.'

'You worked 'ard. Just remember, 'ard work always reaps its rewards. Go and fetch that lad in for 'is money. Ee's been working 'ard an' all.'

'Oh lor, he'll want me to go to't pictures with

’im now ee’s got some money,’ young Molly said.

‘Well, you’ve been giving ’im the come on, so what do you expect?’ Lily reminded her.

‘I ’ave not.’ Molly turned the same colour as the cranberries.

‘So why are yer titivating yer ’air before you fetch ’im in then?’

Molly escaped and went to find Larry. She hoped he did ask her to go to the pictures; she really liked him and she might not see him for ages after today. She only got called in to help at the hall on special occasions such as last night. Molly wished she could work here all the time like their Lily, but her mam said she was needed at home. She frowned. Her mam wouldn’t let her go out with Larry anyway. Molly was considered too young to go out with boys. It wouldn’t prevent her from liking him though.

Molly wasn’t the only one harbouring romantic thoughts. Nellie Gabbitas had never felt like this before. Her heart fluttered every time she thought about Mr Johnson. She didn’t even know his first name. Even if she saw him again – which she wasn’t likely to – he wouldn’t look twice at someone like her. She wished she had done her hair in a different style before going to the office. Oh well, it wouldn’t have made any difference.

When Larry came in Nellie questioned him about the remaining motor. She knew most of the dinner guests had already left and wondered if it belonged to Mr Johnson. ‘Whose is that motor, Larry?’ she said. ‘I thought everyone had left.’

‘It belongs to somebody called Mr Johnson. Mr Smith asked me to take special care of it because ee's a friend of 'is and ever so posh.'

'I wonder where he comes from to own a motor like that. I've never seen one in Sheffield.'

'Blackpool,' Larry said.

'Blackpool?' Mrs Cooper almost choked on her tea. The mention of the seaside resort brought back memories so poignant she had all on to conceal her emotion. Fortunately young Larry chatted on and gave her time to recover.

'Aye, ee came out first thing when I was cleaning it. Ee said when ee comes again ee'll bring me a stick of Blackpool rock. Whatever that might be.'

'It's to eat, yer daft haporth. I 'ope yer were polite.'

'Aye, course I was. I wish I could 'ave a ride in it.'

Mrs Cooper laughed. 'Wishing'll not bring rewards, so hurry up and finish yer tea and get on wi' yer work.'

Larry sighed. He had a hedge to cut and the stables to muck out. No matter how hard he worked he knew he would never own a motor like that. The most he could hope for was that Mr Smith would buy one and let him learn to drive it. In the meantime he would work hard and earn some money. He finished his tea and blushed as he wondered how he could get to know Molly better. 'Right then, I'll go get on,' he said as he pulled on his boots on the doorstep.

'I'll 'ang that washing out for yer before I go,' Molly told her sister. The cloths from the night before had been boiled in the fireside boiler and Lily was lifting them out, filling the kitchen with the smell of Rinso and steam. Once they were rinsed they would be put through the great mangle out in the yard.

'Go on then.' Lily smiled knowingly at Molly, who hurried out with the clothes line and peg bag. She made a show of stretching up to the clothes post, giving Larry an excuse to come and help.

''Ere, let me.' He reached up and wound a bit of line round the post, securing it with a knot. 'Do yer ever go out on a Saturday night?' He blushed as he got the words out.

'Only sometimes with our Sally, if there's a social at chapel.'

'Will yer go to't pictures with me tonight?'

Molly sighed. 'Me mam won't let me. She says I'm too young to go out wi' lads.' Then she had an idea. 'I could say I was treating our Sal out of the extra money I've earned. We'd 'ave to meet you inside though.'

Larry grinned. 'Aye, that'd be grand. I don't mind your Sal coming as long as she lets me sit beside you.' He might even hold her hand.

'I'll see yer tonight then.'

Larry whistled merrily as he went back to work. It had worked even better than he had hoped. If he was meeting Molly inside he wouldn't have to pay for her. He watched her come out with the clothes basket and help Lily fold the snowy white cloths, then she threaded them through the rollers whilst Lily turned the handle. Molly then secured them on the line with dolly pegs. She was lovely was Molly, with her long wavy hair hanging almost to her waist. If her mother didn't let her go out with boys yet, it didn't matter. Larry would work hard and wait until she was allowed. Molly was worth waiting for. He went to the stables, not minding the horse muck this morning. After all, Mrs Cooper always said that where there's muck there's money, and Mrs Cooper was usually right.

Molly was just securing the last cloth when Mr Johnson came round the corner into the yard. 'Good morning,' he nodded to the girl and opened the door of his car. Molly thought he was the loveliest man she had ever seen and, becoming all flustered, she curtsied as she bid him a good morning. He hesitated and then closed the car door and came towards Molly. 'Do you know where I can find Miss Gabbitas?'

Molly nodded and ran towards the kitchen. 'Nellie, come quick, you're wanted, come on, hurry.'

Nellie wiped her hands and followed Molly outside. Her heart seemed to miss a beat as she saw Mr Johnson standing there.

'Hello again,' he smiled and Nellie marvelled at the way he seemed to smile with his eyes as well as his lips. Oh God, her stomach seemed to be turning a cartwheel. 'I wondered,' he paused, not really knowing what to say. He only knew he couldn't go home without getting to know Miss Gabbitas, or at least speaking to her again. 'I wondered if I might take you to dinner tonight?'

Nellie was speechless. When she at last found her tongue she stammered, 'Who, me? Well I don't know. I mean I've only just met you. I don't even know your name.'

'Thomas, but my friends call me Tom. I assure you my intentions are entirely honourable.' He offered her his hand and Nellie thought she might faint at his touch. 'Please, Nellie. I can't go home without seeing you again. Please say you'll come.'

'Well, as it's Saturday I suppose I can take a few hours off.'

'Good. I shall be here to pick you up at seven if that will be convenient?'

'Yes, thank you.'

'No! it is I who should be thanking you, for the privilege of being allowed to escort the girl of my dreams out to dinner.' He glanced towards the house and grinned as he saw three inquisitive faces at the kitchen window. 'Till tonight then.' Thomas ran to the motor, jumped in and tore away down the long, tree-lined drive.

Nellie went in to be interrogated by Mrs Cooper and to plan what she would wear to be taken out to dinner for the first time in her life.

As it happened, Mrs Cooper was almost as excited as Nellie about the invitation. She realised that the gentleman must be fairly wealthy and she considered Nellie to be most worthy of such a husband. She also thought it her duty to warn the girl to be careful and that even the best of men could be carried away when in the company of a pretty girl.

During Ben's absence Emma Scott was taught to make pastry almost as light as Lucy's. First a potato pie, then one made of rhubarb from Mr Slater's allotment. Another Sunday she helped the sisters make a dish of brawn, using a sheep's head, onions, herbs and lots of salt and pepper. When it was cooked Lucy packed it tightly into a basin with a plate on top, then she stood the flat iron on the plate to press it down.

'You can make brawn with any old stuff,' Lucy said. 'Cow heels, pigs' feet – it still turns out good.' Lucy sighed with satisfaction. 'There'll be enough here for our snaps for a week.' When it was cold she gave Emma a slice to take home.

Emma was delighted to be learning how to become an efficient housewife. All she needed now was a wedding, but neither Ben nor her were free to begin married life, what with her mother to care for and Ben's responsibility to his family. Even though Emma was willing to have William to live with them, Ben had explained that his sisters would be turned out of their home if the house wasn't transferred to Will. It seemed to Emma that the solution was for John to marry Lucy and take over the house, but of course Lucy was still rather young. One day Jane had asked why Evelyn Smithson had a house when there was no one working at the mine and Ben had explained that Evelyn's father had been killed in a roof fall, so the management had made the house over to his dependants for as long as required, so long as the rent was paid. Lucy had considered his answer. 'Our dad was killed in the pit too,' she said.

'Don't be daft. Our dad died of consumption,' Jane said.

'That's what we were told, but we all know it was the coal dust that killed him.' Lucy had had tears in her eyes as she added, 'That's why me mam wanted something different for our Will.' Nobody had known what to say to that and the conversation had been brought to an end.

Chapter Ten

It was not only Emma's mind that was on marriage. John Grey would have married Lucy at a day's notice, but Lucy at eighteen was enjoying life. She was happy in the umbrellas where although they worked hard, the girls were a friendly and jolly bunch of work mates. Lucy was proficient at her job and could earn a decent wage, so she was at last able to spend a little on clothes and be a normal teenager.

Lewis Marshall still teased Lucy, but had grown to like John Grey and had accepted that the couple were now courting and he had no chance as far as Lucy was concerned. He had moved from the umbrella shop to the spring mill where he now worked on three shifts so that he saw less of Lucy. However, Lewis knew that he would always be there for her should she ever need him and if John Grey made her happy, then that was all Lewis cared about. The crowd now went dancing every Saturday either at the Victoria Hall or at Cragstone or Longfield.

Sometimes John and Lucy, accompanied by Jane and James, would go to Sheffield on Saturday afternoons, have tea in one of the restaurants and then go to see a show at the Empire or to the cinema. Mrs Slater never minded keeping an eye on William and he usually ended up staying the night, sharing a bed with Ernest. William was a good lad, working hard for Mr Brown and dreading leaving school in summer and starting work at the pit.

It was one Friday when Mr Brown was – as usual – making his last call of the day on Top Row. He had dropped off a box of bruised fruit and vegetables at Evelyn Smithson's, knowing the girl was struggling to make ends meet. Then he knocked on the door of the Gabbitases, hoping they would be home by this time. 'Anybody in?' he called as he opened the door.

'Come in.' It was Ben who answered, 'All right?'

'Aye, not so bad. I'm glad it's thee who's in, Ben. Can I 'ave a word?'

'Yes, take a seat. Is owt wrong? Our Will 'asn't been up to owt, has he?'

'No, lad, just the opposite. I know ee's about to leave school and I don't want to lose 'im. I'd like to tek 'im on full time. Me business is doing right well, what with the new 'ouses up on't hill. And I've got a contract to supply't canteen down at works. Well I've decided to get meself a motor instead of t'owd horse and cart. If your Will came to work for me I'm thinking o' taking a stall in't market on Fridays and another in Cragstone on Thursdays. It's a damn good market there, tha knows, what with cattle market an' all.' Mr Brown paused to get his breath back, then continued, 'I'd learn 'im to drive when ee's a bit older. Well? What does tha think?'

Ben knew what he thought. It would make their Will the happiest lad in Millington. He also knew it was never going to happen. Ben couldn't put off marrying Emma for much longer or he was likely to lose her. Much as Ben loved his family, he loved Emma Scott more.

'I'm sorry Mr Brown, but our Will'll 'ave to go to't pit. Not that I want a collier's life for him, but the house depends on it.'

The greengrocer's face showed how disappointed the man felt. 'Well, I don't know what I shall do then. I shan't find another lad as willing or as quick as your Will.'

A movement outside heralded the arrival of the girls. They looked surprised to see Mr Brown sitting on a kitchen chair he was usually in a hurry to get home for his tea. Lucy glanced from one to the other, searching for an explanation.

'I was just telling yer brother.' Mr Brown was still hopeful. 'I want to give your Will a job when ee leaves school. A proper, responsible job, running a market stall two days a week and 'elping me on't rounds for't rest of the week.'

Lucy's face lit up like a sunflower as she realised what this would mean to William. Then the look on Ben's face warned her that there was no point in becoming excited. Jane took off her coat and beret and hung them on the hook behind the door. 'We shall have to think about your offer,' she said. 'It's very kind of you to consider employing, our Will.'

'Nay, lass, it'd be your Will doing me a favour if ee came to work for me. I can trust 'im you see.' The man frowned. 'And I shan't get another like 'im.'

'Well, like I say we shall think about it and let you know.'

'There's no point in building his hopes up,

Jane.' Ben looked as troubled as he was feeling.

'Have you mentioned it to our William, Mr Brown?' Lucy asked.

'No, lass. Not yet.'

'Well please don't; it'll only upset him if we have to disappoint him.'

'Aye, very well. I'll leave it with yer then.' The man picked up his flat cap and prepared to leave.

'What do we owe you?' Lucy looked in the cardboard box on the table.

'Oh it's nowt but a few leftovers.'

Lucy picked out a cooking apple. 'This apple's perfect – not a bruise to be seen – besides we can afford to pay you. How much?' Mr Brown had gone by the time Lucy had found her mam's old leather purse in which they still kept the housekeeping money. They heard the horse clip clopping along the row.

'Well?' Jane looked from one to the other.

Ben couldn't meet his sister's eyes. 'What good's a well without a bucket?' He attempted a joke but it fell on deaf ears.

'We ought to at least consider it.'

'It's what me mam wanted, something better for her youngest.' Lucy felt the tears gathering.

'Right then, I'll just 'ave to put off marrying Emma and remain an old bachelor,' Ben sighed.

'No, Ben. You must many Emma. There must be another way. Perhaps if we approach the pit management. Tell them we'll pay the rent regularly.'

'It won't work. There're men waiting for these houses.'

'Oh! If only we could find another house to rent.' Jane paced the floor. 'There's none to be had anywhere. They're snapped up as soon as they become vacant.'

'Have you and James been looking for one?' Lucy was surprised.

Jane blushed. 'Well, we've made a few enquiries.'

'What about you, Ben? Where will you live?'

'With Emma's mother. She needs someone with her because of the fits she keeps 'aving. Besides, it's her own 'ouse and it'll be Emma's one day.' Emma ran a general grocers and lived with her mother in accommodation attached to the shop.

'So you'll be able to leave the pit and work in the business then?'

'Well I daresay I could, but I shall probably stay. I'd miss the pit, and the men.'

'And our Will'll be unhappy there.' Lucy took a hot pot from the oven; it had been simmering all day. The aroma wafted out of the house and along the row, greeting William and Ernest Slater as they came home from chopping wood for Mrs Rawlings. 'That smells good,' Ernest said.

'Aye, better than me mam used to make. She's a good cook, our Lucy.' William was oblivious to the problem facing his brother and sisters. 'See yer later.' The lads had the few coppers they had earned from the wood chopping, enough for a game of billiards.

Nellie Gabbitas collected the letters from the postman. 'Kettle's boiling,' Mrs Cooper called. The postman propped his bike against the wall and came into the kitchen. Nellie hurriedly sorted through the envelopes, hoping for one with her name on it. Young Lily stood watching her, almost as excited as Nellie.

'Come on then, Lily, get that tea mashed. Posty'll be parched after peddling all't way up that hill.'

The man wiped the sweat from his forehead with his cap. 'Aye, I'm right ready for a drink and no mistake. It's been a busy morning. Somebody's sent letters to all the houses on't new estate at Millington. Advertising summat or other, but I'm not sure what. I think it's advertising a delivery service but I could only see a bit of writing through the envelope.'

Nellie found what she was looking for. 'I hope you don't sneak a look at everybody's letters,' she said good-naturedly, happy now there was a letter for her with a Blackpool postmark.

'Eeh no, lass, only the ones going to all the 'ouses. Never the personal ones.'

Lily handed him a pot of tea. She wished he would hurry up and go so she could hear what was in Nellie's letter. She thought it was the most romantic thing she had ever heard of. Except for Catherine and Heathcliff in *Wuthering Heights*. Mr Smith was good like that, letting them borrow books from his library.

'What's he say?' Lily asked as soon as the postman had gone.

'I don't know, I haven't read it yet.'

'Oh go on Nellie; read it, please.'

'Shut up, yer nosy haporth. Nellie'll read it when she's good and ready. Anybody'd think it were you ee was writing to.'

'Ooh, I wish it was.' Lily wasn't concentrating on her work.

'There'll be no potato left when you've done peeling it. Yer asking for a clout, you are.'

Lily knew Mrs Cooper would never hurt her but she'd better behave. Her mam wouldn't only clout her, she'd murder her if she got the sack. 'Sorry, Mrs Cooper.' She peeled the rest of the vegetables as thinly as she could, keeping an eye on Nellie all the time in case she decided to read her letter.

My dear Nellie,

You may consider it presumptuous of me, writing without your permission; if so I apologise. The truth is you are on my mind all my working day and in my dreams at night. Your face is there in my mirror as I make myself presentable in the morning and there before me as I conduct my business at the garage.

I think I am in love. I know I am in love. Dare I hope that you feel for me just a little of what I feel for you? If so, then maybe you will have dinner again with me, this Saturday at eight o'clock. I shall call for you at seven and we shall take the road to Derbyshire to an old coaching inn where I shall make a reservation.

Dear Nellie, please don't disappoint me. I have sought permission for you to leave by Mr Smith. I shall be waiting daily for your reply.

Your loving servant,
Tom Johnson.

Nellie didn't tell Lily or Mrs Cooper what was in the letter. All she told them was that she had been invited to dinner. All the same it was enough to send Lily into a frenzy of excitement as she decided what Nellie should wear. In anticipation of a further meeting with Thomas Johnson Nellie had taken a trip to Judith McCall's and bought a new dress; it had taken most of her savings, but she didn't care. The new dress was of salmon pink crepe de Chine trimmed with brown velvet braid. It fit Nellie like a second skin and the back was bare almost to the waist, so that it was impossible to wear the satin brassiere Nellie usually wore. Miss McCall said it didn't matter; she said Nellie looked like one of the mannequins who modelled her gowns. As Miss McCall's gowns were all exclusive designs Nellie had every confidence in her judgement. She had also bought a pair of leather shoes with a bar across in the same shade of brown as the trim on the dress. Nellie had sent for them on impulse to Daniel Neal's in London and still felt guilty about paying thirty-five shillings for a pair of shoes. On her last date with Thomas Johnson Nellie had worn a short dress and he had been unable to tear his eyes away from her long, shapely legs. Well now he had seen them she decided to keep them hidden and assume a more demure look. If Nellie had but realised, the long, skin-hugging dress turned her into a woman as glamorous as any film star, which was what young Lily told her when Nellie tried on the dress.

'Oh Nellie, you ought to be on't pictures,' she exclaimed, jumping up and down in the kitchen until Mrs Cooper put a stop to her enthusiasm.

'Well, I must admit yer do look lovely. Fancy 'im coming all't way from Blackpool just to take you out for yer supper.'

'Dinner.' Lily corrected Mrs Cooper, 'He must be madly in love, just like Heathcliff.'

'Oh I suppose he was coming to Yorkshire for some other reason, not just to see me.' Nellie blushed.

'Well, whatever he's coming for ee won't be disappointed. And don't you forget, mek sure ee keeps 'is 'ands off yer bits and pieces.' Mrs Cooper's advice set Lily off giggling.

'Are you going to stand theer all day laughing like a hyena or are yer going to fetch that washing in before it gets mucky again?'

Lily scurried off with the clothes basket; she felt as excited as if Mr Johnson was taking *her* out to dinner. She thought she might have her hair cut in the same style as Nellie and then she might attract someone like Mr Johnson.

On Saturday night Nellie's heart was beating fifty to the dozen. Lily had forgone her evening off so that she could see the couple set off on their evening out. At five to seven Lily's sharp young ears heard the motor coming up the drive. 'Ee's 'ere.' She called Nellie, who had gone for yet another look at herself in the long hall mirror.

Young Larry was waiting to open the door of the car. 'Oh lor, it's like a peep show.' Mrs Cooper complained about the youngsters but had adjusted the curtain so that she didn't miss anything.

Nellie picked up her evening bag – another waste of her savings, she thought – and went to meet her escort.

Thomas took her hand, kissing it before helping

her into the car. 'Oh Nellie,' he whispered. 'You're even more beautiful than I remembered.'

'Thank you,' Nellie smiled. 'I expect it's my new dress.'

'I hadn't even noticed your dress, though yes, it is lovely. I was looking at you.' His eyes searched Nellie's and she blushed as he held her gaze. Then she waved at the audience she knew was watching as she and Thomas set off to the Strines Inn and dinner. Nellie vowed that on Sunday she would go and tell her sisters about her new romance.

Mr Grundy had gone off on a rare trip with his wife, leaving Robbie in charge of the joiner's shop. He had plenty of work to keep him occupied but hadn't had time to get on with it with a steady stream of customers demanding attention. He seemed to have spent all morning weighing out nails and screws and cutting small sheets of emery cloth and large sheets of plywood. Now at last he was finding time to get on with doing what he liked best: making things. This time it was a bookcase, a beautiful oak affair. He had just finished smoothing down the last shelf ready for polishing when a knock came at the door.

'We're closed, sorry,' Robbie called, annoyed at being disturbed. The knock came again. He opened the door to find Prudence Goodman standing there. 'What do you want?' Robbie asked, rather ungraciously.

'Nothing. I was just out for a walk and found myself passing.'

'I'm busy.' Robbie noticed she had dolled herself up more than usual and let down her hair.

He still didn't find her attractive.

'I thought as it was time you were going home we might as well walk home together.'

'I might not have finished for some time.'

'I'll wait.' Prudence perched herself on top of a pile of floorboards, prepared to wait all night if necessary, so long as she was in the company of Robbie Grey. The attraction she had felt for him at first had intensified and she found it difficult not to reach out and touch him. The romantic passages in the love books she had read were nothing compared to the feelings taking place inside Prudence Goodman – the stories had awakened her awareness to the opposite sex. Now she would do anything to awaken those same feelings in Robbie. She took off her coat and he noticed her blouse buttons had been left undone. 'Are you going to stop working and come and sit beside me?' Prudence crossed her legs, revealing a pair of bare thighs. Not half as shapely as Dot Greenwood's, Robbie thought. He put down the sandpaper and stood up, grabbing his jacket. 'All finished,' he said. Prudence still sat there. 'Well, are yer coming or aren't yer? I'm waiting to lock up.' He stood waiting for her to move. 'Right then, stay, but I shall 'ave to lock you in.'

Prudence stood up and flounced towards the door, pausing to block his way. 'Why don't you like me, Robbie?'

Robbie was embarrassed by the question. 'I do. I mean, you're all right. I just like Dot more.'

'Oh, her again. She's common, she's loud – how can you like her more than me?'

Robbie almost told Prudence it was because she

was a bitch, a spoiled, selfish bitch. 'I don't know, I just do. Come on, let's go home.' He hurried down the hill with Prudence almost running in order to keep up with him. She was fuming inside, vowing that no matter what she had to do and who she had to hurt, one day she'd have Robbie Grey.

Chapter Eleven

Ben confided in John Grey his worries about William. 'It isn't right that he can't take advantage of the job Mr Brown has offered 'im.'

'Lucy's worrying about him too,' John said. 'She doesn't think he'll be suited to pit work.'

'I know. I've decided not to marry Emma and give 'im a chance to better 'imself. After all, it was what me mother wanted. And besides, look what this job did to me dad.'

John wiped sweat from his upper lip with his sleeve, leaving a whiter patch of skin in contrast to the rest of his face. 'Ben, you can't not marry Emma; you've a right to a life of yer own.'

'I don't 'ave any choice. I can't see any other solution to the problem.'

'I can. If only your Lucy would marry me I could take over the house. I'd take care of your Will and he could go work for the greengrocer. The trouble is she's in no hurry to be wed.'

'There'd be our Jane to consider. I can't see you wanting to start married life with a ready-made family.'

'Course I would. Jane'd be welcome for as long as she needed a home, though I don't think she'll be long before she's married herself. I know for a fact she and James've been looking for a house.' John grinned. 'I wish your Lucy was as eager to marry as Jane is.' The two men carried on with their work, both lost in their own thoughts. It seemed to them that only Lucy could solve the problem, and although Lucy loved John she just wasn't sure she was ready yet to be married.

On Saturday John and Lucy went to Sheffield. Each week they added something to their bottom drawer and Lucy loved searching among the market stalls for any bargains. On this occasion it was a mirror that caught her eye. Lucy picked it up. 'Oh look John; it would be just right over the fireplace.' It had a beautiful gilt frame and a picture on each end of it, of a lady in a garden. 'Oh John, I love it. Can we buy it?'

'If it's what you want.' John haggled with the stallholder until he managed to knock off a couple of shillings from the original price. Lucy looked at her reflection; her eyes were shining. She had never noticed before but out here in the brightness of the day she was startled by the beauty of the girl gazing back at her. The man wrapped the mirror in brown paper. 'Just be careful if yer 'ang it over't fireplace like yer said. I shouldn't like yer to set yer frock on fire. Don't want a lovely lass like you getting burned.'

'I won't,' Lucy smiled. 'We've got a fire guard.'

'That's sensible. Are yer planning on getting wed, then?'

'She won't 'ave me,' John grinned.

'Well, if she won't 'ave you perhaps she'll 'ave me.'

Lucy giggled. 'Well aren't I the lucky one, two handsome men offering me their hands. Come on, you, let's go and have some tea.'

'Will yer marry me, Lucy? Please.' John stopped and turned her to face him. 'I love you.' He wanted to point out that Will would be able to take the job he desired if only Lucy would marry him. However he knew that if she did marry him it must be because she loved him and not for any other reason.

Lucy sighed. The desire she felt for John was growing with each passing day, and she wanted him more than anything in the world. 'I'd have to look after our William. I promised me mam.'

'Course we'd look after him. We'd look after him together. Does that mean you'll marry me then?'

Lucy smiled a smile that lit up her face. 'All right, if you insist.'

'Oh Lucy, I do, I do insist.' He lifted her off her feet and spun her round, right there in the middle of the market. 'She said yes,' he shouted to the marketeer.

'It's the bloody mirror; it's a wishing mirror, didn't I tell yer?' Then he began to sing, ''Ere comes the bride, bowlegged, cockeyed.' The other stallholders joined in and a flower seller in a large straw hat gave Lucy a bunch of Sweet Williams. 'Look,' the woman said, 'she's on her way to 'er wedding.' Lucy blushed as everyone called out to wish them well.

''Ere,' a man on another stall came over and gave them a baby's chamber pot. 'I expect that'll come in 'andy before't year's out.' Lucy didn't know what to do with the enamel pot but she thanked the man for his kindness and managed to stuff it into the carpet bag she was carrying. 'Oh, John,' she said, 'of all the places to propose you had to choose the middle of a market.'

'Sorry.' John looked shamefaced.

'No, oh no. It's lovely – all these wonderful people wishing us well; you couldn't have picked anywhere better. They're the salt of the earth, these market traders.'

Aye, thought John, feeling happier than he could ever remember, and your William'll soon be one of 'em.

The news that Lucy was arranging her wedding filled Jane with envy.

'It should have been me first; I'm the eldest,' she grumbled.

'Well if we've to marry according to age that means we'll be waiting for ever. Our Nellie's not even courting.' Now Lucy had made up her mind she couldn't wait to marry John.

'If only we could find a house,' Jane sighed.

'You could always live here,' Lucy pointed out. 'It's your home as well as mine and there'll be me mam's room empty once our Ben's gone. I expect he will once John takes over the house. Our Will prefers the attic.'

'No, James wants a home of our own.'

'John would have lived in Barker's pig sty so long as we could be married.'

Jane knew James wasn't in too big a hurry to be married – willing but not eager. 'No, we'll wait until we find a place of our own,' she said.

Ben was as eager as John. At church the following Sunday the banns were called for Ben Gabbitas and Emma Scott. Also to the surprise of the congregation, for John Grey and Lucy Gabbitas. The brother and sister had decided to make it a double wedding, and because Herbert Goodman was to conduct the ceremony at Millington Church Emma was forced to reside in the town for a few weeks before. Emma decided to stay with Mary and Jacob, travelling back and forth each day to her mother and the shop. Ben realised that travelling to the pit each day once he moved to Emma's would be awkward and on the Saturday previous to the wedding he came roaring on Top Row on a motorbike. This was such an unusual event that everyone came out to see what all the noise was about and Ben spent Saturday afternoon giving rides to Will and his pals, with warnings from parents to hold tight and be careful. Ben could hear mutterings of how he would end up killing somebody before he'd done.

The wedding was to take place on the last Saturday in July. Mary made Lucy a beautiful white satin dress with long narrow sleeves and a skirt that flared ever so slightly at the hem. She had a waist-length veil and Mr Brown was to make her a bouquet of red carnations.

Emma, being better off than Lucy, had bought a dress but Jane said she couldn't possibly look any more beautiful than Lucy. Jane had got over the envy and was thrilled with the blue bridesmaids' dresses she, Kitty and Nellie were to wear. James, of course, was to be best man for John and Will for Ben. Robbie Grey was to be groomsman. All that was needed now was the sun to shine. Jane was becoming annoyed with Lucy's 'What if the car doesn't turn up? What if the caterers forget? What if Mr Crossman forgets to bring his gramophone?'

'For heaven's sake, Lucy. I'm sure Emma isn't making so much fuss. Tomorrow'll be fine. Besides, as long as you and John are married nothing else matters, does it?'

'No, Jane, you're right. I'll stop worrying.' But she didn't. She did however look into the new mirror, already taking pride of place over the mantelpiece, and ask for everything to go well on her wedding day. The stall man had said it was a wishing mirror and Lucy Gabbitas believed that wishes could come true, otherwise she wouldn't be preparing to marry the man she wanted to spend the rest of her life with.

The sky was as blue as Lucy's eyes when she woke on her wedding day. In a flurry of excitement Jane and Kitty washed her hair and set it in waves using sugared water, then they did each other's, laughing at the sight of them all done up in metal curlers. Will had taken off in the company of Albert Marshall to do some jobs for the greengrocer.

'I'm not stopping in there,' he said. 'It's like a women's hairdresser's.'

At first the pair had protested at the idea of having to get dressed up but then one day the lads had been taken to be measured for suits – with long trousers – with instructions for them to be made with room enough to turn down the legs and sleeves as the lads grew. The promise of a proper man's suit had been enough to make the pair behave themselves and as Kitty had warned them, conduct themselves in a proper manner. If not, they had been told, they would have to make do with short trousers.

At quarter to two the car arrived and Will proudly escorted Ben and the bridesmaids into the ribbon-trimmed vehicle. Then he came back for Lucy and Mr Slater, who had been asked to give Lucy away. With Ben being the groom Mr Slater and his wife were proudly standing in for Lucy's parents. Lucy shed a tear as she wished her father and mother here, especially her father. It would have been nice if Aunt Kate could be here too but that was one wish the mirror couldn't possibly grant.

'Eeh, lass, I'm sure you must be missing yer mam and dad on this special day, but I'm sure they'll be watching from wherever they are. In their absence I'd be most 'onoured if yer'd let me take yer dad's place, and I shall be just as proud as ee would 'ave been.'

'Oh Mr Slater, I couldn't ask for anyone better.' Lucy wiped her eyes just as Will charged in. 'Come on, Lucy. Oh I've never seen as many people in all me life. Emma's already there. She looks lovely, but not as lovely as you.' Will blushed at the first compliment he could ever remember paying his sister.

'Come on then, let's get it over with.' Lucy was

smiling again. She took a final look in the mirror and they were off.

Reverend Goodman was as proud as if he was conducting the marriage of his own son. John, along with his brothers, had filled a gap in the vicar's life. A daughter was all very well, but he would dearly have loved a son. It wasn't to be and he knew God must have his reason.

Emma and Ben made their vows first, followed by Lucy and John. The congregation thought a double wedding was the loveliest thing they had ever seen. Aunts, uncles, cousins, friends and even people none of them recognised had turned up to watch the unusual ceremony. Then they were on their way to the photographic studio for pictures to be taken of their special day. When all the formalities were over and they were in the car to the Guild Hall, where the reception was to be held, John gave in to temptation, took Lucy in his arms and kissed her. 'Lucy Grey, I love you and I always will.'

'Even when I'm old and wrinkled?'

'Yes,' he answered. 'Will you love me when I'm old and bald?'

'I might,' Lucy teased. 'On the other hand I might run off with Lewis Marshall.' Lewis was a standing joke between them.

'Ah, but you're forgetting Lewis'll be old and bald too.'

'Oh dear, well I'll just have to find myself a handsome young stud then, with some hair.'

'Don't you dare.' Then they were at the Guild Hall.

'Thank goodness,' Will said as he opened the car door for the newlyweds, 'I'm starving.'

'Well, no change there then.' Lucy kissed her brother on the cheek, causing his face to turn the colour of the carnations in her bouquet. 'By the way,' she told him, 'I've a surprise for you tomorrow.'

'What is it?'

'I said tomorrow.'

Will wondered what it could be. Whatever it was it wouldn't stop him worrying about starting work in the pit. Not even a new suit and two weddings had been able to do that.

'Oh no.' John could see Daniel the bird man standing amongst the onlookers. As soon as Dan saw them he made a rude gesture with his fist, first at Lucy, then at John. Lucy felt herself growing hot with embarrassment. Fortunately the crowd put Dan's action down to the fact that they were newlyweds and thought it was amusing. 'I bet he'll be doing that every time he sees us for the rest of our lives,' Lucy whispered.

It wasn't until they reached the reception that Nellie was able to introduce Tom Johnson to her family. She had asked if she could invite a friend, but none of them had expected a male friend, especially one as suave and handsome as Tom. 'Where did you find him?' Lucy whispered.

Nellie shrugged. 'I suppose we just found each other.'

'Well he's lovely. Is it serious?'

'I suppose so. He's coming over most weekends so I guess it must be.'

'Coming from where?'

'Blackpool. He owns a garage there.'

'Goodness, hang on to him.'

'I will if I can. I really like him, Lucy.'

'Well it's obvious he likes you. I should say more than likes.'

Nellie smiled. Lucy had never seen her looking so radiant.

The fresh aroma of cucumber salad greeted the guests as they entered the Guild Hall. The tables looked beautiful with two wedding cakes set out on the top table.

John went to thank Emma's mother, who had insisted on supplying the tea. 'We really appreciate this,' he said. 'It must have cost a small fortune. I wish you'd let me contribute.'

The lady smiled. 'It didn't cost all that much. I've contacts in the catering trade so it's all been supplied at wholesale. Besides, it hasn't cost any more for the two of you than it would have for a single wedding. I daresay there'd have been the same number of guests, and anyway, you paid for the hire of the hall and the cars so we'll call it quits. It's lovely to meet all Ben's family and friends and I'm so grateful to be here without embarrassing everyone. The trouble with epilepsy is that I don't have any warning. I dreaded having a turn in church.'

'Well you didn't. It's lovely to meet you too. And thanks again. I doubt we could have afforded a spread like this for so many people.'

Mrs Scott leaned towards John and whispered 'Well I can, and who else have I to spend it on except my only daughter. Shall we eat?'

The guests were finding their places at the long

tables. John went to find Lucy. He hadn't eaten all day and was famished.

When the ham, cakes and trifle had all been demolished and the tables cleared, the dancing began. Mr Crossman, a fellow miner from over the hill in Warrentickle, had brought his large collection of records and his gramophone. Music was his hobby and providing entertainment was a good way of spending Saturday nights. He began with 'Teddy Bears' Picnic' for the children. As the evening wore on and more and more Pale Ale was consumed the music changed and the floor became crowded. Miners, umbrella girls, cousins from Cragstone and neighbours from the rows all joined in the dancing. Even Prudence Goodman had one or two partners. Robbie hoped she would find a boyfriend and leave him in peace. The only girl he wanted was Dot Greenwood. 'You're the prettiest girl in the room,' he told her as he took the opportunity to hold her close in a waltz neither of them knew how to do.

'No, I think both brides are the prettiest,' Dot argued. 'And what about the bridesmaids? They look lovely in their blue dresses.'

'Aye they do, but I'm not bothered about dresses. You look just as pretty when you're mucking out or stacking the hay.'

'Oh, so you fancy me in wellies then?'

'Aye, I fancy you in owt.' The couple laughed and moved closer. Boadacea Greenwood sighed contentedly at the sight of her daughter and the handsome young lad. Then as the music changed she dragged little Arthur on to the dance floor for the Hokey Cokey.

Prudence Goodman fumed. She knew she was looking her best, and Robbie Grey hadn't even noticed.

When Will woke at seven the next morning he could see a rook pecking at the window above his bed. Then another came, fluttering and fretting to join its mate. They came from the tall trees opposite the Memorial Gardens. One Sunday the gang had counted nine nests altogether. His dad had once told him they had nested there for at least fifty years. Will had tried to count the birds but it was impossible. The birds on the roof flew away and Will suddenly remembered the surprise Lucy had promised him. He hurried out of bed and into his old trousers. She would have a fit if his new suit wasn't hung on a hanger and kept for best. Jane heard the scuffling in the attic above her and then Will calling 'Lucy!' She caught him on the landing just as he was about to barge into the bedroom where John was in the throes of his fourth climax.

'No, Will, ssh. You mustn't go in our Lucy's room anymore.'

'Why?'

'Well, our Lucy's married now. Come into my room and let's have a chat.' Jane guessed Will might be jealous of John after being doted on by Lucy for so long. Jane hopped back into bed and Will perched on the bed beside her. 'Oh, I see. You think they might be doing it.' Will blushed as he realised what he had said.

'Well, it's possible I suppose. It's a natural thing to happen once two people are married. But, no,

I wasn't thinking that. I just thought we'd let them have a lie in after such a busy day yesterday.'

'I suppose so, but our Lucy said she'd a surprise for me today. Can I open the curtains?'

'What, and have old Lanky on Next Row seeing me in me nighty? Anyway, I can tell you about the surprise. Our Lucy won't mind.'

'Go on then.'

'Well, how would you like to work for Mr Brown instead of at the pit?'

Will wondered if Jane was having him on. His eyes filled with tears. 'You know how I'd feel, but I've got to go to't pit.'

'No, you haven't. That's the surprise: you've got a job working for Mr Brown, starting tomorrow.'

Will stared at his sister. 'You're not 'aving me on are yer, Jane?'

'Oh, Will. Do you really think I'd be so cruel?'

Will's face lit up like a beacon. 'I'm just going to tell Ernie.'

'He might not be up yet. Oh, and by the way, what do you know about doing it?' Jane nudged Will with her elbow.

'Everything.'

'I doubt that. Look, shall I ask James to have a word and explain things to you? So that you do know everything.'

'OK, but I expect I know already.'

'Oh I expect you do, but just to make sure.'

'I'm going to Ernie's.' Will set off down the stairs.

'Will!' Jane called after him.

'What?' He was impatient to be off.

'Don't you think you ought to put a shirt on in

place of your pyjama jacket?' She heard him clomp up to the attic. A young boy, content at last.

The house resembled a gift shop. Presents covered the table in the kitchen and also the polished, posh table in the front room. Even the dresser was overflowing with brown paper parcels and objects that had been handed over unwrapped but with much love.

'What's that?' Now the cloud had been lifted from Will's shoulders he was taking an interest in the proceedings.

'It's a toast rack,' Lucy said. 'If you unwrap anything remember who it's from; I shall need to thank them.'

'Are yer going to put toast in a rack now you're married then? Why don't yer put it on a plate and eat it like we always do?'

'Good question,' John laughed. 'But it's nice of cousin Polly to buy it for us, whoever she is.' John had lost track of all the friends and relatives. The umbrella girls had bought them a lovely pair of lace-edged sheets. The shock came when Lucy opened the box Nellie and Tom had given them. Inside was the most beautiful dinner service imaginable, fine bone china, decorated with twenty-two-carat gold. 'Oh John, look at this; it must have cost a fortune. I shall never dare use it.' There were soup bowls, tureens, dinner plates and dessert dishes. 'I bet our Ben's been given the same.'

'It's really good of them. He must be worth a bit, that friend of Nellie's.'

'He owns a garage.'

There was also a tea set from Mary and Jacob,

bone china patterned with roses.

'I'll tell you what: I'm going to get our Robbie to make us a cabinet to put all this on display.'

'Oh, that'll be lovely and it'll be safe.'

Both Lucy and Ben had received a cheque from Aunt Kate, who regretted missing the weddings and wished them all well. Auntie Kate had found herself a rich husband over in America. Lucy said John should bank the money for emergencies, but John said they weren't going to think about emergencies the day after their wedding. John Grey was the happiest man in Millington. He had a wife most men could only dream of. He had a new family and a house full of love. He had been accepted by the people of Millington and he vowed to look after Lucy and her brother to the best of his ability. John had considered the death of his parents a tragedy from which he would never recover. Now he realised that being made homeless had been the beginning of a new and wonderful life. He prayed that his brothers would find the same fulfilment.

Chapter Twelve

If John Grey was the happiest man in Millington, Will Gabbitas was certainly the proudest as he clambered in and out of the brand new lorry, selling the fresh greens to both old and new customers. Mr Grundy had fashioned a series of shelves on the back of it so that customers could see everything on display. Will went up and down the streets knocking on doors. 'Anything today?' Most of the housewives would come out and see what was on offer – even if they didn't buy much it was an excuse for a gossip and Mr Brown would pass on any news he picked up on the way. Will would weigh out the fruit and vegetables with either the large black weights or the small brass ones. He would then carry the merchandise back to the doors for the ladies. Most would enquire about how the weddings had gone, or how their Mary or Nellie were keeping these days. One even had the audacity to ask, 'Not got a bun in the oven yet, your Mary, then?'

Will thought the new council houses were ever so posh with the big gardens and lavs just inside the back door. Back in the truck he thought about what the woman had said. Evelyn Smithson had told Kitty that she had got caught with a baby the first time she had done it. Kitty had told their Albert and Albert had told Will. So why hadn't their Mary got a bun in the oven? Perhaps she and Jacob didn't do it. Maybe it wasn't as much fun as everybody made out. Perhaps it even hurt. He decided to ask James when they had their talk.

'We'll put the plums down to 'alf price now Will. Them bloody wasps ave been at 'em so we'd best get rid.'

'All right, Mr Brown.'

'Tha'd better start calling me Fred if we're to be working together.'

'All right, Mr Brown. So long as yer don't think I'm being cheeky; our Lucy warned me about that.'

'No, I won't. I just thought it'd be more friendly, like.'

'All right, Mr ... I mean Fred.'

''Ow does tha feel now tha's nearly got first week over? Are tha going to like it?'

'I love it, especially the markets. I'll try not to mek a mistake next week.'

'Mistake? Why, did tha mek one this week?'

'Aye. I sold a whole bag of onions at a penny a pound too much. It were yer writing, yer see. I mistook a five for a six.'

Mr Brown let out a guffaw of laughter. 'Did anybody complain, lad?'

'No. Mind you, I made 'em all laugh with me jokes so I don't suppose they noticed.'

'Tha can mek a few more mistakes like that, lad. I shan't complain.' He looked at his gold pocket watch. 'Right then, we'll do the four rows now and then we'll call it a day. I like to finish early on a Saturday. Tha's worked 'ard enough this week so I'll sort lorry out today. I think we're going to do well me and thee, lad. Once we get into a routine we'll be grand.'

'Thanks Mr ... Fred.'

By the time they reached Top Row the truck was almost empty. There wouldn't be much left for the greengrocer to sort out by the time he'd given stuff to the poor families. At present there were about fifty children living on the row and by the look of it, all of them were out in the yard on this lovely August afternoon – girls playing hop-scotch or skipping, boys playing football. The Holmeses and Murphys against the Marshalls and Cartwnghts. When the truck trundled along the row the game was forgotten as they all came to take a look at the brightly painted vehicle. To celebrate Will's first week on his new job Mr Brown gave every child an apple. He knew the mothers would appreciate his generosity; besides, they were almost past their best anyway. He'd start on a new box on Monday.

William went off to join the Marshall team. 'We're losing two nil,' Ernie Slater moaned.

'Oh, it's only a game,' Will consoled him. Nothing could upset him today. He had done well on his new job, and that meant he would never again have to worry about going to work down the pit.

Lucy was also brimming over with gladness after her first week of married life. Mary had prepared her for what would happen on her wedding night, but she hadn't told her how exquisite love-making would be. There again, perhaps it wasn't like that for everyone, only her and John. Lucy giggled at some of the things they had got up to in the privacy of their bed. And not only in bed. On the pegged rug in front of the wardrobe mirror where they could see themselves. She blushed as she remembered how their nudity had excited them. The only problem had been the lack of sleep. John, who had been on morning shift and had to be up at five, couldn't possibly have had more than a couple of hours' sleep. Oh well, he could make up for it this week on afternoon shift; he could stay in bed in the mornings. Lucy had officially finished work now, as all married women were expected to do.

However, a large order had come in and Mr Blackmore had asked Lucy to stay on until the order was completed. She was happy to do so but John wouldn't like it when he was on night shift and she was on days. They would hardly see each other, but would no doubt find time to make love, between John coming to bed and her getting up. Lucy wondered what her mother would have thought of her. She thought Annie would have considered it sinful to be thinking about making love all the time the way Lucy did. She smiled to herself as she imagined Annie calling her a brazen hussy. Lucy thought she might be, but she didn't care; she loved John and he loved her and she considered herself the most fulfilled woman in Millington, or maybe the whole county of Yorkshire.

The house was looking attractive. The atmosphere also seemed lighter now that Lucy had decided to throw out the old cracked crockery and use some of the new. She had replaced the faded tablecloths and frayed towels and placed a vase bought by the Goodmans in the centre of the dresser where it was reflected in the mirror. She had gathered a bunch of purple heather and arranged it in the vase, adding a few springs of lavender to scent the room. Upstairs their bed had been dressed with new linen and a lovely gold eiderdown, which reflected the morning sun. The carnations from her bridal bouquet were beginning to fade; when they died she would press them between the pages of her bible – her Sunday school prize when she was twelve. She would give the Gabbitas family bible to Ben on his next visit and her mother's hymn and prayer book to Will.

Lucy combed her hair in front of the wishing mirror, took off her apron and took a chair outside. She sat in the sun, watching her husband and brother kicking a ball about in the yard. Dustbins were being used for goal posts and by what she could make out the Holmes team were winning by ten goals to two. Kitty came and brought a stool to join Lucy, laughing as her brother aimed for the goal and missed. 'They haven't a chance against the Holmeses; young Harry's scored all ten.'

Lucy sighed. 'I reckon Mrs Holmes'll have trouble with that one. He's too good-looking for his own good.'

'Aye, and he's after the lasses already. He is handsome though. He'll be a right charmer in a few years' time.'

'So will his brother.' Not as nice-looking as my John though, thought Lucy, already thinking about bedtime.

Mary felt the familiar crampy pain and knew that once again she had failed to become pregnant. Jacob would be just as disappointed as she was, but would hide his feelings as usual and tell Mary it didn't matter. They both knew it did, not only to them but to Jacob's parents who were yearning for a grandchild. If Mary looked a bit tired they would take it as a sign that a baby was in the offing. If she put on a few pounds they would notice and become excited. Sometimes she thought it might happen if only everyone would forget about it. She knew Jacob was on the verge of telling his mother to back off and Mary would hate to fall out with her in-laws. She looked at the crowd of ragged children who lived down in the shadow of the steelworks. She knew the families down there had all on to make ends meet, yet God blessed them with one child after the other. Jacob, a hard worker, would feed his children well, dress them warmly and be the best father in the world, yet it seemed as though it wasn't to be. She put on her coat ready for work. Like Lucy she was back working on the urgent order for parasols. The wealthy ladies wouldn't like their delicate skins to be spoiled by this bout of hot weather. Mary couldn't believe people still had time to bother with parasols in this day and age. When she had a daughter she would buy her the best Millington parasol she could afford. In the meantime, work would help distract from her inability to conceive. She had Jacob, the kindest, most caring husband she could wish for. What more did she need?

Thomas Johnson had been captivated by Nellie's family and astounded at the number of wedding guests. He had been overwhelmed at first, but as first one then another relative had introduced themselves he had realised, as an only child, just what he had been missing all these years. Oh, he knew how fortunate he was to have been left a legacy by his maternal grandfather. Enough to start a garage just when motor vehicles were proving to be the transport of the future. Not only was the filling station thriving but he had orders for a number of cars and motorcycles. However Tom had realised during his time in Millington that he would forfeit all his wealth for a family like

Nellie's. He wondered what Nellie would make of his parents and the grand house in the most select area of Blackpool. It never entered his head to wonder what his parents would think of Nellie, a working girl from a mining family. It wouldn't matter anyway. Thomas had already made up his mind that Nellie Gabbitas was the girl he was going to marry. The following week he invited Nellie to Blackpool to meet his parents. Tom offered to fetch her on Saturday and bring her back on Sunday, but Nellie told him she was quite capable of travelling by train. She knew Tom had a couple of men working for him, but as he had mentioned Saturdays could be quite busy she knew he would be more useful working than trailing all the way to Millington and back. 'You don't mind me taking a weekend off, do you?' she asked Mrs Cooper.

'Course I don't mind. Not a day's holiday 'ave yer taken in all the time you've been 'ere.' Mrs Cooper had every intention of encouraging the friendship between Nellie and Mr Johnson. It wasn't nice living the life of a spinster with neither child nor chicken to call her own, and besides Mr Johnson was nice, with no side to him despite his wealth. 'Theer's nowt special 'appening anyway. I expect it's the time of year they all pop off on their 'olidays.'

Nellie was apprehensive about meeting Tom's parents; they sounded ever so posh. She hoped she didn't embarrass him in any way. When she voiced her concerns to Mrs Cooper, the housekeeper said, 'Embarrass 'im'? They'd 'ave all on to find anybody better.'

'I hope you're right.' Nellie wasn't convinced. She packed her bag and decided to wear her new costume in a lovely fawn colour; she had bought a hat from Daniel Evans in Sheffield to match the brown velvet collar. Nellie had spent more in the last couple of months than in all her working life, but she really did want Tom to be proud of her. If he was she knew it would have been money well spent.

He was waiting for her when she left the train. He held out his arms and gathered her to him, revelling in the scent of her. Nellie had never been to Blackpool before – or any other seaside resort. She didn't see much of it as he drove through the back streets. She could however see the tower looming tall and straight in the opposite direction from where they were heading. 'We'll go to the tower later,' Tom promised. When they drew up outside the large detached property set in the colourful, well-kept garden, Nellie blushed as she wondered what Tom's parents would think of the house on Top Row.

Tom felt the trembling of her hand as he helped her out of the car. 'You're trembling,' he said, concerned for her. 'There's nothing to be nervous about. I daresay my mother's even more anxious than you about making a good impression.' Nellie doubted it. Then they were in the hall where Tom's parents were waiting to greet them.

'So you're Nellie. We've heard so much about you.' Margaret Johnson held out a pale, smooth hand, at the sight of which Nellie already felt at a disadvantage. Still, she supposed there were servants to do all the rough work in a house like this.

'Lovely to meet you.' Nellie smiled and the woman returned the smile, entranced by Nellie's beauty. Mr Johnson placed a kiss on Nellie's cheek. She thought she detected the smell of petrol on his clothing. He took her hand and led her into a large, well-furnished room. 'Welcome to Oak House,' he said.

'It's a lovely house,' Nellie said. She could hardly resist staring round at the furnishings but managed to concentrate on the feel of the thick pile carpet and the warmth of the fire, which she suspected had been lit more for her pleasure than from the need of it on this August afternoon. 'I'll show you to your room, then we shall have tea.' Mrs Johnson led her back into the hall and up the stairs. 'You have a view of the park from this room.'

'Oh, it's lovely,' Nellie answered truthfully, but thought she had a much better view from her room at the manor, of the moors and Cragstone. Nothing, in Nellie's opinion, could compare with the stark beauty of the Pennine moors.

During tea, Tom sniffed at his father, 'You've been at the garage again, haven't you?'

'Aye, how do you know?' Henry Johnson looked puzzled.

'Because you smell like a petrol tank,' Tom laughed.

'What did I tell you?' His wife shook her head. 'He's supposed to have taken early retirement in order to relax a little in his old age and he's gone and found himself another job, helping out at the garage.'

'It isn't a job, it's a hobby.'

'What did you find to do this afternoon then, whilst my back was turned?' Tom laughed.

'Served a few customers, polished that Morris in the showroom. Watched Fred fit a gasket on a bike. I'm learning all the time.'

'Look, Dad, if you enjoy it so much I'll put you on the payroll, part time.' Tom watched his father's eyes light up.

'Oh I don't want paying, son. But I would like to work regular hours. It would give me a purpose in life.' He looked across the table at Nellie. 'I'm not cut out for retirement, Nellie. Margaret doesn't understand that a man needs to feel useful.'

'Oh I do, I do understand. It's just that I thought we could enjoy some time together before we're too old to enjoy it. What do you think, Nellie?'

Nellie blushed, thinking she was between the devil and the deep blue sea. 'Well,' she considered the question, 'I think a few hours' work won't hurt. You can perhaps work in the mornings and relax in the afternoons. Of course that's only my opinion.'

'It's a damn sensible idea.' Mr Johnson was glad Tom had found himself a sensible girl instead of a lazy layabout.

'Yes, but you could always give private tuition for a few hours to suit you,' Mrs Johnson suggested.

'Private tuition be damned. Sorry Nellie, but I never wanted to teach in the first place, only did it to suit my parents. I imagine I'd have been much happier in a job where I could wear dirty overalls.'

Nellie felt sad as she wished her dad had lived

to enjoy his retirement, but remembering her mother she didn't think he would ever have been allowed to retire. 'So you were a teacher then, Mr Johnson?'

'Headmaster. Never got a chance to mucky my hands in my life.'

Nellie smiled. 'Unlike my father and my brother. I'm a miner's daughter. My father died before he reached retirement.'

'I'm so sorry. You can be proud, though. Where would we be without the miners?'

'Where indeed?' Tom squeezed Nellie's hand under the tablecloth. Nellie wasn't sure yet about Tom's mother, but she had taken an instant liking to his father. All the same she was relieved when the meal was over and Tom suggested a walk along the promenade. 'Put something warm on, Nellie. There's always a cold wind on Blackpool front,' Mrs Johnson advised.

'Best air in England,' her husband added. 'Without exception.'

The salty Blackpool air was certainly bracing. The sun was just going down, turning the wide expanse of sea to liquid gold. They stood leaning on the sea wall and watched it change to orange, then crimson. 'That's even more breathtaking than the sunsets over Cragstone.' Nellie was whispering, as though words spoken out loud might make the colours disappear and turn the water black.

'Wait until it's stormy; you'll really see something then. We wouldn't be able to stand here or we'd be washed away. The waves cover the prom at this point and reach the road at the other side.'

'Goodness. I never thought the sea would be so frightening. I imagined it to be still like the reservoirs.' Tom didn't answer. He couldn't imagine anyone never seeing the sea. The sun seemed to be sinking more rapidly now and then disappeared altogether. Still they stood hand in hand, feeling the magic of the night and being together.

'I love you, Nellie Gabbitas.' Tom turned her towards him and kissed her, filling her with a passion frightening in its intensity. 'Will you marry me? Nellie?'

'What? But you hardly know me! I mean, what would your parents say?'

'You wouldn't be marrying my parents, you'd be marrying me. Besides, they like you.'

'How do you know? I mean, they'd hardly be ill-mannered enough to show their feelings in front of me.'

Tom laughed. 'You don't know my mother; she'd have found some way to make her feelings known. I know from past experience.'

'So how many other girls have you invited home?'

'Not many. Three, or maybe four if you count the spotty girl when I was fourteen.'

'What about the others? Didn't your parents find them suitable?'

'No! And they were right, none of them were, until I met you. I dread to think what life would have been like if I'd married one of them instead of you. Fancy some chips?'

'Yes please, they smell delicious.'

'Best fish and chips in England.' They ran

across the promenade and then across the tracks, dodging the open-topped tram. 'We'll take a trip on that on your next visit.'

'So I'm invited again, then?'

'Well, you have to come again to give me your answer, haven't you? Just one little word, yes, or no.'

'Yes...'

'You've decided already. Oh Nellie.'

'No. I meant yes I have to come and give you my answer. Oh now I'm all confused.' She began to laugh. 'All right, yes, I will marry you Thomas Johnson, not in a rush though. We need somewhere to live.'

Tom bought two lots of fish and chips, oozing vinegar which dripped through the newspaper onto their shoes. 'We'll take a look on our way home. There are bound to be properties for sale.'

It was a long walk up the main street and after a while Tom turned off up a road where large houses stood in their own grounds. Nellie was relieved that none of them seemed to be vacant; she much preferred the ones near the shops and the sea front. Besides, it all seemed to be happening in too much of a rush. 'Tom,' she said. 'Let's not tell your parents just yet.'

'All right.' Tom pulled her closer, his arm circling her waist. 'So long as you don't change your mind.'

'I won't. I certainly won't.' Nellie only hoped his mother would approve, but even if she didn't it wouldn't make any difference. Like Tom said, she wasn't marrying his parents.

Lucy saw Evelyn hanging out the washing. 'Fancy a cup of tea?' Evelyn nodded and finished pegging out the snowy sheets. She supposed Lucy wanted to cancel her washing now she wasn't working regularly.

'Come and have five minutes.' Lucy poured tea into two pretty, rose-patterned cups. Evelyn was gratified to see her gift of a biscuit barrel had been put in use – it had been all she could afford.

'First of all, thanks for your lovely wedding present,' Lucy said.

'Oh, it isn't much.' Evelyn blushed.

'Well, I'll tell you what, it'll be used, and not stuck up in the cupboard like our Polly's toast rack.' The girls giggled and sipped their tea. 'I wanted to ask you something.' It was Lucy's turn to blush now. 'It should have been my monthly a week ago and it hasn't come yet. Does that mean I'm expecting?'

Evelyn grinned. 'By gum, that's quick work. Well, to answer your question, probably. Do you feel sick in the mornings?'

'Not that I've noticed.'

'Well it's a bit early for morning sickness. Do yer feel sore round 'ere?' Evelyn touched her breasts.

Lucy blushed. She did, but had put it down to John's lovemaking. She nodded.

'And are yer weeing a lot?' Lucy nodded again. 'Well then, I should imagine you are. Oh Lucy, I'll bet you're thrilled.'

Lucy was too shocked to be thrilled. Then she looked at little Bernard munching away at a biscuit on his mam's knee and decided that if she could bear a child like Evelyn's son she would indeed be thrilled and she guessed John would too.

'Oh I am. It's just a bit quick, that's all.'

'Like me, the first time I suppose. Only in my case it was the only time.'

'I don't know. To tell you the truth we've been at it like rabbits.' Lucy wouldn't have spoken of that to anyone else but Evelyn. They giggled and Bernard laughed with them as though he understood what they were talking about, which made them laugh all the more.

'You enjoy it, Lucy. At least you've a man who loves you and will be there for you.' Lucy detected sadness in Evelyn's voice. She looked at the little boy.

'What happened to his dad?' The subject had never been discussed before to Lucy's knowledge.

'Took off, didn't he? As soon as he found out I was up the club. Never heard a word from him since. Not that I care. He promised me the earth. A child's better off without a father like him.'

'Well, Bernard's certainly happy enough without him.'

'I try my best, but it's hard making ends meet. It'll be easier when he goes to school. I might find a job to fit in with the school hours then.'

Lucy hadn't the heart to tell Evelyn they would be doing their own washing from now on. She would keep Evelyn on for a while in case Mr Blackmore sent for her again. If she was expecting though, Evelyn would have to be told eventually. 'I'll tell you what.' Lucy had an idea. 'I'll look after Bernard for you tonight and you can go out to the pictures. Or to the dance on Saturday if you prefer.'

'Oh I don't expect you to do that.'

'Oh, go on. It'll be experience for me for when I get my own.'

'I'd love a night out, if you're sure. Though I won't go dancing or the gossips'll have a field day.'

'Let them gossip. There's nothing they enjoy more.'

'Oh well. Come on, Bernard. I've a tub to empty and the ironing to do.'

'And your glad rags to get ready for tonight.'

'Only if you're sure.'

'I am. John won't be home until eleven. He calls at the Rising Sun when he's on afters, only for one pint, mind.'

'I know. He's a good man, Lucy. Look after him.'

'I will.'

Robbie had just finished patching up the roof of the hayloft when Dot climbed the ladder with a jug of homemade lemonade. ''Ave yer finished?' she enquired as she offered him first drink from the jug.

'Just.' He threw the hammer and nails back into his tool bag. Dot flopped down in the hay and Robbie came to sit beside her. Her shapely legs glistened brown in the dim light and Dot drew them up beneath her summer dress, embarrassed at Robbie's eyes on them. The strong scent of hay made him sneeze. 'I hope I haven't got hay fever,' he laughed. 'It would never do for a farmer's son-in-law to suffer from hay fever.' Dot knew he wasn't serious but she blushed all the same. 'Just joking,' he said.

'You'd better be; we're far too young to be thinking things like that.'

'Yes I know.' Robbie took a gulp of lemonade. 'But maybe one day, in a few years' time.'

'Oh yes, maybe then.'

'I really like you, Dot.' He had been trying for ages to tell Dot Greenwood how he felt about her, but had never found the courage before. 'I know we're too young now, but will you consider yourself my girl?' Robbie sighed. 'Oh, I'm no good at this. I just want you to know that I shall never ever want another girl, so if you'll consider yourself my girl I shall 'ave something to look forward to in the future. I know I'm rambling on but...' Dot interrupted him by putting her finger to his lips.

'I already consider myself your girl, and I can't see meself ever wanting anyone else either. We can plan for the future together, all right?'

Robbie relaxed. 'All right.' He grinned, then became serious again, drew Dot into his arms and kissed her, a long, sensuous kiss that stirred feelings in both of them, feelings Dot had never experienced before. It was fortunate that Boadacea's voice interrupted the proceedings. 'Dot? Robbie? Are yer up there?'

'Yes, Mam. Just coming.'

'Not far off,' Robbie muttered to himself.

'What?' Dot straightened her dress and set off down the ladder.

'Nothing, just muttering to meself.' Dot

wouldn't have understood if he tried to explain. She might know about animals, but when it came to humans Dot Greenwood was an innocent girl, and would remain one until her wedding day if Robbie could manage to control his feelings; he made a vow that he would try. He loved Dot Greenwood and would prove it. Besides, the Grey brothers had been brought up to show respect for the opposite sex – he wouldn't be the one to let his late parents down.

'Tea's ready,' Boadacea called, in a voice fit to be heard all over Millington. The old dog started barking as the couple came into view. Boadacea glanced from one to the other. She hoped they hadn't been up to owt. She'd keep an eye on those two. She'd seen a spark between them the first time they set eyes on one another, just like her and Little Arthur and she remembered all too well what they had got up to in that very same hayloft. She smiled to herself. He might not be very big in stature but Little Arthur was well enough endowed where it mattered.

Chapter Thirteen

'Potatoes locally grown and only picked yesterday.' Will's voice rang out across Millington market. 'Lovely Bramleys. Come on ladies, make a pie for yer owd man's tea.' Lucy watched her brother proudly as he weighed out the goods and emptied the scoop into a woman's shopping basket. 'Who's next then? Is it you, Mrs Sykes? How's your Maisy? All right?' Will picked out the largest turnip. 'How's this for a whopper? Only picked yesterday up at Barker's Farm. Can't get much fresher than that now, can yer?'

'Eeh, yer'll tell us owt, Will Gabbitas.' The woman laughed and held her bag open for Will to drop the monster inside.

'Now yer know I wouldn't tell you owt that was untrue, Mrs Sykes. I mean, look at these oranges: picked 'em at three o'clock this morning, up't Donkey Wood.'

The women in the queue laughed and Mrs Sykes gave Will a playful slap and giggled, 'Eeh, you are a one.'

Will weighed out more potatoes for the next customer whilst Mrs Sykes fumbled in a worn leather purse to pay the boy. Two young women with a baby in a pram nudged each other and one of them called out, 'Come on Will, give us a kiss for me birthday.'

'All right, Jessie, but you'll 'ave to wait yer turn like everybody else. How old are yer then? Sixteen?'

The woman giggled more than ever. 'Sixteen? I'm twenty-four, I'll 'ave you know.'

'Twenty-four? Never, you're 'aving me on.' Into the bags went carrots, onions, rhubarb, lemons, fresh green beans from Mrs Barker's vegetable plot, long and straight enough to win prizes at the annual show.

'Your Will's a natural,' Evelyn grinned as she and Lucy joined the queue at the fish stall for herrings. The two women always shopped together these days, each enjoying the other's company. John was also becoming fond of little Bernard, often keeping him occupied whilst his mother shopped with Lucy.

'I know, and have you seen how he charms the ladies? He's got them eating out of his hand.' Lucy couldn't believe the change in her brother now he had been freed from the threat of the mine. Will loved his job, especially the market at Cragstone. Cragstone was an old market town, the centre point being the parish church. In front of the church was the town square with the bank on one side and the Golden Eagle opposite, the Crown Inn in competition on the east side and a number of shops and a bus stop on the other. On Thursdays the square was brimming with shoppers, housewives on their way to the market and farmers to the cattle market, some to sell and some to buy. Some were just using market day as an excuse for a few hours in the company of other farmers, to be followed by a good booze up at one of the inns. Mr Brown had secured a stall in the best position, where everyone, housewives and farmers alike, had to pass by the stall as they entered or left the market. Even after just a few weeks Will had become well-known for his joviality. Other stallholders would come for a chat with the likable young lad. They would bring him a pot of tea and share a joke, some of which Will considered too coarse to repeat; others he would memorise and relate to customers the day after in Millington. Even in pouring rain Will would don himself up in an oilskin and sou'ester and could be heard belting out 'On Ilkley Moor

Bah't 'at.' The truth was William Gabbitas considered himself the most fortunate person in Yorkshire, if not the whole world.

When Jane came home from the dance one Saturday Lucy and John were already in bed. Jane knew how important it was to give the couple privacy, but she couldn't wait to tell her sister the news. She listened outside the bedroom door but all was silent. She tapped gently on the door and waited.

Lucy wondered if something was wrong. 'Hello.'

'Lucy, it's only me. Can I tell you something?'

Lucy hopped out of bed and opened the door. 'Is something wrong?'

'No, oh no. I haven't interrupted anything, have I?' Jane blushed.

'No, no.' The sisters came downstairs and Jane poured tea into two cups. 'I'm getting married, Lucy. We've got a house.'

'Oh Jane, where? That's wonderful.'

'The school house. Well, there's a caretaking job to go with it but I don't mind that. When I leave the mill I can do that instead, and James will help me with anything heavy. Oh Lucy, it's a lovely little house and I shall be able to carry on with the work even if we start a family.'

'Jane, that's ideal. Besides, you like cleaning; you always preferred it to cooking.'

Jane wrinkled her nose. 'Oh the cooking, I shan't like that.'

Lucy hugged her sister and grinned, 'It comes with marriage I'm afraid. So when will the wedding be?'

'As soon as it can be arranged. Oh, isn't it good of Reverend Goodman to let us have the house and the job? Oh Lucy, I love that school. I shall keep it spotless.' She frowned. 'Whoever did the cleaning before never cleaned the cloakroom properly. The sinks were always slimy and brown. Oh, I can't wait.'

'Hold on, we've a wedding to arrange first.'

'You won't mind if we don't have a fancy wedding, will you? We just want the family, nothing posh.'

Lucy couldn't believe how Jane had changed; she'd always been the one to go on about wedding dresses and bridesmaids. 'But you always wanted a large wedding.'

'Not now. I just want James. He's all that matters to me. We'd much rather spend the money on the house.'

'Right, but you are having a white dress; you're the prettiest of the four of us and I can't wait to see you in your finery.'

'All right. I'll have our Nellie and Dot for bridesmaids. After all, it looks as though Robbie and Dot are serious and she may well end up as our sister-in-law one day. But that's all, just a family tea. We'll ask our Nellie for some advice on the catering. James says we can have it in the school room.'

'You shall have a lovely tea and our Mary'll make your dress.'

'Our Nellie may well be married herself by then; she's spending a lot of time with Tom Johnson. I bet she won't have to worry about paying for her wedding.' Jane smiled. 'I wouldn't swap James for him though.'

'Jane, if you're short of cash there's the money in the bank.'

'No, that's our Will's. You have your share if you like but I don't want any of it. We shall manage. After all, unlike in the mill, I shall have a job for life as a caretaker. How many women can say that?'

'And I shall soon have a job for life too,' Lucy smiled. 'I'm having a baby. You're not to tell anybody else yet though.'

Jane threw her arms round her sister, her eyes filling with tears. 'Oh Lucy, can you remember when we were little girls and we used to wish for something nice to happen and it never did? Well now all the nice things are happening at once.'

Lucy turned to the mirror over the fire and saw their reflections: two sisters who had been through the dark times and were now coming out into the light. 'It's the mirror, Jane. It's a wishing mirror, you see.'

The next day being Sunday, Nellie brought Tom on a visit to see her sisters. When the car turned the corner onto Top Row children seemed to come from all directions to admire the vehicle. Tom sat in the driving seat, fascinated. 'Where've they all come from?' he enquired of Nellie. 'I feel like the pied piper.'

'They all live here,' Nellie laughed. 'On the four rows.'

'All of them?'

'Oh I should imagine there'd have been a few

more had it not been Sunday. Some of them'll be out for a walk with parents or at Sunday school.' By this time some of the men had come out to examine the car and Mrs Slater had come out to scrutinise Nellie's young man. Mrs Slater wasn't interested in the car, or the fact that the young man was obviously well off. It was his character she was bothered about. Nellie ran towards her mother's friend. 'Mrs Slater, I'd like you to meet my friend Tom Johnson.'

'Ow do yer do.' Mrs Slater shook him by the hand.

'How do you do, Mrs Slater. I know you've been a good friend to Nellie's family. It's lovely to meet you.'

Mrs Slater liked a man with a firm handshake and she wasn't disappointed. 'I were only repaying Nellie's mam for the help she gave me when times were hard.'

'Well it's good to help each other.'

'Gi' us a ride mester.' A little boy with his jumper on back to front tugged at Tom's trousers.

'Not now love, go and play,' Nellie told him kindly. 'They'll be queuing up all afternoon if you encourage them,' she laughed.

Tom felt in his pocket and brought out a sixpence. He bent down and whispered in the boy's ear, 'Will you keep my car safe for sixpence?'

'Sixpence?' the lad's eyes widened. 'I sure will, mester.' He sat himself down with his back resting on the bonnet. 'Nobody'll touch it or I'll bash 'em.' Tom followed Nellie, laughing, into the house.

‘Oh, Nellie, thank goodness you’ve come.’ Jane couldn’t wait to tell her sister the news. ‘Will you be my bridesmaid?’

‘Well I will if you insist, only I’d really like to buy something I can wear later. It’s just that I’m saving up for a wedding dress myself.’

‘Oh Nellie, that’s wonderful! I told you, Lucy: good things are happening to all of us. So shall I ask Kitty? To be my bridesmaid, I mean.’

‘Only if you don’t mind,’ Nellie replied.

‘I don’t mind. I just want to marry James, Nothing else matters. So when is your wedding to be?’

‘As soon as she’ll have me,’ Tom said. ‘And as soon as we find a house.’

‘Oh, Nellie, we shan’t see you once you move to Blackpool.’

Nellie felt a sadness pass over her but Tom said, ‘Of course you will. We can come over any time Nellie likes. Besides, you can come and stay with us. You’ll always be welcome.’

John looked questioningly at Lucy and Lucy nodded. ‘Actually, Lucy and me have some news too. Lucy’s having a baby.’ He placed an arm protectively round his wife.

Nellie kissed her sister, her eyes filling with tears. ‘Oh Lucy, that’s wonderful, but just when I’m thinking of going away! Oh Tom, I’m going to be an auntie.’

‘It’s all right, I’ll spoil it for you,’ Jane said. ‘Oh I wish our Mary was here. We could celebrate then.’

William came in at that moment. ‘Shall I fetch ’er? It’ll be quicker if Tom gives me a lift.’

Tom laughed at Will's hint for a ride. 'Come on then. You're right, it will be quicker but you'll have to show me the way.'

Will was out of the door like a shot, asking Tom questions about the car. 'How many miles does it do to the gallon? How fast can it go on the flat?' Tom answered as best he could and Will told him about Mr Brown's truck. He was disappointed when they reached Mary's and had to change the subject. 'Our Nellie says you've to come cos we're celebrating.'

Jacob asked Tom the same questions he had already answered on Will's behalf but he didn't mind. Just like Jacob, he was heartened to be included in Nellie's family. He almost wished he was moving to Millington and becoming part of the Top Row community. However his livelihood was in Blackpool and, God willing, he might have children one day who would join him in the motor business. He followed his passengers into the house and took his place at the table as Lucy poured the tea. At home they would have toasted any celebration with sherry or port wine, but there was one thing for sure; it wouldn't have tasted anywhere near as good as this cup of tea in the company of the Gabbitas family.

Tom parked as usual in the seclusion of the lane alongside the dam. It was unusually cold for October and the windows were opaque with steam. He drew Nellie into his arms, the need for her almost unbearable. 'I can't keep leaving you like this, Nellie.' He kissed her hungrily then drew away. 'We need to talk about the future, not keep putting things off.'

'I know. It's just that it'll be such a wrench, leaving my family and the manor, and Mrs Cooper,' she added.

'Yes I know, but I want you with me. Don't I count?'

'Of course you do. You're right. As soon as we find a house we'll be married.'

'Really?'

'Really. I love you, Tom and I want to be married and be with you. I suppose it's Mrs Cooper I regret leaving the most. She's been like a mother to me. In fact she's been kinder to me than my own mother was for years. The trouble is I don't think she'll be kept on at the manor for much longer.'

'Well, I'm sorry for Mrs Cooper, but she really isn't your responsibility, Nellie.'

'I know, but while I'm there I can take some of her burden. But you're absolutely right. Let's go house hunting as soon as I get a day off.'

'Actually I think I've found a house you might like.'

'Oh Tom, where?'

'Well, you wanted to be in the thick of things and you can't get much more central than in a small square just behind the station.'

'Oh, I can't wait to see it. Though I don't know what your parents will think. After all, we haven't known each other for very long.'

'Who cares?'

'I do. I don't want to start off on the wrong foot.'

'We won't. My parents love you, they told me so.'

'Tell me about the house.' Nellie blushed with pleasure at Tom's words.

'Another time. I've other things on my mind right now.'

'Hmm.' Nellie was back in his arms and conversation forgotten.

In Blackpool, Margaret Johnson took off her scarf and removed her gardening gloves. She had been busy all day, trimming old branches from the shrubs and raspberry canes. 'There.' She flopped down on a kitchen chair. 'I think that will be the last of the gardening for this year.'

'I'll make a bonfire tomorrow with the rubbish.' Henry made two cups of cocoa and they sat companionably as darkness slowly gathered. He switched on the light and drew the pretty pink chintz curtains, adding a cosiness to the well-equipped room.

'Do you think there'll have been any developments in Yorkshire this weekend?' Margaret asked.

'Developments? Of what nature?'

'Oh, don't tell me you're not waiting for news too.'

'I don't know what you're talking about.' Henry's eyes sparkled. 'Unless you're thinking wedding bells at last.'

'What do you mean, at last? She's the first girl he's brought home who's been suitable. I just hope he doesn't leave her alone all those miles away for too long, or someone else might find her.'

Henry laughed. 'Perhaps he daren't become too serious about the girl in case you frighten her away like you did the last one.'

'Oh, Henry, you surely didn't want our son to marry that silly scatterbrain of a girl.'

'No, I didn't, and I don't think Tom had any intention of marrying her anyway. But you shouldn't have interfered all the same.'

Margaret blushed. 'I know, but I did it for the best. I'm sure Tom must realise that now.'

'Well we'll see, but you can't blame him if he doesn't include us in his plans this time.'

'Oh, Henry, I do hope he marries Nellie. She's exactly right for Tom.'

'What, a miner's daughter who cooks for a living?'

'Yes, she's all I ever wanted. She may be a working girl but she's had a good upbringing, I can tell. Tom could take that girl anywhere and she'd do him proud.'

'Well, just don't interfere this time. Let him tell us in his own good time. That's if there's anything to tell. After all, it's early days, and we've only met the girl a couple of times.'

'Ah, but look how much time he's spending travelling to Millington and back. What time do you think he'll be home?'

'Not until we're both fast asleep in our beds.'

'Oh, surely we can wait up and see if there are any further developments.'

'There you go again, interfering. Curiosity killed the cat. He'll let us know in his own time if he decides to marry the girl. Now I'm going to my bed with that very good book I'm reading. Coming?'

'I suppose so.' Margaret went to the window

and lifted the curtain but there was no sign of the car. She sighed and followed her husband up the stairs. Henry was right as usual; she was an interfering busybody. She would curb it this time though – she had no desire to frighten Nellie away. She smiled to herself, proud of the fact that she had played a part in keeping her son free for the likes of Nellie Gabbitas.

Prudence Goodman was all sugary sweetness and light. 'Your shoes are covered in sawdust, Robert. Take them off and I'll clean them for you.' Before he could refuse she had knelt down and was undoing the laces of his shoes. He could see down the bodice of her dress, of which she had left the buttons undone again. Robbie didn't know why she bothered – there was hardly anything to see and what there was didn't interest him. He wondered what it was about the girl that made his skin crawl. Fortunately he needn't spend much time in her company, what with his work, and time spent at the farm. Robbie's savings were gradually accumulating in the bank. He wished he was older so that he could marry Dot Greenwood, but of course they were too young and must wait until they could afford a home of their own.

The news that his brother James was to leave the vicarage as well as John had filled Robbie with dread. Although he was treated as a son by Louisa and Herbert, Prudence's thoughts towards him were definitely not those of a sister and he felt uneasy at the thought of being without the protection of James. It was only when Prudence caught him alone that her feelings came to the fore. In the company of her parents she would humiliate him by treating him as an inferior being. A common, working-class woodworker was how she once described him. Of course Herbert had retaliated by saying that Jesus Christ was the son of a carpenter, but she had just stuck her nose in the air and looked at Robbie in that disdainful way she had. Robbie did his best to ignore her but it led to an uncomfortable atmosphere from which he couldn't wait to escape. Secretly, Robbie thought Prudence was slightly unstable and seemed to be getting worse.

When she brought back Robbie's shoes Prudence said, 'I've done a sketch of you, Robert. Would you like to see it?'

'All right.' He couldn't very well refuse without being ill-mannered.

'It's in my room.' She set off for the stairs. 'Come on.' Robbie stood on the landing and waited.

'Come in, I won't bite.'

'No, I don't think it's right for me to come in. You bring it out.' Prudence's attitude changed dramatically. 'You wouldn't refuse an invitation into the whore's room, would you?'

'Don't call her that.'

'I shall call her whatever I like. This is my house; you're only the lodger.' With that she slammed the door of her room, the sketch forgotten. Robbie wondered if she had ever done one. If she had it was never mentioned again.

Lucy was minding Evelyn's child more and more

these days. Little Bernard Smithson was like a ray of sunshine with his ready smile. He had brought his wooden farm animals to play with and kept Lucy entertained by mooing like a cow, baaing like a sheep and quacking and snorting in the manner of ducks and pigs. When his eyes became heavy and he struggled to stay awake, Lucy undressed him and put on his pyjamas, then she rocked him in her mother's old chair, his cheeks becoming rosy with the heat from the fire. Lucy's breasts were becoming heavy now and she wondered what it would be like feeding her baby.

She sang softly, 'Twinkle twinkle, little star,' bringing back a fleeting memory of her mother's voice. She wished her child could have a grandma and a grandad, but even the wishing mirror couldn't grant a wish like that. Instead she made another wish; that her baby would be as healthy as little Bernard. She cuddled him closer. If her baby was as lovable as this little boy she wished for lots of babies. Lucy smiled to herself. She had better be careful; the wishing mirror might give her more than she could cope with. She closed her eyes. She would cope – with a lovely man like John by her side she would cope with as many children as God gave her and enjoy them all.

Mary and Jacob were the only ones who couldn't feel any enthusiasm for the forthcoming events. Whereas Jane's house should have had Mary discussing wallpapers and paint colours, all she could think about was Lucy's pregnancy. She tried not to be envious and bought a few ounces of white wool to begin knitting a matinee coat for the baby, but Jacob saw the tears begin to flow every time she began to knit and confiscated the pattern and knitting rather than watch his wife become depressed. 'It'll happen, Mary, if we stop worrying. Besides we haven't been trying as long as Jim at work and now they've got twins.'

'Oh, Jacob, I know it's silly to worry but I can't help it. I so want to give you a child, and there's our Lucy only been married a couple of months and already expecting. Perhaps there's something wrong with me.'

'Aye, and perhaps it's me there's something wrong with, and perhaps there's nothing wrong with either of us except that we're too impatient. So let's forget about babies and discuss what you're going to wear for these two weddings.'

'All right. I expect it'll have to be something posh for our Nellie's. Oh Jacob! What if she gets married in Blackpool where she'll have none of us to support her?'

'What are yer talking about? It'll be a damn good excuse for a bit of sea air and a couple o' days away.'

'Really?'

'Mary, do yer think I'd let yer miss yer sister's wedding?'

Mary cheered up at the thought of a few days' holiday, babies forgotten for the time being, but Jacob knew the problem would only be postponed until another day. He prayed that Mary would become pregnant before that day arrived.

Ben and Emma Gabbitas were enjoying life to the full. Working alongside her mother in the shop suited Emma. The customers had mainly become friends over the years and because Mrs Scott had allowed them to put things in the book each week until payday, they had resisted taking their custom to the Co-op or other larger stores. Emma was quite capable of running the shop without her mother's assistance, but the busy atmosphere and the gossip meant the elder woman found it difficult to keep away. 'What on earth should I do if I retired?' she asked Emma for the umpteenth time.

'Take it easy, go into town for the day, take a holiday.'

'Oh I expect I will one of these days.' But they both knew she was at her happiest pottering about weighing sugar into blue bags and pats of butter from the huge round block. The shop sold everything from vegetables, which were stacked outside each morning and brought in at night, to donkey stones, candles, wrap-round pinafores and socks. Various tobaccos and jar upon jar of sticky toffee, liquorice sticks and sugar mice filled the shelves behind the counter away from little fingers. Sweeping brushes, shovels and floor mops stood to attention beside the door and in a glass case, gorgonzola cheese, potted meat and a side of bacon tempted the palates of customers. The smell of green soap, moth balls and lavender bags filled the air, vying with the aroma of crusty bread, sticky buns and savoury pies.

Emma loved the shop almost as much as her mother did and now she had Ben she considered herself the most fortunate woman alive. She wished Ben would leave the pit and join her in the business – it was a thriving concern and she knew it would be even more successful if Ben began visiting the wholesaler's instead of the salesman visiting them. With a van they could begin deliveries too, but Ben declared he was happiest at the pit doing a real man's job. Emma didn't argue; she adored the man in her life and had no desire to change him. Her mother was relieved in a way. She would have felt like an interloper if Ben had taken over the shop. Much as she was fond of her son-in-law it was nice to have her daughter to herself during shop hours. Besides she would be embarrassed if Ben saw her in one of her fits. If Ben did decide to join Emma however, she would retire; the shop was Emma's now and she had no wish to interfere between husband and wife. For the time being, the three of them were content.

Robbie Grey was extremely proud of himself. Mr Grundy had allowed him to make and fit a new front door for Mr Rawlings. Robbie had measured, made and fitted the door all on his own and when his boss went to check on the work he declared the door a perfect fit and a job well done.

'I can see me sen being done out of a job soon,' he told a very satisfied customer. 'He'll be a better joiner than me before long.'

'Well it's you who's trained me.' Robbie blushed at the compliment, which was soon followed by another.

'Aye, tha's found thi sen a good lad theer. If ever tha wants to get rid of 'im ee can come and work for me.' Robbie had no desire to take a job humping bags of coal, but he grinned and shook his head. 'I like being a joiner,' he said to Mr Grundy's relief. The only worry Robbie had at the moment was that his brother's wedding was looking closer, and he didn't like the thought of James leaving the Goodmans' one little bit.

The wedding took place on a lovely Saturday early in March. It was a quiet ceremony with only Jane's family and the Goodmans present. Jane looked adorable in a short white dress made by Mary. She had had her hair cut short and waved, which made her large brown eyes look even larger. James Grey couldn't take his eyes off his bride throughout the ceremony and Robbie was just as entranced by Dot in her dress of powder-blue. Lucy felt like an elephant with her huge pregnant figure, but John said she had never looked lovelier with her clear, unblemished skin and glossy hair. Actually she felt wonderful but wondered what she would be like in a month's time. The flowered smock Mary had made a few weeks ago was already stretched across her belly and the skirt beneath it held together with a huge safety pin. She hoped by the time Nellie's wedding took place in May her baby would be born and her figure back to normal. Kitty had a new boyfriend who had been invited, which was only right, Jane said, with Kitty being a bridesmaid. Only Prudence Goodman put a damper on the party with her constant glances at Robbie and glares at Dot. Jane and James never noticed: they had eyes for no one but each other and couldn't wait to begin life together in the school house.

Evelyn Smithson had a regular night out once a week now, thanks to Lucy. Evelyn and a friend from school days usually went to the pictures, but on this occasion were going to a dance at Cragstone. Lucy was allowing Bernard to be put to bed in the cot Robbie had made for the forthcoming baby and spend the night with Lucy and John. Evelyn was to see a man friend she had met last week and was nervous about the first date she had had since Bernard was born. 'How do I know I can trust him, Lucy? Frank seems nice but so did Bernard's dad. I thought he really loved me, Lucy. He was all sweet talk and then he would change without any reason. He really scared me sometimes. I don't ever want him near Bernard again. How could I trust another man after an experience like that?'

'Evelyn, you can't go through life mistrusting everyone. Just don't take things too seriously until you get to know him better.' Lucy hoped things would work out for Evelyn; she deserved some happiness and little Bernard would benefit from a man in his life. Lucy felt a little bit envious of Evelyn – she looked so pretty when she set off for Cragstone.

The two girls had a lovely time. Frank was attentive to both of them but it was Evelyn he really liked. After the strains of the last waltz faded he set off to Millington, escorting Evelyn's friend safely home before carrying on with Evelyn to Top Row. 'Can I see you tomorrow, Evelyn?'

'Oh I don't know, I can't leave Bernard again. In fact I won't be leaving him anymore because Lucy's ready for having her baby almost.'

'I didn't mean you to leave your little boy. I meant perhaps to go for a walk if it's fine. I thought he might like that.'

'Well, yes I'd love to,' Evelyn smiled. 'If you're sure? It isn't everyone who wants lumbering with a child.'

'It wouldn't be lumbering me; it would give me pleasure. I think you're so brave, Evelyn, bringing your son up on your own. You're not only brave, you're lovely.' Frank took Evelyn in his arms and kissed her, a kiss that left them both longing for more. Evelyn drew away, vowing not to rush into anything she might regret. 'Goodnight,' she whispered.

'Goodnight, until tomorrow. I'll meet you by the clock at two.' Evelyn nodded and actually skipped along the row, feeling happier than she could ever remember. Maybe Lucy's mirror had worked for her.

The row was in darkness apart from the Murphys' kitchen. Mrs Murphy never seemed to go to bed. Evelyn wondered if the poor woman was afraid of becoming pregnant again and was avoiding her husband. She let herself in and decided not to bother lighting the gas and go straight up to bed. Then the knock came at the door. She wondered if it was Frank, who had changed his mind about tomorrow. It was most likely Lucy to say Bernard wouldn't settle.

She unlocked the door and the figure came out of the dark night into the darkness of the kitchen. Evelyn was too surprised to cry out. Then the voice said 'Light the bloody gas.'

Her heart froze. Now of all times he had turned

up. The times she had prayed he would come back and give her and their son the support and love Evelyn had craved... Now, when she had got over him, realised what a rotter he really was, he had turned up. 'What do you want?' She fumbled with shaking hands to put a match to the gas, sending it through the flimsy mantel.

'My kid.'

Evelyn began to tremble. 'What kid?' she forced herself to laugh.

'The kid you were 'aving.'

'There wasn't a child. I lost it.'

'Lost it?'

'Miscarried at four months. I thought you would have heard.'

'How could I 'ave 'eard? I wasn't 'ere.'

'No, so it was a good thing I lost it then, wasn't it?'

'I wanted that kid. She can't have one.'

'Who?'

'The missis.' So he was married then? Evelyn had asked him once but he had denied it. 'She's 'ad her bloody womb took away, growth of some description.' He walked over to the line over the fire and plucked off one of Bernard's little vests. 'So what's this then?'

'It belongs to one of my customers. I wash for folk on the row.' Evelyn began to cry, and pray he wouldn't go into the front room and see the second-hand pram which was waiting to be handed down yet again to Lucy's new baby. 'I lost my job when they found out I was pregnant. I also lost my reputation so that no one else would set me on, and all for nothing. I wanted that baby so much.' She would lie as much as she had to rather than hand over her son. 'Even though it had a bastard for a father.'

Evelyn saw his fist coming towards her face, then felt the blow that knocked her backwards, but then she knew no more. She didn't feel herself falling; she didn't feel the metal fender as her head hit the sharp corner of it. She didn't feel her life's blood seeping away onto the hearth. Evelyn Smithson was dead. Just when she had found somebody to cherish her in the way she deserved.

Mrs Murphy had been full of condemnation when she heard the male voice coming through the wall. Would Evelyn never learn? The lass had been caught once and would be again if she weren't careful. Not that she wasn't a good mother to little Bernard, but nobody knew better than Mrs Murphy how hard it was to make ends meet with a house full of kids, or how easy it was to get them. That was why she often slept in the chair by the fire instead of enduring the fumblings of her husband, who always wanted it but couldn't always manage it. Then when he finally tired of trying and fell asleep the snoring would start. No, it was easier to sleep in the chair. She relaxed a little when she recognised the voice as that of Bernard's father. Perhaps they would get together again. Not that she'd be happy about that; she had never liked him. Or he had come to offer some financial support? She became concerned when the voices rose and she heard him demanding the child. Mrs Murphy was relieved the bairn was out of the way and thought

Evelyn was right in denying his existence. The man had forsaken her when he was needed – who would give up a child to someone like him?

The sound of a crash set the alarm bells ringing in Mrs Murphy's head, but she relaxed again as she heard him hurrying away along the row, and began to doze in the warmth of the fire. Then she was jolted awake. Something wasn't right. It was too quiet next door and she hadn't heard Evelyn go upstairs. Maybe she was having a bit of supper before going to bed. If there was no sound soon she would go round and investigate. She closed her eyes and listened and waited. But then Mrs Murphy drifted off to sleep. By this time it would have been too late to help Evelyn anyway.

Bernard was dressed and had been fed a breakfast of Post Toasties by John, who was fascinated by the little boy's infectious grin and the way he chatted all the time. 'I've eaten it all up like Goldilocks,' Bernard laughed.

'So you have. It'll make you a big boy.'

'I'm a big boy already now I'm free.'

Lucy thought it strange that Evelyn hadn't fetched him home by this time. Maybe his mother wasn't well. She always suffered severe cramps during her monthlies.

'Watch Bernard,' Lucy said. 'I'll go and see if Evelyn's up yet.'

Lucy's scream could be heard from one end of the row to the other. John grabbed the little boy and ran in the direction of Evelyn's. Lucy was standing in the doorway, her face almost as white as that of the corpse. 'Don't bring Bernard in,' she cried. 'Don't let him see his mam.' Lucy was trembling, almost on the verge of collapsing. John handed Bernard into the care of Mrs Slater and Lucy into the care of Mrs Marshall, then he went into the house. Evelyn's arm was almost on the fire and though only cokes were still smouldering her hand was burned and blistered. 'Fetch the police and a doctor,' John called.

Mr Slater came into the kitchen. 'My God,' he whispered. 'I've sent for't doctor. What does tha think's 'appened, John?'

'I've no idea. She might have fallen backwards but I doubt it. Somebody's struck her in the face and knocked her down, more like. Look at her eye and nose.'

'Who the hell'd do summat like that to a lass?' Mrs Murphy had arrived by this time, weeping and blaming herself for not investigating in time to save the lass.

'It were 'im she used to go with, the bairn's father. I recognised 'is voice. He wanted the babby. It were my fault, I didn't want to interfere but I might 'ave saved 'er life if I 'ad.'

'It weren't your fault, love. It were 'is, the murdering swine.' Mr Slater sat the woman down on a kitchen chair. 'The bobby'll be 'ere soon. I daresay ee'll want to ask yer a few questions.'

Just then a young woman walked in. 'Good morning, I'm Doctor Sellars. I'm new to the practice.' John wished it had been a male doctor – this was no job for a woman – but the lady was already down on her knees beside the body. 'I'd say she's been dead about ten hours. Does anyone know how it happened?'

'Aye, it were about ten hours since, and she was murdered.' Mrs Murphy suddenly became hysterical. 'It wor my fault,' she screamed.

Doctor Sellars opened her bag and took out two pills and then she went to the sink and filled a cup with water. 'Take these,' she said. 'They'll help calm you.'

Mr Murphy came to his wife's side. 'Come on lass, let's get you 'ome.' He had obviously come straight from his bed, with a greyish-coloured singlet half-hanging from his trousers.

'Did the lady witness what occurred?'

'No, she reckons she heard it though. Doctor?' John said. 'Would you go take a look at my wife? It was her who found Evelyn and she's bound to be in shock. Only she's in the last month of pregnancy and I'm concerned about her and the baby.'

'Well I'll see her now. There's nothing can be done for this poor girl. The police will have to be notified of course.'

'Someone's gone for them. They should have been here by now.'

John left Mr Slater in charge and took the doctor to see Lucy. She was cuddling little Bernard – who was trying to free himself from her grip – and rocking frantically in the chair by the fire. John held his arms out for the child but Lucy only held him closer.

'Come along, my dear,' the doctor coaxed. 'Let me take a look at you and see if your baby's all right. You need taking care of too.'

'No, I'm the one who's to take care of him. Evelyn was my friend; it's the least I can do. We'll look after him, won't we, John?'

'Yes, if that's what you want. But let the doctor take a look at you now and make sure our baby's all right.'

'They're both our babies now,' Lucy stated, but she handed Bernard over to John and let the doctor check her over and put her to bed to recover from the shock. 'Your baby's fine,' Dr Sellars told Lucy. 'I can't wait for the delivery, which will be my first in Millington.' My first death too, the doctor thought as she came downstairs – a death she would never forget till her own dying day.

Frank paced the pavement by the clock and wondered what had happened to prevent Evelyn keeping to their arrangement. Maybe her son was ill or had fallen asleep. Maybe visitors had turned up unexpectedly. After ten minutes he perched on the wall and made up further excuses for Evelyn not being here. He considered going to find her, but couldn't bring himself to do so in case she had simply decided she didn't wish to see him again. It would be too embarrassing for both of them if that was the situation. He set off down the hill dejectedly and made his way home. He had thought Evelyn liked him and he liked her, a lot. In fact he was on the verge of falling in love for the first time in his life, with the lovely, desirable Evelyn. Little did he know that the girl who had captured his heart was lying cold and still in the Sheffield City Mortuary.

Lucy hardly stopped crying for a week. Other women on the row took charge of the funeral arrangements, knowing Lucy was in no fit state for anything other than taking care of Evelyn's son. She was afraid to let him out of her sight in case his father came finding him. Lucy knew this was unlikely and Mrs Murphy was adamant that he knew nothing of the child's existence, but Lucy scanned the newspaper each day in case there was any mention of Evelyn's child. John insisted that he wouldn't dare come back to the area after he had committed so vile a crime, but Lucy was hard to convince. It was surprising how much useful information the people on the row managed to give the police, who seemed to have set up home permanently at Evelyn's. Mrs Murphy remembered Evelyn once mentioning that the man came from a place somewhere near Rotherham, though nobody knew the man's name. Someone who had been walking his dog down Side Row on the night of the murder recalled seeing a man run down the hill and roar off on a motorbike. Mrs Slater even found a photograph she had taken a couple of years ago of the kids playing French cricket in the yard. There in the background was the wanted man walking across to the lavatory. The photograph was shown in the newspapers throughout the region; fortunately none of them mentioned Bernard. Jane was uneasy about Lucy keeping the child. 'You're young, Lucy. You'll have a family of your own to take care of, without taking on someone else's. Besides, is it fair to John? After all, you've already given our Will a home.'

But John agreed with Lucy. 'He's ours now, Jane. Evelyn had no one else to care for him. And we didn't give Will a home – it was his home already, more than it was mine. We shall do things properly. We shall adopt Bernard. It would be too heartbreaking if he was taken away later.'

'Well, James and I will support you as much as we can.'

'Thanks, Jane. Lucy will need some support over the next few weeks.'

'Don't worry, she'll get it,' Jane laughed. 'You won't be able to keep the neighbours away when there's a new baby in the house.'

It was Mary however who was there for her sister. She took over the caring of Bernard so that Lucy was free to rest during the week before the baby was born. Lucy hoped Mary didn't become too attached to the little boy and was relieved when her labour began. John had gone on afternoon shift when Lucy's waters broke. The pains came fast and furious and just as Mrs Slater was about to send Mary off for the midwife Lucy gave birth to a daughter. Both mother and child were settled comfortably by the time John came home from work. Bernard was fast asleep and a hot meal was being kept warm in the oven.

'Where's Lucy?' John was alarmed to find Mary there at that time of night.

'In bed.' Mary had decided to surprise John.

'Is she not well?' John was already on his way upstairs.

'She's fine – tired, that's all.'

John crept into the bedroom so as not to wake Bernard, or his wife if she happened to be asleep.

Lucy was sitting up in bed looking flushed and beautiful. She was cradling their daughter in her arms.

'Lucy.' John's eyes filled with tears at the picture they made. He took the baby from his wife. 'Oh, Lucy, are you all right?' He took a tiny hand in his. 'Is it a boy?'

'A girl. Are you disappointed?'

'Delighted, and on your birthday!' Lucy's birthday had been forgotten what with one thing and another, but she was pleased that John had remembered.

'Primrose day,' she said. John examined his daughter, smoothing down her soft hair. 'We should call her Primrose,' he decided. 'Her hair's the colour of primroses.'

'Primrose Grey. It suits her.' Lucy smiled, seemingly for the first time in weeks. 'But it seems a bit prim and proper, a bit like Prudence.'

'Oh no, we can't have her growing up like her.' John pulled a face. 'I like it though, Primrose Grey.'

'Then we shall baptise her Primrose, and call her Rosie.'

John sat on the bed beside his wife, the baby content in her father's arms. 'Rosie Grey, may you grow up to be as beautiful and sweet-natured as your mother.'

'And as kind and lovely as your daddy,' Lucy added. 'We shall take her to the wishing mirror tomorrow.'

'I shall take her to the mirror. You shall stay in bed and get well again; after all, you'll need all your strength with two children to take care of.'

'And a demanding husband.' Lucy's eyes sparkled. 'Our Mary's cooked your supper and she'll be waiting to go home.'

'Aye, she's a good lass.' John prised himself reluctantly from the bed. 'And capable.'

'We were brought up to be.' Lucy gazed at Primrose and wished her parents were here to see their first grandchild – second really, if you counted little Bernard. Yes, Bernard must be counted as her firstborn and treated exactly the same as Rosie. She placed her daughter in the cot beside the bed and hoped Bernard would sleep through the night as he usually did. Before she fell asleep Lucy said her prayers, adding a special one that Mary would be the next Gabbitas girl to become a mother. Lucy had seen the longing in her sister's eyes as Mrs Slater had handed the new baby to Lucy. She wished she could take away the hurt from both Mary and Jacob, but no one could do that, except a child of their very own.

Chapter Fourteen

Nellie stood on the pavement in the quiet Blackpool street and stared wide-eyed at the house Tom was intending to buy.

'This isn't a house for the likes of me. It's more like a guest house.'

'So when we have guests, such as your family to stay, there'll be plenty of room for them.'

'Yes but...'

'No buts; you haven't seen it yet.'

'No, but...'

Tom laughed. 'Shut up. Let's go inside.'

They climbed the steps and he unlocked the front door, then they stepped into a wide, sunlit hall. A thickly carpeted staircase led upwards and a door to the left into a large, beautifully furnished lounge. Another door opened into a huge, well-appointed kitchen,

'This is even better than the one at the manor,' Nellie said. 'Oh, look, Tom.' She pointed through the window to where a rhododendron was just coming into flower. 'There's even a garden.'

'Well yes, a small one.' Tom opened a door to the left. 'This would be our own private sitting room.' The room was furnished with a Chesterfield suite and a glass-fronted display cabinet. 'For when we wanted to escape from our guests and make love in the afternoon.' Tom grinned. 'Come and look upstairs.' It was a tall house with five rooms on the first floor and four on the second, with a bathroom on each.

'Oh, Tom. What would we do with all these rooms?'

'Anything you like, or just close them up and do nothing. Come on, there's more.'

'More?'

'Yes.' She followed him downstairs and he opened a door beneath the stairs and led her down into the basement. It had a high window running from one end of the room to the other so that people walking on the pavement above could be seen and the light came flooding in to reflect on the sunshine-yellow walls.

'Oh, Tom. I thought this would be a dark, dismal cellar. It's beautiful.'

'It was used by the children as a playroom, but

it could be anything we liked. A dining room. A maid's quarters.'

'Maid? We won't have a maid.'

'Well, maybe not at first, but later when we begin a family.'

'Oh! Tom, I don't know. It would all be wasted; we should never use all these rooms. It's more suitable as a guest house.' Tom grinned. 'Exactly.'

'What? You mean we could take in boarders?'

'If you wished. I can't see you being happy doing nothing. It would be entirely up to you, of course.'

Nellie's eyes widened. 'Me? Running a boarding house? I couldn't.'

'All right, if you couldn't we'll look for something smaller.'

'No, wait. Oh, Tom, it's a lovely house but I'd be scared. Besides, it would cost a fortune.'

'Actually, it wouldn't. The family have moved abroad and want a quick sale. Never mind, if you don't want it.'

'I do.' Nellie had fallen in love with the place and was already planning the layout of the dining room in her mind's eye.

Tom lifted her off her feet and spun her round. 'Yippee! I love it, but I had to find out what you thought.'

'I love it too. But I'd be scared of taking in boarders. What if I couldn't cope?'

'You'd have some help of course, and I dare say my mother would find a new lease of life. She can't get enough of entertaining and would be in her glory titivating the rooms and arranging flowers. She doesn't mind cleaning either, not that she'd need to do that. We'd employ a cleaner, maybe two.'

'Oh, I don't know, Tom.' Nellie climbed the stairs to the ground floor and wandered from lounge to kitchen, opening cupboards and drawers, inspecting the walk-in pantry. 'Yes, we'll do it. We shall need a dumb waiter though, down to the dining room.'

Tom grinned. 'What about the furniture? Shall we keep it or renew?'

'Keep it; it's nice, but we shall need the dining room fitting out. Then there'll be the bedrooms to sort out, into doubles, family and single.' Tom's instinct had been right. Nellie would never have been happy with nothing to do.

'And a double for us.'

'Oh yes, definitely a double for us. Let's test the one in the first room; after all we need to know how comfortable it is before we let the room. Oh Tom, it's going to cost you a fortune.'

'Nellie, you're marrying a rich man, my love. Thanks to my grandmother. And I've a feeling that between us we might become even richer. Now, hadn't we better get down to testing the beds?'

The birth of little Rosie had diverted Lucy's thoughts away from Evelyn's death, though Lucy still wasn't happy for Bernard to be out of her sight. When he played in the yard with the other children she was forever looking out to make sure he was safe. He played quite happily with Mrs Cadman's son Donald, who was now a robust and healthy little boy. Mrs Cadman knew what it was like to be anxious after her son's illness and promised she would keep them within her sight. Lucy had regained her slim figure and was excited about dressing up for Nellie's wedding and showing off her new daughter, who seemed to grow more beautiful every day. Lucy had never seen the sea and couldn't believe they were to spend a weekend in Blackpool. The whole family were to travel by charabanc. Mr Smith – Nellie's boss – had arranged the transport and had given his staff a couple of days off as a thank you present to Nellie. Mr Smith, of course, was travelling by train. He was far too posh to ride on a chara. He would be travelling back in a brand new car, bought at a discount from his friend Tom Johnson.

Nellie was at present training a new cook, who would take over at the manor when she left. Mrs Cooper had shed a few tears at the news that Nellie was leaving, but the invitation to the wedding had soon cheered her up. Because Lily and Larry had also received an invitation Mrs Cooper had all on to prevent Lily from going into a frenzy of excitement, which took her mind off Nellie's forthcoming departure.

Nellie's worry was that her new home wouldn't be ready in time to accommodate her family and friends overnight, but Tom had promised to arrange hotel accommodation in the unlikely event that their home was unfinished. Margaret Johnson was ecstatic. Not only was Tom marrying Nellie but the couple had asked her to oversee the alterations to their new home. Nellie had told her what was to be done and to Margaret's delight had asked her advice on a number of things. She was keeping the workmen on their toes and Nellie had given Margaret a free hand to fit out the bedrooms with curtains and bedding. Henry Johnson hadn't seen his wife so animated in years and was able to nip off unnoticed to the garage. Henry had never been as contented as when he was wearing an old pair of overalls and covered in engine oil. Nellie Gabbitas had given both him and his wife a new lease of life, for which Henry would be eternally grateful.

Ben and Emma were just enjoying dinner when Mrs Scott showed two plainclothes detectives through the shop and interrupted them.

'Nothing to be alarmed about,' the tallest assured them. 'We'd just like to know where you were on the night Evelyn Smithson's murder took place.'

Ben was alarmed. 'I was tucked up in bed with my wife by that time.' He told them he was a family friend and that it was his sister who had found Evelyn's body. 'What makes you think I had anything to do with it?' he asked.

'We don't. We're in the process of checking everyone who owns a motorcycle in the Rotherham and Sheffield areas.'

Ben whistled. 'By gum, that'll take some time.'

'Not really; we've eliminated half of you already. We just need to know if you lent out your machine to anyone on that night.'

'No, it's kept locked up in the store room in the yard.'

'Good, that's all we need to know. We won't disturb your lunch any longer.'

'That's all right. I hope you catch the bugger. He should be hung for what he did to Evelyn.'

'He will be, don't you worry.' The men put on their trilbies and made their way back through the shop where Mrs Scott was anxiously serving a customer.

'My word, they look as if they mean business,' the woman said as she looked questioningly at the shopkeeper.

'Oh, just a couple of salesmen.' Mrs Scott loved a gossip, but knew when to keep her mouth closed and when to open it. She was relieved however when Emma explained the visit had just been a routine one and nothing to worry about. At first Mrs Scott had thought the men were the weights and measures inspectors. She would rather have a dozen detectives in the shop any day than one of those.

She waited until Robbie came upstairs and gave him time to undress and get into bed, then Prudence gave a squeal, just loud enough to be heard through the adjoining wall. When there was no response from Robbie she tapped on the wall and called his name.

'Robbie. Help.'

Robbie couldn't very well ignore a cry for help and ran to the door. Tapping on it, he waited.

'Come in. Please help.' Prudence was standing on the bed wearing just a flimsy nightdress, which was almost transparent with the light from over the bed showing through it.

'Oh, Robbie, I'm so scared. There's something in my room, down there in the corner. I think it's a mouse.'

Robbie walked round the bed and looked under the dressing table in the corner of the room, self-conscious in his striped pyjamas. 'I can't see anything.' He stood up. 'Keep quiet a minute and we might hear something.'

Then Prudence began to giggle. 'Oh, Robbie, you look so funny in your 'jamas.' She switched out the light. 'Please, give me a cuddle, just one little cuddle.' Robbie knew then he had been tricked and made for the door. 'Come back here.'

'You're mad, Prudence. Goodnight.'

'Go away.' Prudence raised her voice so that it carried through the silent house. 'Don't ever come to my room again.'

'Don't worry, I won't.' Robbie was just going along the corridor when Herbert Goodman opened his door.

'What's going on?' He looked Robbie up and down, alarmed at his state of undress.

'A mouse in Prudence's room,' Robbie answered and disappeared into his bedroom, closing the door behind him. He must get away from this house. Prudence Goodman was stark raving mad, Robbie was sure of it.

Next morning Prudence never appeared at breakfast and much to Robbie's relief nobody mentioned the night before. As soon as Robbie had left for work however, the conversation turned to the fact that Robbie had been in their daughter's room in his nightwear. 'You'll have to talk to her,' Herbert told Louisa. 'Find out what happened.'

'I'm sure it was entirely as Robbie told you, that

there was a mouse in her room. We shall have to set the traps or we shall end up being overrun like last time.'

'Louisa, this isn't about mice. We can't have Robbie visiting our daughter's room. You must ask her what occurred.'

'If anything, which I don't think for a moment it did. I trust Robert but I'm not sure I trust Prudence.'

Herbert was shocked. 'You're surely not suggesting Prudence welcomed his advances?'

'I'm sure she would, if there had been any. I don't think there were.'

'Well, find out anyway. We must put a stop to whatever happened.'

Louisa sighed. 'Oh very well, I'll talk to her.' She left her breakfast almost untouched and went upstairs. Conversing with Prudence was proving more difficult with each passing day.

'Go away,' Prudence called in answer to the tap on her door. Louisa ignored her and went in. 'So what was Robbie doing in your room?'

'I don't want to talk about it.'

'Well, I do.'

'Go away.'

'Was there really a mouse in here?' Louisa searched the lino for mouse droppings. 'Or was it just a ruse to get Robert in your room?'

Prudence blushed and covered her face with the eiderdown. 'Of course it wasn't. I don't want to talk about it. It was too awful.'

'Why? What happened?' Louisa wondered for the first time if anything had actually happened.

'I can't tell you; I'm too upset. Go away.'

'Prudence, if Robert upset you in any way I need to know.'

'I'm all right. Nothing for you to worry about.'

'Do you want any breakfast?'

'No thank you. I'm tired. I'm going back to sleep.'

'Well, call me if you want anything.' Louisa frowned as she went downstairs. Much as she trusted Robert, she couldn't help worrying. If he had touched Prudence in an offensive way they needed to prevent it happening again. She wondered if Herbert should talk to the boy, or perhaps it would be better to forget the whole thing. The trouble was that Louisa felt guilty because it wasn't Robert Grey she mistrusted; it was her daughter.

Prudence smiled to herself in the privacy of her bed. Her plan was set in motion. If only she could hurry it along, but she must be patient if it was to succeed. And succeed it would – it had to if she was to end up with Robbie Grey.

'What are you doing down there, Herbert?' Louisa called. It was unusual for her husband to venture down into the cellar.

'I'm looking for the poison, just playing safe. We don't want any vermin running wild. It would be a catastrophe if they got in the school. And it's a five-pound fine if we don't take steps to eliminate them.' Prudence heard her father's voice and smiled. Her acting must have convinced her father, even if it hadn't succeeded in enticing Robbie to her bed. It was all the fault of the Greenwood girl. If it wasn't for her, Prudence thought she would have a chance. She would like to use the rat poison on her. A thought suddenly entered her head. She couldn't poison her, but she could make her life unpleasant, take away the smug smile that lit up her face whenever Robbie was near her. Later she watched her father soak pieces of bread in the poison in an old paint can lid and place it under her dressing table, warning her not to touch it. Then she saw him take the Quill poison back down the cellar steps. She could feel the excitement as an idea began to take root in her mind. She decided to take a walk up by Greenwood's farm one afternoon and familiarise herself with the place before putting her plan into action.

A few nights later Prudence waited until the house was silent, then she quietly dressed and sneaked out onto the landing. She remembered that the second and seventh stairs were the ones that creaked and strode carefully over them. The house was in pitch darkness and she fumbled among the hooks on the wall until she found her black coat. Then came the tricky part of her plan – going down in the cellar without stumbling over all the junk that was stored there. She struck a match and found the poison, then she turned and knocked over a wooden clothes horse. Her hair stood on end as she waited for someone to come and investigate but no one did. She tiptoed back up the stone steps, cringing at the creaking door, then let herself out into the moonless night.

Prudence was too excited to feel nervous as she passed the billet mill with its clanging of metal, or at the sound of night creatures in the fields and hedgerows. She walked on the lane to the farm, hoping the dog was indoors – it had barked at her all the way along the lane on her afternoon walk. She had managed to locate the pond and a trough halfway along the lane. The pond was obviously the water hole for all the farm animals and ducks. If she threw the poison in the water the Greenwoods would have no chance of saving their livestock. She carefully removed the heavy chain from the gate stoop and opened the gate. There was no sign of the dog. She went towards the pond, unscrewing the top from the poison as she drew near.

They came round the corner like two great flapping ghosts, pecking at her face, her hair and her ankles. Prudence's heart seemed to stop beating with the shock. Then all she could think of was that she must escape without being seen. She dropped the poison in her attempt to be free of the geese but they clung to her coat and followed her, pecking at her legs all the way out of the yard and along the lane. She heard the dog barking and at last managed to shake off the cackling geese.

She set off running along the lane and over the stile to the path, stumbling in the darkness and falling a couple of yards until she managed to grab hold of a tree branch. Then she sat, tears of rage mingling with blood, before rising to her feet and returning home, wondering how to explain the bruises and scratches on her exposed flesh.

An hour later Prudence, now wearing her night-dress, bumped her way as loudly as possible down the stairs, letting out a scream as she positioned herself in a crumpled heap at the bottom. Herbert was the first on the scene, with Louisa hurrying behind.

'Where am I?' Prudence rose to her feet.

'Prudence, what happened to you?' The concern on her father's face almost made her smile.

'Oh dear, I must have been walking in my sleep and fallen down the stairs.'

'Are you hurt?'

'No, I don't think so. Well, maybe my nose and I must have hurt my hands as I fell. My ankles feel a bit tender, but yes, I'm all right.'

Louisa went to help her daughter to her feet and noticed the mud on her ankles. Then she saw the footprints on the hall floor and knew they hadn't been there when she locked up. 'Prudence, why are you lying?'

'Louisa, have you no compassion? Our daughter could have been killed.' Herbert couldn't understand his wife sometimes. Neither could he suspect his daughter of any wrongdoing. She had always been Daddy's little girl and that little girl was crafty enough to conceal her actions from her father. Louisa, on the other hand, knew how cunning her daughter could be and she was becoming afraid. Afraid that her daughter was not only unusual but was actually mad. Louisa was afraid of what Prudence was capable of next.

'Yes, she could have been killed if she'd fallen down the stairs, but you didn't, did you? You've been out and up to something. Why are you lying?' Louisa went to the hook where Prudence had hung her coat, the back of which was covered in dry mud. 'Well?'

Prudence began to cry. 'I don't feel very well. I'm going to bed.'

'Herbert, aren't you going to ask her where she's been?'

Herbert was red in the face. 'I don't know what's got into you, Louisa. Are you seriously suggesting Prudence is telling untruths? Why should she go out during the night?'

'You tell me, Herbert.' Louisa stormed up the stairs and into the bedroom where she slammed the door, releasing some of her pent-up anger.

Robbie heard the commotion, saw that it was still dark and buried his head beneath the blankets. Whatever was happening, he was keeping out of it. There was no way he was venturing out of his room in the middle of the night, ever again. Especially for someone as crazy as Prudence Goodman.

'Whoever would want to do such a thing?' Little Arthur stood in disbelief, gazing at the poison. His nightshirt, which would have reached the knees of a taller man, was covering his bare feet. He had known something was wrong the moment he had heard the din Genie and Gussie were making. Unfortunately he hadn't been in time to catch the culprit, just to see them hurrying away along the lane.

'Nay, lad, I'm sure I don't know. Oh, Arthur, what if they'd poisoned the pond and we hadn't known? We'd 'ave lost everything. By tomorrer all't cattle and horses'd be dead, not to mention flock. Even the geese depend on that pond for drinking watter. It doesn't bear thinking about.'

Little Arthur suddenly hurried to where his wellington boots stood by the door and slipped them on under his nightshirt.

'What are yer doing, Dad?' Dot had put on her clothes.

'I'm going to cover't horse trough. It'll have to be emptied first thing in't morning in case it's been poisoned, but for now I'll just put summat over it to stop it being drunk out of.'

'I'm going down for the constable.' Dot put on her coat.

'Aye, it should be reported. If there's a lunatic about it might be Barker's farm or one of the others next time. But I'll go. Damn it all, Dot, it's the middle of the night and there's a mad man out theer, somewhere. I'm not 'aving you going by yerself.'

'I'll be OK. I know the path blindfold and can run all the way down. I can come back with Bobby Jones. You and me mam have a hot drink and build the fire up for when we get back.'

'Well, if yer sure.' Dot was already on her way. 'Wait, I'll walk on't lane and stand by't stile until yer get to't bottom. Then I'll put some planks over't trough.'

Boadacea threw a shovelful of coal on the fire and moved the kettle onto it. Then she sat on the bench, her elbows resting on the table, her head in her hands, and tried to make sense of what had happened. Both her mother's family and the Greenwoods had lived on this hillside from the day they were born and in all those years to her knowledge, not one wrong word had been uttered between them and anyone in Millington. Indeed, both she and Little Arthur had gone out of their way to help anyone in need. So why should anybody wish them harm? Try as she might, no sense could be made of it. There was one thing for sure: if it hadn't been for the geese they would have lost everything. Oh well, she'd better get dressed. Boadacea looked down at the voluminous flannel nightie and despite the seriousness of the occasion couldn't help but smile. It wouldn't do for Bobby Jones to see her in her nightwear. No, it wouldn't do at all. It might put him off women for the rest of his life.

She went and put on some clothes, then lifted down a side of bacon from a hook in the low-beamed ceiling. She'd cut a few slices whilst she was waiting. Bobby Jones would no doubt make the interview last until breakfast time and she knew he was partial to a bit of home-fed, a couple of new laid eggs and a few doorsteps. She suddenly experienced a deep sense of relief that her family and livestock were all safe. There were some wicked people in the world but you couldn't go through life worrying about when they might turn up. All you could do was thank God for the good things in life and so long as she had Little Arthur and their Dot she had a hell of a lot to be thankful for.

Constable Jones liked to get his head down for a couple of hours on the night shift. There was never much going off in Millington after the pubs had closed at ten. Except on Saturdays, when there might be a couple of fist fights after the dance finished, usually between the Cragstone lot and the gang from Warrentickle, falling out over a girl. He had sent the lad out for a final check along the main road and had just dozed off in front of the police station fire. He was in the middle of a dream and in another second he would have known the name of the winning horse in the Grand National. So he didn't take kindly to being disturbed. Neither did he fancy the trek up the hill to Greenwood's Farm, but at least he'd be sure of a welcome when he got there. He couldn't believe it when Arthur showed him the poison. No ordinary householder could have acquired such a large quantity. It must have been stolen from a large establishment such as the steel-works or a school. 'I'll ask around and see if there's any gone missing,' he said. 'They'll surely have records at the town hall about who's been allowed such a large amount. Other than that there's not a lot I can do. Now if you had a description of the person it'd be a different kettle of fish.'

'You could keep a lookout and mek sure it doesn't 'appen again.'

'Oh aye, I shall be doing that. I'll put my lad on to keep watch, don't you fret.'

'Aye well then ... seeing as we're all up, what about a bit of a fry up?'

'That'd be right welcome, Arthur. Right welcome.'

Chapter Fifteen

Jane had just finished polishing the teacher's desk in Class Three. Another room done. Only the Baby Class now and she'd done for the weekend. She looked round the room with pride. The windows were sparkling and the wooden floor shone. The cobwebs had been removed from behind the book cupboard and the nasty smell of dirty flower vases and wet raincoats had been eliminated. The headmaster had commented that it was a pleasure coming to school these days and in an effort to help Jane carry on with the good work had told the teachers that each child must put their chair up on the desk before going home. This made Jane's job so much easier and she had never been happier than she was since marrying James and taking over the school. She moved on with her polish and dusters and was just polishing the door of the Baby Class when Robbie came along the corridor.

'Hello, Robbie. You've finished early, haven't you?'

'Aye, I wondered if I could talk to our James, but there's nobody in.'

'No, he's on afters and won't be home till gone ten.' Jane perched on one of the little desks. 'Is there something wrong?'

'Yes, but I'll come back when our James is in.'

'Come on, you can tell me. A trouble shared is

a trouble halved; well, that's what my dad used to say,' she added wistfully.

'My mam used to say that too,' Robbie answered.

'Well, come on then, out with it.'

'I need to move from the vicarage. I wondered if I could move in with you, just for a while until I find somewhere else.'

'Oh?' Jane felt rather threatened. If Reverend Goodman took umbrage at Robbie leaving it might mean them losing their home and her job. 'Well, it could be awkward, Robbie. We shall have to think about it.' Jane had never seen Robbie so downhearted. 'Why do you want to leave?'

'It's OK. Sorry to have bothered you.'

'Here, come back. We need to discuss this. Come on, tell me what's wrong.'

'Prudence. She's pestering me all the time and I can cope with that. But now she's started luring me into her room when she's half-naked, and when I don't respond she makes out it's me who's after her. I wouldn't touch her with that sweeping brush, Jane. She's creepy. Besides, I love Dot. I'm going to marry her when I've saved enough.'

'I see.' Jane frowned. 'I agree, she is creepy and it could cause trouble with Dot. It's just that with us living in church property it could be awkward. Why don't you have a word with Herbert?'

Robbie laughed. 'What? He can't see anything but the light shining out of her backside. Sorry, Jane. Anyway, I can see it could be awkward. Don't you worry about it. I'll be OK.' Robbie went along the corridor and through the cloak-room, which now smelled of bluebells the children had placed in jars, instead of urine and dirty drains. Robbie's shoulders were down and he dragged his feet along the school yard. Jane watched him through the window of the Baby Class – so called because it was where the five-year-olds began their learning. They would have to come up with a solution, but apart from them being in church property, Jane didn't fancy their honeymoon period being gatecrashed by a lodger, even if it was her brother-in-law.

'All aboard,' the driver called as he pulled up on Top Row. The curtains were still drawn at most of the houses, it still not being quite light.

Will carried out the bags for Lucy. Napkins, baby powder, clean clothes and nightwear. 'Blimey, anybody'd think we were going for a month,' he quipped. He went back and fetched a smart attaché case, loaned for the occasion by Mrs Rawlings. In this was packed all the wedding finery. Shirts put away after the last wedding had been brought out again. Clean underwear and Lucy's new dress. All packed carefully to avoid creasing. Bernard stood, still half-asleep, waiting to take his first ever ride.

'Everything on?' the driver enquired. Then came Mr and Mrs Slater and Ernest, who had been invited as Will's friend. The elder Slaters were being left on their own, much to their delight. 'And think on, behave yerselves or else.'

Mr and Mrs Marshall were all dressed up, Mrs Marshall sporting a new hat the colour of Colman's mustard.

'Don't get drunk,' Lewis called out of the bedroom window. Lewis and Kitty had always been closer to the younger girls than Nellie.

'Right then, where to next?' The driver asked when they all seemed to have settled down.

'Our Ben's,' Lucy told him. 'Then to pick up our Jane and Mary, not forgetting Robbie and Dot. After that we need to call at the manor.'

'Fair enough, as long as somebody shows me where they all live.' Will perched himself on the front seat in order to navigate until everybody was on.

Ben and Emma were waiting with a crate of Nut Brown to be consumed on the journey. Mrs Slater warned her old man not to forget he was giving Nellie away. 'Don't you dare get too much ale and show me up in church.'

'As if I would. I'm right proud to be standing in for Bill Gabbitas. The best mate I ever had, and I shan't let his daughter down.'

At the manor Mrs Cooper was trying to curb young Lily's enthusiasm.

'Oh Mrs Cooper, I shall 'ave to go for another tiddle. Don't go wi'out me will yer?'

'Goo on then, and hurry up. Yer'll not be able to be peeing all't time once we set off, yer know.' Larry was almost as bad, hopping from one foot to the other. Mrs Cooper thought it a shame that Molly's mam hadn't let Molly come. The poor lass had been in tears.

'Do I look all right, Mrs Cooper?'

'Course yer do. I've told yer a dozen times. Anybody'd think you'd never been to a wedding before.'

'I 'aven't, nor on a chara.'

'Aye, well, even so stop getting in such a tizzy or yer'll end up being sick.'

By the time they were all aboard and on their way it was coming daylight and the rising sun was colouring the countryside with vermilion and gold. 'Just look at that for a sight,' Mr Marshall said as they followed the road over Woodhead. 'Finest sight in Yorkshire, that is.' It would have been hard to argue at that moment, with the reflecting colours in the reservoir to their left. They could see a train on its way to Glossop.

'Puffer train.' Little Bernard pressed his nose against the window. 'Like Mammie's picture book.'

'Yes,' John agreed, hoping Lucy hadn't heard Evelyn being mentioned. It seemed to upset her much more than it did Bernard. The little boy seemed quite happy to talk about her.

Mrs Cooper had been given a seat at the front with Lily beside her and Lily could hear Larry, Will and Ernest Slater giggling on the back seat. She could feel their eyes on her and longed to go and join the young ones. Mrs Cooper watched Lily fidgeting and turning round, glancing in the direction of the lads.

'Oh, for heaven's sake, Lily, goo and sit at the back if yer like. Yer wearing me out just watching yer.' Lily was off like a tornado, before she'd got the words out. Mrs Cooper sighed and spread her backside across the two seats. 'Ah, that's better.' She watched John trying to keep little Bernard happy. She thought it was daft, him struggling with the little lad on his knee when there was a spare seat beside her.

'Give 'im 'ere; he can kneel up beside me,' she said. Mrs Cooper wished she had grand-bairns of her own. The little boy knelt beside her and chatted away to her about moo cows and baa lambs and then he settled down and slept, his head on Mrs Cooper's knee. She closed her eyes and dozed and stroked Bernard's hair. Give her a toddler any day than a daft giggly teenager like Lily. Even so, she loved the lass just as she did Nellie, and would grow to love the new cook before many weeks had gone by. She would miss Nellie though, who was the nearest thing to a daughter she would ever have. So she would enjoy this day, if it was the last thing she ever did. She would keep her eye on Lily and Larry though; that Blackpool air might make 'em irresponsible and them being like her children, she would make sure they came to no harm. At least she wouldn't have little Molly to worry about.

'I can see the tower, look, over there.' Mr Marshall pointed out the landmark to the youngsters, who had never even seen the sea, let alone the tower. Everyone was relieved to be nearing the end of the journey with a few hours to spare before the wedding. The marriage ceremony might be important to the oldies, but to the youngsters the sea was much more exciting. Lily changed her mind, however, when they arrived at Nellie's new house and Nellie took her upstairs.

'I want you to be my bridesmaid, Lily.' Nellie smiled. 'I just hope your dress fits, that's all.' The dress in question was the most beautiful Lily had ever seen. Lilac satin with a wide sash to tie in a bow at the back. A posy of anemones lay on the dressing table next to Nellie's pink carnations. Lily promptly burst into tears, much to Nellie's consternation. Nellie hugged the young girl, who to Nellie's knowledge had never had anything except serviceable working dresses, and even those probably hand-me-downs. 'Come on,' she said. 'You'll make your eyes all red and they'll clash with the colour of your dress.'

Lily laughed. 'Oh Nellie, I'm so happy; that's why I'm crying.'

'Yes well, come on, let's see if it fits.'

'Oh it's far too pretty for somebody like me.' The dress fit as though it had been made to measure.

'No it isn't. You're not just pretty, you're beautiful, Lily. I'm going to fasten your hair up under the head dress and then you'll see how beautiful you are. You've got to do my hair in return. Like you did when I went out to dinner with Tom.'

'Oh, Nellie. And now you're marrying 'im and I'm going to be all dressed up.'

The others had hurried down for a look at the sea but Lily was quite content making Nellie look beautiful. When they were ready Lily said, 'Oh, I wish me dad could see me now, and me mam and our Molly.'

'They will. I shall send you a photograph when they're developed.'

'Do yer think Ernest'll think I look nice?' Lily blushed.

'Well, he'd have to be blind not to.'

When all the guests had left for church Nellie and Lily came downstairs, where only Mr Slater remained. 'Eeh, lass, tha'r a sight for sore eyes.

And thee an' all, love. Come on, let's not keep that young man waiting any longer.' A wedding car was standing at the bottom of the steps. Nellie Gabbitas was all set to make her marriage vows to the man she adored and who loved her more than life itself.

Margaret Johnson was in her glory; she had taken charge of the catering, leaving Nellie free to put the finishing touches to the house. Some of the guests seemed quite intimidating to Nellie, but Tom introduced his wife with pride and everyone agreed young Tom had done well for himself.

John Grey found himself in conversation with a man quite a bit older than him. The man seemed quite taken with little Bernard, who had a habit of chatting away to everyone. 'Handsome little boy, your son; he'll set a few pulses racing in a few years' time.'

'Yes, I expect he will.' John laughed. 'He isn't my son yet, though.'

'Oh, I apologise. I just assumed.'

'That's all right. His mother died, father unknown. We're about to start adoption proceedings.'

'Hmm.' The man looked at John. 'I know it's a personal question, but how old are you? It's just that you look a bit young and being a lawyer, I do know that as the law stands, no one under the age of twenty-five is eligible to adopt.'

'Oh!' John hadn't known that. 'Not even if the child's being cared for by us because he's no relatives to look after him?'

'I'm afraid not.'

'Surely if I explain, the adoption can go ahead. I'm twenty-four so it's only the matter of another year.'

'Sorry, it is as the law stands at the moment. Best to wait, in my opinion. Actually it could cause problems if you apply too early. The authorities may decide you've no right to be caring for him.' John considered what the lawyer had said. He knew how heartbroken Lucy would be if the boy was taken away now.

'So you think it would be better if we waited a year?'

'Absolutely. Keep quiet is my advice; don't rock the boat.'

'Right. Well, thanks for your advice.'

'You're welcome,' he laughed. 'Not often we give out free advice. Would have cost you a few quid if given in my office.'

'Thanks. Nice to have met you.' John shook his hand.

'You too. Paul Tomlinson, should you ever need a lawyer.' He bent and ruffled Bernard's hair. 'Be a good boy for your father.' He winked at John. 'Good luck.' He went off to refill his glass.

Music had been arranged for the reception in the form of a trio, but it wasn't quite what the younger guests considered up to date and Nellie gave them permission to go and see the sights of Blackpool. Tom's young cousin eagerly offered to take them to the Pleasure Beach. Lily was torn between changing her dress and joining the young ones or staying in and wearing her bridesmaid's dress. Of course Ernest Slater made up her mind for her. He had been eyeing her up all day. Tom gave his cousin enough money for them all to have a few rides at the Pleasure Beach and for their fares on the tram to get there.

'It's a long walk to the South Shore,' Tom told them. None of them minded the walk. They crossed the promenade and walked along the sea front, watching the waves bashing on the sea wall, wetting their best clothes and in Lily's case, her white, uncomfortable shoes she had forgotten to change. 'Does anybody really go swimming in there?' she asked.

'All the time. It's lovely when the tide's out, or on a calm day.'

'Well, you wouldn't get me in there.'

'Me neither,' Dot agreed. 'It looks far too dangerous.'

'Now that's what I'd call dangerous.' Will looked up at the latest ride as they entered the fairground. 'But I'm going on it all the same.'

'Come on then.' Clarence the cousin ran to the kiosk to pay. Lily wasn't sure, but didn't like to be the odd one out. 'What would Mrs Cooper say?' she asked nervously as the ride set off up the steep metal track.

'She'd say, "Yer want yer brains washing."' Larry gave a decent impersonation of Mrs Cooper, making them all laugh. They soon stopped laughing as they reached the top and set off down the other side, with the ride gathering speed as they went. The girls screamed and they all hung on for their lives.

'We do want our brains washing.' Will was as white as Nellie's wedding dress when the ride came to a halt.

'Who's for another go?' Clarence called out, but nobody bothered to reply. After testing a few more rides they took a tram back along the prom and walked up by the station to Nellie's house. All Nellie's family and friends were to stay there for the night. Most of the men were inebriated by this time and the women not far behind them. Rosie and Bernard had been put to bed in the family room and Mrs Cooper, Lily and Dot were to share. The young lads were up on the top floor, where they told dirty jokes and acted the fool until it was almost light. Lily, due to habit, was awake by that time.

'Mrs Cooper,' Lily said as she saw the woman stirring. 'Should I go and cook breakfast for everybody? After all, I am the bridesmaid.'

'Eeh, lass, that'd be a lovely thing to do, and I'll come and 'elp yer.'

'I'll come too,' Dot said. 'I'm not used to lying in bed.'

'Come on then. More the merrier,' Lily giggled.

Mrs Cooper found a tray and set out breakfast for Nellie and Tom. She found a flower and put it on the tray.

'Ooh, Mrs Cooper, doesn't that look lovely? Can I tek it up? I know where their room is.'

'All right, but don't go in until you've knocked and they invite yer in.'

'Ooh no, I'd better not.' Lily and Dot began to giggle.

'And we'll 'ave less of that,' Mrs Cooper said, but the girls noticed the merriment in the housekeeper's eyes. 'Is that batch o' bacon done yet?' she asked Dot.

‘Not quite. Shall I go and wake everybody?’

Lily carried the tray up to the first room and tapped on the door with her toe.

‘Come in.’ Tom’s voice made Lily nervous, but she opened the door with her elbow and delivered their breakfasts without spilling a drop, either of fruit juice or tea.

‘Oh, Lily, how lovely. You’re supposed to be on holiday, not working or waiting on us.’

‘Ooh, I am on holiday. It’s the best time I’ve had in all me born days.’ And not one of the Millington guests would have disagreed.

After breakfast Tom took the men to look round his garage, where Mr Smith had arranged to take possession of a new car. The rest of them made their way to the North Pier – though Larry would have liked to join the men, if only he’d been invited. The sea was calm now and the young ones decided to go for a paddle. Even Lily and Dot couldn’t resist taking off their shoes and stockings and running along the wide expanse of golden sand and standing in the water where the waves rippled round their ankles.

‘Ooh, it’s lovely,’ Lily said. ‘I wish I ’ad a bathing costume, then I could go right in.’ The sea looked so different now it was calm.

‘Aye, I’d go with yer. I bet you’d look all right in a costume,’ Ernest said. It wasn’t much of a compliment but it was enough to send the colour flooding to Lily’s cheeks. They followed the tide mark along the beach, splashing each other and running away. Then Dot saw a gypsy coming towards them dressed in garments of orange, purple and red. The woman was carrying a basket of paper flowers and dolly pegs. 'Me mam told me to look out for the gypsy woman on the sands. I'm going to have me fortune told. She's the best fortune teller in the world is Gypsy Lee.'

'How'd yer know that?' Ernest said.

'Because she told me mam's fortune and everything she said came true. She even knew me mam was named after a queen, without being told.'

'Tell yer fortune, lady?' The gold at the gypsy's wrists and throat gleamed in the sunlight. She came towards Dot. 'Cross me palm with silver.' Dot gave her a shilling. 'Give me yer hand.' The gypsy traced Dot's palm with her finger. 'You've a long and healthy life ahead of you. You'll share it with a tall, dark man. A man who will never cease to be faithful to you.' Dot's heart sang. 'But not yet. Years may pass before you can share your life. Long dark years, all because of the wickedness of a woman.' Dot didn't like the gypsy's prediction now; it was scaring her. 'Stay close to your family, the earth, the green fields. Your man will return; have faith. Beware a tall, slim woman, long-haired and evil. She will fight, but you'll win in the end.'

Dot wished she hadn't had her fortune told now. It had made her sad, spoiled her weekend. Then she brightened. The gypsy had said Dot would win in the end. Besides, she had said he would always be faithful. She didn't mind waiting a few years. In fact she would wait for ever so long as she knew she would eventually share her life with Robbie.

Mrs Cooper finished helping Nellie prepare the vegetables for dinner. Then she put on her coat, hat and gloves. She would go breathe in some of the finest air in England; if that didn't give her an appetite nothing would. She walked on Central Drive and down to the promenade. Every building, every street sign, even the salt air brought a rush of memories, some filling her with joy, others bringing heartache. She endeavoured to remember the good times. The way they had run down the steps to the beach, his hand holding hers, protective yet warm with longing. She remembered how the ripples on the sand hurt her feet. The shock of the cold waves round her ankles. Most of all she remembered the love they had shared on that wonderful week, before he was cruelly snatched away from her. No warning, no signs, just the news that he had died of a heart attack.

She leaned on the railings and looked out to sea. She clutched her hat as the wind threatened to tear it away from her, then she called out across the sand, 'Thank you, Joe, for the love and the memories.' Then she turned and looked up at the great tower, memories flooding through her. They had stood way up there as they tried to locate the Street and the little boarding house where they had stayed with Joe's sister as a chaperon. Joe had pointed out the Isle of Man and North Wales. Then he had taken her in his arms, kissed her and asked her to marry him. 'We shall come back here on our honeymoon,' he had promised. They had danced in the ballroom and he had told her she looked like a queen in her maroon fine wool dress and shoes to match. Then they had returned to Cragstone and heartbreak. Until now, she had never returned to the resort, afraid of the memories, but she would come again, if God chose to preserve her long enough, and next time she would go to the ballroom and relive those wonderful days, in memory of Joe. She sighed and set off back. Nellie would need her help with a house full of hungry guests. Then she smiled to herself; Nellie Johnson wouldn't need an old woman's help. She was young and could cope well enough on her own. She stood waiting for a tramcar to pass and suddenly her hat went flying like a kite along the promenade.

A young couple ran, trying to catch it, but all in vain. 'Eh, love, don't bother. It'll be almost at Squires Gate by now,' Mrs Cooper laughed and they laughed with her. They reminded her of her and Joe all those years ago. She hoped they would have more years together than they had had. It had been so short, but oh so sweet. She wondered where her hat would end up.

She called after the couple, who were walking away, 'I looked daft in that hat anyway.'

Lucy and John had spent an enjoyable hour building sandcastles on the beach for Bernard and Rosie, and burying Bernard up to the waist in sand. Then they had fed the seagulls with bread brought from the breakfast table. Bernard shrieked and waved his arms excitedly at the squawking birds.

'I suppose we'd better go back. Our Nellie said dinner would be ready at one. She should have let us all help.'

John laughed. 'Your Nellie's quite capable of catering for a house full.'

'Oh, John. Have you ever seen a house like it? Tom must be really wealthy to afford a place like that.'

'Well, it's good to see one of the family doing well for herself. He'll make your Nellie a good husband, and a generous one.'

'Yes, it was a lovely wedding and it was good of them to open their home to all us lot.'

'Aye, it was a grand wedding.' John caught Lucy's eye. 'But do you know what?'

'What?'

'I enjoyed ours much more.'

Lucy took his hand. 'So did I, and I wouldn't swap you and our two for anything, not even our Nellie's house, or Tom's car, not even the chance to live here at the seaside.'

'Me neither.' John rose to his feet and lifted Rosie from Lucy's arms so she could put on her shoes. 'But I must admit I'm looking forward to one of your Nellie's dinners. I'm starving.'

'So am I. According to Mrs Cooper it's the Blackpool air.'

John breathed in, filling his lungs with the salt air. 'I think she's right.' He handed Rosie back to her mother and stood Bernard on the wooden steps to shift the sand from his feet. He took off the little boy's clothes and shook them clean, then when they were ready they left the beach behind and climbed the steps.

'Bye bye, birds.' Bernard waved to the gulls. 'Can we come again?' He looked questioningly at John.

'Yes, son, we'll come again. I don't know when, but I promise we'll come again.' Bernard skipped happily by John's side. 'And Rosie, and Mam?' Lucy glanced sharply at John. She thought Bernard had got over Evelyn by now, but he obviously hadn't. Then the little boy looked up at John and said, 'And dad?'

There were tears in the eyes of Lucy and John, but they were tears of joy now they had been accepted by Bernard as his parents. A family at last – albeit not a legal one, but a family all the same.

At four o'clock the chara left Blackpool, with the teenagers high-spirited and richer from the friendships they had made over the past two days, two tired children destined to sleep for most of the journey, and Mrs Cooper reliving the past, uncertain of the future and minus a hat. The rest of them were relaxed and feeling better for the change, but knew they would be back to the grindstone tomorrow, with the benefits of the weekend wiped away by the day-to-day routine.

Lucy lay back and closed her eyes, considering how the Gabbitas family had almost gone. Only Ben and Will now to carry on the family name. God willing, Will would eventually find a loving partner like the rest of them.

'Well, that seemed to go very well.' Tom sank down into the leather armchair and Nellie came and perched on the arm. 'But it's good to have you all to myself again.'

'Thanks, Tom.'

'Thanks? What for?'

'For sharing our honeymoon with my family and friends. Not many husbands would have done that.'

'Nellie, my love, whatever makes you happy makes me happy too. Besides, they're my family too now. It's great to have brothers and sisters at last, even if they are only in-laws.' Tom drew her down onto his knee and ran his fingers up her silk stockings. 'But now, this is where the fun starts.' Nellie kissed him, a deep, lingering kiss, then drew away.

'Oh, Tom, I coped, I really did. I cooked for a full house and it all went well. Do you really think I could manage to take in boarders?'

'Course you could, I never doubted it. Only...'

'What?'

'Not for another month at least. That's how long our honeymoon's going to last. Starting from now.' Tom undid one of Nellie's suspenders, then another and slowly rolled down her stocking. Then the other one. He was just in the process of slipping down her satin French knickers when the doorbell rang. 'Bloody hell. Let them go away. They'll think we're out,' Tom said, pulling Nellie back towards him as she fumbled for her stockings.

'Tom, we can't. Besides, we've a month in which to enjoy ourselves, or so you just promised me.'

'OK, but whoever it is don't make them welcome.'

'We weren't disturbing anything, were we?' Margaret bustled in.

'Not at all.' Nellie ushered her in-laws through to the lounge, hoping her husband had managed to control his painful erection, and that their visitors weren't intending to stay for very long.

Chapter Sixteen

Mr Grundy wondered what was the matter with Robbie. The lad hadn't been himself for a while, but he didn't like to pry. There was no change in his work – in fact he was working harder and longer than ever. As Mr Grundy said to his wife, 'It's blooming unnatural, a lad of his age spending all those hours working. It's as though ee doesn't want to go 'ome.'

'Perhaps ee feels lost now both 'is brothers 'ave married and moved out. I mean, it isn't as though the vicar's 'is kith and kin, is it?'

'No. There is that. But I think the lad's miserable and I might 'ave a word with 'is brother.'

'He might not thank yer for interfering. It might just be that the lad's in love. I know ee spends 'is days off with the Greenwood girl.'

'Aye, maybe you're right, lass. Yer usually are. But I'll keep an eye on 'im all't same.' Mr Grundy filled his pipe. 'Yer see, lass, I think a lot of that lad. I expect ee's become like a son to me.'

'I know. The son we never 'ad. I'm sorry for that.'

'Nay, lass, it were better we didn't 'ave any, what with there being a chance of it not being right. It were my side to blame, not yours.'

'It were nobody to blame. We were just being sensible, that's all.'

'Any road up.' Mr Grundy changed the subject. 'I think a lot of that lad and if I can 'elp 'im I shall. So we'll keep an eye on 'im, shall we?'

'Aye, we'll do that. As it 'appens I've taken to 'im meself. Maybe we should offer 'im a home wi' us.'

'You're a good woman, but like yer said, we'll 'ang on a bit and see.'

Robbie was unhappy. Getting away from the vicarage for the weekend had made him even more unsettled. He wanted to be with Dot all the time, but he'd have been content to wait had it not been for Prudence. Robbie realised the girl was obsessed with him, flaunting herself at every opportunity, yet devious enough to show indifference, even contempt towards him whilst in the company of her parents. The Monday after the wedding he paid a visit to John and Lucy.

'Robert! Come in.' Lucy lifted the kettle off the fire and mashed a pot of tea.

'Is our John at home?'

'Yes, he's just taken Bernard a walk up the allotments. He's after getting one for himself in order to keep some chickens. Sit down. He'll be back in a minute.' Lucy thought her brother-in-law looked a bit miserable. 'Is something the matter, Robert?'

'It's Prudence Goodman. She's trying to cause trouble between me and Dot. I can't stand it for much longer.'

Lucy poured two cups of tea. 'What kind of trouble?'

'Luring me into her room. Undoing her blouse. Oh I know it doesn't sound much, but she's weird.'

Lucy had always thought the vicar's daughter weird. 'Oh, I thought she'd become a bit more normal now she's started helping in the library.'

Just then John returned with Bernard perched up on his shoulders. The child whooped with delight as he lowered him to the ground. 'Hiya, Robbie, you OK?'

'No, he isn't. He's unhappy because of Prudence Goodman. I think he should move out.'

'Yes, but where to?' Robbie looked close to tears.

'Hey, we can't have that girl making you miserable.'

'No, you're right, John. It seems to me she's trying to split up Robbie and Dot's relationship. So are we going to let her succeed?'

'I asked Jane if I could stay with them for a bit, but she says it isn't possible because of it being church property.'

'Well perhaps it could be awkward. No, you must move in with us.'

Robbie beamed. 'Really? Can I, John?'

'Well I suppose so, for a while, if Lucy doesn't mind.'

'I won't be any bother, Lucy. I shan't need any dinners cooking or owt. I have them at work during the week and at Dot's on Sundays.'

'All right. That's settled then. Go get your things. You'll have to share with our Will though, up in the attic.'

'Will he mind?'

'Will he heck. He'll enjoy the company.'

'Oh Lucy, it'll be great.'

'Well, go on then.'

'What, now?'

'There's no time like the present.'

'Crikey. Thanks.' Robbie was out of the door like a flash of lightning.

'Oh, Lucy. You're still a young lass and you've already a family of four to see to. It doesn't seem right somehow.'

Lucy smiled. 'The more the merrier, John. I think I was put on this earth to look after people. I wouldn't be happy without a full house.'

'Well we shall certainly have one at this rate.'

'I told you we should be careful with the wishing mirror.' Lucy walked to the fireplace and gazed into the looking glass. 'I wished for a family of my own and that's what I got, and so long as everyone is healthy and happy that's all that matters to me.'

'And if you're content with your lot, Lucy, then so am I.' Bernard held up his arms. 'Let Bernard see.' Lucy lifted him up to look in the mirror.

'There's Bernard.' He pointed to Lucy's reflection. 'And there's Mam.' Lucy hugged him close. 'Let Rosie see.'

'Rosie's sleeping. When she wakes she can look in the mirror.'

'But Rosie can't wish; she's too little.'

'Well, you make a wish for her,' Lucy told the four-year-old. Bernard always wanted to share everything with Rosie.

'I wish Rosie could live in a sandcastle,' he began to giggle, 'and get sand in her toes.' Lucy tickled him and he laughed louder, with Lucy and John joining their little boy in his merriment.

Robbie slowed down as he reached the bottom of the hill, rehearsing what he would say to Louisa and Herbert. He mustn't let them see how miserable he had become. They had been so good to him and his brothers. He would have been happy to stay there for ever had it not been for their daughter, but he couldn't tell them that. He opened the gate and walked up the path, forgetting everything he had been about to say. 'Robert, would you like some tea?' Louisa called as he entered the kitchen.

'Yes please. I've got something to tell you, Louisa.' Robbie was relieved to see Prudence was nowhere to be seen. Then he remembered it was her evening on library duty.

'Nothing bad, I hope.' Louisa sat at the table and poured out the tea.

'No, just that I'm moving out. I think I've taken advantage of your good nature for long enough.'

'Moving out? But why?'

'Oh, it was different when my brothers were here too, but now there's only me I feel as though I'm intruding. I think it's time you had your home to yourselves again.'

'Robert, you must never think you're intruding. We love having you here. Where would you go?'

'To our John's. To tell you the truth I'm missing my brothers.'

'Well, I suppose that's only natural. But won't it be a bit cramped in John's house?'

'Oh no, I shall be up in the attic with Will.' Robbie suddenly thought of another excuse. 'It's just that I thought it might help them financially if I paid my board. I mean, they've been good enough to take on little Bernard and he'll need clothing and feeding.'

'Well, yes, I suppose he will.' Louisa would miss the weekly contribution Robert made, especially as the only meals he ever expected were his breakfasts.

'I shall pay you my board for another week,' Robert told her.

'Oh, I wouldn't expect that, but you're surely not moving out today, are you?'

'Well, yes. That's if you don't mind.'

'No, no, of course not, but we shall miss you, especially Herbert.'

'And I shall miss him, and you. You've been really good to me and I shall never forget the way you opened your home to us.' He smiled. 'But I expect you'll be glad to have it to yourselves again.'

'No, we won't, but I expect you'll call in and see us frequently.'

'Oh aye, and I shall see you on Sundays anyway at church.' He finished his tea. 'Well, I'll go get my things.' He took some money from his pocket. 'Will that be all right?'

'Oh, Robert, I don't want that.'

'Please, I'd like you to have it. I really do appreciate everything you've done for me. Now if you don't mind I'll get my things before I get all upset. I'm not very good at partings.'

'No, neither am I,' Louisa sighed. 'Do you need any help?'

'No, no thanks.' Robert hurried out into the hall. He really was sorry to be leaving, but relieved to be rid of Prudence once and for all.

Louisa wasn't fooled by the excuses Robbie had made. She had an idea it was her daughter who was at the root of Robert's eagerness to escape. She had noticed Prudence's covetous glances in Robert's direction and her obvious hatred of Dot Greenwood. Herbert would never believe any of it – in his eyes Prudence could do no wrong – but Louisa wasn't fooled at all and knew exactly why Robert was going.

Prudence was seething when she found out. She had hoped to tempt Robbie away from Dot Greenwood. It would have been better all round. Now she would have to fall back on her plan, the plan she had set in action a few months ago. At least Robbie hadn't gone to live at the farm; that had been her worst fear.

She smuggled the book to her room. Working at the library had its advantages, even if it was only the books at her disposal. She just hoped the librarian hadn't noticed her slipping it into her bag; it would never do for the vicar's daughter to be caught stealing. She bade her parents good-night, saying she was feeling tired and would have an early night. Her plan would be set in motion immediately.

Will was delighted to have a room mate, especially one whom he could talk to about things that had been bothering him. Robbie's chat with James had never materialised. Will had long since realised that Jane was quick to make promises but rarely followed them up. Not that she wasn't trustworthy, just a scatterbrain who thought about herself before anyone else, unlike

Lucy. Will thought Jane had been selfish not to offer Robbie a home when they had so much more room at their house. 'I'll bet she never even asked your James if you could stay,' he said to Robbie. 'He wouldn't 'ave turned you away.'

Robbie agreed, but would never criticise Jane to her brother. 'Oh, well it could have been awkward like she said.' He grinned. 'Anyway, I like it better here. This is the happiest house I know.'

'Aye, yer right there. It wasn't like this when me mother was alive though. A bloody owd slave driver, that's what she were.' Then Will felt guilty. 'She was all right though, I suppose.'

Robbie considered what Will had said. 'It's funny us both becoming orphans at about the same time. Not funny to laugh about – I mean strange.'

'Aye, thank God for our Lucy and your John. Where would we be without 'em?'

'Well, you'd be OK; you've got Ben and Mary and Nellie. Hey! Yer might have ended up living in Blackpool.'

'No, I like it 'ere. Besides, our Mary's a bit sanctimonious sometimes, and our Ben's no room, what with Mrs Scott living there and only one spare room for when they 'ave a family. No, I like it 'ere with our Lucy. I 'ope you do an' all.'

'Oh I do. Like I said, it's a happy house. I couldn't have stood it with Prudence Goodman for much longer.'

Will laughed. 'She's not bad-looking though.'

'You 'ave her then.'

'No thanks. I wonder if she's all there. It's her eyes; they're all cold-looking and staring.'

'She's not all there – you're right.'

'Besides, you've got Dot. Who'd swap her for Prudence? Or for anybody else, come to that?'

'Well I wouldn't swap her for anyone in't world. I love Dot, yer see.'

Will blushed as he wondered if he dare ask. ''Ave you ever? Yer know.'

'What?'

'You and Dot? I thought with yer being a few years older, yer might 'ave.'

'Oh, that?' Robbie shook his head.

'I thought being as yer love 'er, yer might 'ave.'

'No. I might if I didn't love 'er, but I'll not spoil things. I respect her, that's why.'

'I just thought yer'd know what it was like, that's all.'

Robbie suddenly felt rather stupid. He supposed it was unusual not to have had sex at his age. 'I could have had it if I wanted to,' he told Will. 'Prudence Goodman was asking for it.'

Wilt's eyes widened. 'She actually asked you to do it?'

'Well, not asked in so many words. Just flaunted herself at me, showing all she'd got, more or less.'

'So does that mean they're asking for it if they show all their private bits?'

'Usually.'

'Only, Mrs Pattersall up in't new houses always invites me in when I deliver her greens, then she perches on't edge of the table and lifts 'er frock up so that I can see 'er thighs over 'er stocking tops. She always pretends to be fastening 'er suspender. Does that mean she's asking for it?'

'Probably, but if she's married you'd end up in

trouble, perhaps in hospital if her old man found out, so I shouldn't bother if I were you.'

'No.' Will was disappointed. 'Only I keep wondering what it'd be like. What with all me mates 'aving done it except me.'

Robbie laughed. 'Is that what they tell yer? Don't take any notice of 'em. The more they brag about it the less likely they are to 'ave done it.'

Will brightened up. 'Really?'

'Well, I wouldn't tell anybody even if I had.'

'So I'm not different then, from everybody else?'

'Don't be daft. When you meet the right girl things'll work out, you'll see. Anyway, I shouldn't be telling you about me love life. But if you're ever worried about anything you can always tell me and I'll tell you if I am worried, OK?'

Will grinned. 'OK.' He felt a lot better for his chat with his new room mate. Robbie was right: it was a happy house and even more so now he had someone to talk to.

'Why aren't you eating?' Louisa watched her daughter toying with her boiled egg.

'I'm not feeling too good this morning.'

'In what way?'

'I feel like I might be sick.'

'Oh dear, perhaps you shouldn't go to the library today.' Herbert was concerned about his daughter.

'No, I shall be all right. I'll just drink my tea, although even that's making me feel queasy. I'll go get ready.' Prudence smiled to herself as she left the table. She hoped she could smuggle the medical book back onto the library shelf without being seen. She had found all the information she needed within its pages and it wouldn't do for her mother to find the book in her room. How devious she was becoming in her attempt to win Robbie Grey. She smiled maliciously as she thought of the bloodied blanket squares of her last two menstruations she had washed herself in the small hours rather than leave them for her mother to launder; they had been folded neatly and replaced in the drawer. That had been the first stage of her plan – now it was time to move a stage further. Prudence considered herself clever. In fact the poor girl desperately needed help for her obsession.

Lucy had been sick for the last three mornings, but unlike Prudence had told no one. It was Enid Slater who heard her retching in the lavatory as she was hanging out the whites on the line. She waited for Lucy to come out. 'Are yer all right, love?'

'Not really. I think I must have eaten something that didn't agree with me.'

'Come on, let's 'ave a cuppa.'

'No, you come to ours – the little ones'll be waking soon. I'll make one. I'm feeling better now.'

Mrs Slater searched Lucy's face. 'Are yer sure it's summat you've eaten and not summat you've done that's brought it on?'

'What do you mean?' Lucy looked puzzled, then she blushed. 'Oh, oh Mrs Slater, I can't be pregnant again so soon, can I?'

'Well, if you'd been breastfeeding I'd 'ave said no, but seeing as Rosie's on the bottle I'd say possibly.'

'But I had to put her on Allenbury's; I didn't have enough milk. I so wanted to breastfeed but I couldn't.' Lucy was almost in tears.

'And no wonder, you were still in shock over Evelyn, and looking after Bernard an' all. 'Aven't yer seen the curse since Rosie was born?'

'No, it must have happened on our Nellie's wedding night.' Lucy was terribly embarrassed. Mrs Slater must think they were sex mad. 'That was the only time we've...' She couldn't say any more to Mrs Slater but the woman didn't seem at all disgusted.

'Nowt to be ashamed of, love. After all you are married. Anyway it looks to me as though there might be another little Grey on the way. On the other hand, it could be summat you've eaten, like yer said.'

'No. Now I think about it I feel pregnant. I've been in and out to use the po umpteen times these last few nights, just like I was with Rosie.'

'Do you mind, love? About 'aving another so soon?'

'No, not at all. More the merrier. I wished for a large family and it looks like I'm going to get my wish.'

'Well, I suppose they'll bring each other up, like the Murphys.'

'Oh, Mrs Slater, I shall never sit about all day letting them run riot like Mrs Murphy does. Although they all seem happy and healthy.'

'I know, love, only kidding. If I saw you sitting

down for five minutes I'd think the world was coming to an end.'

'I wonder what John'll say. I hope he's pleased.'

'Too late now, even if he isn't.'

'Oh, and what will our poor Mary think? She wants a baby so much, it doesn't seem fair, somehow.'

'No it doesn't, but don't let it spoil your carrying of the child. It's God's will, after all.' Rosie suddenly let out a wail, then they heard Bernard pattering about the bedroom. Enid Slater laughed as Lucy jumped up and ran upstairs. Lucy was going to need all that spare energy with a husband, two strapping lads, a toddler and two babies to see to. She took the empty cups to the sink and washed them. The lass would need a bit of help at times, and while Enid continued to enjoy reasonable health, she would make sure she was there to offer it.

The first week in July Nellie welcomed her first paying guests into her home. The advert in *The Lady* had attracted enough holidaymakers to fill the guest house until the end of August. Nellie began with three married couples, two elderly sisters and a family of four.

'That'll be enough for the first week,' she told Tom. 'I'll see how I cope before filling all the rooms.'

A cleaner had been employed but Nellie hadn't found a suitable girl to wait at the tables and assist in the kitchen. One applicant had seemed a bit scruffy and another had begun making eyes at Tom, even during the interview. For the time being Margaret Johnson was quite enjoying working alongside her daughter-in-law, though she wouldn't like to be tied permanently, not at her age. Nellie's set menu at breakfast seemed to suit all the guests and with two choices at dinner everyone seemed satisfied. The compliments on her cooking delighted Nellie. The family with the two little girls and the elderly ladies took advantage of the light supper, which was served in the comfort of the lounge where the guests could chat or listen to the wireless.

Nellie decided she would go shopping for some toys and board games so that the children would be entertained. The three couples were never seen after dinner – they were probably dancing on the pier or seeing a show. Tom gave them all a key to the front door so they could come and go as they pleased. 'No use expecting visitors to Blackpool to be in by a certain time,' he said.

At the end of the first week the two ladies booked for another two weeks in September and in the visitors' book commented on the comfort of the rooms, the friendly atmosphere and Nellie's cooking.

'Well, I think that went rather well.' Margaret waved the last of the guests on their way.

'Yes.' Nellie was ecstatic. The real test would come in the next few days though, when she would have to cope with a full house. It was whilst Nellie was on the way to the wholesalers in Tom's car that she had a brainwave. 'Tom,' she said, 'do you think Lily would come to Blackpool?'

'Lily?'

'Yes, as a waitress. She would have to live in of

course, but she'd be ideal.'

'It would take up one of the single rooms.'

'Yes, but there's the attic. You were talking about having it decorated and furnished. What do you think?'

'Well. I wouldn't like any of the guests to have to climb up there but yes, it would make a perfect bedsitting room for Lily. Still, she might not want to leave Cragstone. After all, she's very young.'

'Shall I write and enquire?'

'Certainly, but don't bank on her accepting.'

'How long will it take to prepare the room?'

'Knowing my mother, not more than a week or two. She'll have the whip out otherwise.'

Nellie couldn't wait to see how Lily would respond to the suggestion. 'I shall write tonight,' she said.

'And I'll round up a couple of decorators for estimates.'

Nellie sighed happily as Tom parked the car. Then they went to stock up on food for this week's expected guests.

Chapter Seventeen

Louisa Goodman placed the seed cake in the oven. She must remember to purchase some more caraway seeds when she went shopping. She felt the familiar dull pain that heralded her monthly bleeding and went upstairs to find a cloth and some safety pins. She opened the drawer and felt quite faint as she realised there had been none of Prudence's dirty ones to wash in the last month. Her pulse raced as she thought about the sickness her daughter had experienced over the past few weeks. She slammed the drawer shut and hurried downstairs to where Prudence was as usual enthralled in one of her romantic novels.

'Prudence, when did you last have your period?' she asked.

The girl kept her eyes on the page. 'I'm not sure.'

'You must know if it came two weeks ago when it was due.'

'Oh! I never noticed it was missing.'

'You mean it is now two weeks late?'

'Oh no, more than that,' Prudence answered innocently.

'Prudence, tell me what happened when Robert came to your room.'

'I'd rather not.'

'I shan't ask you again. I shallask Robert.'

Prudence forced the sobs to her throat and tears to her eyes.

Louisa drew her daughter into her arms. 'Why didn't you tell me before?' Prudence's performance would have put Greta Garbo to shame as she cried as if her heart was about to break. 'Prudence, I'm going to get your father and then we must take you to a doctor.'

'No. I can't. No one must know, not when I'm not married. I'd be too ashamed.'

Louisa hurried out and across to the vestry where she knew her husband would be arranging his Sunday sermon. 'Herbert, you must come home. Something terrible has occurred.' Louisa began to panic at the shameful words she was about to utter. 'I believe Prudence is ... I believe she's pregnant.'

'What?' Louisa watched the colour drain from her husband's face. 'What are you saying? Our daughter would never be capable of such a thing.'

'Oh, I think she would.'

Herbert paced the vestry floor, his hands clasped on his chest as if in prayer. 'Robert Grey. I'll kill him for this.'

'And what good will that do? Besides, you're the one who preaches forgiveness. Our daughter is just as guilty. In fact, I wouldn't have put it past her to have seduced him.'

'What are you talking about? What's got into you, woman?'

'Don't call me *woman*.'

'I'm sorry, but well, you are a woman. Oh, Louisa, the shame of it. He'll have to marry her.'

'Yes, but he doesn't love her, Herbert. I know he doesn't.'

'You don't know, and anyway that can't be helped. He should have considered that when he sullied an innocent girl.'

'Innocent? Are you sure about that?'

'Oh, Louisa, I'm not sure about anything. Are you really certain she's...?' Herbert couldn't bring himself to say the word.

'Well she's either pregnant or there's something else wrong with her.'

'She must see a doctor, make certain.'

'She doesn't want to, says she can't, being unmarried.'

'Then Robert must marry her. I'll go see him. There's no alternative.'

'He'll be at work.'

'Oh yes. I'll go later. I'm going to see James. See what he has to say on the subject.' Herbert slumped into his chair, his head in his hands. It was the first time his wife had ever seen him cry. Her heart was breaking as she took her beloved man in her arms.

'Come on, my love, let's go home.'

'They must marry, Louisa. Just imagine the talk amongst the parishioners if our daughter becomes an unmarried mother. I don't think I can bear the shame of it.'

'No, you're right. We must see Robert tonight.' She led her husband out and locked the vestry door, her heart filled with sadness and sympathy for her husband and anger towards the girl who was causing him so much pain. She felt guilty for her thoughts but she knew in her heart that it was all her daughter's fault. Try as she might, Louisa couldn't bring herself to lay the blame on Robert Grey's shoulders.

The atmosphere in the kitchen reminded Lucy of the night her father died. Reverend Goodman had taken possession of her mother's chair by the fire. Robbie was standing face to face with James. His face was deathly white and sweat beads rested on his brow. 'I never touched her, James. I swear I never laid a finger on her.'

'You were in her room undressed, Robbie.'

'I know. Only because she tricked me. She called for help.'

'I would have heard her, Robert. The first I

heard was when she called you to get out.'

'That was only because I wouldn't cuddle her.'

'Robbie, you'll have to marry Prudence. It's matter of honour. When a man's been in a girl's room he must do what is right by her.'

Lucy poured tea into her pretty cups, privately thinking James's attitude was more to do with him losing his home than it was about doing right by Prudence Grey.

'Are you certain she's pregnant? I mean if Robbie says he never touched her...' she asked.

'Well, nobody else has been in her room. My daughter wouldn't lie.'

'I just don't think Robbie would either,' Lucy pointed out.

John had kept silent until then, leaving the matter to his elder brother. 'Lucy, I really don't think it's anything to do with you, love.'

Lucy blushed. 'I'm sorry, John.'

'It's all right.' John smiled sadly at his wife.

'So it's settled then. My brother'll do right by your daughter,' James told Herbert.

'But I love Dot,' Robbie said in desperation.

'So I can arrange the wedding then?' Herbert felt the tension slip away as he prepared to leave.

'I shall be proud to have you for a son-in-law, Robert.' Herbert held out his hand for Robbie to shake.

'But it's not fair. I don't love Prudence.'

Herbert held Robbie's hand and patted the back of it. 'Love will grow, never fear. The child will bring you closer.'

The look in Robbie's eyes almost brought Lucy to tears. He searched the room appealing for help, but none was forthcoming. James couldn't meet his eyes. He knew he was sacrificing his brother's future in order to hang on to his house and Jane's job. He felt bad about doing so but knew if he let Jane down, his own future wouldn't bear thinking about.

When Will arrived home an hour later only Robbie, John and Lucy were in the kitchen.

'What's up?' Will said. 'Has somebody died?'

Robbie stood up and went towards the stairs. 'I wish I had,' he said. 'I wish I was dead.'

Prudence smiled to herself when she knew her plan had worked. All she had to do now was carry on keeping her periods secret and pray she would become pregnant for real after the wedding in a month's time. She could stop feigning sickness now and was eating as much as she could in order to put on weight. The medical book had told her all she needed to know about pregnancy, and most importantly about miscarriage – should that become necessary. If only Robbie would stop acting so unreasonably and begin to look forward to the wedding. Prudence thought he would come round once Dot Greenwood was out of the picture and she gave him the comfort of her body. She sighed in anticipation. Robert Grey would soon be hers, and she couldn't wait to welcome him into her bed.

'Well, I must say this is a right kettle o' fish.' Boadacea poured boiling water onto a handful of camomile flowers to make a cordial. The best thing for shock, and Dot was certainly in shock.

She hadn't stopped crying since dinnertime. Robbie wasn't much better; in fact he looked as though his face had been dipped in the flour bin. Little Arthur had listened intently to what Robbie had to say.

'I never touched 'er. If you get me the bible I'll swear on it.'

'Then don't marry 'er,' Dot managed between sobs. 'She must've been with somebody else.'

'They say I've got to. They're not going to believe me before a vicar's daughter. If I don't marry 'er, our James'll lose 'is home, Jane, her job and everybody in Millington'll hate me. I might even lose me job.'

'Well, isn't that better than losing me?'

'That's not fair, love. Robbie doesn't know whether ee's coming or going. The lad'll be badly with all this upset.'

'I know, Dad. I'm sorry Robbie, but I love yer and I want to marry yer.'

'So do I, Dot. I hate her.'

'It's all that gypsy's fault. She said we would be parted. I wish I'd never had me fortune told.'

'Nay, me duck. She only told yer what was going to 'appen; she didn't make it 'appen.'

'But she did say we would be together one day.' Dot cheered slightly but then began to sob again. 'And she said you would remain faithful to me. How can you remain faithful to me when you're married to her?'

'I can and I shall; I shan't touch her. I can't abide to be near her, ne'r mind touch her. I love you.'

'Well, like I said, it's a right kettle o' fish. But I

can't see what Robbie can do but marry 'er.' Boadacea placed a cup of bitter-tasting tea in front of Robbie. 'We all know 'ow the people of Millington look up to the vicar and Robbie's life won't be worth living if she spreads the word that it's his babby, even if it isn't.'

'Well, nobody mu'n say a wrong word about yer to me, lad,' Little Arthur said. 'And yer'll always be welcome here in my 'ouse.'

'No!' Boadacea shoo'd a ginger cat off the bench and sat down. 'That wouldn't be right. It'd not only give Robbie a bad name but our Dot as well. We can't 'ave that. No, she'll 'ave to get over 'im and when she 'as, maybe find another sweetheart.'

Dot began wailing again. 'I won't. I'll never get over 'im and I'll never love anybody else. I'll remain an old maid until Robbie and me get together again, and we shall. The gypsy said so.'

'That's all very well, but I shall miss thee, Robbie.' Little Arthur looked near to tears himself.

'And I shall miss coming to the farm. It's been like home to me.'

'Well then, tha must continue to come if tha likes.'

'No, thanks, Mr Greenwood, but Mrs Greenwood's right. It wouldn't be fair to Dot and I shouldn't be able to bear it, loving her as I do.'

'Oh, bloody 'ell, it can't be right loving one lass and marrying another. There must be summat we can do.'

'Aye, but what?' Robbie looked hopefully at Little Arthur, but he couldn't come up with an answer. Robbie stood up. 'I'd better go. I've explained now and that's what I came for. I expect I'll see yer in church, Dot. And I shall remain faithful, even if you fall for someone else, which I expect you will, what with you being so beautiful. There's one thing for sure: I shall never in a million years fall for Prudence Goodman.' Robbie had never felt so sad since his parents died, and Dot felt just as bad.

At John's suggestion, to cheer Robbie up a bit, Will and Robbie had taken Bernard out to see the ducks on the reservoir. Lucy had just finished washing up the pots and pans after a delicious Sunday dinner when Mary and Jacob arrived. Mary was all dressed up and Lucy thought it must be nice to have nothing to do except don yourself up in Sunday best and go out for the afternoon. Then she looked at little Rosie, sleeping peacefully in her pram and the slight envy she had felt changed to pity for her sister.

'Shall I put the kettle on?' John asked, knowing Lucy had worked hard all morning and ought to be putting her feet up.

'Yes please.' Lucy laid out the cups and saucers. 'This is a nice surprise, Mary.'

'Aye well, I'll not beat about the bush; we've come to offer our help.'

'Help? I didn't know we were in need of any help.'

'We've come to tell you we've decided to adopt Bernard.'

John dropped a spoon into the sink with a clatter. 'What?'

'Well, with our Lucy expecting another, you'll

have enough on without Evelyn's boy. So we shall help out by taking him off your hands.'

'Oh no. You're not having Bernard. He's mine, and if I have a dozen more, he'll still be mine.' Lucy's face had turned crimson.

'I must say that's a selfish attitude to take, throwing kindness back in our faces.' Mary scowled at Lucy.

'Kindness? Oh I don't think you'd be taking him out of kindness. You just want a child, Mary. And I'm sorry you haven't got one yet, but you can't have ours.'

'Yours? But he isn't yours. Our Rosie's yours, and the one you're carrying. It'll be a hard enough struggle to keep them and we could give him so much more.'

Jacob looked uncomfortable, shuffling from one foot to the other. He hadn't thought this a good idea, but when Mary got a bee in her bonnet there was no holding her. John felt sorry for him and handed him a cup of tea. 'He's part of our family, Mary,' he said. 'Evelyn handed him into Lucy's care. We can't give him away just because we're having another.'

'You mean you won't.'

Jacob spoke for the first time. 'I think you should let the matter drop, Mary. Lucy and John are obviously not interested in your offer.'

'I won't let it drop. Bernard would want for nothing as our son. What can they give him with one in the pram and another on the way? And I don't doubt there'll be another next year and the year after that.'

'Mary.' Jacob's hand landed on the table with a

bang, causing the cups to rattle in their saucers. 'You've said enough.'

Mary suddenly burst into tears. 'You say something then.'

'I think you've said enough for both of us and you should apologise.'

'What for? Offering help? Never.'

Lucy felt immense pity for her sister, and for Jacob. 'I don't need an apology. It was kind of you to offer. Maybe you would be able to give a child more things than we can, but we have enough for his needs, and more importantly he'll have love. He'll also have Rosie, whom he already adores. You can't take him away from her, Mary. I'm sure you wouldn't want to.'

Mary was weeping as though her heart would break. 'We could adopt him properly.'

'No, we shall adopt him. You can apply to adopt another child, but not Bernard. Come on Mary, drink your tea.'

Mary rose to her feet. 'Come on, Jacob. We've made our offer and it's been refused. You can't help some people.' When she reached the door Mary turned, a look of pure hatred on her face. 'And don't come to me for help in the future, when you're bound to need it.' Then she flounced out with Jacob following behind, glancing helplessly back at John.

'Oh John, I feel so sorry for her. Our Mary's turning all bitter. She never used to be like that.'

'No,' John agreed. He shuddered as he remembered the look of venom in the eyes of his sister-in-law. He wouldn't put it past her to try and make trouble over little Bernard. John wouldn't rest now until the boy was legally adopted, and there were still some months to go before he could officially become theirs. Perhaps it wasn't too early to set the wheels in motion, though. He would begin making enquiries.

Dot Greenwood saw Prudence place her hand possessively over Robbie's and watched him stiffen and draw away from her. Dot joined the congregation as they uttered the words of the creed, wondering if she would ever believe in the words 'God the Father' again. Even her respect for Reverend Goodman had wavered as she considered the pressure he had placed on Robbie to marry his daughter. Surely he should have questioned Prudence in order to find out the father of the child. Dot struggled through the final hymn and joined the others as they shuffled their way out into the churchyard. Instead of hanging round to chat to her friends she hurried out of the lychgate and set off for home, unable to cope with their sympathetic glances. Besides, if Robbie Grey so much as looked at her she thought she might burst into tears. If she had but known, Robbie Grey felt exactly the same.

By contrast, Prudence was making sure everyone saw her clinging to Robbie's arm. The excitement of the coming wedding added a glow to the girl and she actually looked pretty dressed in her Sunday best. No one apart from the family knew of Prudence's pregnant condition, all of them being asked to keep silent until after the marriage. Only the friends of Robbie and Dot found it hard to believe that Robbie would leave Dot in favour of the vicar's daughter. They all knew it had been a case of love at first sight for the couple and couldn't understand what had happened to split them up.

Because none of them liked Prudence, most of the group tended to take the side of Dot, which only made Robbie even more miserable. His only consolation was that for now he still had Lucy, John and Will to go home to each night and Mr Grundy's company during the day. He didn't dare to think what it would be like returning to Prudence every evening and just hoped something – anything – would happen to prevent the sham of the wedding from taking place. He walked Prudence back to the vicarage, as was expected of him now she was considered his fiancée.

'Aren't you coming in for supper?' Prudence asked.

'No, I've to be up early in the morning. I'll be getting home.'

'Oh, Robbie, why don't you move back here? After all, this will be your home when we're married.'

'Yes I know, but we're not married yet.' Robbie turned to go.

'Aren't you forgetting something?' Prudence pulled at his sleeve and turned him towards her, throwing her arms round his neck. Robbie cringed as she kissed him on the lips.

'Goodnight, Prudence.' Robbie hurried away, ignoring the glint of anger in her eyes. She might be succeeding in getting him to the altar, but getting him to love and desire her would be a different matter. In fact it would never happen.

His heart already belonged to Dot Greenwood, with or without a wedding ring.

Robbie mumbled his vows and saw Prudence sigh with relief as he placed the gold ring on her finger. The small congregation thought what a handsome couple they made, and as most of them – with the exception of Robbie's family – were friends or relatives of Herbert and Louisa, none of them had any inkling that the marriage might be one of convenience. Robbie had thought, right up to the last minute, that something would happen to stop the wedding. That their James would intervene and put a stop to the proceedings. That Herbert Goodman would believe him and realise the marriage was a mistake, but for all Robbie had protested nobody had called a halt. Now it was too late and whilst all around him people smiled and offered congratulations, Prudence beamed and Robbie Grey sank deeper and deeper into despair.

A buffet had been set out at the vicarage and both John and James were relieved when they could finally leave. The pain in Robbie's eyes haunted Lucy as they climbed the hill with their two weary children. Lucy's feet were beginning to swell in her high-heeled shoes and she couldn't help envy Prudence, who despite being pregnant was still as slim as ever. 'Prudence doesn't look pregnant,' she commented as they reached Top Row, 'and here's me feeling all fat and frumpy.'

John glanced lovingly at his wife. 'You're imagining things. You're still as slim as ever. In fact that brother of Herbert's couldn't take his eyes off you.'

Lucy blushed. 'Yes, I noticed. In fact I had to dodge him once or twice; he couldn't keep his hands to himself.'

John laughed. 'Well what's all that about you feeling frumpy then?'

Lucy shrugged. 'I was just comparing myself to Prudence, I suppose.'

'Hmm, funny you should mention that. She doesn't look very pregnant to me.' John frowned as a terrible thought came to him. What if Prudence had tricked his brother into marriage? He cast the thought away; it was something that didn't bear thinking about. Yet he wouldn't put it past Prudence Goodman – he wouldn't put it past her at all. The tragedy of it was that she wasn't a Goodman any longer; she was a Grey.

Robbie thought Prudence was acting like a whore. She had undressed down to her underwear and was flaunting herself in panties, stockings and suspenders, all of them white lace. On Dot they would have filled him with desire, but on Prudence they didn't look attractive at all. He took off his clothes, leaving on his underpants and got into bed, ashamed to be sharing it with a woman he didn't even like. Prudence climbed in beside him and pressed her body against his. He felt a stirring deep within him and turned away. With his back to her he drew his knees up in an effort to hide his erection.

'Oh, Robbie,' Prudence whispered, 'come on, you know you want to make love to me. I want to touch you and I want you to touch me. It's our wedding night and we might as well try and make it work. I need you so much; that's the only reason I wanted to marry you. Turn this way and feel my body. It's so much more beautiful than Dot Greenwood's.'

Robbie threw back the bedclothes and jumped out of bed. Bending close to her he almost spat out the words, 'Don't you ever mention Dot's name to me. You're not fit to speak her name. And just get this straight: we may be married but I shall never ever touch your body. You disgust me. Do I make myself clear?'

'Oh, come on. I know I've made you cross but now we're married, think of the fun we can have. It will work.'

'It will never work in a million years. Marriage is about love, trust and friendship and I don't feel any of those things for you. I don't even want to have sex with you. You're a liar and a cheat. I've given you my name but that's the only part of me you will ever own. Do you understand that?'

Prudence nodded, shocked at the venom being directed towards her. She had thought Robbie would be easy to manipulate. He was obviously stronger willed than she had imagined. She turned away from him and lay rigidly on the edge of the bed. It would be hard to win him over to her way of thinking, but she wouldn't give in; she was used to having her own way and she wasn't intending to change for the likes of someone like Robbie Grey.

Will had found a potato in the shape of a man's private parts and had hung it over the stall, knowing the women of Cragstone liked a bit of a laugh. The potato had become the talking point of the day.

'Eeh, Will lad. That reminds me of my owd man, and it's same colour.' The potato was a Red King but was more purple than red.

'Aye.' Another woman joined in the fun. 'It's like my owd man's an' all. All balls and nowt where it matters.'

'I expect that'd be more in your line, Polly.' The first woman picked up a carrot.

'Ger away, now this is more like.' Folly grabbed a foot-long leek and held it up for all the queue to see.

Will never uttered a word. He was happy to have given his customers a bit of a laugh, but he was careful never to cause offence. He couldn't help laughing, however, when a woman picked up a couple of tomatoes and plucked a tiny grape off a bunch. 'Now look 'ere,' she said. 'This is more like what my owd man's got to offer and that's on a good night. On a bad one I can't find it at all.' The queue was in an uproar.

'I'll bet young Will 'ere could show us summat to get excited about. Come on now, Will, is this more like yours?' A large carrot was plucked off the stall and held aloft. By this time Will's cheeks were scarlet.

'Now that'd be telling,' he laughed.

'Shall we find out, ladies?' One of the women twinkled. 'Shall we 'old 'im down and find out?'

Will's face was a picture. He wouldn't put it past this lot to do what they were threatening. The woman laughed and held open her shopping bag.

'Eeh, your face, lad. Come on, weigh me a

shilling's worth of taties, and I'll 'ave that one if yer don't mind. I'll give my owd man a bit of a laugh wi' that, and yer never know, it might ger 'im going if I'm lucky.'

Will weighed the crude-looking vegetable in with the rest and emptied them in her bag. A bit of fun was all very well but he'd better be careful in future with this lot. It had certainly been good for trade though; when he cashed up at the end of the day he found the takings were the best yet. He would have to think up something else to get that lot laughing. It seemed the more they laughed, the more they spent. They were a right lot the Cragstone women; they seemed to think of nothing but sex. It must be the fresh air from the moors. He wished he could find himself a Cragstone girl. Then he thought of Robbie Grey and how miserable he looked since he'd married Prudence. Perhaps he was better off as he was. Still, it would be nice to try it once and see what it was like. He could have asked Robbie, but he didn't see much of him these days. He would just have to wait until the right girl came along, although if it made him as miserable as it seemed to have made Robbie, he might not bother.

Mrs Cooper waited until the tea had brewed before opening the letter from Nellie. The anticipation of wondering what the letter contained was in her opinion as good as reading it. Lily poured the tea as soon as it looked thick enough for the housekeeper's taste, wanting to hurry Mrs Cooper along but knowing she would have to wait. Finally, when the tea was milked and sugared the letter was opened.

'Eeh, lass. Theer's another letter in 'ere with yer mother's name on it. I wonder what that is all about.'

Lily looked at the sealed envelope and read her mam's name. 'Can I open it?'

'What? Why yer certainly can't. Yer don't go round opening other folks's private letters.'

'Ooh! But Mrs Cooper, what can she want to write to me mam about? She's never done it before. She doesn't even know 'er.'

'I don't know. It's nowt to do wi' me any road.' But the housekeeper thought she could guess. From the sound of it the guest house was doing right well and it wouldn't surprise her if Nellie was looking for help. She wouldn't get better than Lily. Oh, but what would she do without the lass? Eeh, she was going to be lost if Lily went gadding off to Blackpool. Still, it might be nowt to do with Lily leaving, and even if it was, her mam might not let her go. She knew she was being selfish by hoping to keep Lily here – there wasn't much for the lass to look forward to up here at the back of beyond. No, if the letter contained what she thought it did, she would wish Lily well.

'Come on then, let's see what Nellie has to say.'

'Can I fetch Larry in for 'is tea? He likes to hear what Nellie 'as to say.'

'Goo on then, and hurry up or it'll 'ave gone cold and we'll 'ave to mash some more.'

By the time Lily had found Larry, Mrs Cooper knew her fears were about to be realised. Nellie had explained to the housekeeper that she couldn't find a waitress with half the wits about her that Lily had, so she'd decided to offer the girl a job. So that was what the enclosed letter was about. She decided not to mention that bit of news to Lily; the lass would be too disappointed if her parents refused permission. Besides, there would be nowt done for the rest of the day if Lily got herself all worked up. Eeh, but she was going to miss her; she was getting too old to be training new folks all the time. Especially young folks of today who thought they knew it all. Times were changing and not all the changes were for the better in her opinion. Still, she supposed Lily was right when she kept telling her she was old-fashioned. 'Come on, get it down yer before it's all stewed; theer's nowt worse than stewed tea.'

Lily was so busy informing Larry about the letter to her mam she wouldn't have noticed what she was drinking, and neither the housekeeper nor Lily noticed that Larry had almost seen off the whole of a date and walnut cake.

Chapter Eighteen

Prudence knew she couldn't pretend any longer. She would have to lose the baby. She waited until her monthly bleeding began and put on the act of her life. Seemingly doubled up with pain, she cried out that something had happened. Of course she played the innocent and never mentioned miscarriage, simply saying she was bleeding and in pain. Louisa, who had grown accustomed to becoming a grandmother once the couple were married, unfortunately didn't act according to her daughter's plan. Instead of keeping the whole thing quiet and being relieved to be free of the shame of it, she hurried for Dr Sellars in an effort to save the baby.

When the doctor entered the room Prudence scowled at her mother, 'I don't think I was pregnant anyway,' she muttered. 'I just missed a few periods, that's all.'

'Well, we shall soon see.' Dr Sellars indicated for Louisa to leave the room. 'I must examine you anyway in order to find out what the trouble is.' When the doctor approached her Prudence drew the eiderdown tightly around her. 'No, there's no point.'

'Oh I think there is. If you've missed a few periods there must be a reason why. Either there's something else wrong or you're pregnant and may be losing your child.'

'I can't be pregnant.'

Dr Sellars removed the bedding from over her patient and gently examined her. When she had finished she told Prudence to cover herself.

'Prudence, why did you say you were having a baby?'

The girl blushed and couldn't meet the doctor's eye. 'I didn't. They just assumed I was.'

'But you didn't deny it?'

Prudence shook her head.

'Despite the fact that you're still a virgin?'

Prudence began to cry. 'That's not my fault; he won't come near me. I hate him.'

Dr Sellars didn't know what to make of the

situation and knew the girl's mother was waiting for an explanation.

Robbie saw the doctor's car at the gate and hurried towards the house just as the doctor came downstairs.

'Mr Grey?' The doctor held out her hand to him.

'Yes, what's wrong? Is it Prudence?' He despised his wife, but all the same he didn't wish her any harm.

'She's losing the child,' Louisa told him and came to comfort Robbie.

'No, she isn't.' The doctor was embarrassed at what she was about to say. 'Prudence has never been pregnant. In fact she is still intact. In other words, Prudence has never had intercourse.' She looked questioningly at Robbie.

'What?' Louisa searched her son-in-law's face for an explanation. 'Robert?'

'I told you I hadn't touched 'er, but nobody believed me, nobody except our John and Lucy. And...' He was about to add and the Greenwoods, but thought it would be inappropriate.

'Do you mean to tell me she accused you of making her pregnant?' asked Dr Sellars.

'Yes, yes she did.'

'Oh, but that wasn't a fair thing to do. I can vouch for the fact that Prudence has never had intercourse. In fact she has admitted that her husband has never touched her.' Dr Sellars smiled at Louisa. 'The good news is that your daughter is healthy. There is nothing wrong with her except a perfectly normal period.' The doctor picked up her bag and prepared to leave. 'Congratulations on your marriage, Mr Grey.

Nice to have met you.' Robbie didn't know whether the doctor was being sarcastic in the circumstances, but he thanked the doctor.

Louisa's face was the colour of parchment after seeing the doctor out. 'Oh Robert, what can I say except I'm sorry?'

'Nothing. It's too late to say anything. I'm stuck in a marriage I never wanted. I don't love Prudence. I never did. It's all a sham. Just to please your daughter and prevent our James from losing his home.'

'Robert, Herbert would never have taken their home away. Jane's doing a marvellous job; the school has never been cleaner.'

'Wouldn't he? We shall see, because I can't stay here. Not now you all know I was telling the truth. I can't live with Prudence's lies any longer.'

'No! No, I can understand that. I'm so sorry. I did doubt what she accused you of but Herbert was so insistent. He thinks our daughter can do no wrong.'

'Now he'll know different. Louisa, I think she needs help. Well, I'll go get my things.'

He went to the wardrobe and removed his shirts and suit from their hangers, then he reached up and lifted down the suitcase.

'What are you doing?' Prudence snapped.

'I'm leaving.'

'You can't. What will people say?'

'I don't know and I don't care.' He opened a drawer, took out his underwear and threw it into the case.

'But we can start afresh now it's all out in the open.'

'You expect me to start afresh with a liar and a cheat?'

'Oh, Robbie, you can't walk out on me; you'll shame my parents.'

'No. *You'll* shame your parents, and I'm sorry about that, but perhaps now your father'll believe me.'

'Please don't tell him. We can just say I've lost the baby.'

Robbie slammed the lid of the case shut. 'You never stop, do you? More lies. Do you think a marriage can survive what you've done?' He lowered his voice. 'You're sick, Prudence. You need help. I'm surprised Dr Sellars didn't suggest you seek some.'

Prudence reached out and picked up the alarm clock Will had bought them, and threw it with all her strength in Robbie's direction.

Fortunately he saw it coming and moved out of its way so that it hit the mirror on the dressing table, shattering the glass, just as Prudence had shattered Robbie's dreams. He picked up the case and left the room, the alarm ringing out behind him.

Robbie had been back at Lucy's for a week. He had been welcomed back without question by his brother. John knew better than to ask for an explanation and it was a few days before the story emerged. Lucy was shocked that the vicar's daughter could have acted so despicably and felt sympathy for the Goodmans. Rumours soon spread about the separation, the cruellest being that Robbie had left his wife because she had suffered a miscarriage. Another being nearer the truth: that Prudence had suffered a brainstorm and tried to kill her husband. Apart from Dr Sellars only the Goodmans and the Greys knew the truth, and for the vicar's sake they vowed to keep it that way. The following Sunday the church was full to capacity, but any of the congregation there out of curiosity were disappointed, as the only thing out of the ordinary was Prudence's absence. By the end of evening service the rumour had been altered so that Prudence had left her husband and run off with someone she had met at the library. As it happened, Prudence had been sent away to stay with her aunt in Liverpool. Robbie didn't know and he certainly didn't care. He held his head high and sang with a lighter heart than he had felt for weeks. People watched with gaping mouths as Robbie paused at the lychgate after the service, to be greeted by the vicar and exchange pleasantries with Louisa. Nobody knew what to make of the situation, least of all Dot Greenwood.

Lucy was not only delighted to have Robbie back in the fold but also relieved to have heard nothing more concerning Mary's wish to adopt Bernard. If she had but known, it was all down to Jacob, who had now made it clear that he would never consider the adoption of Evelyn's child. He was suffering for his wilfulness as Mary blamed her husband for refusing to cooperate. Lucy was right: her sister had turned bitter and Mary's mood was reflected in the clothes she wore as well as her attitude. The net curtains were still immaculate, the aspidistra still watered, the cellar steps still scrubbed and donkey-stoned and the house bottomed once a week as usual. But Mary rarely smiled, never stood at her door chatting with the neighbours and had let herself go. She had taken to covering her hair with a mob-cap in the way of a much older woman. Jacob wondered what had happened to the lovely woman he had married and begged her to cheer up and wear the pretty clothes that hung amongst the lavender bags in the wardrobe.

'What does a barren woman want to look glamorous for?' Mary would sigh and either take up her embroidery or bury her head in a book. In the end Jacob went to Lucy for advice, judging her to be more compassionate than Jane. 'I don't know how to handle her, Lucy. She's blaming me for refusing to adopt your little lad.'

'Well, I thank you for that, Jacob. I'll come and talk to her though I don't see as I can help. You must make enquiries about adopting, Jacob. But not Bernard,' she added worriedly.

'She won't even discuss it. She's so withdrawn I can't seem to communicate anymore. And I swear she's as miserable as your mother used to be.' Jacob blushed as he realised what he had said. 'I'm sorry, lass.'

'It's all right. She did remind me of my mother on her last visit. Oh, why can't she become pregnant?'

'Aye, but why can't she be satisfied with what we've got? After all, Jane isn't always hankering after a child.'

Lucy smiled. 'Our Jane has a different outlook

altogether. If the truth be known she wouldn't want anyone intruding in her neatly organised life. Not even a baby. No! She's quite satisfied with being able to spoil my two then go back home to her nice, comfortable life with James. Besides, she's her job to occupy her days. She finds all the satisfaction she needs by keeping the school up to standard. And the children adore her. They bring her flowers, draw her pictures, lots of little things they do out of affection for her. No, our Jane's perfectly happy with the present carry on. Besides, she and James wouldn't be able to go gallivanting every weekend. He's talking about buying a motorbike now; I heard him discussing it with our Ben. Then we shan't see them for dust.' Lucy laughed and she even noticed a smile appear on Jacob's worried face.

'So you'll come and see her then?' he appealed.

'Yes I will, but I might not be welcome. I'll do my best, Jacob. She's my sister and I hate this awkwardness between us.'

'Aye. But it isn't your fault.'

Lucy frowned. 'No, but the trouble is our Mary thinks it is.' Lucy sighed. 'She wanted Bernard and I stood in her way.'

Jacob raised his trilby to his sister-in-law and went on his way. Lucy watched him leave and thought it sad that Jacob's jaunty way of walking had disappeared; his shoulders were rounded and his walk had slowed, as if he didn't really want to go home. And who could blame him, with his wife in her present frame of mind?

'Ooh, Mrs Cooper, it'll be awful leaving you.'

The tears trailed down Lily's face at the thought of not seeing her beloved housekeeper.

'Now stop that. Oh you are a silly Lily. Don't yer see that you'll never get another opportunity to mek summat of yerself and see a bit of life? Why, yer'll be able to go dancing on the pier or in't tower.' Lily thought Mrs Cooper looked sad as she mentioned the tower.

'I can't dance.' Lily's eyes were still brimming with tears, but this time from the onions Mr Brown had delivered that morning and would soon be part of a hot pot.

'Well, it'll not be long before yer can. Yer'll 'ave all't lads in Blackpool running after a pretty lass like you. But yer must behave yerself. They'll be out for a bit of hanky-panky so you just mek sure they don't get any. It's the air, yer see. Finest air in England, and it's got the finest promenade.'

'Has it really? Finest prom in England?'

Mrs Cooper thought she might have exaggerated a bit. 'Well, I can't say I've seen many. Only Whitby. Now I've got to admit that that's a prettier place altogether, what with its harbour and abbey, but as for't promenade, aye I reckon Blackpool's best in England.'

'Yer will be all right won't yer? When I've gone I mean.'

'Course I shall. New cook's shaping up nicely even if she isn't Nellie, and I shall 'ave your Molly to shout at, shan't I?'

Lily giggled. 'Ooh I am glad me dad said she could come and work 'ere. If ee hadn't put 'is foot down me mam'd never 'ave let 'er.'

'I don't think it's good for a young lass stuck at

’ome all day.’

‘I know, but me mam says she needs ’er to ’elp with all’t housework and to look after the little ones. She says she gets backache doing all’t work ’erself.’ Lily giggled. ‘Me dad says the only thing wrong wi’ me mam is idleitis.’

‘There’s only one thing.’ Mrs Cooper frowned. ‘I shall ’ave to keep me eye on your Molly and Larry. What with her fancying ’im and ’im fancying her, I shall need eyes in’t back of me ’ead.’

‘Ooh, I think our Molly’ll behave ’erself. Me dad warned ’er that if she don’t she’ll ’ave to go back ’ome again, and she won’t want that.’

‘Fair enough. Even so, I’d better give Larry a warning an’ all.’

‘What if I can’t do it right?’ Lily looked about to burst into tears again.

‘Can’t do what right?’

‘Serving all them people and ’elping wi’ the cooking and everything.’

‘Why, yer daft haporth. Yer’ve been doing all that for the past year or two.’

‘I know, but people in Blackpool might be posher.’

‘Will they heck as like. Now look ’ere. Nellie and Mr Johnson know ’ow capable you are – that’s providing yer don’t burst into tears every time anybody says owt to yer. Now that’s one habit yer’ll ’ave to grow out of. Yer can’t be dripping tears into’t soup all’t time, now can yer?’

Lily laughed, then she found something else to worry about: ‘Ooh, Nellie says I shall be taking the place of Mr Johnson’s mother. I shall never be able to do all them lovely flower thingies, like she did for't wedding.'

'Flower arrangements, yer mean. Course yer will. They'll not be wanting great fancy arrangements like them, not every day. Just a few flowers on each table and in each bedroom. I expect Nellie'll be doing them in't lounge. Any road up, she'll teach yer all that sort of thing. She wouldn't 'ave sent for yer if she didn't think yer were capable. And stop getting into such a tiswas, yer'll be meeting yerself coming back one o' these days.'

'Ooh, Mrs Cooper, you always say summat to cheer me up, even when I'm scared. I don't know what I shall do wi'out yer.'

'Yer'll manage.' It's me who'll be lost, the housekeeper thought. She sighed as she filled in the week's outgoings in the ledger. Oh well, at least she'd have young Molly. Besides, the new cook was shaping up right nicely; in fact she was growing quite fond of her.

By December, Lucy's stomach felt as big as a sack of potatoes. Her legs continued to swell and John begged her to rest in the afternoon.

'I'm fine,' she told him. 'I've never felt better.' Actually she did put her feet up for an hour every day when Mrs Slater took charge of Bernard and Rosie. Then the two women would enjoy a chat and a cup of tea together as they watched Bernard push the brightly painted wheelbarrow Robbie had made for him up the yard and back again, filling it with stones along the way. 'Just look at them cheeks,' Mrs Slater said. Bernard's cheeks were as red as the gloves and helmet Lucy had knitted over the past week. 'Ee looks, the picture of 'ealth does that little lad.'

'Evelyn would have been so proud of him,' Lucy sighed.

'Oh well, soon be Christmas.' Enid changed the subject as she dipped a digestive in her tea.

'Yes.' Lucy was looking forward to the festivities. 'I should have enough in the Christmas club to get him and Rosie a few presents and something for our Will and Robbie.'

'Has he heard owt yet from that no-good wife of 'is?'

'Not a word. Something'll have to be done, though I've no idea what. He can't go on wasting his life in this way. He's so wrapped up in his work, which I suppose is a good thing as it's taking his mind off the problem, but it needs solving.'

'Aye, a young man like 'im should be on top of't world, whereas Robbie's world is neither one thing or another. What good's a wife who's gone absent?'

'In my opinion she's better absent.'

'Well, that's as may be, but whilst ee's stuck with her he can't be with the lass ee loves.'

'Namely, Dot Greenwood.'

'Aye. According to our Ernest Robbie worships the lass. Eeh, it's wicked what that lass 'as done to 'im.'

Much as Lucy trusted Mrs Slater she sometimes wished she'd never revealed the truth to her about Robbie's marriage; she tended to go on a bit once she got started and it wasn't something Lucy cared to gossip about. 'I've ordered a couple of fowls from Greenwood's farm for Christmas.'

'Aye, I shall 'ave to see about one I suppose.' Mrs Slater took the tea things to the sink and washed them. 'I suppose you'll be 'aving a quiet Christmas Day; I mean you'll be nearing yer time by then.'

'Oh I shall invite our Jane and Ben. I don't suppose our Mary'll grace us with her presence.'

'No improvement then?'

'None. I feel so sorry for Jacob. He really loves this family. I shall invite them all the same. I wish our Nellie could be here; I really miss her.'

'Aye, still the lass is doing well by the sound of it. Yer dad'd 'ave been right proud of her. And yer mam,' she added as an afterthought. 'Oh aye, she'd 'ave been proud of you all, especially that little flower in't pram.'

'Yes, I'm sure they would, but I wish our Mary could have one all the same.'

'Aye, still it'll happen if it's God's will.'

Lucy laughed. 'You sounded just like my mother when you said that.'

'Well I daresay she's 'ere somewhere, putting words in me mouth.'

'Yes I expect she is.' Lucy was surprised how the thought of her mother's presence comforted her. If only Annie Gabbitas's spirit would visit Mary and tell her to buck herself up, otherwise poor Jacob's life wouldn't be worth living.

Dot Greenwood had finished work for the day. The poultry orders had been delivered along with the potatoes and eggs. The farmhouse had been fettled from top to bottom and trimmed with greenery from down the lane. Pies both sweet and savoury were cooling on the kitchen table and muslin-coated puddings were simmering merrily over the fire. Tomorrow would be a busy day with Little Arthur's sister and her family and Boadacea's parents here for the day. Christ's birthday was usually celebrated with one big party and only essential farmwork being done. This year however, everyone seemed to be putting on an act to cheer each other. If anyone had voiced their thoughts they would have admitted that only Robbie Grey's presence would have brought out the Christmas spirit.

Dot wandered out to the derelict old cottage attached to the main house. Not long ago she had imagined her and Robbie living there. The stone walls would have been pointed, the windows and doors replaced – Robbie could have done that easily enough – and the inside walls plastered. That would have been all the work needed to make the sturdy old dwelling habitable. She wandered from kitchen to front room, then up the crooked staircase and into the main bedroom, bending to avoid the low doorway. There was even a wardrobe standing dusty but proud against the far wall. She cleared a patch on the mirror and stared at her reflection, at her hair which needed trimming and the dark smudges beneath her eyes. Christmas Eve and here she was still in her working clothes. It wouldn't do. She would doll herself up a bit and go out. There would be a dance at the Victoria Hall, and after that she would go to midnight mass. She couldn't waste her life away fretting about somebody who was unavailable. It would please her parents if she went out. There was no point in spoiling their Christmas. No, she would put on her powder and her best dress and a smile.

She walked out and into the other bedroom, her working shoes echoing in the empty house. This was the room rumoured to be haunted. People on the opposite hill often reported seeing a light shining in the window on certain nights of the year. Some of the old timers said it was a shepherd who used to live here, lighting his lamp after a day's work. Little Arthur said it was the moon's reflection on the glass but Boadacea said the grime on the window of the old place was too thick to reflect anything. Dot kept an open mind. Sometimes she thought she heard footsteps on the stairs, which were on the other side of her bedroom wall. If there was a ghost, Dot could understand it being unwilling to leave, the view from this room being the finest of the whole farm. Anyway, the spirit of a shepherd would hurt nobody. Someone who cared for his flock and tended the lambs would most likely watch over humans with the same tenderness. She had envisaged the cot there by the window and a rocking horse in the corner.

Now the cottage would stay empty and sad and without Robbie there would be no baby. If she couldn't have him to father her children she would remain unmarried, an old maid. But tonight was Christmas Eve, so she would make the best of things, for her parents' sake, despite the emptiness and sorrow deep within her. She hurried downstairs. She would carry the zinc bath, into the front room and soak in water scented by her mother's herbs. Then she would go and join Mable and the rest of the crowd, and pray that if Robbie happened to be present she would have the strength to act as though she didn't care.

Whilst Will and Robbie were out on the town, Lucy and John were content to sit by the fire, Lucy listening to the wireless and John reading the *Star*. 'Do you think Bernard will be asleep yet?' Lucy couldn't wait to play Father Christmas to the little ones.

'There's no rush.' John rose to his feet. 'I'll go see.' Lucy gazed round the kitchen with pride. It was warm, comfortable and filled with the delicious aromas of spice from the hot mince pies, ham simmering over the fire and oranges waiting to go in the children's stockings. The wishing mirror looked beautiful decked with holly, and in the front room – which had been cleaned and polished within an inch of its life – a Christmas tree filled the air with the scent of pine.

The children were delighted with the twinkling glass ornaments and stars. John had bought a cardboard Santa Claus on a sleigh pulled by reindeers, the bright red of Santa's coat and the brown coats of the reindeers shimmering with silver. It was in the centre of the dresser and Lucy had explained that because Bernard had been a good boy a real Santa would be bringing presents for him and Rosie. 'When we are all fast asleep he will fly on a sledge pulled by reindeers up onto the roof, then he will climb down the chimney and bring you presents.' Bernard had looked at the Santa on the dresser and thought about the fireplace in the bedroom and decided that the real Santa must be much thinner than this one, otherwise he would never fit down the chimney.

'He will because he's magic,' John had reassured him, considering that for someone of only four years old Bernard was not someone to have the wool pulled over his eyes. However the little boy had hung up the clean pillow cases on the bed knob and Rosie's cot and hoped that Santa didn't fall down the chimney and wake Rosie.

'They're both fast on.' John went to the cupboard near the fire and brought out the toys, accumulated over the past weeks. A teddy bear for Rosie and a push-along horse – made by Robbie – which would no doubt help Rosie to walk during the next few months. Jane had bought brightly-coloured building bricks and Will a squeaky duck for the bath. For Bernard there was a pedal cycle painted bright red, which the little boy had long considered his favourite colour. A *Playbox* annual and a box of crayons and colouring book, an orange, an apple and a sugar mouse completed Bernard's gifts.

'We're so fortunate,' Lucy said when they were once more settled by the fire.

'Aye.' John looked at Lucy, her face flushed in the firelight. 'I reckon I'm the luckiest man on earth.' He went into the front room and came back with a bottle of port wine, poured two small glasses and handed one to Lucy. 'Happy Christmas, my love.' He clinked his glass against hers, took a sip and placed it on the table and took her in his arms. 'I love you, Lucy Grey, and I wish you your happiest year ever.' Then they turned towards the wishing mirror and Lucy said, 'So long as I'm here with you and our children it will be the happiest of years, cos I love you, John Grey, and love is all that matters.' Then she kissed her husband, there in the warmth of the fire, in a kitchen overflowing with love.

The music could be heard along the main road as Dot approached the dance hall. The lights from the high windows welcomed her in the darkness. 'Dot!' The ticket seller called out as she entered the room, 'Long time no see.'

Dot took out her purse and bought a ticket. 'Is Mable here?'

'Was. Nipped out for a quick drink with all your crowd, but I reckon they'll be back any minute.'

Dot smiled and went through to the cloakroom. She was glad she'd arrived late or they would have persuaded her to accompany them to the Golden Ball and Dot never felt comfortable in pubs, not even the Ball, which was considered a more respectable establishment than the Sun. She straightened her dress and powdered her nose, then she ventured out into the dance hall. A barn dance was in progress and one or two of the twirling dancers waved and smiled. One thing about Millington was that everybody seemed to know everyone else. Lewis Marshall sauntered over and stood by Dot. 'All right?' he asked. 'Well, yer look all right. In fact yer look beautiful.' She did.

'Thanks.' Dot liked Lewis. She wished he could find himself a nice girl and settle down, but everyone knew that the girl he wanted had fallen hook, line and sinker for John Grey. Now Lewis was in the same boat as her. A new dance began. 'Come on Lewis, let's do this. I like a foxtrot.' She pulled Lewis onto the dance floor. They chatted about what was happening tomorrow then Lewis suddenly said, 'He loves you, Dot.'

'What?' She stopped dancing and stared up at Lewis.

'Robbie. He'll not rest until he's free to marry you.'

Dot smiled sadly. 'Maybe, but when will that be?'

'I don't know,' Lewis grinned. 'But like my owd dad always says, "Weer theer's life, theer's hope, lad. Weer theer's life, theer's hope."'

Dot giggled at his impression of his father. 'Oh, Lewis, you're lovely, do you know that?'

'Oh aye, I'm lovely, me. Trouble is the lass I wanted didn't think so. So I reckon you're the most fortunate of the two of us.'

Dot squeezed his hand. 'Well, seeing as it's Christmas let's enjoy ourselves. Come on, I'll buy you a lemonade.' As they circled the room and approached the refreshment room Dot saw the door of the cloakroom open and a crowd enter the room. Amongst them Robbie Grey stood out, taller and straighter than the rest. His eyes lit up as he noticed Dot and for a second love was there for all to see. Then they tore their gaze away from each other and Lewis led Dot away for refreshment. She fixed a smile on her face and decided to ignore Robbie; she couldn't trust herself to look at him, let alone try and make conversation. The best thing to do would be to partner Lewis for the evening. They would be a comfort to each other, two lovesick souls together.

Will was in high spirits and intended enjoying himself this Christmas. When he had gone to collect his wage packet this afternoon, Mr Brown had told Will to sit himself down and 'ave a drink to celebrate. Will had sat himself on a hundred-weight sack of potatoes, surrounded by nets of onions and orange boxes and sipped at his drink.

'Happy Christmas, Mr Brown.' He had never got used to using his boss's Christian name; it didn't seem right somehow.

'And to thee, lad. Though it's not the festival I'm celebrating at the moment.' He sipped his drink and rubbed his chin with his thumb. 'I've been thinking, lad. Does tha know, since I took thee on I've been raking money in. That stall at Cragstone's making almost as much in one day as I used to mek in a week. And it's all down to thee.'

Will felt his face growing hot with pleasure. Praise from Mr Brown was praise indeed. 'Well it's good stuff I'm selling; they're always remarking on that.'

'Aye, but it's thee who's selling it. They've taken to thee, Will. Tha's got a way about thee. A born trader, I reckon.'

'Perhaps it's because I like me job. I like delivering to't canteen and going to't wholesale market, but most of all I like doing the stalls.'

'Well, choose how, I'm giving thee a rise. Tha sees I don't want thee leaving and I've been told somebody else's after thee to go and work for 'im.'

'Oh I shan't leave. I love me job.'

'Aye, I've noticed, so I've given thee a rise,

starting from now.'

'Well, thanks very much.'

'And not only that, I'm going to learn thee to drive. And when yer've mastered it I'm going to get thee a van.'

Will was speechless. He gulped as the tears rose to his eyes.

'Oh don't get yerself all excited – it'll be nowt posh, just summat second 'and if I can find owt. Then I can concentrate on the other jobs instead of 'aving to fetch and carry thee about. I thought we might 'ave a stall over in Warrentickle in time, let thee run the stalls full time. Would tha like that?'

'Course I would. I don't know what to say, except thanks.'

'Aye well, don't get carried away. Tha 'asn't learned to drive yet.'

'No but I shall.'

'Well, get thi'sen off then. I've put thee a bonus in for Christmas. Don't spend it all at once.'

'Thanks again.' Will took the pay packet and set off out of the rickety old shed.

'Happy Christmas,' the greengrocer called after him.

'And the same to you.' Will's face was wreathed in smiles. He must be the most fortunate lad in Millington. He might even get drunk to celebrate. Well, perhaps not. He'd go to the dance and maybe find himself a girl. Now that would be summat to celebrate, summat indeed. Will didn't get drunk, but he did have a couple of glasses at the Golden Ball and was feeling slightly merry when he returned to the dance hall with the others. He was standing watching the dancers and enjoying the music when he saw her. It was unusual not to know everybody in Millington, but he hadn't seen her before. Standing near the stage she looked shy and uncomfortable all on her own. Her hair was the most beautiful shade of brown, chestnut actually, and it fell in waves around her shoulders. From where he was standing her eyes looked to be the same warm shade, sparkling in the lights from the stage. Will was no dancer and had never felt inclined to take to the floor but he walked across the room and asked her if she'd care to dance.

Blushing, she looked towards the twirling couples. 'I'd love to but I don't know how to do this.'

Will grinned. 'No, neither do I. I just wanted an excuse to talk to you, that's all. I'm Will Gabbitas, by the way.'

'Pleased to meet you, Will. I'm Elizabeth but everyone calls me Betty, Betty Hague.'

'Well I shall call you Betty Brown Eyes.' He blushed as he added, 'I love yer dress.' It was a pretty dress, the same blue as a summer sky, but it wasn't the dress Will was admiring. It was Betty's face, her slight build and her shapely legs, but especially her eyes. In fact Will Gabbitas – for the first time in his life – was in love, and even the promise of a brand new van couldn't have lured him away from Betty Brown Eyes. They moved on to the dance floor even though they had no idea what the dance was supposed to be. It didn't matter; it was an excuse to be close to each other. It was indeed going to be a happy Christmas for

Will. The happiest ever.

Robbie didn't dance. If he couldn't dance with Dot he wouldn't dance at all, and Dot had dragged poor Lewis onto the floor for everything from the conga to the tango. He watched them twirl by in a quickstep and oh, how he envied Lewis Marshall holding Dot in his arms.

When the last waltz had been played and the national anthem came to an end most of the gang made their way home. A few set off to church, some to St Catherine's, others, including Dot Greenwood, to the parish church. Robbie hadn't intended going to midnight mass. He didn't have the same respect for Herbert Goodman as he once had. Perhaps he should forgive and forget the way he had manipulated him into marrying his daughter. After all, he and Louisa had been good to him and his brothers until Prudence had ruined his life – and that of her parents too he supposed. Yes, he would go to mass. It might make him feel better, though he doubted he would ever feel better again.

James and Jane were amongst the congregation and he went to join them. The strains of 'In The Bleak Midwinter' rose to the rafters of the lovely old church, bringing back memories to Robbie of his mother and father and his childhood. He felt the tears threatening. Tears that should have been shed at the time of his parents' death and had been withheld because of the shock and the loss of their home. Somehow there had never been time to mourn. He felt James's hand grip hold of his and knew his brother was feeling as emotional as he was. He blinked back the tears – he was a man, not a weepy child. He saw Dot across the aisle, standing with Mable. He sighed. Oh he was a man all right, a man who had been duped into a marriage that was nothing but a sham.

The choir began to sing, 'While Shepherds Watched' and the beauty of their voices seemed to lift him out of his melancholy so that he sang out with the other worshippers. Herbert Goodman met his eye and Robbie smiled and nodded. He thought he saw relief in the vicar's eyes and Robbie felt better. Life was too short to bear grudges; besides, he had to start afresh in the new year. He had a divorce to organise, though he had no idea how to go about it or how long it would take. No matter: if it took years to achieve his aim he would in the end be free to marry the girl he loved.

For the first time since her marriage, Nellie was feeling homesick. Even Christmas at the manor had meant she had time to celebrate at least a few hours with her family. She had sent off presents for them all. Warm winter clothes for the children, perfume for her sisters and Emma, and kid gloves for the men. Nellie appreciated how lucky she was to be able to afford such luxuries. Had it not been for her husband she would never have been in this situation. She fixed a smile on her face and accepted that Tom was her family now and he was everything she had ever wanted. Christmas would be lovely in her new home. Even so she would miss Top Row. She would miss her sisters and she would miss Mrs Cooper. Tom's mother was cooking dinner on Christmas Day. Nellie had offered to help, but she wouldn't hear of it. Half a dozen friends and relatives had been invited and Margaret Johnson was in her element. Tom would have liked an excuse to avoid such a formal party and had a feeling Nellie felt the same. On arriving home after drinks with friends on Christmas Eve he broached the subject to his wife, waiting until they were tucked up warm and snug in bed.

'Nellie?'

'Yes?' Nellie snuggled closer.

'Would you like to go for a drive tomorrow?'

Nellie sat up in bed. 'A drive? On Christmas Day?'

'Why not?'

'Well, for one thing we're expected at your parents', and another thing, nobody goes for a drive on Christmas Day.'

'Why not?'

'Well!' Nellie couldn't think of a reason. 'They just don't.'

'Not even to Yorkshire?'

Nellie stared at Tom. 'Are you serious? You'd actually take me home?'

Tom grinned. 'No, this is your home. I mean to Millington.'

Nellie's eyes filled with tears, then she sank back onto the pillow. 'We can't, we can't let your mother and father down. They're expecting us.'

Nellie had grown to love her parents-in-law and they had shown in many small gestures that they were proud of Nellie and that they loved her dearly. Nellie knew they would understand her need to be with her family at this time of the year. Even so she didn't like the thought of neglecting

Tom's parents on such a special day.

'I'm sure they won't mind. In fact I bet they'll be happier with us out of the way. Nellie, they're all of a different generation. Do you really want to spend Christmas Day playing bridge, or charades, or whatever it is people of their age do?'

Nellie giggled. 'Not really, but they'll be upset. I mean, everyone spends Christmas Day with their parents.'

'So let's be different.'

'Really?'

'Yes, we'll take their presents early in the morning and then go.'

'Oh, Tom. I can just imagine their faces when we arrive at our Lucy's.'

'How do you know they'll be in? They might be at Jane's or Mary's, or even Ben's.'

'They won't. Lucy's is the family home. It wouldn't be the same anywhere but at Top Row.'

'Ah, but Lucy might be tired, what with her being pregnant again. And with Rosie and Bernard maybe they won't be entertaining this year.'

Nellie was adamant that Lucy would be at home. 'If we're to be up early we'd better get some shut eye.' She snuggled down again into her husband's arms. 'Although I'm not sure I'm sleepy just yet.' Her hand moved down and she undid Tom's pyjama cord, slipping the bottoms down out of the way. His erection proved that Tom wasn't sleepy either and Nellie lifted the satin of her nightdress and moved astride her husband. 'A happy Christmas, Tom,' she said.

'Oh it's certainly that,' he moaned as they moved together towards another exquisite climax.

It was still not quite light and already the sugar mouse and the rosy red apple had been devoured. If Bernard could have peeled the orange, no doubt that would have been eaten too. Now he was riding round the bedroom on the fairy cycle, ringing the bell which had woken the whole house and set Rosie off screaming at the unfamiliar sound.

'You stay there.' John tucked the eiderdown beneath Lucy's chin. 'It's early and cold and the fire'll need making up.' He lifted Rosie from her cot and examined the toys from Father Christmas, exclaiming in wonder of them, much to Bernard's delight. 'Shall we see what he's brought for Rosie?'

The little boy took the toys from Rosie's pillow case, throwing them aside after a quick glance and returning to his travels on the red bike. Rosie, having been woken too soon, was heavy-eyed and by the time John had placed her back in her cot was already asleep. 'Come on, let's take all these downstairs and play in front of the fire, then when Mam gets up she can see what Father Christmas has brought.'

'I want to carry my bike.' Bernard had no intention of letting go of the tricycle; Father Christmas might come back and take it away again. He struggled downstairs with John walking in front in case he should stumble or drop the precious toy. John built up the fire and placed the drawtin in front. Soon it was roaring away and the kitchen was warm enough for Lucy to come down to a breakfast of toast spread with dripping. The toys had to be enthused over once again and then twice later by Will and Robbie. Lucy looked round at her family with satisfaction and placed a hand on her belly, where it felt as if her unborn child was dancing a jig and joining in the excitement of it all.

After breakfast Will brought out the bag of vegetables he had brought home and began to prepare a mound of parsnips, brussels sprouts and potatoes, enough to feed a regiment. Robbie placed the fowls in the oven, making sure they were covered in goose grease – just as he remembered his mother doing – and then proceeded to set the table in the front room in the manner of Louisa Goodman, with candles and holly for decoration. Lucy was ordered to lie back on the sofa and rest her feet ready for when her company arrived. John, who realised how lost Louisa and Herbert must be feeling, decided to take the children on a visit, which was slow going as Bernard wouldn't be parted from his pedal cycle. The welcome from the vicar and his wife was well worth the drawn-out back-aching walk, especially when Jane and James turned up too, all of them knowing how much the couple must be missing their only daughter.

At twelve Ben and Emma arrived with Mrs Scott in tow. Then James and Jane. Jane filled the house with expensive perfume sent by Nellie. At one she poured the vegetable stock into the fat and made the gravy, its delicious aroma even overpowering her scent. Then she made the sauce for the pudding and all was ready. Jane actually felt quite proud of herself. Lucy was just serving the brown crispy roast potatoes when

Jacob and Mary walked in.

'Oh! You've just come right.' Lucy went to kiss her sister, so relieved she had decided to come, even if it was only for Jacob's sake.

'We shan't stay long,' Mary muttered. 'Only we've brought one or two things for our nephew and niece.'

'Of course you must stay.' John indicated for them to take off their coats. 'There's enough grub to feed an army.' Then he whispered in Mary's ear, 'Thanks for coming; you'll have made Lucy's day. And thanks for these. We've already fed the kids, so if you give them to them now we might get our dinners in peace.'

Bernard's eyes lit up at the sight of the wooden ark, complete with animals and even the fairy cycle was cast temporarily aside as he set out the elephants and lions two by two on the rug. Even Rosie was kept engrossed throughout the meal with the beautifully illustrated nursery rhyme book. Lucy considered it rather too old for her and prayed Rosie wouldn't rip it up or try to eat it until after Mary had gone home, but amazingly she seemed fascinated with turning the pages so everyone managed to enjoy the festive dinner in peace, with Will and Robbie acting as waiters. Will kept them entertained and almost in stitches with a stream of jokes and stories about his Cragstone ladies. The party was only slightly spoiled when Mary nudged a jovial Jacob in the ribs and told him, 'Jacob, stop laughing like that. You'll do yerself an injury.'

Uncharacteristically, Jacob – who had been fortified with a bottle of brown ale – had an answer for his wife. 'Mary,' he said, 'I can't think of a better way to go than to die of laughing.'

Lucy couldn't help but smile at Jacob's response as she piled all the uneaten vegetables into one tureen. Jane placed the large, fruity pudding on the table as Lucy surveyed the leftovers. There was still a whole breast and a leg on one of the fowls.

'There's enough left there for tomorrow's dinner,' Mary said.

'Yes, there is.' Lucy looked thoughtful. 'But I've a better idea,' she said. Lucy knew Mrs Murphy had had a hard time this Christmas making ends meet and would probably be feeding her family with a pan of stew or some other everyday fare. Mr Murphy's chest complaint had worsened in the past year and he had been off work now for months. 'I'm going to take this to the Murphys; the vegetables'll fill them up and the poultry'll seem like a feast to them, even if it's only a mouthful each.'

Jane was just about to dish out the pudding. 'Here, you can take them my portion of pudding.' She patted her flat tummy. 'I couldn't eat another mouthful.'

'Aye,' Mary said, 'take them mine too. I bet the poor little mites have never even seen a pudding, let alone tasted it.' Lucy smiled gratefully at her sisters.

'Well I'm full up to 'ere.' James placed a hand on his chin.

'All right, all right,' John grinned. 'Who wants any pudding?' Nobody answered.

Then Will asked, 'Who wants a mince pie

instead?' Everybody answered at once so Will plucked a twig of holly from the mirror and stuck it in the middle of the pudding. So with John carrying the meat, Lucy the vegetables and Will the pudding, off they went to the Murphys. 'I feel like we're the three kings bearing gifts,' Will quipped.

The Murphys were just saying grace. A hot pot stood in the middle of the table – which for once was covered by a cloth. At the sight of the food, tears filled Mr Murphy's eyes and trickled down to land on his whiskers. 'Praise be,' he said. 'The Holy Mother has answered my prayers and helped to feed my family.'

One of the younger boys, his eyes round at the sight of the first Christmas pudding he had ever seen, answered his father. 'No, Dad. It's not the Holy Mary, it's Mrs Grey.'

'Aye, lad. It might be Mrs Grey, but she's a blooming angel all the same.'

The skinniest of the little girls giggled. 'No, she isn't, she 'asn't got any wings.'

'Wings don't grow until you die,' her brother answered knowingly. 'And then they sprout and carry you to heaven.'

'Is that a real Christmas pie? Like in my nursery rhyme book?'

The book was one of the gifts bought by the eldest of the Murphy girls, who was the only breadwinner in the family at present. She had made sure each of her brothers and sisters had received a present from Father Christmas. The nursery rhyme book – although second-hand – was so precious to the little girl it had remained on her lap throughout the morning. She opened it now and compared the real Christmas pudding to the one in the book.

'Aye, it is that.' Mr Murphy had shared out the poultry, and his wife the vegetables. With a helping of thick gravy from the hot pot there was sufficient for them all.

The Greys had departed with a cheerful 'Merry Christmas' from Will to the family.

'Aye, and the same to you and yours. And may God bless you all. Well then, let's send into this 'ere feast before it gets cold.'

Mr Murphy took a bite of the succulent chicken and gazed round at the children of whom he was so proud, then at his wife, who was so worn down by childbearing and worry about how to make ends meet and had never been known to utter a word of complaint. He hoped things would be easier in a year or two when some of the older ones started work. And maybe God would see fit to give him back his health and strength, so that he could return to the pit. Today however, they would enjoy this meal and afterwards with full bellies they might even enjoy a few carols and a game or two. In fact, this was beginning to seem like a real family Christmas, and it was all down to that lass, Lucy Grey.

Nellie and Tom arrived at the manor in time for lunch, intending to cadge a bite to eat off Mrs Cooper. However, the sound of the car drawing into the yard drew the attention of Mr Smith, who came hurrying down to greet the visitors. He was supposed to be enjoying a relaxing day but was bored, lonely and miserable. In the kitchen he found his housekeeper in tears at the arrival of her beloved Nellie. Mrs Cooper had cooked a brace of pheasants, made succulent by the bacon rashers enfolding them.

'You must join me for lunch.' Mr Smith turned to Mrs Cooper. 'That's if there will be enough for us all?'

'Plenty. Though it's just simple fare, seeing as I've given Cook the day off. I knew I could cope it just being the two of us, like. All there is to do is mek the sauce; that'll tek but two minutes.'

'Well, we weren't expecting lunch, but if you're sure?' Nellie took off her coat and began to make the sauce. 'If you don't mind I'd like to eat here with Mrs Cooper.' She looked at Tom. 'But you go to the dining room and catch up on the news.'

'I have a better idea if my housekeeper has no objections,' said Mr Smith. 'Why don't we all eat here in the kitchen? It's much warmer than upstairs.'

Mrs Cooper blushed the colour of the berries on the holly in the window. 'Nay, it's not up to me to object. You're the boss; choose how.'

'Not today, I'm not. We're four friends about to enjoy Christmas dinner together, on what might have been the loneliest day of the year for me. So when you're ready give us a call. Now, whilst we're waiting, Tom, why don't I take a look at that magnificent motor of yours?'

'Ooh, Nellie, thank goodness ee's gone. Fancy 'im wanting to eat in 'ere with me present. I shall be all fingers and thumbs, a nervous wreck.'

'Don't be daft. Let's all enjoy ourselves; after all it is Christmas. Now is everything ready?'

'Oh, Nellie, it is grand to see yer. I miss yer all't time. Though the new lass is shaping up all right, I must admit.'

'I'm glad. I miss you too, you know. It will be nice to have Lily though. And you are to come and stay when the weather picks up, for as long as you like.'

'Eeh, that'll be right grand, though I shall 'ave to wait until young Molly's got the run of things.'

'Whenever, you'll always be welcome.' Nellie opened the black shiny oven door and released the delicious aroma of pheasant. 'Right, shall I serve?'

'Aye, lass, get it dished up. And don't expect me to join in any conversation; I shall be too busy watching me manners.'

Nellie laughed. 'We shall all be too busy enjoying your cooking to bother conversing. Right, I'll go drag them away from the car if I can. By the way, take off those shoes and put these on.' Nellie undid the laces of the black leather shoes and slipped on the lovely soft carpet slippers. 'Happy Christmas.' She gave Mrs Cooper a kiss and hurried out to find her husband, leaving the housekeeper feeling the most cherished woman in the world. It was a long time since she'd had a pair of new slippers and even longer since she'd had a kiss. Mrs Cooper didn't join in the conversation during the meal, but she had a smile on her face all the same.

As usual the arrival of the car on Top Row sent all the youngsters out into the street. Fortunately most of them had already finished their special dinner, otherwise the mothers would have given Tom Johnson what for. Lucy wouldn't have noticed; all she cared about was that with the arrival of Nellie her family was now complete. 'Oh, Nellie, why didn't you come in time for dinner?'

'It's all right, we've eaten at the manor. But I'd love a cup of tea.' Jane rushed to make one and John handed Tom a glass and a bottle of stout. The kitchen was almost bursting at the seams as the men abandoned their cards on the front room table and left their game of Crib unfinished to greet the unexpected guests.

It wasn't until Robbie took Bernard to feed the flock of recently acquired hens that Nellie asked 'Where's Prudence?'

'Oh!' Lucy realised that nobody had thought to tell Nellie what had happened and a hasty explanation was given. It wasn't until later that John gave Tom all the details and told Tom how worried they all were about the situation his brother now found himself in. 'He needs to divorce her, but how to go about it is beyond me. Actually none of us know anyone who's ever been divorced.'

'If you wish I'll have a word with a friend of mine who's a lawyer.'

'Paul Tomlinson?'

Tom was surprised. 'Yes.'

'I met him at your wedding; he gave me his card. I'd forgotten all about it?

'Would you like me to seek his advice?'

'I would if you don't mind. Our Robbie can't go on like this for ever.'

Young Bernard was still fascinated with the egg

he had brought back from the allotments. 'Look what I've got; it came out of Mrs Hen's bottom.'

Tom laughed and turned to John. 'Leave it with me. I'll do my best.' He took a notebook from his pocket and made a few notes. At that point Ben struck up on the melodion and the party began in earnest. Only Mary refused to join in the singing, but no one took much notice of her, not even Jacob.

Chapter Nineteen

Enid Slater was worried about Lucy. She had never known anyone so big at only seven months gone. She begged the lass to pay Dr Sellars a visit, but Lucy was adamant she was perfectly well. Mrs Cadman was keeping an eye on Bernard and Rosie – who was so placid she hardly needed any looking after at all. Oh well, there wasn't much she could do if Lucy refused to seek medical advice, except give her a hand with the washing and cleaning. The washing was the biggest problem, with three strapping men and two little ones to be washing and ironing for. Not so much the washing but the drying, which usually had to be done indoors in the month of January.

Today for a change had begun as a good drying day, bright and cold with a light wind. But now storm clouds were rolling across the sky from the direction of Cragstone and the wind had risen so that it was wrapping the washing around the clothes line and tangling a sheet round the clothes prop. Enid thought it could blow in some rain later or even some snow, but by then the washing would no doubt be dry. She noticed little Bernard playing on Mrs Cadman's doorstep. If only Evelyn could see him now with his rosy cheeks and ready smile. Enid felt at the washing and unknotted the driest garments off the line. She would get them ironed before taking them in to Lucy's. Like her old mother used to say, a little help's worth a lot of pity. It was a pity Mary Gabbitas – as was – didn't think that way. A right sister that one had turned out to be.

She had finished the pillow cases and started on the shirts when she heard Mrs Cadman calling out, 'Bernard, where are you, lovey?' Enid got to the door in time to see her neighbour hurry into Lucy's and rush out again with Lucy following. 'He was here not a minute since, riding 'is bike,' Enid called. 'Perhaps he's gone into the Murphys'.' All the children liked Mrs Murphy – the house was so untidy she never bothered what they got up to, but Bernard wasn't there. By this time other neighbours had come out onto the street, Mr Marshall, pulling his cap down over his ears waiting to go on afternoon shift, followed by Lewis.

'What's up?' Lewis was by Lucy's side.

'Our Bernard's disappeared.' Lucy was trembling as she went to search the midden and the passage to the lavatories. Her heart almost stopped when she found the tricycle abandoned on its side in the passage. Something abnormal must have happened for him to leave his precious toy behind.

'I'll go up the allotments.' Lewis set off at a run. His father went hurrying down to Next Row.

'I'll go down Side Row.' Mrs Slater's mind was working overtime. What if Bernard's father had got him? As far as anyone knew he hadn't yet been arrested. Her heart seemed to be thumping in her ears; she was getting too old for scares like this. She called out to everyone she saw, 'Have yer seen little Bernard? You 'aven't seen any strange men down 'ere, 'ave yer?' Nobody had. One woman said she had seen a strange woman who she thought was a gypsy but she had hurried inside, knowing what some of them gypsies were like; if yer didn't buy any pegs off 'em they were likely to put a curse on yer.

Lucy went back into the house and upstairs, then back down again and called down the cellar; of course he wouldn't have gone down there in the dark. Oh God, where was he? She thought she was going to faint and sat down to prevent herself from falling. Mrs Cadman ran in, her chest heaving and tears streaming down her face. 'Oh, Lucy, I swear I only took my eyes off him for a minute to knock back my dough and put it to rise again.' She noticed the pallor of Lucy's face. 'Are you all right?'

'Yes, I just felt faint but I'm all right now, if you can just pass me a drink of water.'

Mrs Cadman did so. 'Oh, where can he be? I'm going down to the clock; he might have gone in the gardens.'

'I don't think so. He's never been down there before.'

'Well I'll look anyway and then I'll go down on the main road.' She was off before Lucy could answer. Lucy tried to stay calm – she had her baby to consider, and who was looking after Rosie? The little girl was perfectly safe, having been dumped on Mrs Murphy's knee. The woman was jigging her up and down to Rosie's delight and singing 'Soldiers go gallop, gallop, gallop'.

'Shall I take her now?' Lucy enquired.

'Nay lass, leave her be, yer've enough on yer plate at moment.'

Lucy didn't know where to look next. She saw Lewis slithering down the bank side. Bernard wasn't with him. Lucy felt as though the blood was rushing to her head and then the ground was coming up to meet her. After that she knew nothing until she came round on the sofa, with Lewis, pale and concerned, keeping watch over the girl he would worship till his dying day. 'Lucy? Oh love, are yer feeling better?'

'A bit.' Then she remembered. 'Have you found him?'

Lewis shook his head. 'No but we will, don't fret.' Lucy attempted to stand but the room began to swim again. 'Stay where you are. Me dad's gone for't doctor.'

'But I have to go and look for him.'

'They'll find him. There's everybody and their grandmothers out searching; he can't be far away.'

'Has anyone gone to our Mary's?'

'I don't know.'

'Oh, Lewis, if she's taken him I'll kill her.'

'Nay, love, she wouldn't do that. I mean, what

could she gain by it? She knows you'd fetch 'im back.'

'Will you go and see? Please, Lewis.' He would have preferred to stay by Lucy's side until John came home from morning shift, but he knew she wouldn't rest if he didn't do as she asked. As soon as his mother came back he hurried off down the hill, not thinking for a moment that Mary would have taken Bernard and wondering how best to broach the subject. Mary was emptying the dirty water from the tub and brushing it into the flags with the yard brush.

'Lewis, what brings you here? It's not our Lucy, is it?'

'Well, aye, it is in a way. Bernard's gone missing and she's taking it badly. Me dad's gone for the doctor and we've searched everywhere. I thought I'd better let yer know.'

Mary had already taken her apron off and removed the daft-looking mobcap from her head. She disappeared into the house and scribbled a note for Jacob, to come back seconds later in her coat with the fur collar and black felt hat. Lewis wondered at the change in Mary. At one time all the young lads had fancied her as well as Nellie, but now she had let herself go and resembled an old granny. However, she was striding out and even he had all on to match her steps. 'How long's he been gone?' she wanted to know, and 'Have yer looked up the allotments?'

'We've looked everywhere but there's no sign of 'im.'

'Has anyone fetched the constable?'

'I don't know. They might have by now.'

'If they haven't you can go for him.'

Lewis had always thought Mary was rather bossy; it probably stemmed from her being the eldest. Perhaps it was what Lucy needed at a time like this: somebody to take charge. He prayed as they hurried up past the clock that Bernard was back home safe and well, but on this occasion God didn't seem to be listening and the little boy was still nowhere to be found.

Dr Sellars insisted Lucy take to her bed. Lucy protested, 'I can't; I have to find Bernard.'

'We'll find him, but come on, do as the doctor tells you. You're going up to bed if I have carry you up there myself.' Mary had taken charge on entering the house. To her, Lucy was once more the little girl who could be bossed about, and Mary was the best one to do it. Her sister needed her and as long as she did Mary would be there for her. She was sorry for the upset she had caused everybody, and realised now that this was where Bernard belonged. She had been wicked to try and break up the family; she had acted beyond all reason. Indeed she wondered if she had lost her mind for a time. Well, this was her chance to make amends and when Bernard was safely back she would be happy for them. Oh God, what if he didn't come back? She tucked Lucy up with some hot sweet tea and fetched Rosie from Mrs Murphy's.

'I'll call again tomorrow.' Dr Sellars was worried about Lucy. 'The shock can't be good for her at this stage and the swelling of her ankles isn't normal. You must insist she stays in bed both for her and her baby's sake.'

'Don't worry. I will, even if I've to chain her to the bed posts.'

'Good.' Dr Sellars frowned as she descended the stairs. What a terrible thing to happen, a child missing. Still, she was glad the sister was here; by the look of her she would lay down the law and keep Lucy off her feet.

By the time John returned from the morning shift Bernard was still missing and a search party had been organised. John, still in his pit clothes, went straight out to join the men in the search for his son. When he'd got back, eager to comfort Lucy, Constable Jones was waiting to question him. 'Now then Mr Grey, is there anything you can tell us what might throw some light on where the little boy might be? For instance, is there anybody you can think on who might 'ave taken 'im?'

John's stomach seemed to turn over as he thought of the child's father out there somewhere. Had he found out about his son's existence? Had he decided to risk his freedom in order to gain possession of his son? If the police couldn't find a murderer what chance had they of finding a child-snatcher? John decided to withhold the fact that Bernard was the son of the murdered woman, for the time being. It would be disastrous for the story to reach the newspapers. Of course, if he didn't turn up soon they would need the publicity, but for today at least he would wait and see. He left the constable to get on with his job and set off along the row.

In another hour it would be dark. Surely Bernard couldn't have walked far, but there was no knowing which direction he would have taken. He set off up the hill towards Greenwood's. Robbie had taken him up there sometimes; maybe he had just taken it into his head to go by himself.

Lucy was distraught. 'Oh Mary, it's all my fault. If I'd let you have him he'd be safe now. You were right, I couldn't give him as much attention as you could have done.'

'Now, Lucy, that's not true; I was wrong to say that. Nobody could love the child more than you and John, neither could they have been better parents. There isn't a happier little boy on God's earth, so just you stop saying silly things. I'm sorry for acting the way I did. I hope you'll forgive me and let's be back to normal. I don't think I have been normal for a time, but I realise now how fortunate I am to have Jacob and a loving family. If I can't have children then so be it, and I've still got a nephew and niece and another on the way.'

'But what if we don't get him back, Mary?'

'We shall. Now try and sleep a bit, or at least close your eyes and rest. I'm going to feed Primrose and cook something for John. The lad's done a shift down't pit and he'll be needing some nourishment; so will Bernard when he comes home.' Mary knew her sister wouldn't sleep, neither would John eat until her nephew was back safe and sound, but she had to pretend things would soon be back to normal. The alternative didn't bear thinking about.

'Our Will brought some mussels from the market. They're steeping in a bucket of oatmeal water on the cellar steps; they'll only need rinsing and standing on the fire.'

'I know what to do with a few mussels, Lucy.' Mary went downstairs and cut a pile of bread, holding the loaf against her breast the way her mother used to do. She was rinsing the mussels in the enamel washing-up bowl, making such a clatter that she never heard the door open.

She spun round when she heard a little voice say, 'Look what I've got, Auntie Mary.'

There was Bernard, high on the shoulders of a grinning Dan the birdman. Dan lowered the red-cheeked little boy to the ground. In his other arm was a piece of old sacking wrapped around a black and white puppy dog, not much bigger than Dan's hand.

Mary grabbed Bernard and hugged him close. 'Where on earth have you been?'

'To fetch my baby dog.'

'Did you take him, Dan Higgins?' Mary almost spat the words at the gentle giant, who stood looking too large for the small kitchen.

Dan's lip quivered and his eyes filled with tears in the manner of a small boy. 'Will said.'

'Will? What did Will say?'

Bernard didn't like the sound of Auntie Mary when she was angry. 'He said I could have a baby dog when it came out of Queenie's tummy.' Bernard looked as if he was about to cry too. Mary cuddled him closer. 'Dan took me to choose one.' The words came out muffled in sobs.

'It's all right, Bernard.' Mary turned her attention to Dan. 'You should never have taken him, Daniel; it was a bad thing to do.'

Daniel had been so excited to be taking

Bernard to choose one of the pups it hadn't occurred to him to ask permission, nor had he considered the trouble it might cause when Bernard was missing. Now it was all spoiled and Mary was shouting at him. Dan slumped towards the door, sobbing like a two-year-old instead of a grown man.

'Oh, come back and sit yerself down, Daniel. I'll make us some tea. I don't suppose you realised what you were doing. Besides, he doesn't look as if he's come to any harm. Bernard, go and show your mam your new pet.'

Bernard's face cleared and he made to lift the pup up in his arms. Dan knelt on the floor and gently showed him how to do so without hurting it. Mary waited until she heard Lucy's whoop of joy, then she hurried outside and shouted, 'It's all right. Bernard's back.'

Everybody not out searching ran into the street and cries of 'Is he all reight? Wheer's ee been?' and 'Thank the Lord for that,' could be heard all along the row. Somebody hurried away to call off the search and Dan settled down to enjoy his hot sweet tea. Mary noticed his red chilblained bands and resolved to knit him a pair of warm gloves. Then Dan noticed the pictures on the wishing mirror and jumped up to point out one of the birds hovering in the garden scene.

'A swallow,' he told Mary excitedly.

'Is it really?' Mary didn't know a swallow from a barn owl. She offered Dan a biscuit, which he shoved in his mouth all in one go. Still, there was obviously more to the lad than anyone thought. She hoped John wouldn't be too harsh on him.

Perhaps she should send him home before the searchers returned. 'Go on then Daniel; get off home before it gets any darker. And never, ever take any children away again without asking their mam first.'

Daniel shook his head vigorously and set off for home. Halfway down Side Row he met a relieved John, who had just been given the news of Bernard's safe return. Daniel, pleased to see Lucy's husband, gave him a broad grin and John cringed at the usual lewd gesture which Dan greeted him with, but for once it didn't bother John. So long as his son was safe John couldn't care less about anything else. His main worry now was Lucy.

It wasn't until later that he heard about the part Dan the birdman had played in his son's disappearance, but everyone was so relieved to have Bernard back – and Bernard was so pleased with the funny-looking little mongrel dog – that nothing more was said about Daniel. Besides, John couldn't face being humiliated again in front of everybody. The damned lad must have a memory like an elephant to remember the incident up in Sheepdip Wood. He smiled as he thought what a lovely memory it had turned out to be, and like Dan, John would remember that day for the rest of his life.

His thoughts returned to Bernard; it was time to arrange the adoption. He would look into it as soon as possible. He couldn't risk losing the boy again – the shock had been almost too much for Lucy. She was so relieved at seeing Bernard that she had attempted to come downstairs, but Mary was having none of it.

'She's been ordered to stay in bed,' she told John. 'And stay in bed she shall, at least until Dr Sellars has seen her again.'

It was one in the morning when the pains began. Mary had returned home to her husband hours ago and John had been relieved to be rid of his sister-in-law after such a harrowing day, but now he wished she was here to comfort and reassure Lucy. One good thing that had resulted from today was that the sisters were reunited again. Now, however, he went to fetch Mrs Slater, instinctively knowing that she would be the one Lucy wanted at a time like this. When the woman had finally dressed herself, inserted her false teeth and removed the metal curlers from her hair – which all seemed to take forever – and taken her place at Lucy's bedside, John hurried for the doctor. He knew the baby wasn't due for another two months, but the pains were coming at regular intervals, which Lucy said meant the birth was imminent.

Having missed out at the birth of Rosie, John had no idea what to expect and was shocked at the sight of Lucy writhing in agony and slick with sweat when he returned with Dr Sellars, whose confident manner reassured him slightly that this was all perfectly normal. Mrs Slater ordered him to go make up the fire for some hot water, and despite having to leave Lucy he went without much persuasion, sure that the women would be better off with him out of the way. John paced the kitchen, unable to sit still whilst Lucy was in such pain. A couple of times he went upstairs to check on the children, who were sleeping soundly. It was five o'clock when he heard the sound of a new baby's cry and rushed upstairs to Lucy's side.

'You've got a son, Mr Grey.'

'Is he all right?' John was shocked to see that Lucy still seemed to be in pain; surely that wasn't normal. 'How's Lucy?'

'She'll be fine.' Dr Sellars didn't sound very convincing and Lucy looked anything but fine.

'Go mek a pot of tea, lad.' Mrs Slater almost pushed him out onto the landing. John didn't like the look of things, but did as he was told and made some tea. He didn't know if Lucy would want any, but he made her one anyway and carried the tray with trembling hands up the stairs. Just as he handed over the tea the room was plunged into darkness as the gas went out. John found a couple of pennies in his pocket, felt his way downstairs and then to the cellar. He then hurried to find the matches and relight the gas in the bedroom.

It was then that Lucy cried out and Dr Sellars let out a moderate swearword that surprised them all. 'I can't bloody believe it,' she said in her normal posh way of speaking. 'There's another baby on the way.'

John thought he might faint and Mrs Slater shifted Lucy's clothes off a chair and plonked him down on it. 'Eeh, John, lad, yer don't do things by halves in this house do yer? Yer've gone and caught two birds with one shot; now not many men can brag about that, can they?'

'Come along Lucy, one more push, that's the way. Here it is, a baby girl. Oh Lucy, I've just delivered my first set of twins. Now can we celebrate with that cup of tea, Mr Grey?'

'Aye John, go and mek some fresh, will yer? That lot'll be cold I expect.' Mrs Slater didn't want him passing out when the afterbirth came away. The poor lad was already suffering from shock.

'Are you all right, Lucy?' John came towards the bed. 'We've got twins, love.' He sounded as though it was all his doing.

'Yes, John. I have noticed.' Lucy smiled and took his hand in hers. 'Let me see them.' Mrs Slater brought the girl and Dr Sellars the boy and handed them into Lucy and John's care.

'Will they be all right? Being early I mean.' John searched the small faces worriedly.

'They'll be fine,' Dr Sellars smiled. 'Twins often arrive early but they always catch up. Now I'd love that cup of tea.'

John hurried out of the room, leaving the women to finish the job they'd started, Mrs Slater to the babies and the doctor to the mother, and all Lucy could think about was what their Mary would feel like when her sister could produce two babies and she was deprived of one.

'I'd best get ready for work,' John said when he delivered the tea.

'No point, lad. They'll 'ave gone down by now.'

'Oh aye, I didn't realise it was that time.' He wouldn't be allowed down the pit after six o'clock. Latecomers knew that and were always turned away. Still, it wasn't every day a man had twins, so he would stay with Lucy and take care of Bernard and Rosie. One day off wouldn't hurt. Still, he could have done with the money with two extra babies to keep. Lucy was going to have her work cut out with three under a year and Bernard besides.

Dr Sellars had gone home and Mrs Slater had followed her with the promise to be back in time to give the little ones their breakfasts. It was then that John and Lucy cradled the babies in their arms. 'They're beautiful,' John said. 'What shall we call them?'

'Peter, I love bible names.'

'Yes, I like that. Peter, a rock. And what about you?' John took the tiny hand in his. 'What shall we call you, little daughter?'

'Well, we have a Primrose so what about a Violet?'

'Violet? Aye, she has your eyes which always remind me of violets.' John frowned. 'They're going to be hard work, Lucy.'

'But worth it. It's a good thing we kept the baby clothes we found at Evelyn's, and we've the ones our Rosie's grown out of. We'll need more nappies, though.'

'We've a bit put by and with the lads paying their board we're not badly off. We shall have to be careful though in future. Three in twelve months – that's going a bit.'

Lucy giggled. 'I shall be like the old woman in the shoe if we carry on like this.' Then she frowned. 'I'm dreading telling our Mary. I can just imagine what she and Jacob must feel like.'

'Aye, it doesn't bear thinking about. I shall have to spread the news all the same.'

'Yes, but break it gently won't you, John.'

Surprisingly, Mary took it very well. 'I'll get my

coat,' she said. 'There'll be some washing to do, I expect, and the kids to see to.' She strode out ahead of him. 'You go and break the news to our Jane. It's not many folk who have a new niece and nephew both in one day.'

The letter from Paul Tomlinson arrived on the same day as the twins. The lawyer pointed out that divorces were extremely complicated affairs and he would need to see Robert Grey in person if he was to advise him. Could Robert possibly visit his office at his convenience? He said Nellie and Tom Johnson would be delighted if Robert would stay with them for a couple of days. Nellie wondered if he would do her a great favour and arrange to accompany Lily on the journey. Tom would send tickets for the train as soon as Robert gave him a date. The lawyer also enquired if John had applied to the court yet, regarding the boy's adoption. He offered them any advice they might need in that direction. He ended the letter with regards to John's wife.

The envelope was propped up on the mantelpiece waiting for Robbie to return from work, everybody being far too occupied with the new babies to even wonder about its contents. However, it wasn't only Robbie's spirits which were given a lift as the prospect of being free seemed a little closer. When John was given the letter to read he felt Bernard's adoption also seemed to move closer to reality. The mention that John needed to apply to the court gave him the incentive to do so and he resolved to go ahead as soon as Lucy was up and about again. For the time being though he needed to be on hand for his wife and his four beautiful children. Enid Slater and Mary seemed delighted to cover the hours John was at work, arranging a rota so that Lucy was never left alone. At first Lucy was worried that Mary would become possessive of the children, but she seemed to have accepted the fact that they belonged to her sister and not to her. Jane came and gave the house a good bottoming and then spent a long time gazing in wonder at the twins.

'Don't yer wish they were yours, love?' Enid asked, noticing the adoring expression on Jane's face.

Jane's expression changed to alarm at the very idea. 'Goodness me no; they're so precious I'd be scared to death. Besides, one lot of dirty nappies turn my stomach over – imagine having three lots! No thanks, I'll borrow one of them on the off chance of me ever feeling maternal; that's so long as I can bring them back.'

'Aye, they'll cause a lot of hard work.' Enid spooned mashed up vegetables into little Rosie's open mouth. 'Stands to reason wi' five of 'em.'

'Five? Don't you mean four?' Jane laughed.

Mrs Slater scooped up the small black and white pup into her arms and stroked it gently. 'Five wi' this one. Your Will wants 'is brains washing promising Bernard a dog at a time like this. It's going to cause as much work as a bairn until it's housetrained. And it'll be your Lucy who falls for the extra work, you'll see.'

Mary took away Bernard's dinner plate and gave him a dish of bread and butter pudding. 'I'd work twenty-four hours of the day just to have our Lucy's lot.'

The look on Mary's face made Jane so sad. 'It will happen one day, just you see if it doesn't.'

'Aye love,' Enid said. 'You're no age yet. Try and stop thinking about it for a bit; they say that sometimes works.'

'That's easier said than done with my mother-in-law going on and on about it all the time.'

'Well!' Enid was shocked. 'I would tell 'er where to get off and no mistake. Interfering owd bitch.' Jane looked at Mary and they began to laugh. Enid Slater almost had them in hysterics when she added, 'I don't know 'ow she ever got their Jacob wi' those great big elastic-legged bloomers she used to wear. Even on 'er honeymoon she 'ad 'em hung on the line. I bet they reached from under 'er arms to 'er ankles.'

'Oh, Mrs Slater, you always make me feel better. When I was a little girl I used to come to you instead of my mother if I were ever feeling down,' Jane said.

'Aye well, I expect I 'ad an easier time than yer mam did with the six of yer.'

'Yes, I suppose,' Jane said. 'Which brings us back to where we started and our Lucy's lot.'

'Aye. But you've got to admit they're all lovely.' Mary smiled and tickled the pup behind her ears. 'Even you, Baby.'

Jane giggled. 'What a name to give a dog. Still, it was Bernard's choice and it's supposed to be his dog. If he likes it I suppose it will have to do. You're a lovely dog aren't you, Baby?' She changed her mind when a stream of urine ran down the front of Mrs Slater's legs.

Chapter Twenty

'Now then, Lily, are yer all packed up?'

'I think so.' Lily was fighting to hold back the tears. Mrs Cooper had warned her that she would have to learn to stop crying all the time. It was all right for Mrs Cooper; she wasn't going to live all those miles away leaving her mam, dad and all the rest of her family and Mrs Cooper besides. Molly was standing there not knowing what to do with herself. It wouldn't be the same when Lily had gone. Not only would she miss her sister, but she would have nobody to tell her if she wasn't doing things properly. Neither was she very keen on having to sleep in a room all to herself for the first time.

'Well then, you'd best get yer coat on.' The housekeeper took a coin out of the pocket of her apron and slipped it into Lily's coat pocket. 'Keep that for ever you're in need of it.' That was the final straw and the tears rushed to Lily's eyes.

'Ooh, Mrs Cooper, I don't want to go. I won't be able to talk to yer if I'm worried and I'm going to miss yer.'

'Course yer going to miss me, yer silly lass and I shall miss you. But we shall get over it. Now then, Mr Smith's back wi' Mr Grey. Yer mustn't keep 'em waiting, not after he's been good enough to give yer both a lift to't station. Well, 'ave yer got everything? Come on then, give us a cuddle and don't start weeping again, yer daft haporth. Say ta ra to yer sister and be off with yer. And behave yerself.'

'I will. Ta ra Molly. I'll write if I've time.'

'Ta ta, Lily.' Molly wished it was her going to live in Blackpool.

Lily picked up her bag as Mr Smith drew up at the kitchen door. It wasn't a very big bag because she didn't have much to put in it. Her dad had done his best and sent her mam to the market to buy Lily two pairs of warm knickers, two vests and two pairs of stockings. Her shoes had had to make do with a new sole and heel. Nellie had promised her a new uniform. 'So long as yer warm underneath yer'll not go far wrong,' her dad had told her. 'I've heard tell 'ow cold it can be in Blackpool.' He seemed to think he was sending his daughter off to the North Pole, Lily thought.

She began to panic as she climbed in the back of Mr Smith's car and wished she could change her mind and not go. Then she calmed down as she remembered Robbie would be there to look after her. She turned and waved to the two figures standing at the door, then at Larry who was clearing soggy leaves off the drive. She ought to have reminded their Molly not to let him take advantage of her, but it was too late now. She was off to Blackpool on a train. Suddenly the apprehension gave way to excitement; she was going to live in Blackpool, she really was. Who would ever have thought it?

The queue stretched from Will's stall to the fish stall and Will was rushed off his feet. He tried to fit in a joke or two between serving – it was what the ladies had come to expect. He threw a turnip on the scale and told the woman how much her goods had come to, then he moved to the next customer; he could be weighing out while the first woman fumbled about in her purse to pay him. Then his customer smiled and the world seemed to stop. 'Betty Brown Eyes.'

'Hello, Will.' Her eyes twinkled as she held out her basket. 'Are you going to serve me or aren't you?'

Will felt his face redden as he gathered himself together. 'Yes. Course I am. It was just a surprise seeing you here, that's all.' Will had thought of Betty constantly but didn't think someone like Betty would look twice at someone like him.

'Well I told you I lived in Cragstone. Now, can I have some spring cabbage?'

Will picked out the best from the box. 'How much do yer want?'

'Well, it's for four of us – my gran's staying for a few days. I think that should do.' Will weighed it and placed it in the wicker basket. 'And I'll take some carrots, a couple of pounds I think.' He took his time, not wanting her to leave. He blushed even more as he plucked up courage to ask, 'Can I meet yer after work?'

On Christmas Eve Betty had hurried away home with her friends before he had had time to ask her out. Now he had been given another chance he didn't intend letting her go.

'Well, yes. It's my day off. What time do you finish?'

'About six, but I'll need to go back to Millington and get changed.'

'So shall I meet you in Millington? There's a bus gets there at half past seven.'

'Sure. Shall we go to the second house pictures?'

'That'll be lovely.'

'Are yer serving me or aren't yer?' A regular customer called out from further up the queue. Betty laughed and handed over half a crown. Will gave her the change with a dopey look on his face and Betty hurried away.

'Who's that then? Yer girlfriend?' the woman asked. Will didn't answer. 'If not, she should be. Nice lass like her is just what yer need.'

'No, Martha, what he needs is somebody like me to show 'im 'ow to go on. Come up next week when our owd man's on nights, I'll show yer, Will Gabbitas.'

'Hey, if Will needs any instructions I'm before you, Sadie Fisher.'

Will laughed and joined in the banter but his mind was on other things. He had a date at last with the most beautiful girl he had ever clapped eyes on. She had been worth waiting for, had Betty Brown Eyes. He couldn't wait to tell Robbie. Then he remembered Robbie was in Blackpool. Besides, it wouldn't be fair to let Robbie see how happy he was, not with a divorce facing him.

Things weren't looking good for Robbie. His case was an extremely complicated one, according to Paul Tomlinson. 'If you had stayed with your wife and she had left you, you would have had a case for judicial separation, but it was you who deserted her. Now was there any cruelty involved?' Robbie shook his head. 'Any adultery on her part?'

'No, not that I know of.'

'On your part?'

'No, I wouldn't do that.'

'Mental illness?'

Robbie looked hopeful. 'She's mad as a hatter.'

'Tell me about it.' Paul waited, pen poised, but Robbie didn't know how to explain.

'Well, she told everyone she was pregnant in order to trick me into marriage, even though I'd never touched her, still haven't.'

'Ah, so your marriage was never consummated?'

'No. I couldn't bear to be near her.'

'Hmm!' The lawyer made notes and played with his moustache as he considered this turn of events. 'Do you have evidence of this?'

'Yes. She was examined by the doctor on the day I left. I haven't been in her company since.'

'But she was willing to submit to intercourse?'

Robbie almost laughed. 'More than willing.'

Paul frowned. 'Unfortunately that changes the situation.'

'How?'

'If she had been unwilling the marriage could have been annulled, if she can be persuaded to apply for an annulment on the grounds of your failure to consummate the marriage that could be the solution.'

'Not much chance of that; she won't want a divorce. She's obsessed with me, insane I shouldn't wonder.'

'Have you discussed any of this with her family?'

'What's the point? It's her father who made me marry her, and he being a vicar doesn't help.'

'I can see that. Well, leave it with me and I'll be in contact. Do you know of your wife's whereabouts?'

'Only that she's in Liverpool.' Robbie rose to his feet, then sat down again, embarrassed as he asked, 'How much is this likely to cost?'

'Well, divorces don't come cheap. Can cost anything from twenty-five to five hundred pounds.'

'Five hundred pounds?' Robbie stammered. 'I don't have that kind of money. I'm sorry, I've been wasting your time.'

'I said it *could* cost that, but it won't. Tom Johnson is a very good friend of mine and so is Nellie. You are part of Nellie's family. If I can help you I shall and I'll keep the costs to a minimum. Just leave it with me.' Paul shifted his chair and rose to his feet and Robbie took the hint that the meeting was over.

'Well, thanks for seeing me, but it doesn't sound too hopeful, does it?'

'It won't be easy and it could take years.'

'I don't care how long it takes, so long as I'm rid of her.'

'I shall certainly do my best. Good afternoon, Mr Grey.'

'Good afternoon, Mr Tomlinson.' Robbie went out into the bitter afternoon. Salty rain lashed against the windows and clouds rolled across the darkening sky. Robbie turned up his coat collar and hurried along the back streets in the direction of the Johnsons' guest house. He thought back to the day not so long ago when he had been here with Dot. What a fool he had been to fall in with the Goodmans' plans. What a bloody stupid fool to ruin his life and that of the girl he loved, for someone as despicable as Prudence Goodman. He felt the tears rush to his eyes and found it difficult to swallow. All the sadness of the last few years rose up inside him, the loss of his parents, his home and Dot. He had had his brothers to lean on after the loss of his mother and father, but no one could comfort him now; he would need to sort out this problem on his own. His emotions threatened to drown him and he cried the way he used to when he was a small child. The rain mingled with his tears so that passers by never noticed them being shed by the tall, handsome, heartbroken man.

Lucy spat on the iron, testing its heat, and stood it on the upturned basin on the table, placing the cooling one in its place on the fire. The fortnight-old twins were sleeping one to each end of the pram and Rosie had been taken by Mary to the Co-op for Lucy's shopping. Bernard was playing with Baby in front of the fire and all was peaceful. Lucy loved the smell of fresh, clean laundry and she delighted in the feel of soft, fluffy napkins between her fingers. She skimmed over anything that wasn't too creased and took extra care with things like shirts and Rosie's dresses. The knock on the door caused one of the twins to jump, but Peter soon settled down again, to

Lucy's relief. It was Louisa Goodman, standing uncomfortably on the step.

'Mrs Goodman.' Lucy smiled and beckoned Louisa into the kitchen.

Louisa relaxed. She hadn't know how she would be received after the fiasco of Prudence and Robbie. 'I should have come before, but Jane said you were receiving plenty of help after the births, so I decided to wait until a time when you might need some assistance. It must be hard with the twins and Primrose and Bernard besides.'

'Well it won't be easy, but I shall get into a routine I expect.' She picked up the iron. At one time she would have hurriedly removed the ironing blanket from the table and set out her best crockery, but she didn't have time for that anymore. 'I'll make some tea in a minute, but I really do need to finish the ironing whilst they are asleep.'

'Of course. Can I take a peep? I promise not to disturb them.' Louisa felt a rush of emotion as she studied the faces and tiny fingers of the sleeping babies. 'Oh, Lucy, aren't they adorable, but so different.'

'Yes, Peter resembles John and Violet's like me, I think.'

'Here, let me do that.' Louisa took the iron off the basin as Lucy smoothed out a pillow case. 'Rest your legs for a while. After all they're no age yet and you must be tired after the births.'

'Oh, everyone's been good, especially Mary, and it must be hard for her facing the children every day when she so much desires one of her own.'

'Well yes, but I expect she gains some satisfaction from being with yours. Still it's sad for her. I so wanted another child, but it never happened. After the way Prudence has turned out I suppose it happened for the best.'

Lucy didn't know what to say. She could see the sadness in Louisa's eyes as she ironed one of Will's shirts. 'Oh, Prudence isn't a bad girl; she just became infatuated with Robbie, I suppose.' Lucy moved the iron and placed the kettle on the fire, 'I'll make some tea.'

'I've brought a sweet cake, I baked it this morning, and if you look in the bag there are some pram sets for the twins.' Lucy opened the bag and took out a brown paper parcel, inside were two snowy white knitted coats, two pairs of leggings and two tiny caps.

'Oh Mrs Goodman, they're beautiful, thank you so much. I shall keep them for Sundays when we go for our afternoon walk.'

'As you wish, but if I were you I would let them wear them as much as possible, after all they grow out of things so fast in the first few months.'

'Yes, maybe you're right.'

Louisa finished ironing the last garment – a tiny dress belonging to Rosie – and folded the ironing blanket in four. 'Now is there anything else I can do while I'm here?'

'No thanks, but let's have some tea.' The kettle was singing on the fire and Lucy lifted it off and mashed the tea. 'Well, how is Prudence?' She wasn't really interested but felt so sorry for Louisa; after all she must be missing her daughter.

'I don't really know. She doesn't say much in

her letters except that she's taken a job in the library. I suppose the experience here helped her to get it. She's always been a strange girl, Lucy. I can't describe the way she is. There's nothing I can pinpoint exactly; she's just strange. Never made friends, always a loner until Robbie came. Then she ruined his life, her own too I suppose. Who will ever want anything to do with a divorced woman?' It was all too much for Louisa and she began to cry.

'Oh Mrs Goodman, I didn't mean to upset you.'

The woman brushed away her tears. 'It wasn't your fault, and please call me Louisa,' she managed between the sobs. 'Nobody ever uses my first name; it's being the wife of a vicar I suppose. It makes it difficult to make close friends. We've plenty of acquaintances but not many friends.'

'Well, you're a good friend to me, Louisa. Now let's drink our tea before the twins wake up and need feeding.' Lucy smiled at the sight of Bernard, who had dozed off on the rug with Baby cuddled up close.

'Are you feeding them yourself?

'Yes, unlike with Rosie I have plenty of milk. I expect it was the shock of Evelyn's death at the time.'

'Bernard's fortunate to have you, Lucy.'

'And we are fortunate to have him.'

'Yes, you are. You're a good girl, Lucy Grey. There are givers and takers in the world; you are one of the givers.'

Lucy considered what Louisa had said. 'Yes, I suppose I am. But what I give out is returned to me twofold. Look at the help I'm receiving now.

From Mrs Slater, Mrs Holmes – even Mr Holmes and Mr Marshall have begun taking Rosie and Bernard off my hands, walking them up to the allotments to give me a break. Even Mrs Murphy's been good, rocking Rosie to sleep by the fire. You'd think she'd have enough on with all her lot.' Lucy paused. 'Oh Louisa, I hope I don't end up like her though, letting them all run wild. Though they're all lovable rogues.'

'Well, I don't know the family, them being Catholics, but I'm sure you'll never let your children run amok, and if you ever find them becoming too much for you, you know where I am.'

Bernard was now awake and playing tug of war with Baby, pulling on the end of an old rag. Lucy saw a pool of liquid appear on the rug.

'Bernard, get the floor cloth and the bucket from outside. I don't know what our Will was thinking of, promising him a dog when he's never here to train it. I swear it's more trouble than the children.' She found a bottle of Dettol and poured some into the bucket, adding the water from the kettle.

'I want to clean it up.' Bernard jumped up and down with excitement. 'It's my dog.' Lucy dipped the cloth in the water and wrung it out. 'Let me, let me. I'm a big boy now.' Bernard rubbed at the rug until the patch had disappeared.

'You're a clever boy,' Louisa told him and turned to Lucy. 'And yes, you're both fortunate to have each other.' She looked round the kitchen. 'Is there anything else I can help you with?'

Lucy looked thoughtful. 'Actually there is something you might be able to help us with.'

'Just name it.'

'We're hoping to adopt Bernard and we wondered if you and Mr Goodman would be willing to speak up for us if necessary?'

'Of course, we'd be delighted to.'

Lucy beamed at her friend. 'Thanks. So we shall see you on Sunday at the christening. You will come back to Jane's for refreshments, won't you? Our Jane's insisting on supplying them.'

It was Louisa who was beaming now. 'We wouldn't miss it for the world,' she said.

Both women were relieved that the business of Prudence was out in the open. Louisa knew she needn't have worried about Lucy bearing a grudge. Oh yes, Lucy Grey was a giver all right; she would tell the people that when they began making enquiries about Bernard's adoption.

The double christening attracted almost as much attention as the double wedding. Ben, Will and Robbie insisted on taking on the duties of godfathers and Mary, Jane and Emma were chosen as godmothers.

After the ceremony Ben proudly announced that he was to become a father too. Everybody apart from Mary was thrilled for the parents to be; however she put on a good face and joined in the celebrations. Only Jacob and Lucy understood how difficult it must be for her, and perhaps Louisa Goodman who, having borne a child, was now suffering the desolation of having lost her again.

Lucy was becoming exasperated with Will. Since the dog had joined the family Will had been out every night, leaving everybody else to care for Baby. It was unusual for Will, who usually limited his nights out to the weekends. Now he would arrive home from work, gulp down his meal, a quick wash and change and he was out again. It was Robbie who bought a leash and a collar, Lucy who fed Baby, Bernard who cleaned up after her and John who usually walked the high-spirited little dog.

'I don't know what possessed him to lumber us with a pet, as if we didn't have enough to do,' Lucy grumbled.

'I expect he was just being generous to Bernard.' Robbie and Will were thick as thieves and neither would hear a wrong word against the other. 'Besides, I don't suppose he was intending to be so busy when he promised Bernard.'

'Busy? Gadding off enjoying himself more like.'

Robbie put on Baby's leash and went out to walk her before Lucy could begin questioning him about Will's whereabouts. He knew about Betty Hague and though he was pleased for his friend he missed the game of billiards they used to enjoy and missed Dot more than ever. He found himself heading in the direction of the farm. He didn't know why he came this way it only upset him to be so near Dot and yet so far apart. He wondered if he would ever be free to marry her and worried that by the time he was she might already be married to someone else. He saw the light on in the kitchen and Boadacea moving around. He slowed his walk, hoping to catch a glimpse of Dot but was disappointed.

The flea-ridden old dog recognised Robbie and

began to bark a welcome so Robbie hurried away before Little Arthur came out to investigate. He turned down the path through the fields. Baby wasn't up to a longer walk yet and he would probably end up carrying her anyway. He wondered what was happening in Blackpool. Every day that passed without news from Paul Tomlinson made the future seem more hopeless. Perhaps he should agree to commit adultery and give Prudence grounds to divorce him. The trouble was he didn't think she would be willing to let him go. What a hole he had dug for himself! Baby came to a standstill and refused to move. Robbie picked her up and carried her, her warm little body giving him a measure of comfort, but only a very small measure.

By the time her first birthday came round Primrose Grey had begun to walk. After weeks of shuffling around on her knees she finally gained confidence to rise to her feet. Robbie made a little pen in which Lucy could keep her safe whilst she hung out the mounds of washing and made the beds. Rosie was a placid child and quite content to play with her toys or watch Bernard – whom she adored – playing with his. The twins were thriving and now weighed as much as other babies of the same age. Baby had finally become house-trained, apart from the odd accident, and Betty Hague had been accepted by Will's family.

All was well with Lucy's lot, apart from that she was so anxious about Robbie. Nothing had been mentioned in the letters from Nellie and no news had been forthcoming from the lawyer. Lucy hinted at Robbie's despondency during Louisa's weekly visits but Louisa seemed as unaware of what was happening as Lucy was. Surely Prudence should be receiving advice from her parents, but the couple seemed to be ignoring the situation. Mr Grundy was also concerned about Robbie. The lad was spending so many hours in the joiner's shop he wondered when he found time for any other activities normally enjoyed by a young man of Robbie's age. 'The lad should be out there sowing a few wild oats,' Mr Grundy told his wife.

'The only oats Robbie wants to sow are with the Greenwood girl. And we all know 'ow the vicar put paid to that. It's scandalous if you ask me, the way that lad was cheated out of 'is 'appiness. That man should be ashamed of 'imself; well that's what I think.' Robbie had confided in his boss and of course Mr Grundy had told his wife.

'All't same, churchgoers are.' Mr Grundy was a nonbeliever, but a good and honest man for all that.

'Nay, yer can't paint 'em all with the same brush.'

'I for one would never 'ave forced the lad to marry somebody he didn't love.' Mr Grundy looked at the wife he had worshipped from the day he had first clapped eyes on her. 'Supposed to preach about love, they are, and then to trick somebody into marriage like that. It doesn't seem right to me.'

'Trying to get rid of that lass of theirs, stands to reason. I mean who else would 'ave 'er? You answer me that.'

'Nobody wi' any sense.' The couple drank their evening cocoa and nibbled their digestives, both lost in their own thoughts. Then Mr Grundy said, 'I've a mind to offer 'im some money.'

'Money? How will that 'elp?'

'Buy a divorce, I shouldn't wonder.'

'Will it? Can yer do that? What if she doesn't want one?'

'I don't know, to tell the truth. But you remember what me father told us when we wed. "Always keep summat put by. Money'll buy owt lad, just you remember that."'

'Won't buy love.'

'Not as a rule, but it will in Robbie's case. If it'll buy a divorce he'll be free to marry the lass he loves.'

Mrs Grundy nodded. 'Aye, I see what yer mean. Aye, go on then, tell 'im in't morning. Tell 'im we shall pay for one of them theer divorces. After all, ee's like a son to us and what good's money at our age? We can't take it wi' us when we go.'

'No, but I'm not planning to go anywhere just yet. I want to see young Robbie and Dot Greenwood wed first. Aye, it'll be money well spent.'

Mrs Grundy smiled and nodded. 'Only one thing though: once he gets Dot Greenwood ee'll not be wanting to put all them hours in at work.'

'I know, that's what I was thinking. Costing me a fortune, young Robbie is wi' all that blooming overtime.'

Young Lily thought she had landed in heaven. A sitting room and a bedroom all to herself. And if she stood on a chair by the window she could see the sea. She had become accustomed to the work and had actually managed to control her emotions and avoid crying every time anybody complimented her, or on very rare occasions found fault with her work.

'You were right to send for Lily,' Margaret Johnson told Nellie. 'She's a treasure is that girl. And she adds a touch of glamour to the dining room. You'll have to watch her with the male guests.'

Margaret was right. In her new black skirt and white blouse, with her hair tied up in a black bow, Lily was beautiful. Sometimes she missed her family and Mrs Cooper, but there were lots of interesting things to take her mind off them. Nellie had introduced her to a flower-arranging class where Lily had learned about different types of containers and spiky flower-holders. She had been so proud of the spring flower arrangement she had been allowed to bring home, and even more important, she had made a friend. Phoebe was a chambermaid in the large hotel that stood on the sea side of the promenade.

Nellie had allowed Lily to take her day off to coincide with her new friend's so that the two girls could spend their free time together. They would stroll round the shops, wistfully planning what they would buy if they ever came into money, take walks along the promenade, sometimes to North Shore and other days to the Pleasure Beach. Once they took a bus to Lytham St Annes and ate fish and chips in the gardens, and even though it was a dull day they giggled the whole way as teenagers are apt to do.

Now Phoebe was talking about going in the

tower. 'You should see the ballroom; it's so magnificent it's like a royal palace.'

Lily wondered how much it would cost. She had promised to send home some of her wages to help her mother, but decided to treat herself all the same. After all, it couldn't be right for someone to live in Blackpool and not know what it was like in the tower, which dominated the whole town. 'All right. But don't think you're getting me up in that lift thingy; it doesn't look safe to me.'

Phoebe laughed, knowing that once they were inside Lily would be easily persuaded to take the lift up to the viewing platform. 'Shall we go next Wednesday then?' she asked.

'If yer like. Come on, let's go for a paddle. These shoes are making me feet all hot.' It only took a second to cool down Lily's burning feet. The water was freezing. 'Ooh I can't stand that.' Lily laughed and ran, splashing out of the sea and back to the steps where they had left their shoes and stockings. 'We think it's cold here,' Lily said, 'but Nellie had a letter from Mrs Cooper and it was snowing like mad. Who would believe it? Deep snow in the middle of May.'

'I don't suppose it's all that civilised where you come from with all them moors and crags and things.'

'It's not uncivilised at all, it's lovely.' Lily stuck her nose in the air at the thought of her home town being criticised. 'Still, I suppose it is a bit wild, especially wi' snow in't middle of May.'

'Wait a few months and it'll be warm enough to go right in. I'll learn yer to swim if yer like.'

'What, in a bathing costume?' Lily wouldn't

dare. 'With everybody watching?'

'Well if you'd rather swim wi' out one, that's up to you.' Phoebe always made Lily laugh. She was lucky to have found a friend like her. In fact Lily considered herself the most fortunate girl in the world, and it was all due to Nellie Johnson.

'Come on,' she said, running up the steps to the promenade. 'Let's go on the pier.' Lily had liked Ernest, but he hadn't seemed bothered about keeping in touch. Now Lily had taken a fancy to the son of the man who ran the tea room, and because the lad quite fancied Lily in return he was usually good for a free pot of tea and a toasted tea cake, which the girls shared between them.

The wind almost tugged their hair out by the roots and their skirts up round their waists as they clung together, laughing their way to the tea room, their faces rosy from the cold. Mrs Cooper had been right; Blackpool did have the healthiest air in Britain, but she hadn't mentioned it was also the coldest. Lily didn't mind: She loved Blackpool and had never been happier. Especially when Jim winked one of his gorgeous brown eyes at her from behind the counter.

Chapter Twenty-one

Lucy couldn't believe it. John had been so careful since the twins were born, insisting on withdrawing each time they made love. Now she was suffering all the symptoms again, indicating another pregnancy. She blushed as she wondered what people would say, what with the twins only just over a year old. Most importantly, what would John say? She watched Peter tottering round the kitchen on sturdy but unsteady legs, and Violet following at a crawl. Rosie picked up the building bricks and threw them into the toy cupboard in the corner, ever the little helper, forever tidying after the brother and sister she adored. Lucy frowned as she wondered how she would cope with the twins, Rosie and a new baby. She had managed quite well up to now with a few hours' respite when either Mrs Slater or Mary came to take over. With Bernard settled in at school she didn't have to be watching him all the time.

She smiled as Rosie attempted to wipe Violet's nose and Violet crawled away and hid under the table. They were all beautiful, and if the new baby was half as bonny she would be content. What did it matter what anyone else thought? It would be her and John who were responsible for them. Her only real worry was what John would say, and how they would manage to control themselves in the future. She seemed to catch on if he as much as came near her, but they couldn't continue to breed like rabbits for years on end. Neither could she bear to be deprived of the lovemaking she and John were used to. Life was so unfair. There were Mary and Jacob longing for the child they couldn't conceive and here was she wondering how to prevent it. Well, she needn't concern herself with that for another several months at least. She would keep the news to herself for a while; no point in worrying John just yet, or in upsetting her sister.

She reached for a couple of nappies from the rack over the fire. The twins would need changing and Rosie placed on her potty. Then it would be time for their afternoon nap.

Time to catch up on the ironing and peel the vegetables ready for when the men came home. It was all go in the Gabbitas household. Funny how she never thought of it as the Greys', even though Will was the only Gabbitas left here. By the looks of things it wouldn't be long before he was leaving, then it would really belong to the Greys and no matter how many of them there eventually turned out to be, Lucy vowed it would always be a happy home filled with love.

It was the next afternoon when the adoption inspectors paid Lucy a visit. She was just scrubbing the flags outside with the yard brush. Lucy thanked God it was Friday and the fireplace had been black-leaded and the lino washed. The twins were sleeping after a morning's play and Rosie was looking at a picture book in front of the fire. Lucy's pulse was racing and she wished John were here to deal with such important people. 'Would you like some tea?' Lucy asked as she invited the man and woman inside.

'No we won't trouble you; I can see you're busy.'

Lucy couldn't help admiring the costume the woman wore. She blushed as she realised she was still wearing the floral pinafore with a splash of black lead down the middle. She hurriedly removed it. 'I'm sorry I'm not changed. Friday is one of my busiest days. Well, actually they're all busy days.' She knew she was prattling on and smiled nervously.

'Yes, I'm sure they must be. So with three children of your own why do you wish to adopt another child?'

'We love him. Besides, his mother placed him in our care. We were the ones she trusted to look after him.'

The woman nodded and the man made notes in a book.

'And actually Bernard adopted us, really. He just naturally began to call us Mam and Dad, and he adores his brother and sisters. It would break his heart to be parted from them, especially Rosie. It would break our hearts too.' Lucy's voice broke as she considered such an eventuality.

'Please, Mrs Grey, we're not here to upset you. We are here to make sure you are suitable parents and your home is the right one in which to bring up the child.'

'You can check the rest of the house. We haven't much in the way of luxuries but it's clean.'

'We are aware of that. Your home is also comfortable and warm. We are also aware that Bernard is a happy and intelligent boy. We have spoken to his teacher and as it is a church school we have made enquiries and discovered that Bernard is being brought up in a Christian household.' Peter began to stir and the woman went and peered into the pram. 'All your children are beautiful, Mrs Grey.'

'Yes they are – all our children including Bernard.'

The man closed his book and smiled at Lucy. 'That will be all for now, Mrs Grey.'

'Does that mean we can adopt him?' Lucy

asked excitedly.

'We shall be paying you another visit in the near future.'

'But what shall I tell my husband?'

'You'll be hearing from us soon. Good afternoon.' They walked out of the house, leaving Lucy feeling like a nervous wreck, going over in her mind everything that had been said. Should she have said this? Should she have said that? And after all the mind-searching she was no wiser about whether Bernard was destined to be their son. Only time would tell and if at the end of all the waiting the adoption couldn't take place Lucy knew she would never recover from the heartbreak of losing a child who in every way had become part of her family.

Prudence Grey tore up yet another letter from a lawyer by the name of Paul Tomlinson. She was ignoring the letters, just as she was ignoring the fact that she was a married woman. Her attentions had been transferred to a tall, dark man who could have been mistaken for Robbie Grey. The man was a regular borrower at the library and Prudence imagined he was attending so often because he was attracted to her.

The chief librarian – an aging spinster – considered it scandalous the way her assistant was behaving every time the man returned his books. Had Prudence no shame? Flaunting herself, and she a married woman. She had employed her friend's niece out of the goodness of her heart and this was how she was repaying her. Well, she wouldn't stand for it; she would have to speak to her friend about Prudence's behaviour. Who would have thought the daughter of a man of the cloth would demean herself in such a way? Pouting her lips, titivating her hair and thrusting out her chest at the man. It was disgusting. If the girl continued in this way she would find herself unemployed, as well as deserted by her husband. And who could blame him if this were her normal way of carrying on? Yes, she would certainly pay her friend a visit. It would prove embarrassing, but not as embarrassing as having to witness the carrying on in her library, which had always been a most respectable establishment until the arrival of Prudence Grey.

Will was now a regular visitor at the home of Betty Hague. Her parents were fond of Will and her father had made a few discreet enquiries and discovered Will was a respectable, industrious lad and was the son of the late Bill Gabbitas, which in his opinion spoke for itself. Besides, Betty's father liked a lad with a sense of humour and Will made him laugh. So Will was welcomed into their home and considered to be an eligible young man for their Betty. On Sunday afternoons a fire was lit in the Hagues' front room and the couple were allowed a little privacy, though Mrs Hague made sure no hanky-panky was taking place by conveniently needing something at regular intervals. Sometimes it was the best fruit dishes from the sideboard, or a clean tablecloth in order to set the table for Sunday tea. On this occasion however, the parents had gone out on a visit to Mr Hague's sister, leaving the lovebirds alone for the first time and Betty intended making the most of the empty house.

'Would you like to see my bedroom, Will? I've distempered it myself.' Will wasn't the slightest bit interested in newly distempered walls but had other things on his mind, which would be much easier to manipulate in a room with a bed. So he showed the appropriate enthusiasm in the pretty pink walls and rose-patterned curtains before turning his attention to Betty, who was just as eager to be in his arms.

'Oh, Will. I thought we'd never get the house to ourselves.'

'Me too, though you shouldn't 'ave brought me up 'ere.' He didn't mean a word of it and the young lovers were soon lying on Betty's pink bed. When his hand moved to the bare flesh between Betty's stocking and her knickers she made no resistance and was just as eager as Will to take their friendship a stage further. It was only when intercourse was about to take place that Betty thought better of it and decided things had gone far enough.

Will felt slightly put out that he had been so near fulfilling his dream only to have it curtailed, but he put on a good face and knew that when he finally got round to it, it would be well worth the wait. He loved Betty Hague and the way she had responded to his touch told him that she felt the same. Aye, she had done the right thing by not giving in. He couldn't have lived with himself if he had made her pregnant. There was time enough for that when they were married, and if he had his way a wedding would be taking place in the not-too-distant future.

Will began to panic at the idea of Betty not wanting to marry him and thought he had better find out if she was in the same mind as he was. 'Betty, I love you. Will you marry me?'

'Oh, Will. I wasn't leading you on in order to drag a proposal out of you.'

Will looked put out and Betty smiled at his crestfallen expression.

'I know that, Betty. But I mean it. I love you and I want us to be married.'

'And I love you. I've loved you from the first time I saw you at the dance, and yes, I will marry you. Unless it's just me decorating skills you're after.' Then Will kissed her, this time with a tenderness that told Betty it wasn't only the sex Will was interested in. But by the feel of Will as he pressed up close to her the sex would come a close second and Betty would find it hard to resist him until they were married. But resist she would, even though it would be agony.

'They're home.' Betty hurriedly straightened her clothing and Will thanked his lucky stars that they hadn't been misbehaving after all.

'Hello! What yer doing up there? Everything all right?'

'Yes, Mr Hague, everything's fine.' Betty's dad was already at the top of the stairs. Will looked round the room, indicating with his hand. 'In the pink, Mr Hague.' The man laughed. He should've known Will could be trusted – like his dad, he was.

'I was just showing Will my decorating skills, Dad.'

'Aye, a clever lass is our Betty. Mek a good little

wife one of these days, she will.'

'I'm sure she will.' Will smiled at Betty. 'And I hope I don't 'ave too long to wait.' Will was gratified by the smile that lit up Jim Hague's face. Eeh but they'd had a narrow escape. He wouldn't be visiting Betty's bedroom again until they were married. He couldn't trust himself to behave – not where Betty was concerned.

In January 1936 King George V had breathed his last breath. The lady at the top house of Side Row went into full mourning dress and covered her mirrors with black cloth. Mr Slater said if he went into mourning it would be at the thought of Edward's accession to the throne. 'No good'll come of that,' he predicted. Mr Slater needn't have worried, as it happened. Edward's reign was to prove short-lived.

It was the beginning of April when John arrived home one day with a huge smile on his face. Lucy watched him strip off to the waist at the sink in the corner and rid himself of the coal dust. Then she placed the plate of meat and potato pie – which was more potato than meat – in front of him 'Well?'

'Well what?' John watched the anticipation light up Lucy's lovely face.

'Oh, come on. I know there's something you're holding back.'

'I've been made deputy.'

'What?'

'Your Ben's leaving. Now Emma's looking after little Joyce he's decided to join the business. Mrs Scott has decided she wants to spend some of her money on a van. So he's handed in his notice and put in a good word for me. They've given me his job.'

'Oh, John. It's no more than you deserve.'

'Well it should have gone to somebody who's been there longer than me but two of them don't want to swap shifts and the other one is a poor attender, stays at home most Mondays, prefers to be at the Rising Sun.'

'That's something they can't accuse you of.'

'No lass, drinking on a work day's a fool's game if you ask me. Besides, with our lot there's no money to spare, but I shall be earning more as a deputy. Enough to make a difference between worrying where the next meal is coming from and being able to put a bit away.'

Lucy decided it was as good a time as any to break the news. 'Enough to feed an extra mouth?'

'What do yer mean, love?'

'I mean I'm expecting again. Sorry.' She added the word in a whisper.

'Nay, lass, it's nothing to be sorry about. It'll bring its love with it like the others did.'

'Oh, John, I do love you. You're the kindest, most gentle man in the world.'

John grinned. 'Less of the flattery. When's it due then?' He took another mouthful of pie.

'September maybe.'

John nodded. 'More the merrier,' he said, relieved that he'd be earning a bit more before then, but anxious that Lucy had caught on again after he had been so careful. If they went on like this they'd end up like the Murphys, and they didn't even have the excuse that they were Catholics.

Chapter Twenty-two

Herbert read the letter from his sister, threw it down on the hall stand and went out, down the path and across to the church. Louisa wondered what news had caused her husband to return to his prayers when he had only just come home. She picked up the sheet of paper, looked at the signature on the bottom and began to read.

My dear Herbert,

As you know I was delighted to have Prudence come and stay with me after the upset when Robert left the sanctity of their marriage. However Prudence has disappointed me by letting down my friend the librarian, who was kind enough to offer her employment. I'm afraid Prudence is bringing the library into disrepute by acting more like a young teenager instead of a respectable married woman. Indeed she seems to have forgotten – or chooses to ignore – the fact that she is married. In short, she is flaunting herself at one of the patrons at her place of work. Unless Prudence ceases to make a spectacle of herself and conducts herself in a more appropriate manner I fear she will soon be dismissed.

I think Prudence needs your guidance at this time and hope you will consider paying us a visit. Of course I shall look forward to welcoming Louisa too and maybe you can treat this as a short holiday. I fear you are burying your heads in the sand and hoping the problem will go away. This won't do at all, dear brother. A solution must be found. Incidentally, I have discovered Prudence is ignoring correspondence from a lawyer by the name of Paul Tomlinson.

Please inform me of your arrival time.

Your loving sister,

Edith.

Louisa placed the letter back in its envelope and went across to the church. Closing the old oak door quietly, she tiptoed to where Herbert was kneeling at the altar. She knelt beside him and bent her head in prayer. The scent of lilac in a vase close by mingled with the mustiness of old books and polished wood. Louisa loved this church, which usually stilled her mind and gave her peace. Today she found none of the usual calm. She touched her husband's arm and he reached out and clutched her hand. She realised Herbert was crying.

'Don't, please don't, Herbert.'

'Oh, Louisa, what have I done?'

'You? You've done nothing, my love.'

'I have. I've ruined a man's life to save my daughter's reputation. When all the time her reputation was based on lies. And all the time I suppose I knew what my daughter was like – spoiled – because it was I who spoiled her; and devious, though she doesn't get that from me or you.'

'I, I think Prudence needs help, my love. I have thought so for some time, but I went on ignoring the things she did. I believe it was Prudence who tried to poison the livestock at Greenwood's but I didn't want to believe it. I'm as much to blame as you are. She's sick, Herbert, I'm sure of it.'

'What are we to do?'

'Give Robert his life back. Persuade Prudence to give him a divorce. Make sure she has a lawyer, or at least answers the lawyer's letters.'

'I'm not a wealthy man, Louisa. Divorces can cost the earth.'

'There may be a way. We must do our best for Robert's sake.'

'Yes, we shall take a few days' break and go to Liverpool. Edith is right; the problem won't go away.'

'Now my love, let us pray; it may give us comfort.'

Herbert nodded, then he prayed to the God he loved above all else. He knew He wouldn't let him down.

The library was almost ready for closing when the doctor hurried in to collect a book he had ordered. He hoped the assistant wouldn't start flaunting herself and wished now he had sent his wife. The librarian went to find it and hoped Prudence wouldn't make a spectacle of herself again. The poor man had been embarrassed enough on his last visit by her shocking behaviour. In order to prevent a repeat performance she turned to her assistant. 'You can go now. It's almost closing time anyway.'

The doctor was relieved and smiled at his benefactress, who was surprised when Prudence didn't hang around but simply put on her coat and left. The girl waited outside the building, convinced that the man who so resembled her husband was attracted to her. After all, he always smiled when she removed the cards and handed him the chosen books. She watched him leave the library and set off along the street, then she began to follow him, deciding to surprise him by calling at his home. Unlike Robbie Grey, he wouldn't turn her away; he desired her – she had seen it written on his face. She watched him take out his key and unlock the door. After he had let himself in she waited a few minutes whilst she studied the name plate on the door. Then she rang the bell, already undoing her coat.

Prudence was confused when a woman answered the door, a plump young woman. Then her confusion turned to anger – what was she doing here? He was meant to be alone.

'Yes, can I help you?'

'No, not you. I want him.'

'I'm sorry, surgery's closed for the night, but if you're ill I'm sure my husband will see you.' She turned and called his name. 'Laurence, there's a patient to see you.'

'I'm not a patient, and you're not his wife. He loves me. Why would he marry someone like you? Look at you, you're fat.' Prudence took off her coat, then undid the button on her skirt and slipped it down. Next she took off her blouse. 'See, I'm slimmer than you and much more attractive.' She continued to undress as the doctor's wife looked on in horror.

'Laurence. Please, where are you?'

'Coming.' He came to an abrupt halt at the bottom of the stairs.

'What the...?'

‘I don’t know, she says...’ The woman burst into tears. ‘She says I’m fat and you’re attracted to her.’

‘Good lord. The girl’s ill; she must be. Please put your clothes on.’

‘No!’ Prudence placed her hands on her hips and posed in a sexual manner. ‘You know you want me. Well, I’m here now.’

The door on the left opened and a pretty little girl came out into the hall. ‘Daddy, why is that lady getting undressed? Is she going to sleep here? Is that why?’

‘He’s not your daddy; he doesn’t belong to any of you. He loves me.’

The doctor scooped his daughter up in his arms and took her back into the lounge. ‘Be a good girl and play with your toys, darling. The lady’s sick. We’ll make her better.’ Then he addressed his wife, who was trying to place Prudence’s coat round her now naked body.

‘I’ll ring for an ambulance, Joan.’ He picked up the phone and Prudence hurried forward and knocked the instrument from his hand. Then she spun round and slapped Joan sharply across the face, leaving the doctor’s wife shaking with fear. She backed away as her husband managed to make the call for an ambulance and the police. The girl was ill, mentally ill. She needed restraining and he doubted he could accomplish that on his own. The best thing in his opinion was to humour her. ‘Look, Joan will make us some tea and then we will all sit down and discuss what we are going to do. We’ve both been working all day and you are obviously overwrought.’

‘No, I’m just in love, that’s all. We’ll go away,

you and me, leave the fat woman here, the one who calls herself your wife.' Prudence began to laugh. 'As though you would want her when you can have me! She must be mad to think such a thing.' The doctor wished he could sedate the girl but everything he would need was kept in the surgery. By this time Prudence was laughing hysterically. The ambulance came at that point.

'Thank you God,' the doctor sighed with relief. He realised the situation could have turned out a lot worse; patients in her condition were sometimes driven to serious assault and if Joan had been alone in the house he dreaded to think what might have happened.

Prudence fought like a wild cat, but between them the two ambulance men and the doctor managed to get her in the vehicle. She was still declaring her undying love for a man she had barely spoken half a dozen words to until tonight. Indeed, if he had met her out in the street the doctor doubted he would have recognised the assistant librarian. He only hoped Joan would believe him when he told her he had done nothing to encourage such behaviour.

Joan was a compassionate woman, not given to jealousy. In fact she possessed all the qualities necessary in the wife of a doctor. All she could think of was the poor woman, knowing it would be a long haul back to sanity.

By the time Prudence was carried, struggling into hospital she had already threatened to kill the fat woman, strangle someone called Dot Greenwood and invited the youngest of the ambulance men to make love to her, in language strong enough to make the young one blush and shock the older one.

The next morning Reverend Goodman received a telegram from his sister which was short and to the point.

Come at once STOP Edith.

Within an hour, the verger had been put in charge of the church and Jane in charge of the house. The rector from Cragstone had promised to hold the Sunday services and Herbert and Louisa were on their way to the station. They realised they could ignore the situation no longer, but little did they know how ill their daughter was, or that she was in a secure room at the mental hospital. Louisa had been right: Prudence did need help, urgently.

At the beginning of the year Nellie had wondered if the bookings would justify all the money Tom had spent on the guest house, but by Easter the rooms were already being booked for the summer season, and four family rooms and two singles already occupied for the Easter holiday. Lily had discovered a way of making a bit of extra money, by offering a childminding service so that the parents could take advantage of the entertainment Blackpool had to offer. The children would be put to bed by the parents and all Lily had to do was patrol the rooms at regular intervals and comfort any of the restless ones. Because Lily loved children she considered it to be the easiest way possible of making a little extra spending money. She still insisted on one night a week off however, so that she and Phoebe could get dressed up and go out, sometimes to the dances on the pier or the Winter Gardens, other times to the pictures. Once they went to the Pleasure Beach where they rode on the Flying Machine, but mostly they would simply wander along the Golden Mile with Jim and his mate Stan, who quite fancied Phoebe, though Phoebe couldn't make up her mind whether she fancied him. Lily wished she would decide to have him for a boyfriend; it would be nice if they could be two courting couples. Anyway, she thought Jim was ever so romantic; they would stand by the railings looking down at the sea whilst the brass band played and Jim sang to the music. He made her blush sometimes when he gazed at her with his big brown eyes and sang romantic love songs. Lily thought he should be singing on the stage, so beautiful was his voice. Phoebe would giggle but Lily didn't care – she thought Phoebe was a little bit jealous because Stan didn't sing to her.

Nellie was thrilled that the guest house was proving a success, forever commenting on how fortunate she was, not realising that it was nothing to do with luck and everything to do with her cooking. Tom said there wasn't a restaurant in Blackpool that served better food, and he should know as he had dined in most of them. When Lily and Phoebe compared menus they found that Nellie provided almost as wide a selection as the larger, posher establishment said to be in the finest position in the resort. Nellie was surprised and delighted at Lily's discovery. Still, Nellie wouldn't have liked a larger place, preferring to offer a more homely atmosphere.

It came as a shock at the end of June when Nellie discovered she was pregnant. Tom considered Nellie to be the cleverest woman in the world and wanted to rush around spreading the news to everyone. Margaret was in tears at the thought of a grandchild and Henry experienced such a rush of emotion he threw his arms round Nellie and almost smothered her with kisses.

Nellie thought she must be the only one who had considered the implications. Not that she didn't want Tom's children, but how would she cope with the cooking whilst being a good mother to her child? Fortunately it would be born out of season, so this year's guests wouldn't be affected, but what of next year? When she voiced her fears to Lily she was amazed when the girl said, 'What a pity Mrs Cooper doesn't live 'ere. It'd be right up her street being a kind of nanny. She could wheel the baby on the front and sit in one of them theer shelters with the pram. Oh, it would be nice for 'er. Mrs Cooper loves Blackpool so much it meks tears come to 'er eyes.' Lily almost had tears in her own eyes at the thought of the woman she had grown to love. 'Do yer know what I think, Nellie? I think Mrs Cooper was in love when she came to Blackpool.' Just like I love Jim, Lily thought.

'Oh I don't know about that,' Nellie answered, but she was thinking about what Lily had said. The girl was right: Mrs Cooper would be ideal to take care of her baby, just for the few hours Nellie would need to cook the main meal and breakfast. She would be a kind of grandmother, a doting one no doubt. It would also solve Mrs Cooper's problem of where she would go when a younger woman took over at the manor. Nellie realised she was becoming carried away with the idea. She couldn't expect Tom to take the woman into their home. Besides, where would she sleep? It would mean taking up one of the bedrooms. No, she would have to come up with another solution; there was plenty of time before the baby was born.

Lily might have been a mind reader, for she sighed and said. 'Ooh it would be lovely if Mrs Cooper was 'ere, and theer's plenty o' room for another bed in my room.'

For the first time in ages Nellie saw the tears filling Lily's eyes and realised that it wasn't just Lily who was missing the elderly housekeeper. Nellie was too.

Chapter Twenty-three

'Pretty Betty, don't fail,
'Let me carry your pail,
'To the banks where the primroses grow.'

Little Peter laughed and swayed to the rhythm as his uncle William sang tunelessly. It was a beautiful morning and Will had been up with the lark, intent upon enjoying every moment of his day off. He had placed Peter in the battered old pushchair that had been handed down by a woman on Side Row. The twins were too big now to sit end to end in the pram and were wheeled out in turns by an army of volunteers from Top

Row. Rosie had gone with Mr Slater to the allotments, Violet to Mary's and Bernard to play at Mrs Cadman's. Will could hear the bell ringing for morning mass at St Catherine's and though it sounded more like an old tin can, the familiarity of it comforted William and the memories of his childhood came rushing back. He could hear his dad now as he bade him get ready for a Sunday walk to Sheepdip Wood. It had been Lucy who had washed his face and combed his hair, always Lucy, the little mother. He wished there was some way of repaying her for all the loving care she had handed out to him over the years.

Even though Will had had a hard childhood, he considered himself the most fortunate of all the family. Not for him the horror of the coal mine or the earsplitting sound and heat of the steelworks, but a job he loved. And now he had Betty with whom to share his happiness. He looked out from the rock he was resting on and could see the road winding up the valley between Millington and Cragstone. He had visions of the two towns being joined together in the not too distant future by red brick houses, which would rob both places of their harsh beauty and character. He could just see the chimneys of the little cottage in which he and Betty were about to begin married life together. Betty's father had surprised them by handing over the deeds to the small stone property. 'Not very big I admit,' – he had apologised even though the couple considered it a grand place – 'but there's plenty o' room to build on with a garden that size.' There was too, and Will could hardly believe they would never have to worry about paying the rent. Will didn't know anyone else who owned their own house; well, Mr Brown probably did, and Smiler Grundy, but as for people of his class! It was almost unthinkable. When he had tried to express his gratitude Mr Hague had dismissed his thanks with a wave of the hand.

'Eeh, lad,' he had said, 'if I can't spend me hard-earned brass on me only daughter, it's coming to summat. If yer want to repay me, just you concentrate on making our Betty happy. That's all I ask.'

Will let down the back of the pushchair as he noticed Peter had fallen asleep. He had just made the little lad comfy when a voice called out, 'Is it Annie's youngest lad?'

'Aye, Mrs Greenwood. It is.'

'Well, lad, it's some time since I saw you to talk to.'

'It'd be when I came tatie picking, Mrs Greenwood. That's a few years since.' Will could remember how back-breaking the work had been and he smiled as he remembered Little Arthur calling out to the pickers, 'All reight lads, heads down and arses up.' Apart from the money they had been given a bucket of potatoes for their efforts. Some of the lads had been too exhausted to carry them home and had refused them. Will had carried them home despite his aching limbs and his mother hadn't even acknowledged them, let alone thanked him.

'Where yer going, Mrs Greenwood?' Boadacea was wearing a wrap-round pinafore covering her frock, wellington boots and one of Little Arthur's flat caps. She was brandishing a stick in her hand.

'Going 'ome, Will. Just been to tek cows onto't long field. Are yer coming to 'ave a sup o' tea with us?'

'No, thanks all the same. Perhaps another day.'

'Aye, Little Arthur'd be pleased to 'ave a bit of male company for a change. Our Dot prattles on a bit and gets on 'is nerves sometimes.' The woman's face clouded. 'Though she's not been 'er normal self since she and Robbie split up. It's a right rum do is that.'

'Aye, it is. Robbie's not the same either. He really loves your Dot, Mrs Greenwood. And he'll sort something out, don't you worry. He's in touch with a solicitor fellow all the time. Three letters he's had in the last few weeks. Don't know what's in 'em of course – he doesn't say – but summat's happening.'

'Well, if you say so.' Boadacea perched herself on the rock next to Will. 'And who's this little love, then?'

'One of our Lucy's lot.'

'Aye, he's a Grey all right; no mistaking that dark hair and that skin.' Until the split-up Boadacea had had visions of a grandson of her own looking like that. The pair sat in contemplation for a while.

'My grandmother could remember when that road down there was just a dirt path wi' foxgloves and honeysuckle growing on it. Oh aye, it was nowt but a path in her day. Blackberries, hazelnuts, eeh I bet it was a picture. Mind you, that was before the thick yeller smoke from the works killed 'em all and they widened it to mek the road.'

'Aye, but you know what they say: "Where there's muck there's money."' Will looked out at the view. 'It's lovely up 'ere though, despite the works. I bet you've the best view in Millington.'

'Aye, it'd take some beating. The works and reservoir might be a godsend now, but they could prove a danger in the not too distant future. Well that's what my Little Arthur thinks.'

'In what way?'

'War, lad. He thinks there'll be one before long.'

'There's already a war, Mrs Greenwood.'

'Oh aye, the Spanish war, and that's bad enough, but when that Hitler gets going we shall be in for it right. That's what my little Arthur thinks, and ee's not usually far wrong.'

'I hope not, Mrs Greenwood.'

'So do I, lad, so do I.'

'I'd best be getting back.'

'Aye, lad. Give my regards to yer family.'

'I will.'

'And tell Robbie we wish 'im well.'

'I'll do that.' Will took the brake off the push-chair and set off for home. It would be dinner-time when they got back. Then he was off to see Betty. They'd be going on about frocks and wedding cakes, her and her mam. It would all be worth it though when he and Betty were man and wife. He hoped Little Arthur was wrong, though. Once he'd got Betty he didn't fancy having to leave her again, and that's what would happen if there was a war.

Robbie was feeling much happier now he had

heard the Goodmans had gone to visit Prudence. Surely they would try and persuade their daughter to end her marriage, or at least discuss the situation with Paul Tomlinson, or a lawyer of their own. Robbie had been touched when Mr Grundy had offered to pay for a divorce for him. He had refused his offer, pointing out that nothing could be done at the moment and that by the time a divorce could go ahead Robbie would probably be able to afford the expense himself. Mr Grundy said the money was there anyway, should it be needed.

He turned the corner of Top Row, where a young lad was throwing a ball at the wall and catching it. Two others were watching and willing him to drop it so they could have a turn. The lad was chanting to the rhythm of the ball-throwing.

'Every day old Smiler Grundy

'Hammers nails, except on Sunday.

'How many nails does Smiler knock?

'How many times does he play with his–'

'Hey.' Robbie stopped the lad just in time. 'Have a bit of respect for Mr Grundy and the people who can hear yer.' He wondered why Mr Grundy was made a figure of fun when he was one of the nicest people you could wish to meet.

'Aw, Robbie, we were only 'aving a bit o' fun. I only meant an owd crowing cock, not his...' The lad realised he was making things worse and ran off round the corner with the others following. Robbie could hear them laughing and grinned to himself, wondering which of the three was the budding poet. On entering the house his eyes went straight to the mantelpiece, but there was no letter waiting for him. He glanced at the mirror and as always made a wish that he could be rid of Prudence and free to marry Dot. He must be going soft in the head to be wishing in a mirror, but Lucy believed it was a wishing mirror and who was he to deny it?

If John was on night shift and Will out courting, Robbie would take Baby out for her last walk. Tonight he found himself – as usual – taking the lane towards Greenwood's. He could see a light shining in the window of the old derelict cottage. Dot had had such plans for the place. Perhaps she was in there now, thinking of him just as he was thinking of her. At times like this he was tempted to seek her out and tell her how much he loved her and longed to be with her, and most of all seek reassurance that she still felt the same about him. Would it be so wrong to meet her occasionally? Yet he knew he never would. He had her reputation to consider. He was still a married man, albeit not a normal one, but he would wait, only go to her when he was free to marry her.

Baby began to jump about with excitement as they neared the farm and old Bob ran barking towards them. Baby had taken a fancy to the old dog on their late-night walks. Robbie never failed to hope that one of these nights Dot might come out to the yard; just a glimpse of her would be something to be going on with, but she never did. They had to be satisfied with a few words on Sundays at church, which he supposed was better than nothing. Besides, Dot was there in his thoughts from waking in the morning to retiring at night. Every detail of her face was vivid in his mind. The light in the cottage had been extinguished. He wished he could extinguish Prudence as easily.

'Come on, Baby. Let's go home.' The little dog ran slipping and sliding down the steep path, pulling Robbie behind her.

Chapter Twenty-four

It was when Will went to collect his wages that he heard the news from Mr Brown. 'I 'ear they're selling your 'ouse, Will.'

'What?'

'Your 'ouse and t'other one.'

'Which other one?'

'I don't know which one. I only know they're the only ones the pit still own and they want rid.'

'But I thought they owned the whole row.'

'Eeh, no lad. Most of 'em 'ave been sold on to a private landlord over the years. Been 'anging on to the last two, hoping prices'd go up I expect. I suppose it's all the talk of a war that's persuaded 'em.'

'But what'll happen to us? We won't be thrown out, will we?'

'Eeh no lad. I'll tell yer summat though, yer can bet the rents'll go up. Whoever buys 'em'll want to mek their money back.'

Will began to sweat at the thought of John having to fork out more, and just when Will was about to leave. His board had been a help towards household expenses, and then there was the new baby expected any day. He realised Mr Brown was still talking to him. 'Sorry, what did you say?'

'I was just saying, they're good 'ouses. Eighteen-inch-thick walls they 'ave. Be a good investment for't future, especially wi' 'aving sitting tenants. They'll not fetch as much as if they were vacant.'

'When are they to be sold? I don't think our Lucy knows.'

'On the fourteenth, by auction. Saw it in't *Cragstone Express*.'

'How much do you think they'll go for?'

'Eeh, I don't know, lad. Like I say, without vacant possession they won't fetch as much. Depends who turns up on the night.'

Will was quiet as he collected his wages and set off for home. Being quiet was highly unusual for someone like Will. He didn't say anything about the sale to Lucy or John. He didn't want to worry them about who was likely to be their future landlord. Instead he went to see Jane; he would ask her advice before he did anything, but if she was agreeable he had a plan forming in his mind.

Andrew Grey was born on the seventh of September, a twelve-pound baby who caused Lucy three days of pain and a hell of a lot of stitches. Dr Sellars was worried for a time, but Lucy soon recovered from her ordeal and everyone was full of admiration for their fine son.

'Now we've got Peter, Andrew, James and John in the family,' Lucy told Mary, who had turned up once again to take charge.

'All the saints,' Mary remarked.

'And me, don't forget Bernard,' the little boy reminded them.

'No, we won't forget you. You're a nice cuddly Saint Bernard,' Lucy laughed.

'And don't forget my sisters.' Bernard idolised Rosie and Violet and everything had to be fair in order to keep him happy. Lucy hugged him close and wondered how she would cope if the adoption was refused. She changed her position so that Bernard had room to climb on the bed and winced at the soreness, causing Mary to warn the boy to sit still because his mam wasn't very well.

'That's because baby Andrew came out of her tummy and it had to be stitched up like in the story about the wolf.'

'Who told you that?'

'Nobody, I just guessed because your tummy was fat and now it's all empty.'

Mary tutted. 'He's been here before has this one.' Lucy nodded and smiled, but she wondered how long it would be before he began asking questions about what happened to Evelyn and who his real father was. When he looked at the picture of Evelyn these days he called her his old mam, the one before his new one. Lucy just prayed that by that time Bernard wouldn't be with mam number three.

'Of course I don't want the money. Both our Lucy and me told you the money was yours. It's in your name, Will. In fact I'd forgotten all about it. You do whatever you like with it.' Jane frowned. 'It's a big step to take, though. Why don't you ask our Ben what he thinks? Or Jacob? He's the one to advise you about financial matters.'

'Aye, you're right. I'll ask Jacob. What do you think, though?'

'I think it's a marvellous idea, so long as you don't land yourself in debt.'

'I shan't; that wouldn't be fair on Betty, but the money's just stuck there doing nothing. Think of the peace of mind it would give our Lucy and John. I'll never be able to repay them for keeping me out of the pit, and never once has she complained about all the washing and cooking she's done for me over the years, so if I do this for 'em it'll make me feel good. Besides, some of the money should be hers by rights.'

'Then do it, but talk to Jacob first. I'm sure we shall all be relieved to know our Lucy and John have security for the future. With all their lot they're going to need it.'

Will beamed at his sister. 'Don't tell her yet, though. I want it to be a surprise if I'm successful.'

'All right, but don't get too excited. Don't forget there'll be others with more money than you have.'

Will nodded and went off to Mary's, hoping Jacob would be home by now. The precious bank book was secure in his jacket pocket.

The tap room at the Golden Eagle was packed and it was difficult to breathe in an atmosphere thick with smoke. Will's heart sank at the sight of the crowded room. 'We won't stand a chance, Jacob.'

'Oh stop worrying. Auctions always attract the crowds, mostly just here for the beer, or out of curiosity. Now just remember, don't bid until I say so. And for goodness' sake sit still, or you'll have placed a bid inadvertently.'

Beside him, Ernest was trembling; he had never felt so nervous. He could feel the sweat dripping off his hair. It was the scariest thing he had ever considered doing in his life. When Will had told him of his plan to buy the house for Lucy he had thought it a crazy idea, but when Will told him about the money in the bank it hadn't sounded so crazy after all. Then when he had realised their house was the other one to be sold he had put the suggestion to his father that Ernest might make an offer, expecting his father to ridicule his plan. Instead Mr Slater had worked out how much he could chip in, how much Ernie had to spare and had made enquiries about a loan. 'It'd be a sound investment for't future, Ernest. And it'd set me mind at rest knowing you'd 'ave a roof over yer head when me and yer mother're pushing up daisies.'

'No, Dad. I'm buying it for you and me mam. If I shift out it'll be yours.'

'Aye but yours, one day. And if yer do buy it it'll be in your name or none at all.' Ernest wished now he had never suggested it.

'Right, it's coming up next,' Jacob whispered. 'Ours first.' Jacob waited, satisfied that there were only a couple of bidders. It was what he had expected. Mid-terraced houses weren't expected to attract the property owners, especially with sitting tenants. The two men bid against each other and then Will nearly fell off the stool when Jacob nudged him. Will raised his arm. He had no idea what he was bidding – the auctioneer was going too fast for him and he couldn't make out a word of what he was saying. He heard a cough from one bidder and saw the other nod his head. Jacob nudged him again and he raised his arm. The first bidder shook his head and the nodder made no response.

'Going once. Going twice.' The auctioneer thumped the table with such force Ernest thought he might suffer a heart attack.

'Sold to the gentleman on the right.'

Jacob thumped Will on the back. 'Congratulations. You've just bought your sister a house.' He heard the voices abate and told them to shush. It was Ernest's house coming up next. Will wanted to ask how much he'd paid for the property, but Jacob was concentrating now on the next lot.

'Well,' Jacob grinned, 'are yer going to buy me a pint after all that?'

'I'll buy yer a half a dozen,' Ernie laughed. 'Bye, but we've got a bargain there, Will.'

Will had never in his life felt so elated. He would still have something left in his account even after the expenses. He'd been surprised at the interest accumulated over the years. He thought he would leave that in the bank in case Jane wanted anything; after all, he was earning a good wage these days.

Ernest said that by the time he had paid the deposit the loan repayments would be no more than they would have been paying in rent. To tell the truth, Ernest didn't understand anything about mortgages – in fact he had never even heard of one until he and his father had made an appointment with the bank manager. Ernest actually felt a bit put out because he'd got his house for ten pounds less than Will. He couldn't understand why, when the houses were identical. Jacob laughed and said he should be thankful. Actually Jacob thought that one of the bidders had wanted both houses and had lost interest after the first one was sold for more than he was prepared to pay. All good news for Ernest.

'So when are you going to break the news to Lucy?'

'Now. But first it's my round, so let's have another and then I'm off.'

Jacob grinned. Will was a character and no mistake. Who else would have considered buying a house with money he could have spent on frivolities? He was proud to have Will for a brother-in-law and by what he had seen of his fiancée, Betty Hague was every bit as generous-natured. She would be a welcome addition to the family.

The house deeds had been handed over to John and Lucy with advice from the solicitor that joint ownership was wiser. Ernest Slater had been given a little green Building Society payment book with instructions to pay at the old chapel on the last Friday of each month. Ernest was not only proud to be a house owner, but also relieved not to be living in a tied house anymore. He could now leave the coal mining job if he wished. Lucy had argued that Will should never have spent his nest egg on her and John, but there had been tears in her eyes as she kissed her brother and thanked him, especially when Will said, 'You've been like a mother to me, Lucy. It's the least I can do.' John had told him that the door would always be open to Will and his family and Will had laughed.

'And where would we sleep? The way you and our Lucy are carrying on you'll need a tent in the garden in a few years' time.'

Lucy had blushed and hugged her brother and Will had turned all serious and said, 'But I'll tell you this, Lucy: I'd rather bring my kids up in this house than any other in Millington, even if we had to sleep in the cellar. It's a house with love in it and that's what makes it a home.'

'Ah, Will, that's a lovely thing to say.'

'It's true. Just look around at your lot. I've seen a lot of families when I was out on my rounds but not one as contented as yours. I'll tell you summat: if I can mek Betty as happy as John has made you I shall be well satisfied.'

'So have you named the day for the wedding?' John asked. He was embarrassed by the compliments Will was handing out and relieved to change the subject.

'We will as soon as the house is ready; it'll be at Cragstone of course, with Betty residing there. I say, the Goodmans are taking their time aren't they? I thought they were going for a few days. Do yer think they're sorting things out for Robbie?'

'I've no idea but I certainly hope so.' John frowned. Robbie's problem was on his mind the whole time. Little did he know the mountainous problem Herbert and Louisa were coping with in Liverpool. In comparison John's worry was little more than a mole hill.

Chapter Twenty-five

'Ooh, Nellie, we shall never be straight again.' Lily was scurrying around like a scalded hen trying to tidy up after the workmen, even though Nellie had told the daily cleaning woman to leave the mess until the job was done. The lift was installed and working, all the way from the dining room to the attic, and all they were waiting for now was for the plaster to dry and then Nellie could patch up where the wallpaper had been soiled.

'Lily, come and sit down. I need you to cut the edges off this roll of wallpaper.' The girl was making Nellie's head spin with all the rushing around. Lily found the scissors. 'Ooh, it will be good for the owd ones not to 'ave to go up and down stairs. Fancy me living in a 'ouse with a lift in it.'

'It'll be good for all of us, Lily. Just think, you'll be able to carry everything up and down in half the time.'

Lily looked shocked. 'Ooh no, I shan't use it. What if it broke down and got stuck in the middle? No, I shall still walk up and down stairs.'

'That'd be silly, Lily.'

'Mrs Cooper used to say that: Silly Lily. Ooh I do miss Mrs Cooper, even more than me mam. Do yer think that's awful of me?'

'No, Lily. If the truth be known I miss her more than my mother too.' Nellie picked up the baby coat she was knitting and for once Lily was silent, as the pair both thought about how much they missed Mrs Cooper. Nellie knew she should have broached the subject to Tom of what would happen after the baby was born but she had just kept putting it off. She would talk to him tonight after they had eaten. He would have been mellowed then with a glass of wine. The more she considered bringing Mrs Cooper to Blackpool, the more sensible it seemed. Though what Tom would think of the idea she couldn't even guess. She couldn't really blame him if he didn't want another woman in the house. Tom had never denied her anything in all the time they had been married – there was bound to be a first time, and she would abide by his decision. All the same she would be so disappointed if he said no.

'Why do they put edges on wallpaper in't first place when we 'ave to cut 'em off again?' Lily enquired, her tongue keeping time to the opening and closing of the scissors.

'I don't know.' Nellie had often wondered that herself. 'Probably to prevent the wallpaper edges becoming damaged.'

'Aye, I suppose.' Lily carried on cutting. 'Still, I expect rich folk who can afford wallpaper 'ave plenty o' time to sit and cut, or somebody to do it for 'em. Poor folk 'ave to mek do wi' whitewash.'

Nellie felt quite shocked as it occurred to her that she was now considered one of the rich folk Lily was talking about. Well, she was working hard for it and employing two cleaners and Lily.

Perhaps the money Lily was sending home might one day buy a few rolls of wallpaper for her mam. But no, according to Lily, poor folk had no time to sit cutting paper.

The girl blushed as she realised what she had said and tried to make it better. 'Not that me mam'd paper't walls even if she could afford to; she's too bone idle. Not like you, Nellie, not like you at all.'

Just then they heard Tom's key in the lock and Lily gathered up the wallpaper and scissors to go up to her room. She had never been asked to leave; she just did so automatically whenever Tom entered the room.

Lily loved her room at the top of the house and it was no hardship for her to respect her employers' privacy. She had a wireless and a shelf full of books and she could sit and think about Jim. It would be nice though if Mrs Cooper was here.

'Tom.'

'Yes, my dear?' Tom had his head hidden in a newspaper, probably the motoring adverts.

'What am I going to do when the baby comes?'

'You will love it and cosset it, just as I shall.'

'I know that, but what about when I'm cooking? Lily won't have time to look after the baby; she works just as hard as I do.'

'Well!' Tom folded the newspaper and leaned back in his chair. 'There's one thing for sure; as much as I love my dear mother, I don't want her taking over my child. Borrow the baby she may, but a few hours regularly would become all day. I don't want that.'

'Your mother wouldn't want it either, she enjoys all her activities too much. So what do you suggest?'

'Either stop taking in guests for a few years, or...'

'Oh Tom, after all the money you've spent on the place it would be such a shame.'

'Or. Stop interrupting and let me finish. Ask the wise young owl up there in her nest.' Tom pointed up at the ceiling, a wicked gleam in his eye.

'Lily? Has she been talking about it?'

'Oh no, not talking about it. Just dropping hints every time she's within hearing distance. "Ooh, I do miss Mrs Cooper. Ooh, wouldn't it be nice if Mrs Cooper could be 'ere to 'elp Nellie when the baby comes? Ooh, if only Mrs Cooper could 'ave a bedroom like mine."'

Nellie couldn't help laughing at Tom's impression of Lily.

'So,' Tom said, 'it might not be a bad idea at that. I know how much you miss her and I should feel easier in my mind with a capable woman at hand when the baby's here. Besides, after going to all the expense of having the lift installed...'

'You mean you had Mrs Cooper in mind all the time?'

'Well, it doesn't go all the way up to the attic for Lily's benefit.'

'Oh, Tom. Are you sure you won't mind?'

'If it will make you happy I don't mind.'

'Do you know? You're the loveliest man I've ever met in my life.'

'I should hope so, Nellie Johnson. I should certainly hope so.'

Lucy was surprised to hear Mr Holmes coughing his way to her door. He wasn't a man to come calling, especially at this time of the morning. He knocked, opened the door a couple of inches and called, 'Lucy, are yer there, lass?'

'Come in, Mr Holmes. Is anything the matter?'

'No, lass. It's summat in't paper you ought to see.' He opened the paper and pointed to one of the columns. Lucy sat down at the table and read, her face turning pale as the news sank in. 'The man wanted in connection with the murder of Millington woman Evelyn Smithson has been killed in a motorcycle accident on Sunday evening. The accident happened on Attercliffe Common. The vehicle was thought to have been stolen.'

Lucy felt faint with relief and couldn't read any more. 'Oh, Mr Holmes, he's gone at last. You don't know how relieved I am that he won't be able to take Bernard away. Oh I'm so glad you noticed it or it would have been on my mind for ever.'

'Are tha all reight, love? Shall I get thee a drink or summat?'

'No, I'm fine, thank you. Unless you want one?'

Mr Holmes didn't want to leave the lass on her own. It must have been a shock for her. 'Aye, I could do wi' one. Just you sit there and I'll make it.' He lifted the kettle off the fire, checking that it held enough water. 'I don't think the news is summat we should draw anybody's attention to, or your little Bernard might get to hear of it.'

'No, Mr Holmes, you're right. At least when he

does start asking questions now I can truthfully tell him his dad is dead.' The two neighbours sat together, not needing to talk, each glad of the other's company, then he said, 'You're a sensible lass, Lucy and a right good mother to your lot.'

'I do my best, Mr Holmes. If they grow up as well as your four I shall be well satisfied.'

'Aye, we all do our best, but it doesn't always work.'

'I'm sure it worked for you.'

'Oh I don't know. The lasses have never given us any trouble, but I worry about our Harry.'

'Your Harry?' Lucy grinned. 'I'm sure you needn't worry about him. He's a good worker, according to John, and he'll have the pick of the girls with his handsome looks.'

'He's a cocky young bugger.' He realised what he had said and looked shamefaced at Lucy. 'Sorry lass, don't tell our Lizzie about me bad language, will yer?'

'I won't.' Lucy heard the twins and knew it was time to begin the day's toil. Today she would carry out her tasks with a lighter heart: Bernard was safe. He might not be theirs yet, but at least he didn't belong to a murderer anymore.

Mrs Cooper read the letter for the fourth time and was still in shock at the contents. Nellie needed her. Not just needed her – wanted her. Actually wanted her to go and live in at the guest house, as a sort of part-time nanny when the baby came. Nanny be damned; if she went it would be as a granny, not a nanny. Oh, to think of her being given the chance to care for Nellie's child. Nellie, who was like a daughter to her. Tears trickled down her cheeks at the joy of it. She read the words again, trying to read between the lines and discover what Tom Johnson thought about his home being invaded by an old woman. After all, it was his house. It was his money that had paid for the property and all the work that had been done to it, and now he had apparently had a lift installed, right up to the room she would be sharing with Lily. A sort of flat, was how Lily described it, every bit as posh as Mr Smith's room.

She frowned, wondering what would happen if she became ill and couldn't fulfil her duties. She would need to ask questions before she upped and went. Still, what would happen if she became ill whilst she was here? Mr Smith couldn't be expected to keep her on. No, the time was coming when she would have to make way for a younger woman. Oh, the relief at knowing there was a welcome waiting for her at Nellie's! She would enquire about a few things before she decided, though. She had a week before Tom and Nellie came, a week in which to come to a decision one way or the other. As far as she was concerned, she had already decided. If Tom Johnson agreed with Nellie that she was needed, then she would go to Blackpool. To the place with the memories, and who knows, she might make even more, memories associated with being a granny.

She would need to go shopping, buy herself some new clothes; after all, she didn't want to show Nellie up. She might even go and have one of them Eugene permanent waves. If she dared. Mrs Cooper felt alive for the first time in years.

Reverend Goodman was back in Millington in time to call the banns for Will and Betty, and to baptise Andrew Grey. The vicar and his wife seemed to have aged and lost weight in the few weeks they had been away. Lucy invited Louisa to be godmother to her son in an effort to cheer up the woman she now considered her friend. Only Robbie was told the news about Prudence when he enquired about her health. The news that his wife was in an asylum and had been prescribed barbiturates in an effort to sedate her came as a shock to Robbie.

'I'm so sorry,' he told Herbert, who was having trouble containing his emotions.

'Not half as sorry as I am for the trouble I've caused you, Robert.'

Robbie didn't answer. He just felt sad that the man who had given him and his brothers a home had ended up in such a tragic position.

'We have met with Paul Tomlinson and have done everything we can to sort out the problem we caused. It came to our attention that our daughter had destroyed all the correspondence from the lawyer. Her illness obviously accounted for her actions. We are, however, doing our best to make amends. It will of course take time. Mr Tomlinson will be in touch, eventually.'

'And what about Prudence? Will she recover?'

'It is highly unlikely. Apparently she has been of unsound mind for a long time, probably all her life. Unfortunately I ignored her condition, unlike Louisa, who has been worried about Prudence for some time. My fault entirely. I'm so sorry.'

'Oh I expect it was only natural to hope it would go away. Do you think I ought to go and see her?' It was the last thing Robbie wanted, but after all she was his wife.

'No, it wouldn't do any good. She wasn't even aware that we were there. She seems to have become obsessed with one of the doctors, says he's going to marry her. There wouldn't be any point in you visiting her. She's quite content planning her wedding.' Herbert smiled through the threatening tears. 'You're a good man, Robert. I hope you'll be able to begin anew in the near future.'

'Well, I'm sorry the news isn't better about Prudence.' Robert genuinely was sorry. He wouldn't wish insanity on his worst enemy.

'Keep of good heart, Robert. I am praying for you, and for God's forgiveness for myself.'

Robert nodded and went home. He wasn't much wiser about where he stood with his marriage; all he could do was put his trust in the lawyer and wait.

As usual Christmas Day had been a hectic one for Lucy with four little ones and Bernard besides. Even though Andrew was only three months old the family had taken it for granted that Christmas Day would be spent on Top Row as usual. Mary and Jacob had turned up first, with gifts for everyone and a bag containing a cold cooked ham, a loaf and a large tin of My Lady peaches. Then came Jane and James, whose presents had already been sent to Father Christmas. Emma and Ben arrived in the van with baby Joyce, announcing that they hadn't come to stop as Lucy had enough to do without visitors. But thcy stayed anyway. The women had taken over and produced a mountain of sandwiches, a sliced up fruit cake and peaches and cream.

Lucy had been forced to take it easy and enjoy the company of her brothers and sisters whilst the men played nursemaids in the front room. The highlight of the day had been the arrival of an extremely pregnant Nellie and her husband. Lucy had surveyed her family all around her and had found it difficult to suppress the threatening tears. The sight of Nellie and Tom – who had so much – so obviously enjoying their hospitality, humble as it was, gladdened her heart. Glancing up at the mirror, Lucy made a silent wish for health and happiness for everyone here. The mirror had been decked with holly by Will and Robbie, and Lucy added an extra wish that by next year's celebrations Robbie would have found happiness with Dot. The rest of them had all been so fortunate in their choice of partners.

Lily had been ecstatic when Nellie had told her they were taking her home to Cragstone to spend the day with her family. She had rushed out on Christmas Eve and bought presents for everyone. The money Tom had given her for Christmas had soon disappeared, but Lily hadn't minded. She had a lovely new-winter coat, a warm woollen one with a belt that emphasised her tiny waist, and a large collar. Nellie had taken her to one of the posh shops and let her choose it herself. She couldn't wait to see Jim's face when he saw her looking so glamorous. Mrs Johnson had bought her a phial of Mischief, which made her feel even more sophisticated. Actually she had felt quite shy when she arrived back at the little house in Cragstone; her old habit had got the better of her and she had burst into tears, especially at the sight of Molly, who had always been closest to her. Nellie had promised to call for her at seven and take her to visit Mrs Cooper before returning to Blackpool. Lily expected to cry again at the sight of her dear friend.

Actually it had turned eight when Nellie managed to tear herself away from Lucy's, where a party was still in progress. Mrs Cooper was expecting them and had put on a new dress and tried in vain to get a comb through her recently permed hair. It hadn't quite turned out like the poster in Marybelle's window and instead of shiny waves there was a mass of frizz. The disappointment hadn't quelled her excitement at the thought of her visitors. Once everyone had calmed down conversation turned to the important matter which was uppermost in everyone's mind. Was Mrs Cooper moving to Blackpool or not?

'I don't want to be a nuisance.'

'But we're going to need you,' Tom had emphasised, knowing instinctively that the woman was afraid of being a charity case. 'Without your help we shall have to shut the guest house.'

'But what will Mr Smith say? I mean ee's been good to me.'

'Ah yes, but I'm sure there are plenty of people in need of work.'

'Aye, and besides I'm not as young as I was. What if I get poorly? I shall be nowt but a burden then.'

'I'll look after yer, Mrs Cooper.' Lily took hold of thc housekeeper's hand. 'Ooh, yer should just see the room; it's like one you'd see on the pictures. Ooh, please come, Mrs Cooper.'

'Aye, that's as maybe, but it's up to Mr Johnson and Nellie, not you, yer silly Lily.' At the familiar expression Lily looked about to turn on the tears again.

'Well, it looks as though you've no option but to come,' Nellie said.

'So shall I tell your employer? Or will you?' Tom handed Lily a handkerchief.

'I'll do it. Like I said ee's been good to me.'

Mr Smith had been waiting all evening for the expected visitors. Christmas was a lonely time in places like the manor. He would be relieved to move on, if the truth be known. Though what was afoot was a mystery. The news that the place was to be taken over had come a month ago. He wouldn't be at all surprised if it wasn't something to do with the Ministry of Defence. With a war looming ever closer that seemed to be the most likely explanation. He had had no problem finding a new position. He wouldn't be sorry to leave this sprawling mansion. Men of Mr Smith's standing could always be found work with West Riding County Council. The news that his housekeeper was leaving came as a blessing in disguise. Molly and Madge would no doubt still be needed here, but Mrs Cooper would probably have lost her position.

Mr Smith had been anxious about the elderly woman and now the problem had been laid to rest he could sit back and enjoy his evening. He insisted on Nellie and Tom staying the night. Journeying back to Blackpool at this time of night was unthinkable; besides, Boxing Day would be just as miserable as today had been without anyone to share it with.

He rang the bell for some refreshment for Nellie – forgetting his staff were on holiday – and brought out his best brandy for Tom and himself. It came as no surprise when Lily answered the call and delivered the tea and sandwiches. She might be a silly Lily, but she was the most thoughtful and hardest working one Tom Johnson had ever encountered and she brought sunshine into the room every time she entered. Nellie had chosen her waitress well and he only hoped Mrs Cooper would be as happy in his employ. 'It looks like you'll be remaining here for the night, Lily.' Lily's face told him how delighted she was at the chance to gossip with Mrs Cooper to her heart's content.

'This is a drop of good brandy.' Tom held out his glass to his host for a refill.

Chapter Twenty-six

The adoption inspectors couldn't have turned up at a worse time. Monday morning – and a wet one at that. The kitchen was full of steam and the smell of hot soapy water. The door was almost blocked by the wringing machine and the tub and rubbing board. To crown it all Bernard was off school and he and Rosie were wanting to help. Lucy let Rosie stir the starch and Bernard hang the wet washing on the rack, which had been let down so he could reach. When the knock came Lucy prayed it would be someone willing to take one of the twins off her hands for an hour or two.

'Good morning, Mrs Grey.' Lucy's heart missed a beat.

'Oh! Won't you come in? If you can get in, that is.' Lucy forced a smile to her face.

'Yes, we can get in. I can see you're busy and we won't detain you for long. It's Bernard we are here to see this time. Do you think we can talk to him in private?'

'Yes, of course, you can go through here.' Lucy opened the door to the bottom of the stairs and led the man and woman through to the front room. At least it was tidy in here. 'Be a good boy, Bernard, for the lady and gentleman.'

'Thank you. Please carry on with the washing, though it's a typical January drying day.' Lucy wondered if the man was only here for the outing or if he had perhaps lost his voice. It was the lady who seemed to be doing all the talking. Still, no doubt he was taking everything in. She closed the door and left them to it, just in time to keep out the sound of Rosie beginning to wail 'And me, and me.' The little girl hated being parted from Bernard just when he was on holiday from school.

Bernard sat on the edge of the worn, leather sofa, unsure whether he liked the man or not.

'Well, Bernard, have you been helping your mother this morning?'

'Yes.'

'Do you like living here in this house?'
'Yes.'
'Is there anywhere else you would rather live?'
'Yes.'
The man glanced at his colleague and frowned. The woman said, 'Where would you rather live, Bernard?'
'In a gingerbread house.' Bernard giggled and the woman laughed with him.
'Would you like to show me where you sleep?'
Bernard nodded, jumped up and headed for the stairs. 'You'll have to be careful; they're very steep. That's why Mam keeps the door closed, because our Rosie's a clumsy little thing and might fall down.' He held out his hand. 'Hold my hand and then you won't fall.' The woman did so. 'I sleep here in this bed with our Peter.' He jumped up on the bed and bounced up and down, laughing as he added, 'Our Rosie and Violet sleep in that bed and Andrew sleeps in the cot in Mam's room, cos he's only a baby.' He came closer to the lady, who he had obviously taken a fancy to and whispered, 'When Uncle Will gets married I can sleep in his bed up in the garret. Sometimes I sneak up there in the morning while it's still dark. I like it up there. Uncle Will shows me things.' The man cast a look of alarm at his colleague.
'What does he show you, Bernard?'
'Come on. I'll show you.' The three clattered up the narrow stairs to the attic, where Bernard jumped up on one of the beds – which had fortunately been made – and lay flat on his back. 'The clouds, that's what he shows me, and the birds. Uncle Will says they are rooks. I like the

birds. They look at me and I wave to them. Once he showed me the stars. The Milky Way, that's a funny name. And heaven. That's where my old mam is, watching over me cos she's turned into an angel.'

'And what about your old dad?' The man spoke for the first time.

'I haven't got one. I expect he died long ago in the olden days. I've got my new dad now and my new mam.'

'Do you love them?'

'Yes and they love me.'

'I'm sure they do.' The woman ruffled Bernard's hair. 'What's your other name, Bernard.'

'Bernard Smithson.'

'Would you like to be called Bernard Grey?'

'Yes. Then I'd be like my brothers and sisters.'

The inspectors looked at each other, both of the same mind: that the boy was highly intelligent, well-mannered and an entirely happy child.

'Let's go down, Bernard.' The boy ran to the stairs. 'Don't fall,' he warned. Then he led the woman by the hand, carefully down both sets of stairs.

Lucy had managed to tidy up a bit and hoist up the rack, but couldn't do anything about the mangle and tub until all the washing was done. She waited anxiously as she heard the clatter of feet on the stairs.

'Well, Mrs Grey, I think that will be all for now.' The woman glanced at the sleeping baby and bent to touch Violet and Peter on the cheeks. 'You have five very beautiful children; you must be really proud. Good morning.' She waved a hand at Rosie, who waved back.

'What happens now?' Lucy asked as they made towards the door. 'Can the adoption go ahead?'

'You will be contacted.' Then they were gone.

'Oh!' Lucy was more frustrated than before. She was sure the state of the kitchen must have shown her to be slovenly and put them off. It wasn't until the washing was finished and the kitchen tidy again that she had time to go over everything that had been said – not that much had, except to Bernard, and she had no idea what had been discussed in her absence. Then she recalled the words the woman had said. FIVE beautiful children. Did that mean she considered Bernard was already theirs? How long would they have to wait before finding out? She heard the dog scratching at the door to be let in. 'And you're more trouble than the lot of them,' she told the little dog. Then added as an afterthought, 'But we love you all the same.'

'What a performance,' Molly said to the cook as Mrs Cooper went yet again to bring something down she had forgotten. First it had been the picture of her mother which had been hanging over the bed. Then it had been a hat box from the top of the wardrobe, containing a hat she kept for funerals. Now she had gone to check if anything had fallen behind the marble-topped wash stand.

'I should 'ave forgotten that on purpose.' Madge pointed at the photograph in an ornate gilded frame. ''Ave you ever seen such a miserable mug as that? She'd gi' me nightmares if I 'ad her on me bedroom wall.'

'Still, she is her mother.' Molly thought privately that her own mother didn't look much happier. The only time she smiled was when Molly handed over her pay packet or she had received a postal order from Lily. Oh but Mrs Cooper was lucky, going to live at Blackpool in a posh 'ouse with their Lily. Molly would miss Mrs Cooper, who was always kind to her. Nobody knew what was going to happen when she had gone. She expected Madge would be in charge, her being the eldest. Mr Smith had told them they were to be kept on, but what if the new boss was horrible?

Mrs Cooper bustled back in carrying a bookmark carefully in her hand, a look of wonder on her face. 'Eeh, it's a good job I 'ad another check, I'd 'ave 'ated to leave this behind. This, Molly, was given to me by the loveliest man I ever knew.'

'Were yer in love wi' 'im, Mrs Cooper?' Molly's eyes were shining at the thought of something romantic having taken place.

'Yes, Molly I was.'

Madge stopped peeling apples and sat down at the table to listen.

'And ee loved me. We would 'ave got married; I 'ad me dress and me shoes all ready...'

Molly held her breath in anticipation.

'And then ee went and died.' The elderly woman covered her face with her kid-gloved hands, unwilling for her emotions to be seen.

'Oh, Mrs Cooper, don't cry.' Molly picked up the bookmark inset with a pressed bluebell. 'Did ee buy this for yer?'

'No. He made it specially for me. It upset me when I lost it and now I've found it again.'

'So that's all right then.' Molly threw her arms round the housekeeper. 'Was ee handsome?'

'Aye, inside and out, ee was handsome. Tall, thin and kind. Always look for kindness, me duck. Don't forget, handsome is as handsome does.'

'I won't. Now then, are yer all ready? Larry'll be 'ere to tek yer to't station in a minute. Oh I wish yer weren't going.' Molly started to cry.

'Come on, yer daft haporth. Anybody'd think I was off to Timbuctoo. I'll write and yer must write back, think on.'

'I will.'

Madge got all the bags together, not that there were many considering they were all the woman had to show for sixty-odd years of life. Larry drew the car up at the door, proud to have passed the driving test Mr Smith had arranged for him. Mr Smith said he would be able to find a job anywhere now he could drive. He settled Mrs Cooper in the front seat and made sure she was comfortable, all the time preparing himself for a lecture. It wasn't long coming.

'Now look 'ere, young Larry,' she began as they descended the drive. 'Young Molly's a good lass but a bit excitable. Now I'm trusting you to behave yerself. Now I know yer only young and it's 'ard to stop yerself getting carried away, but just you keep that girl pure for her wedding night.' Larry's face was puce. 'Are yer listening, young Larry?' Larry nodded. 'Aye, well, I suppose I'll just 'ave to trust yer. But I love that little lass and yer'd better not hurt her. Do you 'ear?'

'Yes Mrs Cooper, I'll never hurt Molly. I love her as well.'

'Well, that's all right then. I shall go off to Blackpool with an easy mind.'

They drew up at the small station and Larry helped the elderly woman out of the car and into the waiting room where a fire roared and spread its welcoming warmth around the room. Funny, she was usually stiff and often found it difficult to straighten her legs after being cooped up in the car, but she had nipped out like a two-year-old this morning. Larry supposed it was the excitement of going to begin a new life in Blackpool. He wished he was off with her. He carried her assortment of luggage onto the platform.

'Now then, remember what I've told yer. Be a good lad, and this is to tek Molly somewhere nice.' A handful of coins was pressed down into Larry's hand.

'Crikey. Thanks, Mrs Cooper. I 'ope yer like it in Blackpool.'

'I shall, Larry. I shall.' Then she was stepping up onto the steam train, off to her new life on the Lancashire coast.

Nellie's son was born on the fourteenth of February. Of course he was named after his grandfathers, Henry William. Unlike her sister, Nellie had given birth in a nursing home, though she had protested that she would have been just as cared for by Mrs Cooper – who despite having never given birth herself had enough common sense to cope with the situation. Mrs Cooper didn't care so long as mother and child were safe and healthy. Nellie was blooming, 'like a full-blown rose', her mother-in-law said, whilst holding her precious grandson for the first time.

Lily, of course, burst into tears at the sight of the turned-up nose and tiny fingers and toes. 'Can I 'old 'im, Nellie?'

'Of course you can, so long as you don't drown him in tears.'

Lily giggled. 'Ooh I won't, it's just that ee's the cuddliest baby I've ever seen. Ooh, I can't wait for yer to bring 'im 'ome.'

'Well, I don't want you and Mrs Cooper falling out over him.'

Nellie was only half-joking; at the moment she didn't want anyone taking over her son. She just wanted to hold him and gaze at his perfection. No doubt she would be glad of Mrs Cooper taking over after a while, but for now Nellie was so possessive of her child she would have fought anyone who tried to take him out of her sight, even Mrs Cooper.

The housekeeper – who wasn't a housekeeper any longer – was in her glory rearranging the room that had been turned into a nursery, and familiarising herself with the routine of the guest house. At the moment she didn't quite know what to call herself – certainly not a housekeeper, but was she a nanny either? For the time being she thought of herself as a mother's help and in Nellie's absence had taken over the cooking, the planning of menus and the book keeping. Now *that* was one thing she was definitely good at, having kept the accounts at the manor for more years than she cared to remember. The one thing she had to become accustomed to was the telephone, the one at the manor being in Mr

Smith's office. Mrs Cooper complained heatedly to Lily every time the contraption rang. She was gratified nevertheless when she arranged a booking for two gentlemen to stay from the first of April until the last day of September. When she told Tom on his return from work he was amused when she told him the couple didn't mind sharing a room. 'Seems a bit odd that,' she added. 'Perhaps they're economising.'

'They'll be show people,' Tom guessed. 'Some of them have odd tastes, Mrs Cooper, but you'll find they're quite harmless and usually of an extremely generous nature.'

'And they keep their rooms lovely and tidy,' Lily added.

Mrs Cooper was so proud of the way she had managed to cope with the phone and secure the double booking that she didn't quite grasp what Tom was implying, then suddenly the penny dropped and so did her mouth – wide open.

'You're not tellin me they're...' She searched for the right words, her face turning crimson as she failed to find them.

'Pansy boys.' Lily helped her out and giggled. 'Or pansy old men. There's a lot of 'em in Blackpool, Mrs Cooper. They're sometimes famous. From on't Winter Gardens and places like that. They're nice really and you 'ave to laugh at 'em sometimes.'

'Well, I never thought I'd live to see such a thing, and in the same 'ouse as I'm living in.' Mrs Cooper was quite taken aback.

'You'll soon become accustomed to them,' Tom said. 'Actually they accounted for a large amount of our business last year.'

'Ooh, Mr Johnson, they're going to love little Henry; they always make a fuss of the children. Ooh ee's not 'alf going to be spoiled.'

'Oh well, if they're good with childer and pay their bills on time I shouldn't think there'll be much to complain about.' Mrs Cooper thought she'd probably been stuck at the back of beyond for far too long. She'd have to move with the times now she was in a place like Blackpool. Besides, she might even manage to obtain a free ticket to one of the shows if she played her cards right. She might even get used to that flaming telephone an' all, if she lived long enough.

To the delight of the children on Top Row, a street party was organised on the twelfth of May to celebrate the coronation of King George VI and Queen Elizabeth. The men and boys from along the row managed to drag a piano outside and tables were laden with an assortment of food by the women. The woman at the top house of Side Row changed her mourning dress for a smart navy costume, white blouse and a red hat, bought specially from the Co-op. She had also hung a Union Jack from her bedroom window.

One of the Murphy lads, assisted by a pal, had smuggled out one of his mother's sheets and made a banner which they hung on a clothes line, stretched from one block of lavatories to the other. Mrs Murphy had almost had a seizure at the loss of one of her precious – albeit threadbare – sheets. 'Wait till I get my 'ands on 'im.' She hurried as fast as her round frame would allow with the intention of throttling the lad, but when she saw the words GOD SAVE THE KING hanging in all its splendour for everyone to admire, her anger changed to pride and she merely patted her son on his tousled hair and strolled back to her chair. Mrs Cadman, realising how the loss of a bedsheet would affect the family, had presented Mr Murphy with a pair of sheets of beautiful quality, used only once for her mother's laying out. To be truthful she was glad to be rid of them, especially to such a good cause.

A couple of crates of beer had been delivered from the Bottling Company with lemonade to make shandies for the ladies. As a special treat for the kids there was also cherry pop in bottles with a marble stopper. Jack and Harry Holmes organised a darts match and Kitty brought out a huge bull-rope for skipping. With a decent quantity of drink to drive him on, Will had everyone in stitches as he reeled off one joke after the other. 'He ought to be on't wireless,' Mr Holmes laughed. 'Ee's a right comedian is that one.' He was trying hard not to slur his words but Mr Holmes had consumed a few bottles more than usual, not just to celebrate the crowning of the king but also the birth of his first grandchild, a baby girl born to his daughter Marjory.

When darkness fell and the dancing began, Robbie took the little dog for a last walk of the day. The sight of couples in each other's arms was too hard to bear. Baby knew the way by now and set off excitedly in the direction of the farm. Robbie couldn't believe his luck when he climbed the stile and came face to face with Dot.

'Robbie!'

'Dot!' Baby and Bob greeted each other and chased off into the long grass. 'Lovely night.' Robbie was lost for words, yet there was so much he wanted to say.

'Beautiful.' Though it was just an ordinary night, not special at all. She stood still, unable to meet Robbie's eyes; if she did she would give herself away, show her feelings, probably cry.

'Oh, Dot.' Robbie moved closer, and placing his finger beneath her chin tilted her face towards him.

His eyes searched hers and suddenly she was in his arms. She could feel his heart beating like a drum and the heat of his body against hers. Her lips searched in the darkening night, hot and hungry for his. He could feel her breasts through her cardigan, her nipples hard against his chest. She felt his erection straining for release and she desired him so much, wanted him inside her, needing release from the months of longing. She drew away. She loved him so much, would always love him, but it was a forbidden love; to give in to such love would be wrong. 'No, Robbie.'

'All right, but please don't go. Just let me hold you. I've wanted to for so long. Just stay close to me.' Robbie breathed in the scent of her hair and Pears soap and closed his arms around her.

Dot fell against him, heavy with longing but for the moment, content just to be with him. They stood looking down at the long, winding road in the valley, then up to the farm.

'Look, there's a light on in the old buildings,' Robbie said. 'Is somebody in there?'

'No, there's no one there, except the shepherd.'
'The shepherd?'
'Aye, the ghost. We can hear him in there sometimes.'
'Wow. Aren't yer scared?'
'No, he's guarding the place for you and me. Keeping it safe for when we're ready to move in.'
'Oh, Dot. If only we could.'
'We shall.'
'How can you be sure?'
'Gypsy Lee said so.' The dogs came charging down the field, barking and disturbing the couple. Robbie released her from his embrace.
'I hope she's right.'
'She's always right. Come on Bob, it's time to go home.'
'Aye, we'd best be getting back.' He kissed Dot one more time then turned reluctantly towards the stile. 'And don't forget, Dot Greenwood, I love you.'
'And I love you, Robbie Grey, and don't you forget it either.'
Robbie almost skipped down the path and back up the hill, lighter at heart than since the day he had last held Dot in his arms.
The celebrations were in full swing when he reached Top Row. He could hear the men gathered round the piano singing 'After the Ball'. Lucy was sitting by the door, listening in case any of the children should wake and need her. Robbie went towards her.
'You look about sixteen, Lucy Grey. If I wasn't in love with somebody else I could quite fancy you.'

'And if I wasn't in love with your brother, Robbie Grey, I could quite fancy you.'

Laughing, he pulled Lucy up the yard. 'Come on, I think it's time I learned how to dance. You never know, I might have cause to celebrate one of these days.'

'I hope so, Robbie. Come on then. Here beginneth your first lesson.' After a few stumbles Robbie got the hang of it and they waltzed round and round, faster and faster until Lucy began to feel dizzy – Robbie content now he knew Dot still loved him, and Lucy just enjoying the dance.

'All right, Robbie, it's my turn now.'

Robbie let go of her and as John's arms gathered her to him Lucy felt the familiar warmth she experienced every time they were together. 'Do you know something?' she said as they moved slowly now to the music, 'I don't think anyone in the whole world could be happier than I am. Not even Queen Elizabeth.'

John pulled her closer. If Lucy was happy then so was he.

It was three o'clock in the morning when the knock came at the door. John was out of bed and pulling on his trousers by the time Lucy had roused herself properly. 'Summat must be wrong.' John hurried downstairs. By the time Lucy was dressed he was back up again. 'Lucy, it's the woman who gave us the pushchair; she's hurt. Can you come?' Lucy was already on her way.

'Oh, come and sit down, Mrs Hakin. Whatever's happened to you?'

At Lucy's kindness the woman burst into tears.

It was the youngest of the four children huddled close to their mother who enlightened Lucy.

'Me dad did it. He got pissed up again.'

The girl who looked about fourteen slapped him on the leg. 'Stop swearing, our Danny.'

'Well, ee did. He always hits somebody when ee's pissed up. This time it wor me mam, last time it wor our Gladys.'

'Stop telling tales.' The girl slapped him again.

By this time Mrs Hakin had recovered a bit and John had begun bathing the woman's eye and washing the blood from her cheek. 'I didn't know where to go, Mr Grey. He's chucked us out and locked door. It was our Jane who said that Bernard's mam'd look after us.' Jane was in the same class as Bernard and often shared a meal with them rather than go home. Now Lucy realised why the little girl spent a lot of time away from home.

'She did right to tell you that. We'll manage for tonight,' John frowned, 'but after that...'

'Oh, ee'll be all right when he's sobered up. It's just the drink that affects 'im.'

'Well then, let's get you lot to bed.'

'Oh I didn't expect that.'

'You girls can squeeze in with Rosie and you two lads can go in with Bernard.'

Jane began to protest. 'I want to sleep wi' Bernard. 'Ee's my friend.'

'Shut up and do as Mr Grey tells yer.' Gladys pulled her sister after her towards the stairs.

Mrs Hakin sat on the sofa. 'I'll be right grand 'ere, thanks.' Finally they were all settled, until Andrew, disturbed by the noise, decided he had slept long enough.

Two days later Lucy had to get out the nit comb and vinegar.

'So much for doing someone a good turn,' John said as she poured vinegar water over his head.

'God will repay us one day.' John hoped Lucy's philosophy proved to be right.

Chapter Twenty-seven

On a lovely September day William Gabbitas and Elizabeth Hague were married. Most of Cragstone turned out to see the popular marketeer and the pretty local girl tie the knot and with Will's family and friends from Millington the church was more crowded than it had been for many years. For once, Herbert Goodman was amongst the congregation and the memory of his daughter's wedding brought pain to him and Louisa. Mr Brown felt quite emotional at the sight of Will and Betty's obvious happiness. The bridesmaids, including Primrose Grey, looked as pretty as a picture in lemon satin dresses and juliet caps and muffs made by Mary. Will never noticed, having eyes for no one but his bride.

A straight-faced photographer had been hired, but by the time Will had done playing the fool and making a joke of the whole procedure, even he had a smile on his face. The Cragstone housewives had donned their finery to watch their favourite greengrocer become a respectable married man and poor Betty had to cope with a barrage of ribald remarks. Fortunately she was as broad-minded as they were and though she seemed to ignore them she couldn't help smiling at remarks such as 'We's 'ave to mek do wi' one of them there carrots now young Will's out of bounds, Polly.'

Polly's answer of 'Nay lass, a cucumber'd be more like,' brought smiles to the faces of the by-standers. Broad-minded Betty might be but she found herself blushing to think that the vicar and his wife were listening. However, Will held her hand and gazed adoringly at his new wife and Betty couldn't care less about anyone except him.

The reception was still in progress when the couple slipped away. They could hear the Lambeth Walk as Betty's father opened the car door for them. 'Well lass, what does it feel like to be a married woman?' He looked lovingly at the daughter he was going to miss so much.

'Ask me when we come back from Blackpool, Dad.'

Then they were at the station and on their way to Nellie and Tom's, the honeymoon being a wedding gift from the Johnsons.

'Oh, and Dad.' Betty's eyes were filling with tears. 'Thank you for making this a wonderful wedding day for us.'

'And for the house,' Will added as he shook his father-in-law's hand.

'You're welcome, lad. Like I said, just take good care of my lass. So long as she's looked after I shall be content.'

'She will be, I promise. The train's coming.

Better get the bags out.'

'Yer going to be tired by the time yer get to Blackpool.'

Then they were on their way, alone in a carriage with pictures on the wall of Buxton and Harrogate and Robin Hood's Bay, and the blinds lowered at the windows. 'Well, Mrs Gabbitas, are we going to wait for a nice feather bed in which to consummate our marriage?'

'Nothing wrong with this seat as far as I can see.'

'Nothing wrong at all.' And then Betty was in his arms and for once in his life, Will Gabbitas was silent. He had more important things on his mind than making witty remarks. In fact he had never felt more serious about anything in his life. Betty was his and he was about to find out at last what lovemaking was all about. Betty's dad had been right: they were tired by the time they reached Blackpool.

Mrs Cooper had settled in remarkably well and had fallen completely in love with little Henry. On fine days she wheeled him on Central Drive and down onto the promenade. She couldn't help showing off a bit with the Silver Cross pram when she sat in one of the shelters to rest her feet and have a bit of a gossip with other pram pushers, or other elderly people simply out for a brisk walk and a bit of sea air. She made friends with a grandmother and both women tried to outdo each other with how much weight the babies had gained, or which one had slept through the night, or smiled their first smile. Both women were wise enough to realise the smiles were only wind.

Nellie was careful to claim back her son after the hours allotted to Mrs Cooper, afraid that her baby might become fonder of the helper than he was of Nellie. She was also careful not to tire her or take advantage of the older woman's kindness. She needn't have worried; Mrs Cooper seemed to have more energy than she had had for years. She was delighted now to take bookings over the phone, keeping tabs of which rooms were reserved and which were vacant. Nellie was astounded to find the big blue account book balanced week by week, and she seemed to keep the cleaners in order. Tom laughed one day when he came home early to find one of the women applying brasso to the letter box and house number. 'I've never seen the cleaner do that before,' he told Nellie.

'No, but Mrs Cooper told them she thought it was time it was done. Said it would have been done every week in her day.'

'Well, it certainly looks better. I just hope she doesn't upset our staff, or they may decide to leave.'

'Oh she won't, she's started making them tea and biscuits halfway through the morning. They seem to work all the harder after that.'

Nellie frowned. 'Do you think I should have given them a tea break?'

'I don't know. My staff at the garage just brew up when they like. Anyway, Mrs Cooper seems to have everything sorted.'

'And she's so good with Henry. Oh, Tom, he's such a contented baby.'

'He's loved, that's why. Lily adores him too.

He's going to get spoiled with all you women fussing round him.'

'Oh he's not short of male adoration either; Cyril and Sydney demand a cuddle every morning.'

'If you can call them male company,' Tom grinned.

'Well, not only them. There's the sergeant major. Surely he's man enough; he'll have him running round playing at soldiers as soon as he can toddle. He tells Mrs Cooper to let the boy exercise his lungs and that all her mollycoddling'll never make a man of him. She usually takes notice of him and puts Henry back in his pram.'

'He must like it here to decide he'll stay permanently. A few more like him would be a good thing if there's going to be a war.'

'Well, I think it was Mrs Cooper's persuasion that did it. All her talk about it being the finest air on the planet and me being the best cook in Blackpool. Although in my opinion it's just that they've taken a fancy to each other. Anyway, there won't be a war, will there?'

'I'm afraid there will, Nellie,' Tom sighed, 'but we shall worry about that when it happens.'

Nellie was quiet as she wondered what would happen in the event of a war starting. It was all very well Tom telling her not to worry, but they had a son to consider, and a guest house with so many overheads. She picked up her son and cuddled him close. He and his father were so precious to her, and they might neither of them be safe if a war began. 'Oh, well, it's time you were fed, big boy, so let's get that bottle made, shall we?'

'Can I feed him?' Lily had finished setting the

tables in the dining room and there was nothing morc to be done until high tea.

'If you like.' It would give Nellie a chance to finish the trifle and she knew Lily enjoyed giving Henry his bottle. She didn't indulge Lily very often, so feeding Henry would be a treat. The girl's face blossomed as she settled the baby in the crook of her arm and gave him his milk. Henry's large blue eyes fixed on Lily and as of old, emotion brought tears to her eyes. 'Ooh, Nellie I wish ee was mine. He's the sweetest baby in the whole wide world.'

'I agree, Lily, he is. But you'll have one of your own soon enough. Don't be in a hurry, love. Enjoy yourself whilst you're young.'

'Ooh, I am. I never thought I'd enjoy meself as much. It's being 'ere with you, and now Mrs Cooper's 'ere too. It's like I've a new family of me own.'

'Don't you miss your own family?'

'I miss me dad but not me mam, and I miss our Molly and the others, but I've grown to love being 'ere. Besides I've got Jim and I've grown to love 'im too.'

'Oh! And does Jim love you?'

'Well ee says ee does. But don't worry, we're not thinking of getting married or owt daft like that. Jim wants to save up for a café of 'is own and somewhere to live. So it'll take years for that to 'appen. So we're just enjoying our lives. I shall 'ave a baby like Henry one day though. That's if war doesn't start. It wouldn't be fair would it, 'aving a baby with Jim going to war?'

'Let's not talk about war, Lily. It might never happen.'

'Sergeant major says it will. He was telling Cyril and Sydney they'll be entertaining the troops before next year's out.'

Nellie stuck a few sprigs of fresh mint in the pan of new potatoes and carried on slicing the ham. She hoped all this talk of war turned out to be nothing but talk. 'I should get his wind up now, Lily.'

Lily removed the bottle and held Henry over her shoulder, gently patting his back. Henry gave a huge burp, causing Lily and Nellie to burst into laughter. The subject of war was put on one side for the time being.

This was the quietest Christmas for a long time, if ever. Ben and Emma were recovering from influenza and wouldn't risk Lucy's family becoming infected. Will and Betty were spending the day with her parents and Nellie and Tom couldn't make the journey this year. So it was Mary, Jacob, Jane and James who were the guests at Lucy's. Nevertheless it was a joyous occasion as the children played with their toys from Father Christmas and the adults drank and ate too much. After lunch the men played Crib and the ladies caught up with the gossip.

'It's quiet without our Will and Ben.' Mary had Andrew on her knee, showing him a book about animals and revelling in the scent of his newly washed hair. Mary had at last resigned herself to the fact that she would probably remain childless. She had told Jacob's mother in no uncertain terms never to mention the subject again and both Mary and Jacob felt much better without the fact being constantly referred to.

It had just turned eight when Mr and Mrs Marshall, Kitty and Frank walked in. 'We came for a bit of a sing song, lass. But it doesn't look as though the musician's turned up,' Mr Marshall said.

'No, but we can sing without him,' John said. And they did. All the old favourites and new ones besides.

When Jacob put on his trilby and reached for his coat to go home, Kitty said, 'Well actually I came to tell you Frank and I are to be married.'

'Oh, Kitty, that's marvellous news! When is it to be?' Lucy hugged her.

'We thought as soon as possible, what with the threat of the war hanging over us.'

'This calls for another drink.' John went for some clean glasses.

So Jacob took off his hat and coat and the party continued well into the night.

'Can I be a bridesmaid and wear a white dress?' Rosie shyly asked Kitty.

'You surely can, and Violet too. You'll be the prettiest bridesmaids ever to walk into Millington Church.'

Rosie and Violet giggled and forced their heavy eyes to stay open so as not to miss a moment of this exciting day.

When the visitors did finally decide to leave, James said, 'It's been another right grand day, John. Not many of the family here this year but a grand day all the same.'

Lucy looked round at the children – at Rosie and Violet, at Andrew asleep on the sofa and Bernard and Peter playing with Baby on the rug in front of the fire.

'These are my family, James. So long as they are content, then so am I.'

Everything seemed to be going smoothly since the old year had drawn to a close. Lucy was pleased to think John had finally got the hang of being careful and no more babies were on the horizon. Mrs Slater wondered if Lucy's last difficult confinement was the more likely reason. All the children were thriving and once Rosie realised that temper tantrums wouldn't help in her endeavour to attend school with Bernard, she turned out to be a great help to her mother. Rosie would help dress the younger ones and keep an eye on the twins, who now delighted in playing outside. Rosie's favourite task was to be given a bucket of water on washday and a yard brush with which to scrub the step and the outside flags. The fact that she usually ended up saturated didn't bother Rosie, and Lucy simply hung the wet garments to dry on the fire guard.

The twins didn't seem to need much attention from anyone except each other. They were content to play the same games, go to bed at the same time and learn at the same rate. When Peter had begun to walk, Violet followed, and when Violet started to talk, her brother copied. When Bernard contracted measles the twins fell ill on the same day. Fortunately Andrew and Rosie escaped the illness. It was difficult enough keeping the twins in a darkened room, without the baby becoming infected. All three patients recovered without any long-lasting effects, much to Lucy's relief. Little Andrew looked as if he would never suffer a day's illness in his life and seemed to grow heavier and taller by the day.

Far more worrying than the measles was the time a few months later when Lucy was woken in the early hours by Rosie. 'Mam, our Violet's sick.' Lucy was out of bed before the words were out. She could hear her daughter's racking cough echoing through the house. She was used to dealing with croup and decided to take Violet down to the kitchen. Lucy filled the boiler by the fire to heat up the water. With another kettle on the fire it should provide enough steam to allow Violet to breathe freely again. Sometimes the walls and windows were running with steam by the time the bout of croup had passed. This time was different. Violet had vomited all over the pillow, a mixture of vomit and mucus. The little girl was hot and seemed to be fighting for breath.

Lucy hurried back to her room and shook John awake. 'John, I think we should have the doctor. Our Violet's sick.' John pulled on his trousers and hurried to where the child's coughing resembled the sound of a barking dog.

'You're right. I'll fetch Doctor Sellars.'

Lucy attempted to wipe up the mess, then decided to strip off the covers and replace them with clean ones. 'Go sleep in our bed, Rosie. There's a good girl.' Rosie didn't need telling twice. She loved the warmth and special scent of her mam's bed. In fact it was a treat for any of the children to be allowed to snuggle down in the warm place their mother or father had vacated.

By the time John arrived with the doctor

Violet's head was being held over a basin of steaming water, but still the coughing continued. 'It's croup again, doctor.'

'No, Mrs Grey, not this time. I'm afraid it's Whooping Cough.'

'Oh no.' A child on Second Row had died of the complaint only a few days ago. 'What can we do for her?'

'There isn't a lot we can do except keep her warm and dry. I can prescribe a mixture, but I'm afraid only time will heal; normally it takes about six weeks. Unfortunately it is highly contagious, so your other children will probably have already been infected. You could of course isolate Violet and hope the others escape this distressing illness. Though it may already be too late. Please keep the boy away from school. If we can avoid an epidemic it will be for the best. If you can send someone for the medicine it will be ready in the morning.' By this time Violet seemed to have got over the coughing bout.

'Now, I suggest you try and get some sleep whilst you can.'

'I'll fetch the medicine in the morning then. Thanks for coming, doctor.' John went to see the doctor out.

'You're welcome.'

Violet was asleep when John went upstairs. The little girl was flushed and exhausted. 'I'll stay with her.' John lay down on the bed by his daughter's side. 'You go back to bed, Lucy. It'll be a busy day tomorrow what with Bernard off school and trying to keep them apart. Get some sleep.'

‘Thanks, John.’ Lucy was dreading the next coughing fit and the thought of the others already being infected. There was also the dirty bedding to be laundered. Oh well, she had never expected having children to be all a bed of roses. So long as Violet recovered, nothing else mattered. Lucy slipped into bed next to Rosie and felt her daughter’s arms encircle her. The children might bring her worry on occasions, but on the whole they gave her more joy than pain. Lucy made herself comfortable and was on the verge of dozing, off when Rosie began to cough, a nasty whooping sound. Lucy said her prayers for her daughters to recover, and for her boys not to have already caught the frightening illness.

Miraculously, the boys remained healthy and Rosie didn’t seem as badly affected as her sister. However Violet sometimes seemed on the verge of suffocating and on one occasion the poor child had turned blue in the face. Mrs Greenwood sent up an infusion of red clover, which she swore would relieve the symptoms and it certainly seemed to help. The neighbours rallied round as usual; Mr Marshall remembered taking Lewis up to a spring on the common and believed it had helped the boy get better in record time.

As soon as the girls were well enough to walk so far, Lewis volunteered to take them and let them drink the pure spring water. For the next month he continued to take them whenever he had the opportunity, by which time they were not only looking and feeling better but Lewis had also built up a close friendship with the little girls. He pointed out the wild flowers and insects they encountered on the way and once when a red admiral settled on Violet's cheek, Lewis told her it was giving her a butterfly kiss. After that, Rosie would ask for a butterfly kiss each time they passed that particular spot. Lewis would bend and flutter his eyelashes on each girl's cheek. 'There,' he said. 'We don't need a butterfly to give you a kiss; my eyelashes work just as well.' The girls would squeal with delight and Lewis would wish the girls were his daughters and Lucy his wife. He realised he had the next best thing when suddenly they began to address him as Uncle Lew. Soon the boys were following their example.

Both John and Lucy were pleased their children were giving Lewis the affection he so deserved, When the weather was good John and Lewis would relax up at the allotments, competing good-naturedly as to whose vegetables thrived the best, and sharing everything they grew. Lewis's lettuces heartened in their frame and his beans grew long and straight enough to win a prize at the local show. John produced the finest crop of peas anyone had seen for years; unfortunately the kids got to them and ate the lot. The only things to fail – and the one thing Lucy requested, to add colour to her salads - were the radishes. Lewis tended them with care and John even sent Bernard after the ragman's horse with a bucket and spade, but even the horse droppings couldn't improve the thin, puny-looking radishes

'A waste of good growing ground,' Mr Marshall admonished.

Still, for Lucy's sake the men persevered, and failed. The friendship between John and Lewis, however, grew from strength to strength, and John and Lucy's children grew as dear to Lewis as if they were his own.

Chapter Twenty-eight

It was almost the end of 1938 when the telegram came for Robbie and it was short and to the point.

'MEET MY OFFICE TEN AM THURSDAY URGENT STOP P TOMLINSON STOP.'

Robbie immediately arranged time off work, rang Nellie to arrange lodgings and caught the first available train to Blackpool.

When Louisa paid her weekly visit to Lucy she told her friend she was optimistic that Robbie would return home a free man. Lucy wasn't convinced. From what she had heard of divorces they were long drawn-out affairs and could take years. However, Louisa proved to be right. Paul had greeted Robbie warmly and with an air of optimism.

'Well, Mr Grey, I think you may soon have cause for celebration.'

'You mean I can have a divorce?'

'No, Mr Grey. I mean I doubt very much that you will need one.'

'What?'

'With the cooperation of Prudence's father, I sought an annulment of your marriage. For two reasons. The first being that Prudence Goodman was of unsound mind and had been for some time. The second reason being that the marriage had never been consummated. A certain Doctor Sellars has provided evidence of that. I am fairly confident that at eleven thirty this morning the Probate, Divorce and Admiralty Division of the High Court will declare your marriage to Prudence Goodman null and void. So, Mr Grey, shall we be on our way?'

Paul picked up his briefcase and bustled out to his car with Robbie hurrying behind, trembling so much he could hardly open the car door. He was still trembling when they arrived back at the lawyer's office two and a half hours later. 'Well, I don't know what to say except thank you.'

'Oh I think it's Reverend Goodman you should be thanking. Without his help, a divorce would certainly have been necessary.'

Robbie couldn't help thinking it had been Herbert's fault in the first place. He only realised how shocked he must have been afterwards, when he remembered running his hands over the solid oak desk in Paul Tomlinson's office and casually remarking on what a magnificent piece of furniture it was, and how much work had gone into the making of it. It was then that the lawyer insisted on Robbie taking a tot of brandy. It was after he had almost choked on the potent spirit that it suddenly dawned on Robbie that he was a free man, no longer shackled to Prudence and free to marry Dot. He seemed to shed the weight that had lain so heavily on his shoulders. His spirits lifted and Robbie grinned at the man who had been worried about his mental state just moments before.

'I can't believe it.' Robbie took the lawyer's hand and shook it warmly. 'Does this mean I am free to marry again? Immediately?'

'Well, yes it does, but damn it man, I should think twice before doing so for a second time.'

'Think twice? I've thought about nothing else for twenty-four hours of the day, every day.' Robbie took out his wallet. 'Now, how much am I in your debt?'

'Nothing. Let us put it down to experience. It's certainly been a new one for me. The first null and void marriage I've come across. It just proves the old saying that we're never too old to learn. No, Robert, you don't owe me a penny; I'm more than happy to know that right has prevailed.'

Robbie was pleased at the lawyer's use of his christian name and read the documents Paul had given him. 'But what about the court costs?'

'Forget them. I might need a favour myself one of these days. Besides, I'm feeling quite proud; these cases are extremely rare you know.'

'Well, at least let me take you out to dinner. It would have to be tomorrow though, then I need to go home. I'm sure you'll know of a decent place.'

'Very well, I shall bring my wife and you must invite Tom and Nellie. I'll ring them when I've made a reservation.' He grinned at Robbie. 'I'm warning you it won't come cheap.'

Robbie grinned back. 'It'll be worth it, whatever it costs.'

'To marry the girl you love? Yes it will, if you truly love her.'

'I do, I definitely do.'

'Now, let me run you to Tom's.'

'No, thanks all the same. The last time I left your office I felt like throwing myself from the top of the tower. Now I feel like I could climb to the top. I'd like to walk.'

'Very well, and if you should ever need my services again, you know where to find me.' The two men shook hands again, both satisfied with the outcome, but sorry for the Goodmans who, despite making things right for Robbie, must be feeling nothing but despair at the whole sorry episode.

Robbie called at a toy shop before going to Nellie's and bought a teddy bear for the baby. He opened the door of a jeweller's but then realised he had no idea what size ring Dot would require, so closed the door again, cringing as the shop bell rang out, leaving an assistant glaring at him through the glass. He breathed in the salty air and threw back his shoulders. A couple of teen-age girls stared at him and giggled as he gave them a wink. Robbie Grey was a happy man.

Nellie was delighted to see Robbie and catch up on the news from home. She was even more pleased that their friend had solved Robbie's problem so satisfactorily. He insisted on paying for his bed and board despite Tom's protests, but agreed to eat with the couple rather than in the guests' dining room. When he told them he had decided to go to Liverpool and visit Prudence, Tom insisted on driving him there the following morning. 'I don't think it's something you should do alone,' Tom said. 'I doubt it will be a very pleasant experience.'

'I know that, but it's something I need to do. If I don't it'll be hanging like a cloud over me for ever.'

'Very well, but I'm going with you. Besides, we shall be there and back in half the time the bus takes.'

As it happened the visit wasn't as horrendous as Robbie had feared. Prudence was seated in a pleasant room, working on her crocheting. When Robbie walked towards her she glanced at him and carried on.

'Hello, Prudence. How are you?'

'Fine. Do you like the mat I'm making?'

'It's pretty.' It was just a long tangled length of silk thread.

'It's for my house when we move in.'

'Your house?'

'Yes, haven't they told you I'm getting married?' A porter wheeled a patient into the room. 'Maurice.' Prudence beckoned him over. 'Come and meet this man. I forget his name but I think he used to be a friend of mine. This is Maurice, the man I'm going to marry. Isn't he handsome?' The porter grinned.

'I sure am. Though not the marrying type, I'm afraid. Still, it gives young Pru here something to look forward to. Pleased to meet yer. Did you know Pru back in Yorkshire?'

'Yes. Actually we were married for a time.'

The porter laughed nervously. 'Sorry, but I didn't know any of her husbands were real. According to her, she's had at least half a dozen husbands. I'm apparently about to be the seventh. Not blooming likely. Still, it keeps her happy, all the arranging.'

Prudence beckoned for her visitors to come closer. 'Don't tell my father, but we're going to have a baby.'

'Oh, when is it due?' Robbie asked.

'Any day now.'

'Well I'm pleased for you.'

Prudence counted out the chains. 'One, two, three.' However she seemed oblivious now to anything happening around her.

'We're going now, Prudence. Goodbye.' There was no reaction from the patient. Robbie looked questioningly at the porter.

'Don't worry about Pru, she'll be all right. She's had electric shock treatment and it takes their memory away for a while but it'll come back eventually.'

Robbie frowned, concerned. 'Isn't that painful?'

'No, I don't think they feel anything.'

Tom wondered how he could know that if he had never had the treatment himself. The porter went off to help another patient.

'Come on Robbie, let's go.' Tom led Robbie from the room. They encountered the porter again on the way out.

'Look after her, Maurice, won't you,' Robbie said.

'Oh, don't worry about Prudence; she's happy enough up there in the clouds, so long as she's a wedding to plan.'

'All the same.'

'She'll be well looked after here. It's a good place this, and so it should be considering how expensive the care is. Her aunt seems to gain some satisfaction by keeping her here - seems to be worth a few quid with nobody else to spend it on, which is fortunate for Pru.'

'Well thanks anyway, for humouring her, I mean.'

'No problem. Good for the ego to think she fancies me.' Maurice laughed and left them to see themselves out.

Robbie was surprised to realise how sorry he felt for Prudence and her parents. Even so, the relief that she was out of his life at last was tremendous.

'Come on, let's go. It's all over, Robert, and now you can begin again.'

'Yes, I know.' Even so he couldn't control the emotion. He sat in the passenger seat of the car, his head in his hands, and wept. All the tension of the past months escaped at last. 'Come on, Robert. I'm sure she doesn't remember anything that happened. Like the man said, she's oblivious to it all.'

Robbie nodded. Prudence might not remember but he would. He would never forget the horror of it all, even if he lived to be a hundred.

By the time they reached the guest house Robbie was feeling better and looking forward to dinner that evening. Lily was looking forward to babysitting little Henry and Mrs Cooper to going to the pictures with Edith, the grandma she had met whilst on her daily walk.

The restaurant was the poshest he had ever set foot in and Robbie felt out of his depth at first, but the food was so delicious and the conversation so stimulating he soon forgot his nervousness. Besides, Nellie had come from the same humble background as him and she was holding her own. It was when the talk turned to the inevitable war that the two ladies became quiet. Tom and Paul didn't seem to notice and carried on discussing the fact that the British navy had been mobilised, so Robbie intervened.

'I think we're upsetting the ladies with all this talk of war. But if we must, let's look on the bright side: they're forecasting an end to the Spanish War in the next few months.'

'Ah, you're right. We shouldn't be discussing such morbid subjects on what's supposed to be a celebration dinner.'

'Hurrah. At least Robbie cares about us. It's marriage, Robbie: it makes men blind to our feelings. When you marry Dot you must remember that and don't become complacent.'

'Who's become complacent? You know I love you, darling wife, more than life itself.' Diana was the light of Paul's life and a good friend to Nellie.

'Ah, yes, until someone more stimulating comes along to talk of warships and Hitler and the Munich Agreement.'

'Sorry, my love. So let's all have some more wine and talk about Robbie's forthcoming marriage. When is the wedding likely to be?'

'I haven't asked her yet. In fact she doesn't even know I'm here.'

'Let us know as soon as she accepts your proposal and we can keep a room vacant for your honeymoon. That's if a Blackpool honeymoon would be to your liking,' Tom smiled. 'It will be our wedding gift to you both.'

'Why thanks, it would be great. It might be quite soon actually; I want to be with Dot so much and if there is going to be a war I don't want to waste any time.'

'There's no IF about it, Robbie.'

'Oh now we're back on that subject again,' Diana said.

'Sorry.' Robbie apologised to Paul's wife.

'Apology accepted. Anyway I agree; don't leave it too long.'

'Easter would be nice,' Nellie said. 'Besides, we aren't quite so busy then.'

'OK, I'll suggest Easter. Thanks, Nellie.'

'Another poor bachelor going to the gallows.' Paul pulled a face and his wife gave him a playful punch on the arm.

'See what I mean? She's even attacking me now.'

The meal continued with much laughing and drinking. When the bill came Robbie thought it might have been cheaper to pay the lawyer's bill than the one for the restaurant. It was still worth every penny to be free to go home and marry the girl he loved.

The next morning, even the thought of Dot couldn't take his mind off the hangover, especially with the train journey to face.

Lucy threw her arms round her brother-in-law at the news. 'Oh Robbie, that's the best news we've had in ages. Do Louisa and Herbert know?'

'Yes. I've just called and told them – well, thanked them actually. It must've been an ordeal for them. Paul said it would have been so much more difficult without Herbert's cooperation.'

'Yes, well, don't forget it was his fault it happened in the first place.'

'Oh, Lucy. I don't know why they didn't realise how ill Prudence really was. They must have noticed, being with her all day.'

'I don't expect they'd want to admit what she was like. Or maybe they thought the love of a good man might be the making of her.'

'She'll never be cured. In fact she's much worse. I feel so sorry for them all.'

'Yes, but it's over for you now.'

'Aye. I'm going to have a pot of tea and a couple of aspirins and then I'm going to see Dot. Well, Little Arthur really.'

'Better get my best hat out then.' Lucy looked at herself in the mirror. 'I know you'll laugh but the wishing mirror's worked again.'

'I'm not laughing. I've wished in it every day since the trouble with Prudence began.'

'Really? So you don't think I'm daft, then?'

'You're not daft, Lucy. You're the nicest, most sensible and kindest sister-in-law a man could wish for. In fact I love you Lucy Grey, but I love Dot Greenwood more. So,' Robbie gulped down his tea and carried the pint pot to the sink. 'I'm off to ask her to marry me.'

Little Arthur was leaning on the gate of the long field, deciding whether to plough half of it or leave it all as pasture. The dog left his side and ran to meet Robbie, circling him in excitement. Little Arthur's face lit up when Robbie came and leaned on the gate beside him.

'All right, lad?'

'Aye, are you, Mr Greenwood?'

'Fair to middling.'

'Mr Greenwood; I know I've caused you all a lot of grief in't past but I can assure you I love Dot and I promise as long as I live I will never hurt her again. Mr Greenwood, can I 'ave your daughter's hand in marriage?'

Little Arthur looked questioningly at Robbie, the young man he had grown so fond of. 'So yer free to marry 'er then?'

'I am. I wouldn't be 'ere otherwise.'

'Then aye, yer can marry me daughter. That's if she'll 'ave yer.' He grinned at Robbie and held out his hand. Robbie shook it eagerly, once again surprised at the strength of a grip in so small a man.

'So can I go and ask 'er then?'

'Aye, and let's 'ope she starts to smile again. She's been like a bloody wet weekend these past months, not like our Dot at all. Well, goo on then, if yer gooing.'

Robbie grinned and set off along the lane. Gertie and Gussie came to meet him, flapping and pecking at his legs. Bloody geese.

Dot was carrying a bucket of mash towards the chicken huts. He followed her slowly, intending to surprise her, but the geese were making such a din she turned to see what all the noise was about.

'Robbie?'

'Dot.' Robbie knelt down on one knee in the churned up mud – or was it cow dung? 'Dot Greenwood, will you marry me? I promise never to do anything again to cause you pain. And I shall love you to my dying day.'

Dot stood there for so long he thought she was about to refuse. In truth she was in shock. Then she knelt down in the sludge in front of him, uncaring that the knees of her overalls were becoming saturated. 'Oh Robbie, do you really need to ask? Of course I'll marry you. And in case you're wondering, I love you too.'

He held out his arms and Dot leaned closer until their lips were touching. He kissed her tenderly and then fiercely, with all the passion withheld over the past months. When Dot withdrew she looked down at the ground and they began to laugh until they seemed close to hysteria. Dot rose to her feet. 'Do you really want to marry me? Looking like this?'

'No! I shall expect you to put on a dress.' This set them off again, bringing Boadacea hurrying out to see what all the laughter was about.

'What the hummer thumps is going off here? Did yer fall down or summat?'

'No, Mrs Greenwood, the only falling I've done is falling for yer daughter, so I've just been on my knees proposing to her.'

Boadacea's face broke into smiles, 'Eeh, lad, couldn't yer have found somewhere not quite as mucky?'

'Couldn't wait. I thought I'd waited long enough. Besides, all this cow muck might bring us luck.' Robbie hugged his future wife close. 'In fact it's brought me luck already. Dot's accepted me.'

'Well, thank heavens for that. She might put a smile on that miserable mug of hers now for a change; she's been about as happy as a wet haystack since you left her.' She looked the couple up and down. ''Ere, yer not coming in my kitchen caked up in cow muck. Get them trousers off and let's get 'em cleaned.'

Robbie clung like glue to his trousers. 'No, it's all right, Mrs Greenwood. I'll stop out 'ere.'

'I've heard of some strange places for proposals but this one takes some beating.'

Little Arthur came into the yard. 'Well, Boady, lass. Tha knows that bottle of rhubarb wine tha made after our Dot was born? Well I think this is a good time to open it. Come on, let's go inside.'

Robbie glanced at Boadacea. 'It's all right, Mr Greenwood; I'm all mucky. I'll stop out here.'

'Will you 'ell as like. You'll come inside. I insist.'

'All right, but I won't sit down.' Boadacea didn't object so they all trooped inside, the muck on their knees stiffening by the second.

Little Arthur lifted up the pegged rug and opened a trapdoor which led down into the cellar. When he climbed back out again he was carrying two bottles, both as clear as spring water. 'Now then, let's get this poured and drink to the happiness of our Dot and Robbie.'

'Nay, me duck, we mustn't drink two bottles. It'll be potent after all these years. We shall be three sheets to the wind after one.'

'I know that. This 'ere other one is for Robbie to take 'ome. His lot'll be wanting to celebrate as well. I expect they'll be as glad to 'ave our Dot in the family as we are to 'ave Robbie.'

Boadacea got out four crystal glasses and poured the wine. 'You can take the bottle of elderflower, Robbie,' Little Arthur said. 'It's just as good as the rhubarb.' He raised his glass. 'And now, to Robbie and Dot's future 'appiness, and may all their troubles be little ones.'

Dot giggled and Robbie blushed and took a swig of the wine, almost choking on its strength.

'What did I tell thee? A drop of good stuff is this. If it doesn't mek thi 'air curl nowt will. Anyway, lad, welcome to the family.'

'We'll need to find somewhere to live first,' Robbie said.

'Eeh, that won't take long; our Dot's been working on that ever since that there gypsy told her fortune.'

Dot's face turned red. She hoped Robbie didn't think she was too forward at surmising he would marry her.

'What does yer dad mean?'

'Come on, I'll show you.' Dot led the way to the old cottage next door. The walls had been plastered by a farmer's son Little Arthur had met at Cragstone cattle market. Dot had distempered them and scrubbed the flagged floor, which was now covered by a carpet square. The only furniture was a table – but Robbie could see to the furnishings. The range had been scoured to remove the rust and blackleaded until it shone. Pretty chintz curtains hung at the windows. Dot led him into the other room, which was just as empty and just as clean and bright.

Robbie went to the window and looked out at the view, the same view he had first seen when he came over the hill from Lincoln. He couldn't believe so much had happened in so little time. He turned to the girl he had loved since the day he first set eyes on her. 'Is this for us?'

'Course it is. You don't think I'd go to all this trouble for somebody else to live here, you idiot. Come upstairs.'

The wardrobe was still there, less dusty. It had been too good to burn; in fact it looked almost new after a good going over with Boadacea's homemade polish. They went into the other room.

'You must have been working in here when I saw the light, on the nights I was walking Baby.'

'There's never been a light on in here. There's no lamp, no candles and certainly nothing as posh as electricity up here.'

'But...'

'I told yer, it's the ghost of a shepherd who once lived here. I hope it isn't going to put you off.'

'No, no it's grand. It'll be heaven waking up to that view every morning.'

'I shall be just looking at you.' Dot grinned. 'So how long have we to wait before we can plan the wedding?'

'We don't have to wait at all. We could be married tomorrow if yer like. But I wondered about Easter.'

'An Easter wedding? Oh Robbie, it'll be lovely.'

'Aye. What do yer reckon to a honeymoon in Blackpool?'

'Really? Can we afford it? I never expected a honeymoon.'

'It'll be with the compliments of Nellie and Tom. Though I shan't notice where we are; we shall probably stay in bed all day.'

Dot kissed him. 'Stop talking about beds. You're giving me ideas.'

'I don't need a bed to give me ideas, but we'd

better go. Besides, I don't fancy an old shepherd watching me perform.'

'We won't be in this room. The children will be in here.' Dot glanced at Robbie, all the love shining in her eyes. 'We shall have children, I hope.'

'Oh aye, as many as you like.'

Boadacea thought they had been gone long enough. They might be engaged but they weren't married yet. 'Are yer coming for yer teas?' Her voice echoed through the empty house.

Dot pulled a face. 'Do yer think you can cope with living next door to me mam?'

'I'd live next door to Bel Vue Zoo as long as I were with you.' Bel Vue Zoo in Manchester had more animals than almost anywhere in the country.

'It might be quieter.' They ran laughing down the stairs, the cares of the past behind them and all the joys of the future ahead.

Chapter Twenty-nine

A few days before Christmas a court order was made allowing the adoption of Bernard Smithson by John and Lucy Grey. The adoption, regulated by the Adoption of Children Act, 1926, meant a Christmas free from wondering if it would be the last one for Bernard in the Greys' home.

They decided to tell Bernard they had chosen him to be their little boy and he would now be staying with them for ever. Bernard said he had better write and tell Father Christmas his new name or he might be looking for Bernard Smithson when there wasn't one anymore. The lctter was written in large, uneven letters, signed Bernard Grey and sent up the chimney by Lucy. That seemed to be the end of the matter and to Lucy's knowledge was never mentioned again.

Christmas was all the more joyful now that Andrew was two and able to understand and open his presents. Once again the family arrived at teatime, this time with two new members, Betty and Dot. Only Nellie failed to make it this year; after all she had her all-the-year-round boarders to keep happy. With Cyril and Sydney extending their stay in order to play the ugly sisters in panto, and the retired sergeant major there for good, the festivities were planned around them and included Margaret and Henry in the party. An awkward moment arrived when Cyril began 'Cutchy cooing' to little Henry and the sergeant major said to him, 'What the hell do you think you're doing? Trying to turn him into a cissy? Give him here.' When Henry was comfortably seated on the man's knee he began to bounce the little boy up and down, singing in a voice loud enough to waken the dead, 'Oh the grand old Duke of York.'

Henry gurgled up at the sergeant major, who carried on with the song. Then he glared at Cyril and announced, 'Leave the boy to me and I'll make a man of him. Won't I, my little man? We've enough of the other kind in the house with their pantomime frocks and their stage make-up.' Then he astounded everyone with a request to Sydney: 'Any chance of tickets for us all for tomorrow's performance? My treat.'

Nellie choked on her tea and Sydney said he would do his best.

'Nothing like a good pantomime on Boxing Day. Haven't been for years. Haven't had any friends to go with, not the same on yer own. Now I've all of you, not only Cyril and Sydney but dear Mrs Cooper and Lily. And I hope I'm not being presumptuous if I class you, Mr and Mrs Johnson, as my friends.'

'Of course we're friends, but I think it's time we began using our Christian names if you intend staying here indefinitely, so please call us Tom and Nellie. And you are?'

The sergeant major turned crimson and muttered, 'Marmaduke.'

Lily spluttered and hid her chuckle with a coughing fit. 'Marmaduke? Goodness, I thought Cyril was bad enough.'

'No, Lily, Marmaduke's err, quite unusual,' Nellie offered.

'It's bloody awful.' The sergeant major began to guffaw and the rest of the company joined in. Then Lily recovered from her outburst and kindly as ever said, 'I think we should cut out the marmalade and call you Duke.'

'Now that's a champion idea, young Lily. Duke! Aye, I quite like that.' Then he began again, bouncing Henry until Nellie thought he might be sick. 'And when they were only halfway up they were neither up nor down.'

Mr Grundy noticed the change in Robbie immediately he returned to work. He had missed the lad, but it was worth it to see Robbie smiling again. Instead of finding excuses to stay over at work he was now eager to be on his way home and meet Dot. Mrs Grundy, on hearing about the forthcoming wedding, had what she called a sideation and presented Robbie with a pile of bedding and table linen, most of them completely unused. Dot was thrilled with the gift and insisted on paying a visit one Sunday afternoon to thank the lady personally. When Dot casually mentioned that they were now the proud owners of the beautiful lace-trimmed linen but had no bed to put it on, Mr Grundy said he would buy them a bed for a wedding present. He then set about working on a bed head to go with the spring mattress he ordered from Lewis's Department Store. 'Nowt but the best for that lad,' he told his wife when she remarked on the quality of the wood. 'Like a son to me he is.'

'And to me,' Mrs Grundy agreed, 'and that young lass is just as sensible.'

'It's a poor time to be starting off together, though. They'll not be together long before they're parted again.'

'Will ee be forced to go? Won't ee be exempt? I mean there'll be a lot of building work needed if there's any bombing, and there's always coffins needed.'

'Nay, lass, Robbie's not the type to be finding excuses. I doubt he'd shirk his duty even if he had chance.'

'Just like you then.'

'Aye, but I pray he won't see the same horrors that I saw, lass.'

'But you got through it, and Robbie will too. You'll see.'

'I hope so, lass. Because I 'ave a mind to mek 'im a partner in a few years. Not 'aving a son, like. It'd be a relief knowing't business won't come to an end when owt 'appens to us.'

'Aye it would; we'll look into it then. In't meantime will you be able to manage on yer own if ee has to go?'

'Well, I managed before, lass, and with most of the men away there'll not be much woodworking done. Oh aye, I reckon I shall manage until ee comes back.'

'And he will come back. I've got a feeling in me bones.'

'I've got a feeling in mine an' all, but mine's bloody rheumatics.'

Mrs Grundy smiled at the husband she idolised. If Robbie and Dot were half as happy as the Grundys they wouldn't have much to grumble about.

Though the wedding arrangements were going well, the news in February that air-raid shelters were to be provided to thousands of homes put a slight damper on the proceedings. Dot dismissed thoughts of Robbie having to go to war, determined to enjoy the time they had left. The wedding was planned for Saturday the twenty-fifth of March. An awkward moment came when the couple went to ask Herbert about blessing their marriage after the register office wedding, but Herbert wished them well and said he would be delighted. At first Dot had been angry at the heartache Reverend Goodman had caused, but she never stayed angry for long and now felt immense pity for the family. Louisa felt the rift had finally been mended when Boadacea sent them an invitation to the reception, which was to be held in the huge front room of the farm. The room was rarely used, but was beautifully furnished with a dresser filled with blue and white porcelain and a highly polished mahogany table. 'This table's been known to seat eighteen, twenty at a pinch,' Boadacea said. 'But on this occasion it'll be a help-yerself do. Everything home-made though, and homegrown, think on.'

Little Arthur got out his best suit, the one he had been married in and hadn't worn since. 'If yer can give it a good airing to get rid of the smell of moth balls, all it'll need is a bit of a press wi' brown paper; nobody'll be any the wiser.'

'What? Yer never intending wearing yer own wedding suit for our daughter's wedding. Well I never heard owt like it. Yer'll get yerself down to't Co-op and be measured for a new one, if I've to drag yer there on our Bob's lead.'

Little Arthur hummed and hawed a bit, but did as he was told, as usual.

John had also bought new clothes for all the children, though Lucy proudly announced that she could fit into her best clothes for the first time in years and there was no reason to waste money on new ones. John's own wedding suit was indeed pressed with brown paper and being of a more fashionable style than Little Arthur's, nobody would be any the wiser.

Because both Robbie and Dot hoped to avoid

attracting much attention Boady had limited the number of guests to the immediate families and the Slaters. Mable had been chosen to be a bridesmaid along with Rosie and Violet, and her boyfriend Harry was of course invited. Lucy wondered if Mable's might be the next wedding to take place.

After the meal, Little Arthur was delighted to escape and take all the children on a tour of the farm. Bernard was curious to know if any of the animals had babies in their tummies and Rosie laughed at the idea. 'Babies don't come from tummies; they come in Dr Sellars's black bag.'

'No they don't.'

'Yes they do. Anyway, they would smothercate inside a tummy.'

'They would not. Baby chicks don't suffocate and they're inside eggshells. Anyway there's no such word as smothercate.'

'Ooh, Bernard Grey, you think you're so clever just because you're dopted.'

'I don't. They do grow in tummies, don't they? Mester.' Bernard did wonder though, why mothers bothered to eat their babies in the first place when they knew they had to come out again.

Little Arthur didn't want to become involved in the argument but told Bernard that if Uncle Robbie brought him to the farm in a couple of months he could see the new lambs.

'And me?' Rosie enquired. 'And Violet and Peter and Andrew?'

'And Joyce?' Bernard insisted. He liked everything to be fair.

'But not Henry, because he lives too far away,'

Rosie explained to Little Arthur, who had no idea who all those children were. 'Oh just bring 'em all,' he said, hoping he didn't have to wait too long for a grandchild of his own.

'Dad. We're ready for going.' Dot told the children to go and get some lemonade. She wanted some time with her father.

'Eeh, lass. Yer look a sight for sore eyes.' His daughter had changed into a suit of kingfisher blue and a pink blouse.

'I just wanted to say thanks, Dad.'

'What for?'

'For the wedding, but not only that: for being there for me and for having faith in Robbie.'

'I know a good lad when I see one.'

'I know that, but I 'aven't been easy to live with at times.'

Little Arthur nudged her with his elbow as they leaned on the wall. 'Yer never 'ave been. A right mouthy little madam you were at times.' He grinned. 'Just like yer mother. That's why I love yer so much.'

'Oh, Dad. Yer making me cry now, then I shall set off on my honeymoon looking a mess.'

'Tha couldn't look a mess if tha jumped into't cesspit. It's always stumped me how I ever produced a beauty like thee, love.'

'Well, yer did get me, and I couldn't have had a nicer dad if I'd chosen one meself. I'd better go; Tom and Nellie are needing to be off, what with the little one.'

'Aye, it were good of 'em to come all this way and take yer back with 'em.'

Dot couldn't remember the last time she had

kissed her father, or her mother, but she kissed him now. And the loving smile he gave her was worth all the embarrassment of it. They walked through the yard with the familiar sounds and smells. Dot loved this place and didn't think she could have borne to leave it for good.

'Dad?'

'Aye, love?'

'I'm not really as mouthy as me mam, am I?'

Little Arthur chuckled. 'Not now, yer not. I think it's young Robbie who's tamed yer. I should 'ave tamed yer mother but I suppose I loved her just the way she is. Don't tell 'er though; she'll be mouthier than ever if she knows that.'

Dot kissed her mother, who was trying not to cry. 'Oh go on, yer sloppy thing.' Boadacea pushed her daughter towards the car but Dot knew she was pleased at the loving gesture. They had never been a kissing family, not needed to be really, but Dot vowed that if she and Robbie were fortunate enough to have children they would bring them up to demonstrate their feelings, like Lucy and John. She waved to Lucy, who she knew would miss Robbie almost as much as Boadacea would miss her. Then they were on their way to Blackpool, and married life.

Lucy did miss Robbie. Even five children in the house couldn't make up for Robbie, or Will. It was the grown-up conversation she missed most. The laughter Will used to cause with his stories about the markets. With Robbie it was the local gossip from the customers using the workshop. The twins kept asking when Uncle Robbie was coming back and after a few days without her dog-walker Baby went into a sulk.

A bit of good news came a few days after the wedding when the Spanish war came to an end, with Franco taking Madrid, but news on the home front was not so good. The mutual assistance pact signed by Britain, France and Poland in case of attack only seemed to make the war seem more threatening, especially at the end of May when a further pact was signed by Hitler and Mussolini.

Chapter Thirty

Mrs Cooper had never been more content. Her days were full now and interesting. She had pushed all her aches and pains out of her mind until one fine May morning as she was having a tussle with a deckchair on the promenade. She usually managed to get the contraption up after a few attempts but on this occasion a pain in her chest caused her to double up in agony and abandon her attempt.

'Eeh, what's wrong? Jessie?' Edith watched the colour drain from her friend's face. She put up the deckchair without any bother and helped her friend down onto the canvas.

'I don't know, Edith. I've had it before but nowt as bad as this.'

'Look, you keep yer eye on the bairns and I'll nip and fetch a jug of tea off the pier.' Edith set off as fast as her swollen legs would carry her. When she returned she was carrying two cups and young Jim was following with a jug of hot, milky tea.

'Shall I fetch a doctor, Mrs Cooper? Or Lily or somebody?'

'Shall yer heck. I shall be right as rain when I get this down me. And don't tell Lily either, about me pain. Yer know what that lass is for worrying.'

'I know, but she thinks a lot of you; I ought to tell her.'

'Don't you dare. I expect it wor a bit of indigestion. I'll tek some bicarb in a drop of milk when I get 'ome.'

'So we won't be going to't tower then?' Edith asked.

'Course we will. I'm all right now.'

Edith was uncertain. She'd become fond of her friend and thought maybe she ought to take things easy for a while.

'Look 'ere Edith,' Mrs Cooper said. 'I've waited all these years to go to't tower ballroom and yer promised you would go with me. Well it wouldn't be much fun going on me own, would it?'

'All right, but our Mary says there's a lot of steps to go up.'

'I know. I can remember going up 'em with Joe.' Little Henry woke and pulled himself up in the pram. She turned it round so he could look down to where the donkeys were standing on the beach. 'I need to go, Edith. I need to recall those last carefree days before ee died. Yer see, Edith, sometimes I can't quite remember his face. That face I loved so much and it meks me feel guilty when I can't quite picture it. I think if I go back to where we spent our last days together I might remember.'

'Oh, lass. Don't you 'ave a photo of 'im?'

'No, it'd be different if I had, but the only one I had's got lost. I've searched high and low but I can't find it.' She frowned. 'But even if I found it I still need to go. I just want to feel the atmosphere and see the magnificence one more time.' She felt better after the tea. It must have been indigestion. 'Besides, we can 'ave a dance and if we enjoy it we can go again.'

'Not much point when I can't dance, and I'm too old to start learning now, what with my legs an' all.'

'But we could sit and watch the others. It's so... Oh I can't begin to describe it. Anyway, you'll see for yerself.'

Edith's grandson tried to climb out of the pushchair. 'I'd better be going or he'll start mithering to come out.'

'Aye, I'd better be going as well. So we'll meet outside the tower then at seven.'

'If yer sure?'

'I'm sure. I'm going to wear the very same frock and shoes I wore for Joe.'

Edith sniffed. 'If they fit yer after all those years.'

'I 'aven't put all that much weight on.'

'No, but I mean none of us look like we did before middle-age spread took over. All right, yer've no need to yell, we're going.' Both babies were making themselves heard. They made their way across the prom and along the Golden Mile, wheeling the pushchair in and out between the early holidaymakers. If it hadn't been for the blooming pains that occasionally caused her such agony Mrs Cooper would have been the happiest woman in Blackpool. She would ask Nellie where she could find a doctor, but not today when she was about to fulfil her dream and visit the tower.

By the time she had helped Lily clear the tables and do the washing up Mrs Cooper felt much better and at quarter to seven she set off to meet Edith.

'What yer got in yer carrier bag?' Edith enquired.

'Me dance shoes.'

Edith pulled a face. 'Can't see anybody asking us to dance.'

'Come on.' Mrs Cooper moved with growing excitement towards the kiosk, thinking it was a bit expensive. 'Two please.'

''Ere, I'll get me own ticket.'

'No, Edith, it were me who wanted to come so I'll pay.'

'I don't know how families manage a holiday at these prices,' Edith said.

'Aye, but as Joe used to say, there's enough to keep you occupied all day once you're in.' The music wafted towards them. 'Can yer feel the atmosphere? It's like no other place I've ever been in.' Then she stared in dismay at the mountain of steps. She couldn't remember there being so many when she had come with Joe, but she'd been too much in love to notice anything on those occasions.

'Well, are yer coming or aren't yer?' Edith set off. 'Though what my legs'll be like when I reach the top doesn't bear thinking about.' They stopped halfway up to tidy their hair in the mirrored wall. The wind and the salt air hadn't been kind to either of them but Mrs Cooper's was the worst. She got out a comb and did her best.

'Don't ever 'ave one of them perms, Edith; my hair's never been the same since I had mine. I'd better not wear a green frock or they'll think I'm a dandelion clock.'

Edith laughed. 'Nay, lass, it isn't the perm – that's all worn out long ago. It's the sea air what dries it up. It looks all right now you've combed it.' They scrutinised themselves as they regained their breath. Their faces were flushed, either from the wind or from the stair climb – they weren't sure which. 'I don't reckon we look bad for our age.'

'No, we'll pass. Come on.' After a few more steps Mrs Cooper knew she should never have attempted the climb and when she reached the top she leaned on the window ledge until she felt better. She gazed out at the wide expanse of stormy grey sea. Waves galloped like white horses onto the promenade then rolled back again to continue their never-ending journey. Edith stood beside her, as mesmerised as she was.

'Once Joe hired a landau to take us from one end of the prom to the other. Tucked up in blankets just like royalty we were. Then ee took me to a wine bar and bought me a cocktail wi' one of them fancy names. We went under't pier after that for a cuddle.'

'I'll bet yer did more than cuddle.' Edith nudged her friend and giggled.

'No, we didn't, but do yer know Edith, I've always regretted that we didn't. It was a lovely moonlit night and all we did was talk about what we would do when we came back to Blackpool on our honeymoon. He promised me we would go dancing in the tower.' She sighed. 'Then he went and died, before we even had chance to be married.'

'Aye, but you were fortunate all't same. In all those years I was married, my owd man never did owt romantic, not once.'

The music beckoned them on. Edith gazed in awe at the magnificence, her eyes taking in the red plush seats, the ornately gilded ceiling and balcony. 'Eeh, lass, you weren't exaggerating.'

'Yer see that bit of balcony that curves out by the stage? That's where ee first kissed me. He said I looked like a princess in the royal box.'

'Do yer want to go up there for owd times' sake?'

'No, Edith. I couldn't make it up any more stairs.' She didn't want Edith to know about the pain that had come on again during the last climb; it would be foolish to intensify it. 'Come on, we'll sit 'ere.' They removed their coats and she changed her sturdy, laced-up shoes for the maroon ones, coaxing her bunions into them.

'What are yer putting them on for if we aren't going to be dancing?'

'Because they match this frock, which was Joe's favourite.'

'Well I'm going to 'ave a lemonade. Shall I get you one?'

'Aye, that'd be nice.'

The young man looked round the ballroom for a partner; he doubted if the giggly young girls near the stage would know the steps and most of the others seemed to be couples. Then he saw the old lady. She looked lonely all on her own and rather odd in a dress that looked as if it had come out of the ark and was at least two sizes too small. Still, she wouldn't be here if she didn't like dancing.

Mrs Cooper felt a little dizzy as the dancers whirled past her and things seemed a little hazy somehow. Then she saw him approaching her, immaculate as ever in white shirt and dark suit. She noticed he needed a haircut, not that she intended mentioning it tonight. Nothing was going to spoil tonight. Alan touched her arm. 'Would you like to dance?' he asked, taking her hand and whirling her away onto the dance floor.

She forgot about the pain in her chest and squashed-up toes and matched her steps perfectly to his. Alan thought the old girl was certainly light on her feet and ever so pleasant – in fact he imagined she must have been quite a beauty in her younger days. The dance changed to a Viennese waltz and Mrs Cooper smiled radiantly as her partner gathered her to him. 'Oh, listen Joe. They're playing our tune.' Then she sank, suddenly, peacefully into Alan's arms.

Edith had been watching Jessie, wishing it was her who was dancing with the handsome young man. Then she saw the commotion, watched her friend lowered to the floor and a first-aid man rush to her side. Edith hurried as fast as the slippery floor would allow. Someone held her back and in a daze she watched the uniformed man shake his head. By the time the doctor arrived it was too late. Somebody led Edith to a chair and gave her a sip of something that took her breath away, then they explained that the death had been instantaneous, not that it made the sadness any easier to bear.

Alan was in shock; he was worried that if he hadn't asked her to dance the poor lady might still be alive. 'I never ought to have approached her, but I've no regrets,' he told Edith. 'I don't think I've ever witnessed such joy as the lady displayed when the organist played what she said was our tune. Funny though how she had mistaken me for someone called Joe.'

'You brought her happiness, dear,' Edith told him between the sobs. 'You paved the way for her to be reunited with the one she loved. You've nothing to reproach yourself for, nothing at all.' Then Edith set off to Nellie Johnson's, with the heartbreaking news about the woman she would miss so much. The only consolation was that her friend was now free from pain and hopefully once again with her beloved Joe.

Nellie had just finished reading *Three Little Pigs* to her son when Edith arrived. Tom didn't know the woman, but seeing how distressed she was he brought her inside and alerted his wife. The news devastated Nellie, but she was more concerned about Lily than herself. The girl couldn't stop crying and had to be put to bed with a couple of Genasprins and a glass of hot milk. It wasn't until the next day that the Johnsons got round to discussing funeral arrangements. Tom wondered if they should have Mrs Cooper taken back to Cragstone for her burial.

'Ooh, yer mustn't do that, Mr Johnson. She said she's never been as happy as she has since coming to Blackpool. She said for the first time in her life she was part of a family, and besides she said Blackpool was where her happiest memories were.' Lily was adamant.

This set Nellie off weeping again and then when Lily started crying again little Henry joined in. Partly because he didn't like it when his mother was upset and partly because he hadn't seen his beloved Coopy all day.

Tom arranged the funeral as he thought best and when the day arrived he was gratified when Mr Smith turned up with Molly and Larry. Mourners were few, apart from Nellie, Tom and his parents, Edith, Lily and her boyfriend and the three boarders; only the three from Cragstone and Lily followed the coffin. However the funeral of Jessica Jane Cooper was conducted with the dignity the lady deserved. Of course Lily was taking it badly and couldn't stop crying; even the appearance of her sister hadn't done much to console her, so after the refreshments had been devoured Tom suggested Lily take Molly and Larry on a tour of the resort. 'Go and show them the sights of Blackpool,' he said. 'Mrs Cooper wouldn't like them to travel all this way and not see the place she loved so much.'

'Ooh, Mr Johnson, would it be right on such a sad day?'

'Oh, goo on, Lily, I've never seen the sea,' Molly pleaded.

'All right then.' Lily didn't need much persuading. She would show them the tower where Mrs Cooper had died and then they would go on the pier. Jim said that as they were special visitors he would serve them the special afternoon tea. Molly liked Lily's young man, nearly as much as she liked Larry, but not in the same loving way. Whilst they were finishing off their cream buns Molly asked why Mrs Cooper always called herself Mrs when she had never been married.

'Housekeepers always did. Nellie says it was a tradition from the old days when housekeepers were supposed to be married to the house they were looking after.'

Molly began to giggle and then thought it would be inappropriate to be laughing on such a sad day. She couldn't control her excitement however at being here in Blackpool, even if it had been Mrs Cooper's death that had made the visit possible.

It wasn't until a few days later when Nellie and Lily were sorting out Mrs Cooper's belongings that Lily found the photograph. It had somehow worked its way underneath the lining of Mrs Cooper's handbag.

'Ooh, look, Nellie. It's Mrs Cooper and her Joe. Doesn't she look lovely and isn't he handsome? Do yer think they'll be together now?'

'Yes, Lily. I'm sure they will. Love doesn't end when someone dies; it lasts for ever.'

'Can I keep it?'

'What?'

'The photo.'

'Oh, yes of course.' Nellie was relieved to see a smile light up Lily's beautiful face for the first time in days.

'We'll chuck this owd handbag away though. Nobody'd be seen dead with an owd-fashioned thing like this over their arm.'

Nellie smiled. Lily was certainly back to her normal self.

In readiness for the blackout which would surely come, white lines were painted down the middle of the main roads and the day after the evacuation of over a million children began. Lucy said she would live down the cellar permanently before parting with her five. Mrs Slater said she didn't think evacuation from Millington would be necessary.

'We were safe enough in the last war,' she pointed out.

Mr Slater wasn't so sure. 'I don't think we shall be safe anywhere wi' all these modern aircraft.'

Jane arrived at Lucy's in a state, with the news that when the war came, James had decided he would be among the first to enlist. 'He says women will be able to do his job and because we have no children he feels it is his duty to go.' Jane began to sob. 'He doesn't care about me at all.'

'Course he cares. I think you should be proud of him. Send him off with a smile, after you've told him how much you love him of course.'

'It's all right for you. John won't be going, will he?'

'No, but John's a miner; he'll be needed. I don't suppose women could do John's work.' Lucy sighed. 'Look, Jane, I think you should tell James how proud you are. After all, it won't be easy for him either.'

'Yes, Lucy. You're right as usual. After all, our Will's already prepared, with Betty running the market stalls almost as well as he does himself.'

'Well not quite, but she's got a school-leaver to help. Mr Brown says he's a good lad and they'll manage between them. After all, it won't be for long.'

'And our Ben and Robbie are ready for their call to duty, and it will be much worse for Emma with little Joyce.'

'Oh our Mary's offered to help out there. To tell you the truth I think it'll be good for her, especially if Jacob enlists too.'

Jane had stopped sulking now. 'You've made me feel ashamed of myself. I should consider myself fortunate with a job I love and with you and John on hand if I need you. It's just that I love James so much.'

'I know. But I'm sure it won't be for long.' Lucy mashed a pot of tea. 'Come on, let's have a cuppa. And just think what it'll be like when he comes home: just like a second honeymoon.'

'Lucy Grey, is that all you think about?'

'Not all, but a lot of the time.' The sisters laughed. Once again Lucy had smoothed things over.

It was the following Sunday when the news came and even though it was expected the shock was still as great. Reverend Goodman made the announcement during morning service. Lucy heard it on the wireless whilst mixing Yorkshire puddings for Sunday dinner. Bernard hurried up the banking to the allotments where John was gathering beans and mint for the potatoes.

'Dad, the war's started.' He was so excited he fell head-first over the cucumber frame. Lewis Marshall left the garden fork sticking in the

ground and came over to John.
'So it's started then?'
'Sounds like it, Lewis.'
'When will the soldiers be here, Dad?'
'Here? Never I hope, son.'
Bernard, disappointed, wandered off to the hens. It didn't look as though the war would be as exciting as he had expected.
That night the blackout began, with the gas lamps switched off and inside lights to be obscured. Places of entertainment were closed and British Summer Time extended for six weeks in order to reduce the number of accidents expected to be caused by the blackout.
As Bernard had said, the war had started and it wasn't exciting; it was scary.

'The job'll be waiting when tha comes back, Robbie.'
'Thanks, Mr Grundy. I shall look forward to coming back.'
'I've been 'aving a natter wi' my missis and when tha comes back we've decided it'll be on a different footing.'
'Oh! Am I not giving satisfaction?'
'Don't talk so daft, Robbie. It's because I'm so satisfied that we've decided to mek yer a partner.'
Robbie almost hit his thumb with the hammer. 'A partner? No, hold on, Mr Grundy. I won't have enough savings to buy a partnership, not with just furnishing the cottage.'
'Who said owt about payment? I didn't buy this business. My old father started it and ee worked bloody hard and ee made a lot of money, and

when I started working for 'im I worked bloody 'ard as well. And me father, God rest 'is soul, wasn't one to part wi' owt, so I 'ad to wait till he'd gone before I got what was due to me. But by heck, I got a shock when I knew what ee was worth. I'm a rich man, Robbie, but I worked bloody 'ard for it, and you're a hard worker an' all. Now I 'aven't a son to pass it on to, so we've decided that you're the next best thing. So we've made a will and left the bulk to you. Wi' a few exceptions, charities mainly. Now I don't want thee to wait until I've gone before tha gets it. I want to see thee and Dot enjoy some of it. So I'm making thee a partner until the time when I finally hang up me hammer.'

Robbie felt so emotional he wanted to cry. 'I don't know what to say. Only that I shall carry on working just as hard if I come back.'

'What do yer mean, if? When, lad, not if. Just one thing, though.'

'Anything.'

'Will yer ask Dot if she'll pay a visit occasionally whilst you're away? Only it's the missis. She's going to miss thee, and it'd be a bit of company for her.'

'Course she will. She'll enjoy coming to see you both.'

'Right then, we'd better get this 'ere coffin finished or poor owd Fred'll 'ave to be buried up to't neck in muck.'

They carried on, one working on the coffin and one on the lid, both wrapped up in their own thoughts of what the future might bring.

Chapter Thirty-one

With the twins now at school and only Andrew at home Lucy could have been taking things easy. Instead she began looking after a few of the children from the rows – children whose fathers were fighting for their country and whose mothers were finding it difficult to make ends meet. One of the mothers went into the steelworks as a crane driver and another into the wire department. James had been right: women were doing his job and doing it just as well.

For the first time since her marriage Lucy was thankful that John was a collier. Though the news of an accident at Hatfield Colliery – when a cage fell a hundred feet to the bottom of a shaft, injuring sixty miners – had filled her with panic. Another six men had been killed at a pit in Nottingham just before Christmas. Lucy realised that being a miner wasn't much safer than being a soldier, but at least John could come home to her and the children at the end of a shift.

At the end of January Lewis came to see Lucy. 'I've just come to tell you I've enlisted, Lucy. I'm off tomorrow.'

'Oh, why? You're a key worker. You don't need to go.'

'I do. There's nowt for me here. It'd be different if I were married, but that'll never happen. The lass I loved went and married somebody else.'

'Oh, Lewis. I'm sorry.'

'No, you mustn't be sorry; you're happy with John and that's all I care about. He's a good man. But it hasn't stopped me loving you. So I'm off.'

'Lewis, I do love you in a way. If I hadn't met John things might have been different.'

'Maybe, but you did meet him. So like I said, I'm off.'

'Well, take care.'

'Aye. You too.' Lewis came towards her and gently kissed her, and for the first time Lucy didn't pull away.

Lewis grinned. 'It's worth going, if only for that. A kiss at last. Yippee!'

'Lewis Marshall, you get dafter.' Lucy knew that if she didn't laugh she would cry. They stood quietly looking at each other, then Lewis walked away, leaving behind the girl he had loved since she was ten years old. It was the last time Lucy was to see Lewis; he was killed somewhere on the French coast four months later.

Before long Lucy had six little ones as well as her own in her care. Sometimes the mothers gave Lucy a shilling or two to pay for their midday meal; sometimes they didn't. She never complained and everyone on the rows agreed that Lucy Grey was an angel. All the children called her Auntie Lucy and would have preferred to stay there in her warm loving care rather than go home. Only very rarely did John complain and that was when he thought his wife looked tired and needed a rest. 'People don't rest when there's a war on,' Lucy said, and carried on. John knew better than to argue with Lucy Grey.

When Tom Johnson came home on leave, looking smart and handsome in his air force blue, Nellie was the proudest woman in Blackpool. Tom's father was coping admirably with the filling station, not that there was much to do with the petrol rationing in force. Still, there was enough trade to keep him and a young apprentice occupied. Besides, Tom thought there would be a boom in the car trade after the war. 'Got to keep it going for little Henry,' he said.

The guest house was just about paying its way. The boarders were mainly show people, now the theatres had been allowed to reopen. The general opinion was that wartime Britain needed entertaining in order to boost morale. Sometimes soldiers turned up with a young woman needing a room for the weekend. Lily'd whisper to Nellie about them not being married and giggle when they yawned and decided on an early night. Nellie would turn a blind eye; who was she to deny a soldier his comfort? They mightn't be alive tomorrow.

The sergeant major had proved a true friend to Nellie. He had more or less taken over from Mrs Cooper in the care of little Henry. He would march the little boy along the prom, issuing orders such as 'tummy in, shoulders back, left, right, left, right'. Henry thrived on the friendship in his father's absence. Nellie thought Duke was gaining as much benefit as her son from the relationship. Being too old for war service didn't sit well on the shoulders of a man who had made the armed forces his career. Duke was also missing Mrs

Cooper and the chats they had enjoyed about their younger days. Nellie was glad Henry was diverting his thoughts and giving him a purpose in life.

Lily's Jim was somewhere in France, but with Phoebe for company the two girls seemed happy enough. They went dancing on the Central Pier, sometimes with soldiers, but both girls made it clear that dancing was the only thing they were there for. The cinema was their main source of entertainment – especially the newsreels, where they searched the faces, hoping for a glimpse of their sweethearts. It was on one of those visits that Lily decided she needed to be doing something more useful with her life.

'I've decided to join up,' she whispered.

'What?'

'I've decided to join up.'

'You can't.'

'Shush,' the woman in the row behind them warned.

'I can.'

'What will Nellie do?'

'She doesn't really need me with only the regulars. I expect she'll be relieved if she doesn't have to pay me.'

'Lily, please don't go. It's dangerous.'

'Be quiet please!' hissed the woman.

'Well it's dangerous for the lads an' all but they've gone. We want the war to be over so we've got to help finish it.'

The usherette came down the aisle and shone her torch on the two girls. They didn't speak again until the end of the film. Then Phoebe didn't have much to say.

'It's no good yer sulking. I'm joining the land army?

'So yer not kidding? You're determined.'

'I am.'

'I'm not stopping 'ere on me own. I'll come with yer.'

'Really?' Lily hugged Phoebe and they danced the Palais Glide all the way along Albert Road and back again. A few days later, amongst much protesting from Nellie and cries of 'Bravo' from Duke, Lily promised she'd be back when the war was over and people began taking holidays again. Then she kissed little Henry and managed to walk away without crying.

With Henry at the garage all day Margaret Johnson was delighted to take Lily's place when a waitress happened to be needed.

Fortunately for Lily and Phoebe, the two girls managed to stay together for the duration of the war and Lily couldn't believe it when she was sent to a farm back in her beloved Yorkshire. Life was hard but the land girls managed to enjoy themselves with dances in the village hall to look forward to on Saturday nights. There were also tears when letters sometimes arrived with news of brothers or sweethearts either missing or killed in action. Lily and Phoebe prayed every night for Jim and Stan to be kept safe. Sadly it wasn't to be. Both soldiers fell to the enemy, though months apart and in different parts of the world.

Both the guest house and the filling station just about held their own until the end of the war. Then Nellie managed to turn the guest house into one of the most successful hotels on the

Lancashire coast. Tom's garage also went from strength to strength, just as he had predicted.

When Lily did return to Blackpool it was to the memories and for a time she found it difficult to cope with the heartache, but Lily had grown up now; she would get over it. Well Mrs Cooper had, hadn't she?

Jacob cowered in the corner of the wooden shack. The earth floor was awash with vomit and urine and the air thick with the stench of diarrhoea. It was hard to tell which was worse: the hunger pains when no food was brought to the prisoners, or the stomach cramps after eating the disgusting slop that was offered on other days. Sometimes Jacob woke up confused in the pale light of dawn and wondered if he had died and gone to hell. Perhaps that would be preferable to this hell on earth here in the Far East. Then in a more lucid moment he would think of Mary and know she would be waiting on his return.

Once he dreamed she came to find him with a baby in her arms and he woke in tears to find her gone. Another time he felt the closeness of her body and drew her into his embrace, only to wake and find one of his comrades dead in his arms. He hoped his closeness had provided a measure of comfort to the dying soldier. He had cried out on that occasion and had been rewarded with the butt of a rifle thrust into his stomach. Last night he had found himself floating, up on a level with the solitary light bulb, looking down dispassionately at his own skeletal body. He had seen an angel beckoning him, and the temptation had been almost more than he could bear, but Mary had called his name and he had chosen her. Where were the letters she was certain to have written? Maybe she thought he was dead. He imagined her in some civilian's embrace and experienced a pain so acute he wondered how he would survive it, but no one ever died from heartache, only from the brutality of this bloody war, and the dysentery which was rife amongst the prisoners here in the camp. He thought of Mary and the love she had shown him on his last leave. To keep her in mind was the only way he could think of to keep him sane in this godforsaken place.

Reverend Goodman lived up to his name throughout the war, working unceasingly with the city's homeless during and after the blitz. He comforted the injured and the bereaved both in the shelters and the hospitals. Sometimes Louisa didn't see him for days on end, so she decided to make herself useful and joined the Women's Voluntary Services. Serving hot drinks from a mobile canteen she was astounded at the satisfaction she gained, not only from the comfort they gave to the destitute, but from the camaraderie of the other volunteers.

When news came that Prudence had been killed along with three more patients during the bombing of the nursing home in Liverpool, her work provided the salvation she needed. Herbert comforted her with the words that God had been merciful by taking his daughter into His loving care. It was at that time that Louisa's work took her to the Wharncliffe Hospital, where she helped to care for the soldiers who had returned from overseas. Some of them were shell shocked, others trying to come to terms with a future without arms or legs. Neither Herbert nor Louisa had time to feel sorry for themselves.

When, after the war, Robbie and Dot took their baby son to visit them, Herbert finally felt he was forgiven for the wrong he had done them. Baby Arthur was a loving and well-loved child, with not only his Grandma and Grandad Greenwood to shower him with affection, but also the Grundys and Goodmans. Two years later when Dot gave birth to a daughter, Robbie Grey's life was complete.

Lucy and John carried on regardless, helping and advising the women whose men were away, and comforting Mary, who didn't know if Jacob was living or dead, having heard nothing since his last leave.

After a long shift at the pit John would be up all night fire-watching. Even so he realised how fortunate he and Lucy were, with a family who never seemed to cause them much trouble and he being at home rather than in some godforsaken war zone. The kids were thriving and doing well at school, so it came as a shock one day when Rosie came home from school and said Bernard had been caned. Lucy had noticed how he had slunk away upstairs and went to investigate.

'All right, what have you been up to?'

'Nothing.'

'Come on, you don't get the cane for nothing.'

'Our Rosie's a tell-tale.'

'So?'

Bernard knew it would come out sooner or later. 'It was Fatty Green's fault. He's so greedy he makes me sick. He pinched my pop, after I'd taken all the bottles back to pay for it. He pinched it and drank the lot.'

'Well if it was him, why did you get the cane?'

'Because I got me own back.'

'So I suppose you were fighting.'

'No.' Bernard didn't want to say any more but there was no escaping his mother's probing. 'He wouldn't 'ave been worth fighting. Ee's a cry baby.'

'So how did you get your own back?'

'I peed in the bottle and left it for 'im to pinch again. And ee did. Then ee was sick all over Miss Mason's shoes and all over Auntie Jane's clean floor. When Fatty told on me she gave me the cane and made me clean it up. But it was worth it,' Bernard added defiantly. Lucy almost laughed, but knew she mustn't. 'Well, it was an awful thing to do, so you got what you deserved. Did he get the cane too?'

'No.'

Lucy made a point to have a word with Miss Mason. In her opinion taking something that belonged to someone else was just as bad as what Bernard had done. 'Well, we'd better not tell your dad or he'll probably give you another walloping.' Lucy knew John would never lay a finger on any of his children, but it wouldn't harm Bernard to think he might. She couldn't wait to hear what Jane had to say about the incident. She had an idea it might have given her a great deal of pleasure. Lucy knew for a fact that neither the spoilt, pampered Frank Green nor Miss Mason were thought very highly of by Jane. She was right. Jane thought even a vomit-splattered floor was worth it just to think of Frank Green's face when he swallowed Bernard's urine.

Chapter Thirty-two

When Jane met James off the train at Sheffield she was shocked at the sight of him and the men who were with him. Some had to be helped off the train and though James was uninjured he looked only half the man who had gone away. However, with Jane's loving care and assistance and encouragement from Herbert and Louisa he was soon able to return to his job. He never discussed the horrors he had witnessed; perhaps it would have been better if he had done so. James would never forget, but knew he was one of the fortunate ones, to be home and in one piece. They never did have children; they seemed to be content with each other and if they did feel a need to spoil their nephews and nieces there were plenty of them to choose from. They would set off at the weekends on their beloved motorbike, just Jane and James and the wide open spaces of the countryside, and they were content.

Will had kept the lads of the Royal Signals from becoming too despondent. He had formed a concert party with a group of lads from Wales –

who had voices like angels and a magician who attracted more cat calls than applause. Will's jokes and banter sometimes seemed to be fighting a losing battle as more and more of his comrades lost their lives or suffered appalling injuries, but even on the worst days he forced a smile to his face in an effort to keep up the lads' spirits. Despite a leg wound Will managed to return to Betty in one piece. His wife had grown to love the market life and apart from the years she stayed home to bring up her two boys, she remained by her husband's side working the stalls. Like she said, she and Will had been apart long enough.

It was much later when Jacob came back. Like James, his appearance shocked Mary to the core, but Jacob hadn't only his wife as an incentive to get well. On his last leave the wishing mirror had worked its magic once again.

Lucy had been listening to *Two Way Family Favourites* on the wireless, singing away to the music, 'With a Song in My Heart'. She hadn't heard Mary come in. She could tell by Mary's flushed face that she was excited about something. 'Are you all right? Has something happened? Have you heard from Jacob?'

'No, I've heard nothing since his last leave.' Her face had clouded momentarily, but Mary smiled again as she said, 'But yes I'm all right. I'm pregnant, Lucy.' Mary was trembling by now as she spoke the words for the first time. 'After all the waiting it had to happen in the few days he was home. Oh Lucy, I can't believe it. If only I could let him know, but I don't think he's getting my letters. Well, if he is he isn't answering them.'

'But just imagine the surprise he'll get when he does come home!'

'If he comes home. He might be dead now for all I know. But at least I shall have our child, a part of him.'

'He'll come home, Mary. The wishing mirror has worked again and if I keep on wishing for Jacob to come home he will.' She took Mary by the waist and danced round the table singing to the wireless until Mary asked 'Is something burning?'

'Oh, it's the joint. There wasn't much to start with, what with the blinking rationing, and then I have to go and burn it.' She lifted the small, dried-up piece of beef out of the oven. 'Never mind, we've plenty of vegetables. There'll be no dripping this week though.'

'I'm sorry, I should never have come just at dinnertime.'

'Don't be daft. It's the best news I've had for years.'

They went to tell Mrs Slater. 'Eeh, lass, what a surprise. What will Jacob say? Now if that news doesn't buck 'im up nowt will.'

The trouble was that Jacob didn't hear the news; the letters had never reached him. It was only when he saw Mary standing on the platform on his return some years later that he caught the first sight of his son. The little boy was clinging to Mary's skirt and he thought it must be one of Lucy's lot. Mary, dressed in a smart blue costume, looked more beautiful than he could remember and he forgot about the child when she drew him into her arms and kissed him long and hungrily.

Then she drew apart and lifted the small boy up into her arms. 'Luke,' she said, fighting back the tears. 'Say hello to your daddy.'

Jacob felt faint for a moment, then he held out his arms to the child he had longed for for so long. It had been worth all the suffering just to come home to the wonderful news that he was a father.

Ben Gabbitas eventually became a wealthy man, and when a few years after the war he and Emma had a son to carry on the Gabbitas name their life seemed complete. Lucy's heart would miss a beat sometimes when she looked at her brother. He was the image of the father she'd so adored. At those times she wished John'd leave the muck and danger of the coal mine behind and find a more healthy occupation. She got her wish when Mr Grundy asked Robbie one day 'Does tha think your John'd be interested in coming to work for us?'

'Our John? Well I don't know. I shouldn't think he's ever thought about leaving the pit.'

'I shouldn't think ee'll 'ave any option if the rumours I've 'eard turn out to be true.'

'What rumours?'

'That the Sheepdip might be closing in't next few years. Course it might prove to be nowt else but rumours, but as I think we should be setting somebody on, I thought ee might be interested.'

'Don't yer think we're managing all right between the two of us?'

'Aye, lad, and I dare say we could go on managing, but I'm ready for a rest. Me missis wants to travel a bit and I don't blame 'er. I've never taken 'er anywhere, always been too busy, so I'm thinking of becoming semi-retired. Oh I'll never leave altogether, can't. This workshop's more of a home to me than me house is. But we're going to be busier. We're going to need to expand to deal with all the new building that's planned for the future. And what with 'im being an 'ard-working sort I just wondered if he'd be interested.'

'Well, I don't know. If he came we should have to train him up. But you're right, he's a good worker is our John. So shall I mention it?'

'Aye, lad. let's give him a try.'

John was alarmed at the thought of learning a trade at his age. But he was even more alarmed when Robbie mentioned the rumour about the pit closure. When Robbie told him how much he would be paid he knew Lucy would never let him turn down the offer of leaving the place she had always believed killed her father. Besides, with Bernard and Rosie both at grammar school he couldn't afford to be out of work.

Lucy reassured him that he could tackle anything once he made his mind up and sighed with relief when he handed in his notice at the pit. She turned out to be right, and John had never been more content. The two brothers worked together well. Being of the same temperament they could work for long periods in companiable silence, both lost in the pleasure of their work. Sometimes Robbie would think of Prudence with sadness, but he resolved to put the past behind him and look to the future with hope that his children would never see another war.

John, on the other hand, would sometimes think about the men he had worked with at the pit, missing the banter and camaraderie they had shared, but most of all he missed Lewis. He had taken over Lewis's plot at the allotments and found a measure of consolation from working the same earth as his friend had once worked. Sometimes on Sunday mornings the boys would come and give him a hand and the girls had taken over the care of the chickens, for which they all received spending money on a Friday. It was Lucy and the girls who decided to accompany him one lovely sunny day. 'I can bring the peas back and you can stay here whilst I cook the dinner,' Lucy said.

When they reached the plot John couldn't believe his eyes. There, peeping through the rich dark soil were row upon row of beautiful scarlet radishes. The seeds John had scattered on the ground – without any hope of them making anything – had taken root and were a treat to behold.

'It's a bloody miracle,' John spluttered.

A butterfly fluttered about among the radishes, then came to settle on Violet's cheek. Rosie danced with excitement. 'It's Uncle Lewis; he's grown the radishes for my mum. Now he's sent the butterfly to give us a sign. Look, he's giving her a butterfly kiss, just the way he did before he died.' The butterfly came to settle on Rosie's hand, fluttering its wings before flying away down the bank where the wild flowers grew. Lucy felt the tears gather and roll down her cheeks.

'Why are you crying, Mum?' Rosie asked, taking hold of Lucy's hand.

'Because she's sad that Uncle Lew died,' Violet answered.

'No, not because I'm sad. I'm crying because he's still here amongst us. I'm sure you're right. The radishes and the butterfly really are signs that he's here. I'm sure of it.'

Lucy expected John to laugh at such nonsense, but he was standing there staring unbelievingly at the scarlet globes, as if they were liable to disappear if he turned away. He blinked his eyes, but the radishes were still there in all their glory. 'Well, Lew,' John whispered. 'Between us, we've managed to grow the bloody things at last.'

Chapter Thirty-three

Peter and Bernard had been to Longfield for a Christmas tree and trimmed it with baubles and tinsel. It stood in the corner of the front room and glittered in the firelight's glow. Andrew had been to the Donkey Wood for holly and ivy and had decorated the pictures and the wishing mirror. Rosie and Violet had spent the morning making a mound of sandwiches using a fowl and a leg of pork – courtesy of Little Arthur. The aroma of spice from the hot mince pies filled the house with the scent of Christmas.

There were far too many now for a sit-down meal and Lucy had decided it would be a help-yourself do. John had shoved the three-piece suite back to the wall, making more room for the youngsters, who had claimed the front room as their own. Shrieks of laughter and cries of 'I got a six, I go first' filtered through to the kitchen. Due to the war it was the first time all the cousins had been together. This year it seemed even more important than before to celebrate Christ's birthday.

In the kitchen a couple of Nut Brown Ale crates were serving as extra seats and Will had even brought in the wash tub and perched himself on that. Nellie, Tom and Henry had arrived in time for lunch. Sadly Duke had passed away a few months ago following a stroke. Cyril and Sydney were dining out with friends. Mary had invited Tom, Nellie and Henry to stay at their house for the night. After the trifles had been devoured and cups of tea – or something stronger – had been handed round, Ben asked if he could fetch down the old melodion. Once the children heard the sound of carols they left their games behind and came to join in the singing. When the warblers finally paused for breath Will kept them entertained with stories about the market.

On the row parties were taking place at most of the houses. The Murphys' was overflowing with all the married ones visiting on this special day. The Marshalls and Slaters were having a combined do with not only Mable's young man and Kitty's husband present but also Lily. With a bit of conniving from Molly and Larry – who were now engaged – Lily and Ernie had now been reunited. Mrs Slater was delighted. It wasn't right, according to her, for a man of Ernie's age not to have a wife. At the Holmeses' the old harmonium sounded as if it was being strangled and further on the row a couple of teenagers were locked in an embrace, regardless of the cold.

Ben had just struck up with 'I've Got Sixpence' when a knock came on the door. Joyce – who was nearest – went to open it.

'Aunty Lucy, it's a lady in a fur coat, with a fur hat and fur boots.'

'Sounds more like a bear than a lady,' Will whispered. 'Be careful she doesn't bite.'

Lucy didn't know the stranger at first. 'Yes, can I help you?' she asked.

'Well I certainly hope so.' It was the American accent that alerted Lucy to who this strange woman with the heavily made-up face was.

'Auntie Kate? It is. Oh come on in. I didn't recognise you.'

'Well, you wouldn't. You were only eight years old when I left. I'd still know you, though. You're the one with your dad's eyes.' Kate drew Lucy into her arms as her other nephews and nieces came to embrace their late father's sister.

'Rosie, make your great aunt a cup of tea.' Lucy drew Kate towards a chair.

'How did you get here?' Mary asked when her aunt had removed her coat and been given something to eat.

'I hired a taxi. He's coming back for me at eleven; is that all right?' Kate laughed. 'It's costing me double seeing as it's Christmas, but it's worth it to see you all together.'

'You could have stayed the night,' John said. 'Where are you staying, by the way?'

'We're booked into a hotel, the Grand.'

'Blimey,' Will whistled, 'that's grand.'

'What about Uncle Gregory? Aren't we ever going to meet him?' Mary had read about Aunt Kate's husband in her letters but that was all.

'Yes, I shall bring him to see you all before we go home, but tonight he's visiting his sister in Barnsley. It will probably be a tearful experience after thirty years.' Kate sighed. 'We've been wanting to visit the old country for some time, but it wasn't possible what with the war. So we've decided to take the plunge before it's too late; after all we're both getting on in years.'

'Well, you don't look it.' Jane wished she had a coat like Aunt Kate's and dared to smoke like the stars did on the pictures. Kate had taken out a cheroot from a silver case and offered them round. Only Ben and Jacob accepted. Kate put on her coat and made for the door. 'I never smoke indoors,' she said. 'It makes me smell.'

'Well, I'll come outside with you then.' Lucy followed her aunt out into the cold.

'Oh, the memories this place brings flooding back,' Kate sighed. 'You wouldn't believe how many children lived here at one time, or the fun we had, even though some of them were desperately poor.'

'Well we never had very much,' Lucy said. 'But I remember a time when we were extremely happy, but then...'

Kate took hold of Lucy's hand. 'I know, and then it all changed. But you mustn't blame your mother, Lucy. It was when our William was born; before that she was a lovely wife to our Bill. And a perfect mother. She was pretty, kept herself smart and her home comfortable for you all. She worried about your dad's health and begged him to take time off work. Sometimes he coughed so much it seemed he would eject those dust-eroded lungs altogether. They were one of the most loving couples I ever knew. Well-loved by the neighbours, always helpful.'

'Then why the change?' Lucy whispered.

'It was when William was born. She had developed a sore on her leg, but nothing serious, or so we thought at the time. We expected it to heal after the baby was born. She became despondent after the birth, worrying about the least little thing. She knew your father's days were numbered and was anxious how she would cope without him. And when the sore didn't heal she worried about what would happen if she died. Who'd keep you? Would they take you all to the orphanage at Longfield?

'I told her I would take care of you all. Then she said I wasn't fit to bring up children, that I was a loose woman, just because I worked for an elderly gentleman and I lived in. There was no foundation to her accusations. We had been friends from childhood and I couldn't cope with the terrible things she said. Then my employer died and left me a large sum of money and I gave some to your mother. She said it was dirty money and wouldn't touch it, but I left it anyway. I thought it would take away her worries and she would get better. She didn't. She was never the same again. Poor Annie. You mustn't blame her. The condition is recognised now in America, if not here, and is a type of depression caused by childbirth. Some get over it pretty quickly, but Annie didn't. I know she would never have acted the way she did if she had been well; she loved you all so much.'

'And she suffered all those years with a bad leg before she told us.'

'She thought the Borax would work.'

'The money you gave her went towards the purchase of this house.'

'Oh, I'm so glad. So she did well by you after all.'

The tears were rolling down Lucy's cheeks by now. 'Oh, Aunt Kate, I'm so glad you've told me. We thought she was just being spiteful and miserable.' Lucy threw her arms round the older woman, taking in the expensive perfume as she hugged her.

'Come on, let's go in. I want to spend some time with the rest of my family.'

Inside, a game of charades was in progress. The game soon came to a standstill when Kate's large leather bag was opened and she brought out a huge box of chocolates and a bottle of brandy. 'Come on, help yourselves, and whilst we're at it I want to know all your names. I've a lot of catching up to do.'

Lucy thought how lovely Aunt Kate was – in fact just as nice as her late brother. 'This is the best Christmas we've had ever,' she said.

'You know,' Kate replied, 'this is what I miss most in America: a real old-fashioned family Christmas.'

Chapter Thirty-four

It was Lucy's thirty-seventh birthday, which she would have preferred to forget, but as it was also Rosie's eighteenth some sort of celebration had been called for. Lucy had woken early and had lain drowsily reflecting on her life and her family. They had been fortunate - apart from the usual infectious diseases her children had been exceptionally healthy. Now they were growing up and making their own decisions on what each wanted from their lives.

Bernard was a mechanic, back now after completing his national service in the Royal Engineers as a driving instructor.

Rosie, after leaving school, had secured a receptionist's job in the offices of the steelworks.

Peter, despite being a twin, was quite content with his own company so long as he had a stack of drawing material at hand. He was training now to be a draughtsman; it was all he had ever wanted to be.

Violet, with eyes to match her name, was the beauty of the family, and was enjoying making other people beautiful too, in her training to be a hairdresser.

Andrew, the tallest and broadest of them all, didn't seem to be able to make up his mind. He was working at the moment as a brickie on the new housing estate being built between Millington and Cragstone, but was intent upon joining the navy, 'To see the world'. Or so he told them at least once a week. Lucy was praying he would change his mind but John said whatever Andrew decided to do he would get by. Andrew was blessed with the Gabbitas spirit, especially the same sense of humour as his uncle Will.

Lucy wondered why she had never had another child. They hadn't taken precautions for ages. She wouldn't have minded another, though she wouldn't have wanted to carry on as they had in the first few years. Lucy looked at her husband: still in dreamland, still as handsome as ever. He looked so much healthier now he was at Grundy's. She knew he sometimes missed his mining days, miners being the best mates a man could wish for. Anyway the mine was closed now and he still met up with them on Saturdays on their visits to the Working Men's Club. John would join them in a game of billiards in the games room whilst Lucy gossiped with other wives and listened to turns such as singers and comedians. Last week it had been a group belting out music so loud that the elderly members had withdrawn to the back of the room and stuffed hankies in their ears. Lucy had quite enjoyed it; if they booked another group she might even get up and have a dance – after all, she didn't feel her age.

She looked at the clock; she'd better get up. It would be a busy day. By eleven the house was full of flowers. Vases had been borrowed from Mrs Slater to accommodate them all. The ones taking pride of place were in a small Wedgwood jug, a present from the twins – a bunch of primroses, from John. Visitors never stopped arriving all day: friends of Rosie's, Kitty and her son, Herbert and Louisa and all the Gabbitas lot, except Nellie who sent cards for them both. Mothers with children she'd cared for over the years, some of them grown up now but none of them forgetting Auntie Lucy.

It was quiet now. The children had gone out to a Youth Club dance in the school room, except for Bernard who had recently acquired a girl-friend and had gone to the Cutlers Hall. The Youth Club had been started by John and James in an effort to keep the kids off the streets and was proving popular, especially the dances. Ben had bought the group a Regentone record player and the members would bring their own records to play. It was James's turn to be on duty tonight. 'We ought to have gone with them tonight, Lucy. With it being Rosie's birthday I mean.'

'No. They'll be smooching by now to The Four Aces, or having a bop, whatever that might be. And our Violet'll be crying along with Johnny Ray, her latest heart-throb. They wouldn't want us watching over them.'

'They do want us, Lucy. All five of them. We couldn't have more loving kids. Well, they aren't kids anymore, are they?'

'No. And that's why they don't want us spoiling their night out. Besides, after all today's excitement, I thought it would be nice to stay in with you. I might have filled the house with children over the years, but you're the only one I need really, all I ever needed.'

'Aye, it is nice to be on our own.' Suddenly John sat bolt upright in the, chair.

‘What’s wrong?’

‘Nothing, just that for a second I could have sworn I saw my mother and father in the mirror. I’ve had too much to drink, what with the celebrations.’

‘No. I often see images in that glass, people who have passed on. My mam and dad especially. Once I saw Evelyn and once Lewis.’

‘Oh well, Lewis’ll never leave as long as you’re here.’ John laughed.

‘There’s something weird about that looking glass, though. It’s as if as well as reflecting our images, it’s reflecting the people who are in our thoughts and in our hearts.’

‘Ah, we’ve had too much to drink, love, that’s all.’

‘Yes, I suppose that’s it. Still, as long as it keeps making our wishes come true, we’ll keep it.’

‘It’s looking a bit tarnished now. I suppose it’s to be expected with all the steam it’s been subjected to over the years. I wish I had a shilling for all the washing that’s been hung on the rack over that mirror. I ought to buy a new one.’

‘Oh no you don’t. It reminds me of the day you asked me to marry you.’

John’s eyes swept over his wife, looking still as desirable as she had on that day, in her new dress bought to match her eyes. ‘Are you tired, Lucy?’

‘No, not really. Why?’

‘So shall we be going up? They know where the key is.’

Lucy saw the look in John’s eyes and knew it wasn’t sleep he was thinking about.

‘All right. But before we go, let’s make a wish.’

'What for? There's nothing we need, is there?'

'That they stay out for a couple of hours at least, the whole lot of them.'

The mirror might be old and tarnished, but it continued to work its magic.

The publishers hope that this book has given you enjoyable reading. Large Print Books are especially designed to be as easy to see and hold as possible. If you wish a complete list of our books please ask at your local library or write directly to: